D1016521

Lisa Jackson is a #1 *New York Times* bestselling author of more than eighty-five books, including romantic suspense, thrillers and contemporary and historical romances. She is a recipient of the *RT Book Reviews* Reviewers' Choice Award and has also been honored with their Career Achievement Award for Romantic Suspense. Born in Oregon, she continues to make her home among family, friends and dogs in the Pacific Northwest. Visit her at lisajackson.com.

B.J. Daniels is a *New York Times* and *USA TODAY* bestselling author. She wrote her first book after a career as an award-winning newspaper journalist and author of thirty-seven published short stories. She lives in Montana with her husband, Parker, and three springer spaniels. When not writing, she quilts, boats and plays tennis. Contact her at bjdaniels.com, on Facebook or on Twitter, @bjdanielsauthor.

#1 *New York Times* Bestselling Author

LISA JACKSON

BEST-KEPT SECRETS

Previously published as *The McCaffertys: Thorne*

**HARLEQUIN
BESTSELLING
AUTHOR
COLLECTION**

**HARLEQUIN®
BESTSELLING
AUTHOR
COLLECTION**

Recycling programs
for this product may
not exist in your area.

ISBN-13: 978-1-335-40622-4

Best-Kept Secrets
First published as The McCaffertys: Thorne in 2000.
This edition published in 2021.
Copyright © 2000 by Susan Crose

Second Chance Cowboy
First published in 2008. This edition published in 2021.
Copyright © 2008 by Barbara Heinlein

For questions and comments about the quality of this book, please contact
us at CustomerService@Harlequin.com.

Harlequin Enterprises ULC
22 Adelaide St. West, 40th Floor
Toronto, Ontario M5H 4E3, Canada
www.Harlequin.com

Printed in U.S.A.

CONTENTS

Also by Lisa Jackson

Visit her Author Profile page at Harlequin.com,
or lisajackson.com, for more titles!

BEST-KEPT SECRETS

Lisa Jackson

Prologue

Last summer

"The truth of the matter, son, is that I've got a request for you," John Randall McCafferty stated from his wheelchair. He'd asked Thorne to push him to the fence line some thirty yards from the front door of the ranch house he'd called home all his life.

"I hate to ask what it is," Thorne remarked.

"It's simple. I want you to marry. You're thirty-nine, son, Matt's thirty-seven and Slade—well, he's still a boy but he is thirty-six. None of you has married and I don't have one grandchild—well at least none that I know of." He frowned. "Even your sister hasn't settled down."

"Randi's only twenty-six."

"High time," J. Randall said. A shell of the man he'd once been, J. Randall nonetheless gripped the arms of his metal chair, often referred to as "that damned contraption," so tightly his knuckles bleached white. An old afghan was draped over his legs though the temperature hovered near eighty according to the ancient thermometer tacked to the north side of the barn. Across his lap was his cane, another hated symbol of his failing health.

"I'm serious, son. I need to know that the McCafferty line won't die with you boys."

"That's an archaic way of thinking." Thorne wasn't going to be pushed around. Not by his old man. Not by anyone.

"So be it. Damn it, Thorne, if ya haven't noticed I don't have a helluva lot of time left on this here earth!" J. Randall swept his cane from his lap and jabbed it into the ground for emphasis.

Harold, J. Randall's crippled hunting dog, gave off a disgruntled woof from the front porch and a field mouse scurried into a tangle of brambles.

"I don't understand you," J. Randall grumbled. "This could have been yours, boy. All yours." He swept his cane in a wide arc and Thorne's gaze followed his father's gesture. Spindly legged colts frolicked in one pasture while a herd of mottled cattle in shades of russet, black and brown ambled near the dry creek bed that sliced through what was commonly referred to as "the big meadow." The paint on the barn had peeled, the windows in the stables needed replacing and the whole damned place looked as if it were suffering from the same debilitating disease as its owner.

The Flying M Ranch.

John Randall McCafferty's pride and joy. Now run by a foreman as he was too ill and his children too busy with their own lives.

Thorne regarded the rolling acres with a mixture of emotions running the gauntlet from love to hate.

"I'm not getting married, Dad. Not for a while."

"What's the wait? And don't tell me you need to make your mark. You've done it, boy." Old, faded blue eyes rolled up to look at him, then blinked when rays from a blinding Montana sun were too much. "What're ya worth now? Three million? Five?"

"Somewhere around seven."

His father snorted. "I was a rich man once. What did it get me?" His old lips folded back on themselves. "Two wives who bled me dry when we divorced and a bellyful of worry about losin' it all. No, money isn't what counts, Thorne. It's children. And land. Damn it all—" biting his lower lip, J. Randall dug deep into his pocket "—now where in tarnation is that— Oh, here we go."

Slowly he withdrew a ring that winked in the sunlight and Thorne's gut twisted as he recognized the band—his father's first wedding ring; one he hadn't worn in over a quarter of a century. "I want you to have this," the old man said as he held out the gold band with its unique silver inlay. "Your mother gave it to me the day we were married."

"I know." Thorne, sensing he was making a serious mistake, accepted the ring. It felt cold and hard in his fingers, a metal circle that held no warmth, no promise, no joy. A symbol of broken dreams. He pocketed the damn ring.

"Promise me, boy."

"What?"

"That you'll marry."

Thorne didn't bat an eye. "Someday."

"Make it soon, will ya? I'd like to leave this earth knowin' that you were gonna have a family."

"I'll think about it," Thorne said and suddenly the small band of gold and silver in his pocket seemed to weigh a thousand pounds.

Chapter 1

Dr. Nicole Stevenson felt a rush of adrenaline surge through her blood as it did each time accident victims were rushed into the emergency room of St. James Hospital.

She met the intensity in Dr. Maureen Oliverio's eyes as the other woman hung up the phone. "The copter's here! Let's go, people!" The hastily grouped team of doctors and nurses responded. "The paramedics are bringing in the patient. You're on, Dr. Stevenson."

"What have we got?" Nicole asked.

Dr. Oliverio, a no-nonsense doctor, led the way through double doors. "Single-car accident up in Glacier Park, the patient's a woman in her late twenties, pregnant, at term. Fractures, internal damage, concussed, a real mess. Membranes have ruptured. We'll probably need to do a C-section because of her other injuries. While we're inside, we'll repair any other damage. Everybody with me? Dr. Stevenson's in charge until we send the patient to O.R."

Nicole caught the glances of the other doctors as they adjusted masks and gloves. It was her job to stabilize the patient before shipping her off to surgery.

The doors of the room flew open and a gurney, propelled

by two paramedics, flew through the doors of the emergency room of St. James Hospital.

"What have we got here?" Nicole asked the nearest paramedic, a short red-faced man with clipped graying hair and a moustache. "What are her vital signs? What about the baby?"

"BP normal, one-ten over seventy-five, heart rate sixty-two but dropping slightly…" The paramedic rattled off the information he'd gathered and Nicole, listening, looked down at the patient, an unconscious woman whose face once probably beautiful was now bloody and already beginning to bruise. Her abdomen was distended, fluid from an IV flowed into her arm and her neck and head were braced. "…lacerations, abrasions, fractured skull, mandible and femur, possible internal bleeding…"

"Let's get a fetal monitor here!" Nicole ordered as a nurse peeled off.

"On its way."

"Good." Nicole nodded. "Okay, okay, now, let's stabilize the mother."

"Has the husband been notified? Do we have a consent?" Dr. Oliverio asked.

"Don't know," a grim-faced paramedic replied. "The police are trying to locate her relatives. According to her ID, her name is Randi McCafferty and there's no indication of any allergies to meds on her driver's licence, no prescription drugs in her purse."

Oh, God! Nicole's heart nearly stopped. She froze. For a split second her concentration lapsed and she gave herself a quick mental shake. "Are you sure?" she asked the shorter of the two paramedics.

"Positive."

"Randi McCafferty," Dr. Oliverio repeated, sucking in

her breath. "My daughter went to school with her. Her father's dead—J. Randall, important man around these parts at one time. Owned the Flying M Ranch about twenty miles out of town. Randi, here, has three half brothers."

And Thorne's one of them, Nicole thought, her jaw tensing.

"What about the husband or boyfriend? The kid's got a father somewhere," Dr. Oliverio insisted.

"Don't know. Never heard of one."

"We'll figure out all that later," Nicole said, taking charge once more. "Right now, let's just concentrate on stabilizing her and the baby."

Dr. Oliverio nodded. "Let's get that fetal monitor on here! STAT."

"Got it," a nurse replied.

"BP's falling, Doctor—one hundred over sixty," a nurse said.

"Damn." Nicole's own heart began to pound. She wasn't going to lose this patient. *Come on, Randi,* she silently urged. *Where's that good ol' McCafferty fight? Come on, come on!* "Where's the anesthesiologist?" Nicole demanded.

"On his way."

"Who is he?"

"Brummel." Dr. Oliverio met Nicole's gaze. "A good man. He'll be here."

"The monitor's in place," a nurse said just as Dr. Brummel, a thin man in rimless glasses, pushed his way through the doors. "What have we got here?" he asked as he quickly scanned the patient.

"Woman. Unconscious. About to deliver. Single-car accident. No known allergies, no medical records, but we're checking," Nicole said. "She's got a skull fracture, multiple other fractures, pneumothorax—so she's already entubated.

Her membranes have ruptured, the kid's on his way, and there might be more abdominal injuries."

"The mother's BP is stabilizing—one hundred and five over sixty," a nurse called, but Nicole didn't relax. Couldn't. In her estimation Randi McCafferty's life wasn't yet certain.

"Keep your eye on it. Now, what about the baby?" Nicole asked.

"We've got trouble here. The baby's in distress," Dr. Oliverio said, eyeing the readout of the fetal monitor.

"Then let's get it out of there."

"I'll be ready in a minute," Dr. Brummel said from behind his mask as he adjusted the breathing tube. Satisfied, he glanced up at Nicole. "Let's go."

"We've got a neonatologist standing by."

"Good." Nicole checked Randi's vital signs one last time. "Patient's stable." She glanced at the team, then met Dr. Oliverio's eyes with her own. Randi McCafferty was in an uphill battle for her life. As was the baby. "All right, Doctors, the patients are all yours."

Thorne drove like a madman. He'd gotten the call from Slade less than three hours earlier that Randi was in a car accident in Glacier Park, here in Montana.

Thorne had been in Denver at the time, in a private business meeting at the offices of McCafferty International and he'd left abruptly. He told his secretary to handle everything and rearrange his schedule, then he grabbed a duffel bag he kept packed in a closet and had driven to the airfield. Within the hour he was airborne, flying the company jet directly to a private airstrip at the ranch. He hadn't bothered checking with his brothers again, instead he'd just taken the keys to a pickup that was waiting for him, tossed his duffel bag into the truck then taken off for Grand Hope and St. James Hospital where Randi was battling for her life.

He stepped on the accelerator, took a corner too fast and heard the tires squeal in protest. He didn't know what was going on; the phone call from his brother Slade had been broken up by static and eventually disconnected as cell service wasn't the greatest here. But he did understand that Randi's life was in question and that the name of the admitting doctor was Stevenson. Other than that, he knew nothing.

Night-darkened fields flew by. The wipers slapped sleet from the windshield and Thorne's jaw grew hard. What the devil had happened? Why was Randi in Montana when her job was in Seattle? What had she been doing in Glacier Park, how serious were her injuries—was she really in danger of losing her life? A piece of information that finally pierced his brain from his conversation with Slade burrowed deep in his brain. Hadn't his brother said something about Randi being pregnant? No way. He'd seen her less than six months ago. She was single, didn't even have a steady boyfriend. Or did she? What did he really know about his half sister?

Not a helluva lot.

Guilt ripped through him. *You should have kept in contact. You're the oldest. It was your responsibility. It wasn't her fault that her mother seduced your father over a quarter of a century before and broke up John Randall's first marriage. It wasn't her fault that you were just too damned busy with your own life.*

Dozens of questions burned through his conscience as he saw the lights of the town glowing in the distance.

He'd have his answers soon enough.

If Randi survived. His fingers clenched around the

wheel and he found himself praying to a God he'd thought had long ago turned a deaf ear.

Thorne McCafferty.

The last person on earth Nicole wanted to deal with. But, no doubt, he'd be here. And soon. As she tore off her surgical gloves, she told herself to buck up. He was just another worried relative of a patient. Nothing more.

Nonetheless Nicole didn't like the idea of facing him again. There were too many old wounds, too much pain she'd never really resolved, too many emotions that she'd locked away years ago. She'd realized when she moved here after her divorce that she wouldn't be able to avoid Thorne forever. Grand Hope, despite its recent growth, was still a small town and John Randall McCafferty had been one of its leading citizens. His sons and daughter had grown up here.

So she'd have to face Thorne again. Big deal. It was only a matter of time. Unfortunately the situation—with his sister struggling for her life—wasn't the best of circumstances.

Nicole stuffed her stethoscope into her pocket and braced herself. Not only would she have to face Thorne again, but Randi McCafferty's other distraught brothers as well—men she'd known in a lifetime long, long ago when she'd dated their older brother. Her time with Thorne had been short, though. Intense and unforgettable, but thankfully short. His younger brothers, who had been caught up in their own lives at the time, might not remember her.

Don't believe it for a minute. When it comes to women, the McCafferty men were almost legendary in their conquests. They'd known all the girls in town.

Another painful old scar ripped open because Nicole had

come to face the fact that she had been nothing more than another one of Thorne McCafferty's conquests, just another notch in his belt. A poor, shy, studious girl who had, for a short period one summer, caught his eye.

An archaic way of thinking, but oh, so torturously true.

Through a high window she saw the movement of stormy gray clouds that reflected her own gloomy thoughts. Though it was only October the weather service had been predicting snow.

She'd been in the ER all day, had nearly finished her shift when Randi McCafferty had been brought in.

Nicole's feet ached, her head pounded and the thought of a shower was pure heaven—a shower, a glass of chilled Chardonnay, a crackling fire and the twins cuddled with her under the quilt in her favorite rocker as she read them a bedtime story. She couldn't help but smile. "Later," she reminded herself. First she had serious business to attend to.

Randi, still in recovery, wasn't out of the woods yet, nor would she be for a while. Comatose and fighting for her life, Randi would spend the better part of the next week in ICU being monitored, her vital signs watched twenty-four hours.

The good news was that the baby, a robust boy, had survived the accident and a quick Cesarean birth. So far.

Sweaty and forcing a smile she didn't feel, Nicole slipped into her lab coat and pushed open the doors to the waiting room where two of Randi McCafferty's brothers sat on chairs, thumbing through magazines, their cups of coffee ignored on a corner table. They were both tall and lanky, handsome men with bold features, expressive eyes and worry written all over their faces.

Looking up as the doors opened, they dropped their magazines and climbed hastily to their feet.

"Mr. McCafferty?" she asked, though she'd spotted them instantly.

"I'm Matt," the taller of the two said as if he didn't recognize her. Maybe that was for the best. Keep the situation as professional as possible. Over six feet, with dark-brown eyes and near-black hair, Matt was dressed in jeans and a Western-cut plaid shirt with the sleeves rolled up. Cowboy boots covered his feet and a stir-stick, chewed flat, was wedged firmly in the corner of his mouth. "This is my brother Slade."

Again, no hint of recognition lit Slade's gaze. The youngest of the McCafferty brothers, he'd been tagged as the hellion. He was shorter than Matt by less than an inch and a thin scar jagged down one side of a face distinguished by hawkish features and deep-set, startling blue eyes. Wearing a flannel shirt, faded jeans and beat-up tennis shoes, he shifted nervously from one foot to the other.

"I'm Dr. Stevenson. I was on duty when your sister was brought into the ER."

"How's she doin'?" Slade asked anxiously. His eyes narrowed a bit as he looked at her and she realized he'd started the recognition process. It would take a while. It had been years since she'd seen him, her name was different, and there were dozens of women he would have to sift through unless she missed her guess.

She didn't have time for any of that now. Her job was to allay their fears while explaining about Randi's condition. "The surgery went well, but your sister was in pretty rough shape when she was brought in, comatose but in labor. Dr. Oliverio delivered your nephew and he seems healthy, though he'll be given a complete examination by a pediatrician here on staff.

"Randi's prognosis looks good, barring unforeseen complications, but she's survived an incredible trauma." As the brothers listened grimly, Nicole described Randi McCafferty's injuries—concussion, punctured lung, broken ribs, fractured jaw, nearly shattered femur—the list was long and grave. Concern etched in both brothers' features, storm clouds gathering in their eyes. Nicole explained the procedures that had been used to repair the damage, using as many lay terms as possible. Matt's dark skin paled slightly and he winced at one point, looking out the window and chewing the stir-stick until it was thin as parchment. On the other hand, the younger brother, Slade, stared her straight in the face, his jaw clenching, his blue eyes rarely blinking.

As she finished, Slade let out a soft whistle. "Damn it all to hell."

Matt rubbed the stubble on his chin and stared at her. "But she will make it. Right?"

"Unless she takes a turn for the worse, I think so. There's always a question with head injuries, but she's stabilized."

Slade frowned. "She's still in a coma."

"Yes. You understand that I'm the emergency room physician, and other doctors have taken over your sister's care. Each of them will contact you."

"When?" Slade demanded.

"As soon as they can."

She managed a reassuring smile. "I'm going off duty soon. Randi's other doctors will want to talk to you as well. I came out first because I knew you were anxious." *And because, damn it, I have a personal connection to your family.*

"Anxious doesn't begin to cover it," Matt said and glanced at his watch. "Shouldn't Thorne be getting here by now?" he asked his brother.

"He said he was on his way." Slade's gaze swung back

to Nicole. "Our oldest brother." His eyebrows knit a bit. "He'll want a full report."

"No doubt," she said and Matt's eyes narrowed. "I knew him. Years ago."

She could almost see the wheels turning in the McCafferty brothers' minds, but the situation with their sister was too imminent, too dire, to be distracted.

"But Randi, she's gonna be okay," Matt said slowly, doubts shadowing his brown eyes.

"We're hopeful. As I said, she's stabilized, but there's always a question with head injuries." Nicole wished she could instill more confidence, allay their worries, but couldn't. "The truth is, it's gonna be touch-and-go for a while, but she'll be monitored around the clock."

"Oh, God," Slade whispered and the words sounded more like a prayer than a curse.

"I—we appreciate everything you and the other doctors have done." Matt shot his brother a look meant to silence him. "I just want you to know that whatever she needs, specialists, equipment, whatever, we want her to have it."

"She does," Nicole said firmly. In her estimation the staff, facilities and equipment at St. James were excellent, the best she'd seen in a town the size of Grand Hope.

"And the baby? You said he's okay, right?" Matt asked.

"He seems fine, but he's being observed for any signs of trauma. He's in pediatric ICU, as a precaution for the next few hours, just to make sure that he's strong. From all outward appearances, he's healthy and hale, we're just being doubly cautious especially since your sister was in labor and her water had broken before she got to the hospital. Dr. Oliverio will have more details and of course the pediatrician will get in touch with you as well."

"Damn," Slade whispered while Matt stood silent and stern.

"When can we see Randi?" Matt asked.

"Soon. She's still in Recovery. Once she's settled in ICU and her doctors are satisfied with her condition, she can have visitors—just immediate family—for a few minutes a day. One at a time. Again, her physician will let you know."

Matt nodded and Slade's fist clenched, but neither argued. Both brothers' jaws were square and set, the McCafferty resemblance impossible to ignore.

"You have to understand that Randi's comatose. She won't respond to you until she wakes up and I don't know when that will be—oh, here we go. One of Randi's doctors." Spying Dr. Oliverio walking down the hallway, Nicole took a few minutes to introduce the McCafferty brothers, then, excusing herself, made her way to her office.

It was a small room with one window. It barely had enough space for her desk and file cabinet. She usually transcribed her own notes and after shrugging out of her lab coat, flipped on the computer and spent nearly a half an hour at the keyboard writing a report on Randi McCafferty. As she finished, she reached for the phone. Dialing her home number by rote, she massaged the back of her neck and heard the strains of piped-in music for the first time since she'd walked into the hospital hours before.

"Hello?" Jenny Riley answered on the second ring. Jenny, a student at a local community college, watched Nicole's twins while she worked.

"Hi. It's Nicole. Just wanted to know what was going on. I'll be outta here in about—" she checked her watch and sighed "—probably another hour. Anything I should pick up on the way?"

"How about a ray or two of sunshine for Molly?" Jenny

quipped. "She's been in a bad mood ever since she woke up from her nap."

"Has she?" Nicole grinned as she leaned back in her chair so far that it squeaked in protest. Molly, more precocious than her twin sister, was known to wake up grumpy while Mindy, the shier half of the two girls, always smiled, even when rousted from a nap.

"The worst."

"Am not!" a tiny, impertinent voice disagreed.

"Sure you are, but I love you anyway," Jenny said, her voice softer as she turned away from the phone.

"Am not the worst!"

Still grinning, Nicole rested a foot on her desk and sighed. The struggles of the day melted away when she thought of her daughters, two four-year-old dynamos who kept her running, the reasons she'd stayed sane after her divorce.

"Tell them I'll bring home pizza if they're good." She listened as Jenny relayed the message and heard a squeal of delight.

"They're pumped now," Jenny assured her and Nicole laughed just as there was a sharp rap on the door before it was pushed open abruptly. A tall man—maybe six foot three or four—nearly filled the frame. Her heart plummeted as she recognized Thorne.

"Dr. Stevenson?" he demanded, his face set and stern before recognition flared in his eyes and for the briefest of seconds she saw regret chase across his face.

"Look, Jenny, I've got to go," she said into the receiver as she hung up slowly, righted her chair and dropped her feet to the floor.

"Nikki?" he said, disbelieving.

Nicole stood but on her side of the desk, her barely five-foot-three-inch frame no match for his height. "Dr. Stevenson now."

"You're Randi's doctor?"

"The ER physician who admitted her." Why, after all the time that had passed and all the pain, did she still feel a ridiculous flutter of disappointment that he hadn't, in all the years since she'd last seen him, ever looked her up? It was silly. Stupid. Beyond naive. And it had no business here; not when his sister was fighting for her life. "I'm not her doctor, you understand. I helped stabilize her for surgery, then the team took over, but I did stop to speak with your brothers out of courtesy because I knew they'd been waiting a long time and the surgeons were still wrapping things up."

"I see." Thorne's handsome face had aged over the years. No longer were any vestiges of boyhood visible. His features were set and stern, matched only by the severity of his black suit, crisp white shirt and tie—the mark of a CEO of his own little empire. "I didn't know—didn't expect to find you here."

"I imagine not."

His eyes, a deep, troubled gray, held hers in a gaze that she knew was often daunting but now seemed weary and worried sick. "Did you see your brothers in ICU?" Nicole asked.

"I came directly here. Slade called, said a Dr. Stevenson was in charge, so when I got here, I asked for you at the information desk." As if reading the questions in her eyes, he added, "I wanted to know what I was dealing with before I saw Randi."

"Fair enough." She waved him into the office and motioned to the small plastic chair on the other side of the desk. "Have a seat. I'll tell you what I know, then you can talk to Randi's other doctors about her prognosis." As she reached for her lab coat, she leveled a gaze at him that had been known to shrink even the cockiest of interns. She wanted him to understand. She was no longer the needy little girl he'd dated, seduced and tossed aside. "But I think we should get something straight right now. As you can see this is my private office. Usually people knock, then wait for an answer, before they come barging in."

His jaw tightened. "I was in a hurry. But—fine. Next time I'll remember."

Oh, Thorne, there's never gonna be a next time. "Good."

"So she's in ICU?" Thorne asked.

"Yes." Nicole sketched out the details of Randi's emergency arrival to St. James, her conditions and the ensuing procedures. Thorne listened, his expression solemn, his gray eyes never leaving her face.

Once she was finished, he asked a few quick questions, loosened his tie and said, "Let's go."

"To ICU? Both of us?"

"Yes." He was on his feet.

Nicole bristled a bit, ready to fight fire with fire until she spied the hint of pain in his gaze and a twinge of some other emotion that bordered on guilt.

"I suppose I can do that," she agreed, hazarding a glance at her watch. She was running late, but being behind schedule came with the territory. As did dealing with worried relatives of her patients. "Let me make sure she's out of Recovery first." Nicole made a quick phone call, discovered that Randi had been transferred and explained that she and the patient's brother were on their way. For the duration of the short conversation she felt the weight of Thorne McCafferty's gaze upon her and she wondered if he remembered anything about the relationship that had changed the course of her life. Probably not. Once his initial shock at recognizing her had worn off, he was all business. "Okay," she said, hanging up. "All set. Matt and Slade have already seen Randi and the nurse on duty wasn't crazy about a third visitor, but I persuaded her."

"Are my brothers still here?"

"I don't know. They told the nurse they'd be back but didn't say when." She adjusted her lab coat and rounded the desk. He had the manners to hold the door for her and as they swept down the hallways he kept up with her fast pace, his long strides equal to two of hers. She'd forgotten that about him. But then she'd tried to erase every memory she'd ever had of him.

A foot taller than she, intimidating and forceful, Thorne walked the same way he faced life—with a purpose. She wondered if he'd ever had a frivolous moment in his life. Years before, she'd realized that even those stolen hours with her had been all a part of Thorne's plan.

At the elevator, Nicole waited as a gurney carrying a frail-looking elderly woman connected to an IV drip was pushed into the hallway by an aide, then she stepped inside. The doors shut. She and Thorne were alone. For the first time in years. He stood ramrod stiff beside her and if he noticed the intimacy of the elevator car, he didn't show it. His face was set, his shoulders square, his gaze riveted to the panel displaying the floor numbers.

Silly as it was, Nicole couldn't remember having ever been so uncomfortable.

The elevator jerked to a stop and as they walked through the carpeted hallways, Thorne finally broke the silence. "On the telephone, Slade mentioned something about Randi not making it."

"There's always that chance when injuries are as severe

as your sister's." They'd reached the doors of the Intensive
Care Unit and she, reminding herself to remain professional
at all times, angled her head upward to stare straight into
his steel-colored eyes. "But she's young and strong, getting
the best medical care we can provide, so there's no need to
borrow trouble, or voice your concerns around your sister.
She's comatose, yes, but we don't know what she does or
doesn't hear or feel. Please, for her sake, keep all your worries and doubts to yourself." He seemed about to protest and
by instinct, Nicole reached forward and touched his hand,
her fingers encountering skin that was hard and surprisingly callused. "We're doing everything we can, Thorne,"
she said and half expected him to pull away. "Your sister's
fighting for her life. I know you want what's best for her,
so whenever you're around her, I want you to be positive,
nurturing and supportive. Okay?"

He nodded curtly but his lips tightened a bit. He wasn't
and never had been used to taking orders or advice—not
from anyone. "Any questions?"

"Just one," he said slowly.

"What?"

"My sister is important to me. Very important. You
know that. So I want to be assured that she's getting the
best medical care that money can buy. That means the best
hospital, the best staff, and especially the best doctor."

Realizing she was still holding his hand, she let go and
felt a welling sense of disappointment. It wasn't the first
time her ability had been questioned and certainly wouldn't
be the last, but for some reason she had hoped that Thorne
McCafferty would trust her and her dedication. "What are
you trying to say?" she asked.

"I need to know that the people here, the doctors assigned to Randi's care are the best in the country—or the whole damned world for that matter."

Self-impressed, rich, corporate bastard.

"That's what everyone wants for their loved ones, Thorne."

"The difference is," he said, "I can afford it."

Her heart sank. Why had she thought she recognized a bit of tenderness in his eyes? Foolish, foolish, idealistic woman. "I'm a damned good doctor, Thorne. So are the others here. This hospital has won awards. It's small but attracts the best, I can personally assure you of that. Doctors who have once practiced in major cities from Atlanta to Seattle, New York to L.A., have ended up here because they were tired of the rat race...." She let her words sink in and wished she'd just bitten her tongue. Thorne could think whatever he damn well pleased.

"Let's go inside. Now, remember, keep it positive and when I say time's up, don't argue. Just leave. You can see her again tomorrow." She waited, but he didn't offer any response or protest, just clenched his jaw so hard a muscle jumped. "Got it?" she asked.

"Got it."

"Then we'll get along just fine," she said, but she didn't believe it for a minute. Some things didn't change and she and Thorne McCafferty were like oil and water—they would never mix; never agree.

She pressed a button and placed her face in the window so that a nurse inside could see her, then waited to be admitted. As the electronic doors hummed open, she felt Thorne's gaze center on the back of her neck beneath the upsweep of her hair. Without making a sound, he followed her inside. She wondered how long he'd obey the hospital's and the doctor's terms.

The answer, she knew, was blindingly simple.

Not long enough.

Thorne McCafferty hadn't changed. He was the type of man who played by his own rules.

Chapter 2

Oh, God, this couldn't *be Randi.* Thorne gazed down at the small, inert form lying on the bed and he felt sick inside—weak. Tubes and wires ran from her body to monitors and equipment with gauges and digital readouts that he didn't understand. Her head was wrapped in gauze, her body draped in sterile-looking sheets, one leg elevated and surrounded by a partial cast. The portions of her face that he could see were bruised and swollen.

His throat was thick with emotion as he stood in the tiny sheet-draped cubicle that opened at the foot of the bed to the nurses' station. His fists clenched impotently, and a quiet, damning rage burned through his soul. How could this have happened? What was she doing up at Glacier Park? Why had her vehicle slid off the road?

The heart monitor beeped softly and steadily yet he wasn't reassured as he stared down at this stranger who was his half sister. A dozen memories darted wildly through his mind and though at one time, when she was first born, he'd been envious and resentful of his father's namesake, he'd never been able to really dislike her.

Randi had been so outgoing and alive, her eyes sparkling with mischief, her laughter contagious, a girl who wore her heart on her sleeve. Guileless and believing that she had every right to be the apple of her father's eye, Randi Penelope McCafferty had bulldozed her way through life and into almost anyone's heart she came across—including those of her reluctant, hellions of half brothers who had sworn while their new stepmother was pregnant that they would despise the baby who, as far as their tunnel-visioned young eyes could see, was the reason their own parents had divorced so bitterly.

Now, twenty-six years later, Thorne cringed at his ill-focused hostility. He'd been thirteen when his half sister had summoned the gall to arrive, red-faced and screaming, into this world. Thorne had been thoroughly disgusted at the thought of his father and the younger woman he'd married actually "doing it" and creating this love child. Worse yet was the scandal surrounding her birth date, barely six months after J. Randall's second nuptials. It had been too humiliating to think about and he'd taken a lot of needling from his classmates who, having always been envious of the McCafferty name, wealth and reputation, had found some dark humor in the situation.

Hell, it had been a long time ago and now, standing in the sterile hospital unit with patients barely clinging to life, his own sister hooked up to machines that helped her survive, Thorne felt a fool. All the mortification and shame Thorne had endured at Randi's conception and birth had disappeared from the first time he'd caught his first real glimpse of her little, innocent face.

Staring into that fancy lace-covered bassinet in the master bedroom at the ranch, Thorne had been ready to hate the baby on sight. After all, for five or six months she'd been the source of all his anger and humiliation. But Thorne had been instantly taken with the little infant with her dark hair, bright eyes and flailing fists. She'd looked as mad to be there as he'd felt that she'd disrupted his life. She'd wailed and cried and put up a fuss that couldn't be believed. The sound that had been emitted from her tiny voice box—like a wounded cougar—had bored right to the heart of him.

He'd hidden his feelings, kept his fascination with the baby to himself and made sure no one, least of all his brothers and father knew how he really felt about the infant, that he'd been beguiled by her from the very beginning of her life.

Now, as he watched her labored breathing and noticed the blood-encrusted bandages that were placed over her swollen face, he felt like a heel. He'd let her slip away from him, hadn't kept in touch because it hadn't been convenient for either of them and now she lay helpless, the victim of an accident that hadn't yet been explained to him.

"You can talk to her," a soft, feminine voice said to him and he looked up to see Nicole looking at him with round, compassionate eyes. The color of aged whiskey and surrounded by thick lashes, they seemed to stare right to his very soul. As they had when he was twenty-two and she'd been barely seventeen. God, that seemed a lifetime ago. "No one knows if she can hear you or not, but it certainly wouldn't hurt." Her lips curved into a tender, encouraging smile and though he felt like a fool, he nodded, surprised not only that she'd matured into a full-fledged woman— but that she was a doctor, no less, and one who could bark out orders or offer compassionate whispers with an equal amount of command. This was Nikki Sanders, the girl who had nearly roped his heart? The one girl who had nearly convinced him to stay in Grand Hope and scrape out a living on the ranch? Leaving her had been tough, but he'd done it. He'd had to.

As if sensing he might need some privacy, she turned back to the chart on which she was taking notes.

Thorne dragged his gaze from the curve of Nikki's neck, though he couldn't help but notice that one strand of gold-streaked hair fell from the knot she'd pinned at her crown. Maybe she wasn't so buttoned-down after all.

Grabbing the cool metal railing at the side of Randi's hospital bed, he concentrated on his sister again. He cleared his throat. "Randi?" he whispered, feeling like an utter fool. "Hey, kid, can you hear me? It's me. Thorne." He swallowed hard as she lay motionless. Old memories flashed through his mind in a kaleidoscope of pictures. It had been Thorne who had found her crying after she'd fallen off her bike when she'd been learning to ride at five. He'd returned home from college for a quick visit, had discovered her at the edge of the lane, her knees scraped, her cheeks dusty and tracked with tears, her pride bitterly wounded as she couldn't get the hang of the two-wheeler. After carrying her to the house, Thorne had plucked the gravel from her knees, then fixed the bent wheel of her bike and helped her keep the damned two-wheeler from toppling every time she tried to learn.

When Randi had been around nine or ten, Thorne had spent an afternoon teaching her how to throw a baseball like a boy—a curveball and a slider. She'd spent hours working at it, throwing that damned old ball at the side of the barn until the paint had peeled off.

Years later, Thorne had returned home one weekend to find his tomboy of a half sister dressed in a long pink dress as she'd waited for her date to the senior prom. Her hair, a rich mahogany color, had been twisted onto the top of her head. She'd stood tall on high heels with a poise and beauty that had shocked him. Around her neck she'd worn a gold chain with the same locket J. Randall had given Randi's mother on their wedding day. Randi had been downright breathtaking. Exuberant. Full of life.

And now she lay unmoving, unconscious, her body battered as she struggled to breathe.

Nicole returned to the side of the bed. Gently she shone a penlight into Randi's eyes, then touched Randi's bare wrist with probing, professional fingers. Little worry lines appeared between her sharply arched brows. Her upper teeth sank into her lower lip as if she were deep in thought. It was an unconsciously sexy movement and he looked away quickly, disgusted at the turn of his thoughts.

From the corner of his eye he noticed her making notations on Randi's chart as she moved to the central area where a nurses' station had full view of all of the patients' beds. Like spokes of a wheel the separated "rooms" radiated from the central desk area. Pale-green privacy drapes separated each bed from the others and nurses in soft-soled shoes moved quietly from one area to the next.

"Why don't you try to speak with her again?" Nicole suggested quietly, not even glancing his way.

He felt so awkward. So out of place. So big. So damned healthy.

"Go on," she encouraged, then turned her back on him completely.

His fingers tightened over the rail. What could he say? What did it matter? Thorne leaned forward, closer to the bed where his sister lay so still. "Randi," he whispered in a voice that nearly cracked with emotions he tried desperately to repress. He touched one of her fingers and she didn't respond, didn't move. "Can ya hear me? Well, you'd better." Hell, he was bad at this sort of thing. He shifted so that his fingers laced with hers. "How ya doin'?"

Of course she didn't answer and as the heart monitor beeped a steady, reassuring beat, he wished to heaven that he'd been a better older brother to her, that he'd been more involved with her life. He noticed the soft rounding of her abdomen beneath the sheet stretched over her belly. She'd been pregnant. Now had a child. A mother at twenty-six. Yet no one in the family knew of any man with whom she'd been involved. "Can...can you hear me? Huh, kiddo?"

Oh, this was inane. She wasn't going to respond. Couldn't. He doubted she heard a word he said, or sensed that he was near. He felt like a fool and yet he was stuck like proverbial glue, adhering to her, their fingers linked, as if someway he could force some of his sheer brute strength into her tiny body, could by his indomitable will make her strong, healthy and safe.

He caught a glance from Nicole, an unspoken word that told him his time was up.

Clearing his throat again, he pulled his hand from hers, then gently tapped the end of her index finger with his. "You hang in there, okay? Matt, Slade and I, we're all pulling for you, kid, so you just give it your best. And you've got a baby, now—a little boy who needs you. Like we all do, kid." *Oh, hell, this was impossible. Ludicrous.* And yet he said, "I, uh, I—we're all pullin' for you and I'll be back soon. Promise." The last word nearly cracked.

Randi didn't move and the back of Thorne's eyes burned in a way they hadn't since the day he learned his father had died. Shoving his hands into the pockets of his coat, he crossed the room and walked through the doors that opened as he approached. He sensed, rather than saw Nicole as she joined him.

"Give it to me straight," he said as they strode along a corridor with bright lights and windows overlooking a parking lot. Outside it was dark as night, black clouds showering rain that puddled on the asphalt and dripped from the few scraggly trees that were planted near the building. "What are her chances?"

Nicole's steps, shorter by half than his own, were quick. She managed to keep up with him though her brow was knitted, her eyes narrowed in thought. "She's young and strong. She has as good a chance as anyone."

An aide pushing a man in a wheelchair passed them going the opposite direction and somewhere a phone rang. Piped-in music competed with the hum of soft conversation and the muted rattle of equipment being wheeled down other corridors. As they reached the elevator, Thorne touched Nicole lightly on the elbow.

"I want to know if my sister is going to make it."

Color flushed her cheeks. "I don't have a crystal ball, you know, Thorne. I realize that you and your brothers want precise, finite answers. I just don't have them. It's too early."

"But she will live?" he asked, desperate to be reassured. He, who was always in control, was hanging on the words of a small woman whom he'd once come close to loving.

"As I said before, barring any unforeseen—"

"I heard you the first time. Just tell me the truth. Point-blank. Is my sister going to make it?"

She looked about to launch into him, then took a deep breath. "I believe so. We're all doing everything possible for her." As if reading the concern in his eyes, she sighed and rubbed the kinks from the back of her neck. Her face softened a bit and he couldn't help but notice the lines of strain surrounding her eyes, the intelligence in those gorgeous amber-colored irises and he felt the same male interest he had years ago, when she was a senior in high school. "Look, I'm sorry. I don't mean to be evasive. Really." She tucked an errant lock of hair behind her ear. "I wish I could tell you that Randi will be fine, that within a couple of weeks she'll be up walking around, laughing, going back to work, taking care of that baby of hers and that everything will be all right. But I can't do that. She's suffered a lot of trauma. Internal organs are damaged, bones broken. Her concussion is more than just a little bump on her head. I won't kid you. There's a chance that if she does survive, there may be brain damage. We just don't know yet."

His heart nearly stopped. He'd feared for his sister's life, but never once considered that she might survive only to live her life with less mental capabilities than she had before. She'd always been so smart—"Sharp as a tack," their father had bragged often enough.

"Shouldn't she see a specialist?" Thorne asked.

"She's seeing several. Dr. Nimmo is one of the best neurosurgeons in the Northwest. He's already examined her. He usually works out of Bitterroot Memorial and just after Randi's surgery he was called away on another emergency, but he'll phone you. Believe me. Your sister's getting the best medical care we can provide, and it's as good as you're going to get anywhere. I think we've already had this conversation, so you're just going to have to trust me. Now, is there anything else?"

"Just that I want to be kept apprised of her situation. If there is any change, any change at all in her condition or that of the child, I expect to be contacted immediately." He withdrew his wallet and slid a crisp business card from the smooth leather. "This is my business phone number and this—" he found a pen in the breast pocket of his suit jacket and scribbled another number on the back of his card "—is the number of the ranch. I'll be staying there." He handed her the card and watched as one of her finely arched brows elevated a bit.

"You expect *me* to contact you. Me, personally."

"I—I'd appreciate it," he said and touched her shoulder. She glanced down at his hand and little lines converged between her eyebrows. "As a personal favor."

Her lips pulled into a tight knot. Color stained her cheeks. "Because we were so close to each other?" she asked, gold eyes snapping as she pulled her shoulder away.

He dropped his hand. "Because you care. I don't know the rest of the staff and I'm sure that they're fine. All good doctors. But I *know* I can trust you."

"You don't know me at all."

"I did once."

She swallowed hard. "Let's keep that out of this," she said. "But, fine… I'll keep you informed."

"Thanks." He offered her a smile and she rolled her eyes.

"Just don't try to smooth-talk or con me, Thorne, okay? I'll tell it to you straight, but don't, not for a minute, try to play on my sympathies and, just to make sure you're getting this, I'm not doing it for old times' sake or anything the least bit maudlin or nostalgic, okay? If there's a change, you'll be notified immediately."

"And I'll be in contact with you."

"I'm not her doctor, Thorne."

"But you'll be here."

"Most of the time. Now, if you'll excuse me, I've really got to run." She started to turn away, but he caught the crook of her elbow, his fingers gripping the starched white coat.

"Thanks, Nikki," he said and to his amazement she blushed, a deep shade of pink stealing up her cheeks.

"No problem. It comes with the job," she said, then

glanced down at his fingers and pulled away. With clipped steps she disappeared through a door marked Staff Only. Thorne watched the door swing shut behind her and fought the urge to ignore the warning and follow her. Why he couldn't imagine. There was nothing more to say—the conversation was finished, but as he tucked his wallet back into his pocket, he experienced a foolish need to catch up with her—to catch up with his past. He had dozens of questions for her and he'd probably never ask one. "Fool," he muttered to himself and felt a headache begin to pound at the base of his skull. Nicole Stevenson was a doctor here at the hospital, nothing more. And she had his number. Big-time. She'd made that clear enough.

Yes, she was a woman; a beautiful woman, a smart woman, a seemingly driven woman, a woman with whom he'd made love once upon a time, but their affair was long over.

And she could be married, you idiot. Her name is Stevenson now, remember?

But he'd checked her ring finger. It had been bare. Why he'd bothered, he didn't understand; didn't want to assess. But he was satisfied that she was no longer another man's wife. Nonetheless she was off-limits. Period. A complicated, beguiling woman.

He stepped onto the elevator, pounded the button for the floor of the maternity level and tried to shove all thoughts of Nikki Sanders—Dr. Nicole Stevenson—from his mind.

But it didn't work; just as it hadn't worked years before when he'd left her. Without so much as an explanation. How could he have explained that he'd left her because staying in Grand Hope, being close to her, touching her and loving her made his departure all that much harder? He'd left because he'd had a deep sense of insight that if he'd stayed much longer, he would never have been able to tear himself away from her, that he never would have gone out into the world and proved to himself and his father that he could make his own mark.

"Hell," he cursed. He'd been a fool and let the only woman who had come close to touching a part of him he didn't want to know existed—that nebulous essence that was his soul—get away from him. He'd figured that out a couple of years later, but Thorne had never been one to look back and second-guess himself. He'd told himself there would be another woman someday—when he was ready.

Of course he'd never found her.

And he hadn't even worried about it until he'd seen Nikki Sanders again, remembered how it felt to kiss her, and the phrase *what if* had entered his mind. If he'd stuck by her, married her, had children by her, his father wouldn't have gone to his grave without grandchildren. "Stop it," he growled to himself.

Nicole let out her breath as she walked through the maze that was St. James. She was still unsettled and shaken. Used to dealing with anxious, sometimes even grieving relatives, she hadn't expected that she would have such an intense and disturbing reaction to Thorne McCafferty.

"He's just a man," she grumbled, taking the stairs. "That's all."

But she met men every day of the week. All kinds from all walks of life and none of them caused anywhere near this kind of response.

Was it because he had been her first lover? Because he nearly broke her heart? Because he left her, not because of another woman, not because he had any good reason, just because she didn't mean enough to him?

"Fool," she muttered under her breath as she pushed open the door to the floor where her office was housed.

"Excuse me?" a janitor who was walking down the hall asked.

"Nothing. Talking to myself." She offered the man an embarrassed smile and continued to her office, where she plopped into her desk chair and stared at the monitor of her computer. The notes that had filled her head only an hour earlier seemed scattered to the wind and she couldn't budge thoughts of Thorne from her brain. In her silly, very feminine mind's eye she saw him with the clarity of young, loving eyes. Oh, she'd adored him. He was older. Sophisticated. Rich. One of the McCafferty scoundrels—bad boys every one, who had been known to womanize, smoke, drink and generally raise hell in their youths.

Handsome, arrogant and cocky, Thorne had found easy access to her naive heart. The only daughter of a poor, hardworking woman who pushed for and expected perfection, Nicole had, at seventeen, been ripe for rebellion. And then she'd stumbled onto Thorne.

She'd fallen stupidly head over heels in love, nearly throwing all of her own hopes and dreams away on the rakish college boy.

Blowing her bangs out of her eyes she shook her head to dislodge those old, painful and humiliating memories. She'd been so young. So mindlessly sophomoric, caught up in romantic fantasies with the least likely candidate for a long-term relationship in the state.

"Don't even think about it," she reminded herself, moving the mouse of her computer and studying the screen while memories of making love to him under the star-studded Montana sky swept through her mind. His body had been young, hard, muscular and sheened in sweat. His eyes had been silver with the moon glow, his hair unkempt.

And now he was some kind of corporate hotshot.

Like Paul. She glanced down at her hands and was relieved to see that the groove her wedding ring had once carved in her finger had disappeared in the past two years. Paul Stevenson had been climbing the corporate ladder so fast, he'd lost track of his wife and young daughters.

She suspected Thorne wasn't much different.

When she'd moved back to Grand Hope a year ago, she'd known his family was still scattered around the state, but she'd thought Thorne was long gone and hadn't expected to come face-to-face with him. According to the rumors circulating through Grand Hope like endless eddies and whirlpools, Thorne had finished law school, linked up with a firm in Missoula, then moved to California and finally wound up in Denver where he was the executive for a multinational corporation. He'd never married, had no children that anyone knew of, and had been linked to several beautiful, wealthy, career-minded women over the years, none of whom had lasted on his arm too long before they'd been replaced with a newer model.

Yep. Thorne was a lot like Paul.

Except that you're still attracted to him, aren't you? One look, and your gullible heart started pounding all over again.

"Stop it!" she growled and forced herself to concentrate. This wasn't like her. She'd been known to be single-minded when it came to her work or her children and she found the distraction of Thorne McCafferty more than a little disconcerting. She couldn't, *wouldn't* fall victim to his insidious charms again. With renewed conviction, she ignored any lingering thoughts of Thorne and undid the clasp holding her hair in place. No doubt she'd have to deal with him later and at the thought her heart alternately leaped and sank. "Great," she told herself as she finger-combed her hair. "Just…great."

Right now facing Thorne again seemed an insurmountable challenge.

Twenty minutes later Thorne was still smarting from the tongue-lashing he'd received from a very sturdily built and strong-willed nurse who allowed him one glimpse of Randi's infant, then ushered him out of the pediatric intensive care unit. Thorne had peered through thick glass to an airy room where two newborns were sleeping in plastic bassinets. Randi's boy had lain under lamps, a shock of red-blond hair sticking upward, his tiny lips moving slightly as he breathed. To his utter surprise, Thorne had felt an unexpected pull on his heartstrings and he'd promptly advised himself that idiocy ran in the McCafferty family. Nonetheless Thorne had stared at the baby, so tiny, so mystifying, so innocent and unaware of all the turmoil he had caused.

As he'd left the pediatric unit Thorne wondered about the man who had fathered the child. Who was he? Shouldn't he be contacted? Was Randi in love with him? Or…had she hidden her pregnancy and the fact that she was involved with someone from her brothers for a reason?

Thorne didn't care. He'd find out about the kid's father if it killed him. And he couldn't sit idle just waiting for Randi to recover. No, there was too much to do. Ramming his hands into his coat pockets, he took a flight of stairs to the first floor.

"Think," he ordered himself and a plan started forming in his mind. First he had to make sure that both Randi and her child were on the road to recovery, then he'd hire a private investigator to look into his sister's life. Wincing at the thought of prying into Randi's private business, he rationalized that he had no choice. In her current state, Randi couldn't help herself. Nor could she care for her child.

Thorne would have to locate the baby's father, interview the son of a bitch, then set up a trust fund for the kid.

Already planning how to attack the "Randi situation" as he'd begun to think of it, he shouldered open a door to the parking lot. Outside, the wind raged. Ice-cold raindrops beat down from a leaden sky. He hiked his collar more closely around his neck and ducked his head. Skirting puddles, he strode toward his vehicle—a Ford pickup that was usually garaged at the ranch's airstrip.

Then he saw her.

Running to her car, her briefcase held over her head, Dr. Nicole Stevenson—Nikki Sanders once upon a time— dashed toward a white four-wheel-drive that was parked in a nearby lot.

Rain ran down his neck and dripped off his nose as he watched her. Her hair was no longer pinned to the back of her head, but caught in the wind. Her stark white lab coat had been replaced by a long leather jacket cinched firmly around her waist.

Without thinking, Thorne swept across the puddle-strewn lot. "Nikki!"

She looked up and he was stunned. "Oh. Thorne." With raindrops caught in the sweep of her eyelashes and her blond-streaked hair tossed around her face in soft layers, she was more gorgeous than he remembered. Raindrops slipped down sculpted cheekbones to a small mouth that was set in a startled pout.

For a split second he thought of kissing her, but quickly shoved that ridiculous thought from his mind.

She jabbed her key into the SUV's lock. "What're you doing lurking around out here?"

"Maybe I was waiting for you," he said automatically—actually *flirting* with her. For the love of God, what had gotten into him?

He saw her eyes round a bit, then one corner of her mouth lifted in sarcasm. "Try again."

"Okay, how about this? I just got finished dealing with Nurse Ratched up in Pediatrics and was tossed out on my ear."

"Someone intimidated you?" One eyebrow lifted in disbelief. "I don't think so." If she'd been teasing him before, she'd obviously thought better of it and her smile fell away. She yanked open the door and the interior light blinked on. "Now…was there something you wanted?"

You, he thought, then chided himself. What the devil was he thinking? What they'd shared was long over. "I didn't get your home number."

"I didn't give it to you."

"Because of your husband?"

"What? No." She shook her head. "There is no husband, not anymore." She was standing between the car and open door, waiting, her hair turning dark with the rain. His heart raced. She was single. "You can reach me here," she said. "If it's an emergency, the hospital will page me."

"I'd feel better if I could—"

"Look, Thorne," she said pointedly. "I understand that you're a man used to getting your way, of being in charge, of making things happen, but this time you can't, okay? At least not with me, not any more, nor with St. James Hospital. So, if there's nothing else, you'll have to excuse me." Her eyes weren't the least bit warm and yet her lips, slick with rainwater, just begged to be kissed.

And, damn it, he reacted. Knowing that she'd probably slap him silly, he grabbed her, hauled her body close to his and bent his head so that his lips were suspended just above hers. "Okay, Nikki," he said as he felt her tense. "I excuse you." Then he kissed her, pressed his mouth over hers and felt a second's surrender when her lips parted and her breath mingled with his as rain drenched them both. The scent of her perfume teased his nostrils and memories of making love to her over and over again burned through his brain. Dear God, how she'd responded to him then, just as she was now. He was lost in the feel of her and old emotions escaped from the place where he'd so steadfastly locked them long ago. With a groan, he kissed her harder, deeper, his arms tightening around her.

Her entire body stiffened. She jerked her head away as if she'd been burned. "Don't," she warned, her voice husky, her lips trembling a bit. She swallowed hard, then leaned back to glare up at him. "Don't ever do this again. This—" she raised a hand only to let it fall "—this was uncalled-for and...and entirely...*entirely* inappropriate."

"Entirely," he agreed, not releasing her.

"I mean it, Thorne."

"Why? Because I scare you?"

"Because whatever you and I shared together is over."

He lifted a doubting eyebrow as rain drizzled down his face. "Then why—?"

"Over!" Her eyes narrowed and she pulled out of his embrace. Though he wanted nothing more than to drag her close again, he let her go and tamped down the fire that had stormed through his blood, the pulse of lust that had thudded in his brain and caused a heat to burn in his loins. "I don't know what happened to you in the past seventeen years, but believe me, you should take some lessons in subtlety."

"Should I? Maybe you could give them to me."

"Me?" She let out a whisper of a laugh. "Right. Just don't hold your breath."

She slid into the interior of the car and reached for the door handle. Before she could yank the door closed, he said, "Okay, maybe I was outta line."

"Oh? You think?"

"I know."

"Good, then it won't happen again." She crammed her key into the ignition, muttered something about self-important bullheaded men, twisted her wrist and sent him a look that was meant to cut to the quick. The SUV's engine sputtered, then died. "Don't do this to me," she said and he wondered if she was talking to him or her rig. "Don't do this to me now." She turned the key again and the engine ground but didn't catch. "Damn."

"If you need a ride—"

"It'll start. It's just temperamental."

"Like its owner."

"If you say so." She took a deep breath, snapped her seat belt into place and grabbed the handle of her door. "Good night, Thorne." She yanked the door closed, turned the key again and finally the rig roared to life. Pressing on the gas pedal, she revved the engine and rolled down the window. "I'll let you know if there are any changes in your sister's condition." With that she tore out of the parking lot and Thorne, watching the taillights disappear, mentally kicked himself.

He'd been a fool to grab her.

And yet he knew he'd do it again.
If given half a chance.
Yep, he'd do it in a heartbeat.

Chapter 3

"God help me," Nicole whispered, trying to understand why in the world Thorne would embrace her so intimately and more to the point, why didn't she stop him. *Because you wanted him to, you idiot.*

As she wheeled out of the parking lot, she glanced in the rearview mirror, and saw him standing beneath a security light. Tall, broad-shouldered, bareheaded, rain dripping from the tip of his nose and the hem of his coat, he watched her leave. "Cocky son of a gun," she muttered, flipping on her blinker and joining the thin stream of traffic. She hoped Thorne Almighty McCafferty got soaked to the skin. She switched her windshield wipers to a faster pace to keep up with the rain. Who was he to barge in on her, to question her and the hospital's integrity and then…and then have the audacity, the sheer arrogance, to grab her as if she were some weak-willed, starry-eyed, spineless…ninny!

Oh, like the girl you once were, the one he remembered?

She blushed and her fingers curled around the steering wheel in a death grip. She'd worked hard for years to overcome her shyness, to become the confident, scholarly, take-charge emergency room physician she was today and Thorne McCafferty seemed hell-bent to change all that. Well, she wouldn't let him. No way. No how. She wasn't the little girl he'd left a lifetime ago—her broken heart had mended.

As she braked for a red light, she flipped on the radio, fumbled with the stations until she heard a melody that was familiar—Whitney Houston singing something she should know—and tried to calm down. Why she let Thorne get to her, she didn't understand.

She cranked the wheel and turned into a side street where the neon lights and Western facade of Montana Joe's Pizza Parlor came into view.

She pulled into the lot, raced inside and waited in line between five or six other patrons whose raincoats, parkas and ski jackets dripped water onto the tile floor in front of the take-out counter. A gas flame hissed in the fireplace in one corner of the room that was divided by fences into different seating areas. Pickaxes and shovels and other mining memorabilia were tacked to bare cedar walls and in one corner, Montana Joe, a stuffed bison, stared with glassy eyes at the patrons who were listening to Garth Brooks's latest hit while drinking beer and eating hot, stringy pizza made with Joe's "secret" tomato sauce.

As Nicole stood in line and dug into her wallet to check how much cash she was carrying, she couldn't help but overhear some of the conversation of the other patrons. Two men in front of her were discussing the previous Friday's high school football game. From the sound of it the Grand Hope Wolverines were edged out by an arch rival in a nearby town though there was some dispute over a few of the calls. Typical.

Other conversations buzzed around her and she heard the name McCafferty more often than she wanted to. "Terrible accident...half sister, you know...pregnant, but no mention of a father and no husband...always was bad blood in that family...what goes around comes around, I tell you..."

Nicole grabbed a menu from the counter and turned her attention from the gossip that swirled around her. Though Grand Hope had grown by leaps and bounds in the past few years and had become a major metropolis by Montana standards, it was still, at its heart, a small town, where many of the citizens knew each other. She placed her order, lingered near the jukebox and listened to three or four songs ranging from Patsy Cline to Wynona Judd, then, once her name was called, picked up her pizza and refused to think about any member of the McCafferty family—especially Thorne. He was off-limits. Period. The reason she'd responded to his kiss was simple. It had been over two years since she'd kissed any man and at least five since she'd felt even the tiniest spark of passion. She didn't even want to think how long it had been since she'd been consumed with desire—that particular thought led her back to a path that she didn't want to follow, a path heading straight back to her youth and Thorne. She was just susceptible right now, that was all. Nothing more. It had nothing to do with chemistry. Nothing.

Once in her SUV again, she twisted on the key and the engine refused to fire. "Come on, come on," she muttered. She tried again, pumping the gas frantically and mentally chiding herself for not taking the rig into the shop for its regular maintenance. "You can do it," she encouraged and finally, on the fourth attempt, the engine caught. "Tomorrow," she promised, patting the dash as if comforting the vehicle, as if that would help. "I'll take you in. Promise."

On the road again, Nicole drove through the side streets to her little cottage on the outskirts of town. Her stomach rumbled as the tangy scents of melting cheese and spicy sauce filled the rig's interior and her mind, damn it, ran back to Thorne and the feel of his lips on hers. He was everything she despised in a man: arrogant, competitive, in control and determined—a real corporate Type A and the kind of man she had learned to avoid like the plague. But beneath his layer of pride and his take-charge mentality, she'd caught glimpses of a more complex man, a gentler soul who stumbled through the awkwardness of talking to his comatose sister. He'd tried to communicate with Randi, the back of his neck flushing in embarrassment, his steely gray eyes conveying a sense of raw pain at his sister's condition—as if he somehow blamed himself for her accident.

"Don't read more into it than there is," she warned herself as she cranked the wheel and braked in her driveway. She pulled to a stop in front of her garage and made a mental note that between helping at preschool, the twins' dance lessons, the housework and the grocery shopping, she should call a roofer for a bid on the sagging roof.

Juggling her briefcase and boxed pizza, she made a mad dash to the back porch and was able to unlock the door, then shove it open with her hip.

Patches, her black-and-white cat, streaked through the opening and Nicole nearly tripped on the speeding feline. Tiny footsteps thundered through the house. "Mommy! Mommy! Mommy!" the twins cried, flying pell-mell into the kitchen and sliding on the yellowed linoleum as Patches slunk down the bedroom hallway. Molly and Mindy were dressed in identical pink-and-white-checked sleepers that zipped up the front and covered their feet in attached slippers. Their hair was wet and curled in dark-brown ringlets around cherubic faces and bright brown eyes.

Nicole slid the pizza onto a counter, knelt and opened

her arms wide. The four-year-old imps nearly bowled her over. "Miss me?" she asked.

"Yeth," Mindy said shyly, nodding her head and smiling.

"You got pizza?" Molly demanded. "I'm hungry."

"I sure do. Lots of it." She dropped kisses on each wet head, then standing once again, she stripped out of her coat and hung it in a tiny closet near the eating alcove.

Jenny Riley appeared in the archway separating the kitchen from the dining room. Tall and willowy, with long straight black hair and a nose ring, the twenty-year-old had been the twins' nanny since Nicole had moved to Grand Hope.

"How were they today?" Nicole asked.

"Miserable as usual," Jenny said, her green eyes twinkling, sarcasm lacing her words.

"Were not!" Molly said, planting her little fists on her hips. "We was good."

"Were," Nicole corrected. "You were good."

"Yeth," Mindy said, nodding agreement with her precocious sister. "Real good."

Jenny laughed and bent down to retie the laces of her elevated tennis shoes. "Oh, okay, I lied," she admitted. "You were good. Both of you. Very good."

"It's not nice to lie!" Molly said with a toss of her wet curls.

"I know, I know, it won't happen again," Jenny promised, straightening and slinging the strap of her fringed leather purse over her shoulder.

"Want a piece of pizza?" Nicole offered. Using her fingers and a spatula she'd grabbed from a hook over the stove, she slid piping hot slices onto paper plates. The girls scrambled onto the booster seats. Nicole licked a piece of melted cheese from her fingers and looked questioningly at Jenny.

"No thanks, Mom's got dinner waiting and—" Jenny winked broadly "—I've got a hot date after."

"Oooh," Nicole said, licking gooey cheese from her fingers. "Anyone I know?"

"Nope. Not unless you're into twenty-two-year-old cowboys."

"Only in the ER. I have been known to treat them upon occasion."

"Not this one," Jenny said with a wide grin and slight blush.

"Tell me more."

"His name is Adam. He's a hired hand at the McCafferty spread. And... I'll fill you in more later."

Nicole's good mood vanished at the mention of the McCaffertys. Today, it seemed, she couldn't avoid them for a minute.

"Gotta run," Jenny said as Molly reached across the table to peel off pieces of pepperoni from her sister's slice of pizza.

Mindy sent up a wail guaranteed to wake the dead in every cemetery in the county. "No!" she cried. "Mommeee!"

Grinning, Molly dangled all the pilfered slices of pepperoni over her open mouth before dropping them onto her tongue. Gleefully she chewed them in front of her sister.

"I'm outta here," Jenny said and slipped through the door as Nicole tried to right the wrong and Patches, appearing from the hallway, had the nerve to hop onto the counter near the microwave.

"You, down!" Nicole said, clapping her hands loudly. The cat leaped to the floor and darted in a black-and-white streak into the living room. "Everyone seems to have an attitude today." She turned her attention back to the twins and pointed at Molly. "Don't touch your sister's food."

"She's not eating it," Molly argued while chewing.

"Am, too!" Big tears rolled down Mindy's face.

"But it's hers and—"

"And we're s'posed to share. You said so."

"Not your food…well, not now. You know better. Now, come on, there's no real harm done here." Nicole picked off pepperoni slices from another piece of pizza and placed them on the half-eaten wedge that sat on Mindy's plate. "Good as new."

But the damage was done. Mindy wouldn't stop sobbing and pointing a condemning finger at her twin. "You, bad!"

Molly shook her head. "Am not."

Nicole shot her outspoken daughter a look meant to silence her, then picked Mindy up and, consoling her while walking toward the hallway, whispered into her ear, "Come on, big girl, let's brush your teeth and get you into bed."

"Don't wanna—" Mindy complained and Molly cackled loudly before realizing she was alone. Quickly she slid out of her chair and little feet pounding, ran after Nicole and Mindy. In the bathroom, the dispute was forgotten, tears were wiped away and two sets of teeth were brushed. As the pizza cooled, mozzarella cheese congealing, Nicole and the girls spent the next twenty minutes cuddled beneath a quilt in her grandmother's old rocker. She read them two stories they'd heard a dozen times before. Mindy's eyes immediately shut while Molly, ever the fighter, struggled to stay awake only to drop off a few minutes later.

For the first time that day, Nicole felt at peace. She eyed the fire that Jenny had built earlier. Dying embers and glowing coals in deep ashes were all that remained to light the little living room in shades of gold and red. Humming, she rocked until she, too, nearly dozed off.

Struggling out of the chair she managed to carry her daughters into their bedroom and tuck them into matching twin beds. Mindy yawned and rolled over, her thumb moving instinctively to her mouth and Molly blinked twice, said, "I love you, Mommy," then fell asleep again.

"Me, too, baby. Me, too." She kissed each daughter and smelled the scents of shampoo and baby powder, then walked softly to the door.

Molly sighed loudly. Mindy smacked her little lips.

Folding her arms over her chest Nicole leaned against the doorjamb.

Her ex-husband's words, "You'll never make it on your own," echoed through her mind and she felt her spine stiffen. *Right, Paul,* she thought now, *but I'm not on my own. I've got the kids. And I'm going to make it. On my own.*

Every minute of that painful, doomed marriage was worth it because she had the girls. They were a family— maybe not an old-fashioned, traditional, 1950s sitcom family, but a family nonetheless.

She thought fleetingly of Randi's baby, tucked away in the maternity ward, his father not yet found, his mother in a coma and she wondered what would become of the little boy.

But the baby has Thorne and Matt and Slade. Between the three of them, certainly the boy would be taken care of. Every one of the McCafferty brothers seemed interested in the child, but each one of them was a bachelor—how confirmed, she didn't know.

"Not that it matters," she reminded herself and glanced outside where rain was dripping from the gutters and splashing against the window. She thought of Thorne again, of the way his lips felt against hers, and she realized that she had to avoid being alone with him. She had to keep their relationship professional because she knew from experience that Thorne was trouble.

Big trouble.

He was making a mistake of incredible proportions and he knew it, but he couldn't stop himself. Driving through the city streets and silently marveling at how this town had grown, he'd decided to see Nikki again before returning to the ranch. She'd probably throw him out and he really didn't blame her as he'd come on way too strong, but he had to see her again.

After watching her wheel out of the parking lot after their last confrontation, he'd walked back into the hospital, downed a cup of bitter coffee in the cafeteria, then tried to track down any doctor remotely associated with Randi and the baby. He'd struck out with most, left messages on their answering machines and after talking to a nurse in Pediatrics and one in ICU, he'd called the ranch, told Slade that he'd be back soon, then paused at the gift shop in the hospital lobby, bought a single white rose and, ducking his shoulders against the rain, ran outside and climbed into his truck.

"This is nuts," he told himself as he drove across a bridge and into an established part of town, to the address he'd found in the telephone directory when he'd made his calls to the other doctors. Bracing himself for a blistering reception, he parked in front of the small cottage, grabbed the single flower and climbed out of the car.

Jaw set he dashed up the cement walk, and before he could change his mind, pressed on the door buzzer. He'd been in tighter spots than this. He heard noises inside, the sound of feet. The porch light snapped on and he saw her eyebrows and eyes peer through one of the three small windows cut into the door. A moment later they disappeared as, he supposed, she dropped to her flat feet from her tiptoes.

Locks clicked. The door opened. And there she stood, all five feet three of her wrapped in a fluffy white robe. "Is there something I can do for you?" she asked without a smile. Her eyes skated from his face to the flower in his hands.

He nearly laughed. "You know, this seemed like a good idea at the time but now…now I feel like a damned fool."

"Because?" Again the lift of that lofty eyebrow.

"Because I thought I owed you an apology for the way I came on earlier."

"In the parking lot?"

"And the hospital."

"You were upset. Don't worry about it."

"I wasn't just upset. I was, as I said before, out of line, and I'd like to make it up to you."

Her chin lifted a fraction. "Make it up to me? With… that?" she asked, one finger pointing to the single white bud.

"To start with." He handed her the flower and thought, beneath her hard posturing, he caught a glimpse of a deeper emotion. She held the flower, lifted it to her nose and sighed.

"Thanks. This is enough…more than you needed to do."

"No, I think I owe you an explanation."

She tensed again. "It was only a kiss. I'll live."

"I mean about the past."

"No!" She was emphatic. "Look, let's just forget it, okay? It's been a long day. For both of us. Thanks for the flower and the apology, it's…it's very nice of you, but I think it would be best—for everyone, including your sister and her new baby—if we both just pretended that nothing ever happened between us."

"Can you?"

"Y-yes. Of course."

He couldn't stop one side of his mouth from twitching upward. "Liar," he said and Nicole nearly took a step backward. Who was he to stop by her house and…and *what? Apologize? What's the crime in that? Why don't you ask him in and offer him a cup of coffee or a drink?*

"No!"

"You're not a liar?"

"Not usually," she said, recovering a bit. She felt the lapel of her bathrobe gap and it took all of her willpower not to clutch it closed like a silly, frightened virgin. "You seem to bring out the worst in me."

"Ditto." He leaned forward and she expected him to kiss her again, but instead of molding his lips to hers, he brushed his mouth across the slope of her cheek in the briefest of touches. "Good night, Doctor," he whispered and then he turned and hurried down the porch steps to dash through the rain.

She stood in the glow of the porch lamp, her fingers curled possessively around the rose's stem and watched him steer his truck around in her driveway before he drove into the night. Forcing herself inside, she closed and bolted the door. She didn't know what was happening, but she was certain it wasn't going to be good.

She couldn't, wouldn't get involved with Thorne again. No way. No how. In fact, she'd toss the damned flower into the garbage right now. Padding to the kitchen she opened the cupboard under the sink, pulled out the trash can and hesitated. How childish. Thorne was trying to make amends. Nothing more. She touched the side of her cheek, then placed the rosebud in a small vase, certain it would mock her for the next week.

"Don't let him get to you," she warned, but had the fatalistic sensation that it was already too late. He'd gotten to her a long, long time ago.

Thorne parked outside of what had once been the machine shed and eyed the home where he'd been raised, a place he'd once vowed to leave and never return. Though it was dark and the rain was coming down in sheets, he saw the house looming on its small rise, warm patches of light glowing from tall, paned windows. It had been a haven at one time, a prison later.

He grabbed his briefcase and the overnight bag and wondered what had come over him. Why had he stopped at Nikki's? There was more than just a simple apology involved and that thought disturbed him. It was as if seeing her again sparked something deep inside him, something he'd thought had burned out years before, a smoldering ember he hadn't known existed.

Whatever it was, he didn't have time for it and he didn't want to examine it too closely.

Lights blazed from the stables and he recognized Slade's rig parked near the barn. As he ducked through the rain he remembered the first time he'd seen Nicole—years ago at a local Fourth of July celebration in town. He'd been back from college, ready to enter law school in the fall, randy as hell and anxious to get on with his life. She'd only been seventeen, a shy girl with the most incredible eyes he'd ever seen as she'd staked out a spot on a hill overlooking the town and waited for darkness and the fireworks that were planned.

Funny, he hadn't thought of that night in a long, long time. It seemed a million years ago and was tangled up in the other memories that haunted this particular place. As he walked up the front steps he remembered nearly drowning in the swimming hole when he was about eight, hunting pheasants with his brothers and pretending the cold silence between his parents really didn't exist. But the memories that were the clearest, the most poignantly bright, were of Nikki.

"Yeah, well, don't go there," he warned himself as he yanked open the screen door. He walked inside and was greeted by the smells of his youth—soot from the fireplace, fresh lemon wax on the floors, and the lingering aroma of bacon that had been fried earlier in the day and still wisped through the familiar hallways and rooms. He dropped his briefcase and bag near the front door and swiped the rain from his face.

"Thorne?" Matt's voice rang loudly through the century-old house. The sound of boots tripping down the stairs heralded his brother's arrival onto the first floor. "I wondered when you'd show up." Forever in jeans and a flannel shirt with the sleeves rolled up, Matt clapped his brother on the shoulder. "How're you, you old bastard?"

"Same as ever."

"Mean and ornery and on your way to your next million-dollar deal?" Matt asked, as he always did, but this time the question hit a nerve and gave him pause.

"I can only hope," he said, unbuttoning his coat, though it was a lie. He was jaded with his life. Bored. Wanted more. He just wasn't sure what.

"How's Randi?" Matt asked, his face becoming a mask of concern.

"The same as when you saw her. Nothing new to report since I called you from the hospital."

"I guess it's just gonna take time." Matt hitched his chin toward the living room where lamplight filtered into the hallway. "Come on in. I'll buy you a drink. You look like you could use one."

"That bad?"

"We could all use one today."

Thorne nodded. "So where's Slade?"

"Feeding the stock. He'll be in soon. I was just on my way to help him, but since you're here, I figure it won't hurt him to finish the job by himself." Matt flashed his killer smile, the one that had charmed more women than Thorne wanted to count.

Matt had been described as tall, dark and handsome by too many local girls to remember. The middle of the three McCafferty brothers, Matt's eyes were so deep brown they were nearly black, his skin tanned from spending hours outdoors, and the shadow covering his jaw was as dark as their father's had once been.

Sinewy and rawhide tough, Matt McCafferty could bend a horseshoe at a forge as well as he could brand a mustang or rope a maverick calf. Raw. Wild. Stubborn as hell.

Matt belonged here.

Thorne didn't.

Not since his parents had divorced.

"Look at you." Matt gave a sharp whistle. One near-black eyebrow cocked as he fingered the wool of Thorne's coat. "Since when did you become a fashion statement?"

Thorne snorted in derision. "Don't think I am. But I happened to be at work when Slade got hold of me." Thorne hung his coat on an aging brass hook mounted near the door. The long wool overcoat seemed out of place in the array of denim, down and sheepskin jackets. "Didn't have time to change." He pulled at the knot in his tie and let the silk drape over his shoulders. "Tell me what's going on."

"Good question." Together they walked into the living room where the leather couches were worn, an upright piano gathered dust, and two rockers placed at angles near blackened stones of the fireplace remained unmoving. His great-grandfather's rifle was mounted over the mantel, resting on the spikes of antlers from an elk killed long ago. "There's not a lot to tell."

Matt opened the liquor cabinet hidden in cupboards beneath a bookcase filled with leather-backed tomes that hadn't been read in years. "What'll it be?"

"Scotch."

"Straight up?"

"You got it…well, I think."

Matt scrounged around in the cabinet and with a snort of approval withdrew a dusty bottle. "Looks like you're in luck." He reached farther into the recesses of the cabinet, came up with a couple of glasses and, after giving them each a swipe with the tail of his shirt, poured two healthy shots. "I could get ice from the kitchen."

"Waste of time. Unless you want it."

Matt's smile was a slow grin. "I think I'm man enough to handle warm liquor."

"Figured as much."

Thorne took the drink Matt offered and clicked the rim of his glass to his brother's. "To Randi."

"Yep."

Thorne tossed back his drink, unwinding a bit as the aged liquor splashed against the back of his throat then burned a fiery path to his stomach. He rotated his neck, trying to relieve the kinks in his neck. "Okay, so shoot," he said, as Matt lit tinder-dry kindling already stacked in the grate. "What the hell's going on?"

"Wish I knew. Near as the police can tell, Randi was involved in a single-car accident up in Glacier Park. No one knows for sure what happened and the cops are still lookin' into it, but, from what anyone can piece together, she was alone and driving and probably hit ice, or swerved to miss something—who the hell knows what, a deer maybe, your guess is as good as mine. The upshot is that she lost control and drove over the side of the road. The truck rolled down an embankment and—" he studied the depths of his glass "—she and the baby are lucky to be alive."

Thorne's jaw tightened. "Who found her?"

"Passersby—Good Samaritans who called the local sheriff's department."

"You got their names?"

Matt reached into his back pocket and withdrew a piece of paper that he handed to Thorne. "Jed and Bill Swanson. Brothers who were on their way home from a hunting trip. The deputy's name is on there, too."

He read the list of names and numbers, his eyes lingering for a second when he came to Dr. Nicole Stevenson.

"I figured we should keep a list of everyone involved."

"Good idea." Thorne tucked the piece of paper into his pocket. "So do you have any idea what Randi was doing at Glacier or anywhere around here for that matter? The last I heard she was in Seattle. What about her job? Or the father of the baby?"

Matt finished his drink. "Don't know a damned thing," he admitted.

"Well, that's gotta change. The three of us—Slade, you and I—we've got to find out what's going on."

"Fine with me." Matt's determined gaze held his brother's.

"We'll start tonight." The gears were already turning in Thorne's mind. "As soon as Slade gets in, we'll start making plans. But first things first."

"Randi and the baby's health," Matt guessed.

"Yep. We can start digging around in her private life as much as we want, but it doesn't mean a damned thing if she or the baby don't pull through."

"They will." Matt was cocksure as the front door banged open and Slade appeared.

"Thanks for all the help," the youngest brother grumbled as he marched into the room smelling of horses and smoke. He found a glass and poured himself a stiff shot.

"You managed," Matt guessed.

Thorne rolled up his sleeves. "Why are you so sure that Randi and her boy will be okay?"

One side of Matt's mouth lifted. "Because they're Mc-Caffertys, Thorne. Just like us—too ornery not to pull through."

But Thorne wasn't convinced.

Chapter 4

"Don't want to dance," Molly insisted as Nicole shepherded both her daughters from the preschool and into the SUV. The rain had stopped in the night and an October sun peered through high, thin clouds.

"Why not?"

"Don't like it." Molly climbed into her car seat and started hooking the straps together while Mindy waited for her mother to snap her into place.

"Next year you can play soccer and we've got swim lessons in the spring. Until then, I think we'll stick with dance. I already paid for the lessons and they won't hurt you."

"I like to dance," Mindy said, casting her more outspoken sibling a look of pure piety. "I like Miss Palmer."

"I *hate* Miss Palmer." Molly crossed her chubby arms over her chest and glowered at the back of the passenger seat as Nicole slid behind the steering wheel.

"It's not nice to hate." Mindy lifted her eyebrows imperiously and glanced knowingly at her mother. The angel, making sure Nicole knew that Molly was being the embodiment of evil.

"*Hate*'s a pretty strong word," Nicole said and started the SUV. The engine fired on the first try. "Atta girl," she added and Mindy nodded, thinking her mother was praising her. Dark curls bounced around her head as she sent her twin a holier-than-thou look of supreme patience.

"Quit that! Mommy, she's *looking* at me."

"It's okay."

"I want ice cream," Molly insisted.

"Right after dance."

"I *hate* dance."

"I know, I know, we've been over this before," Nicole said adjusting the heat and defrost. Sun or no sun, the air was still cold. She drove over a small bridge and past a strip mall to the older side of town where an old brick grade school had been converted into artists' quarters. She parked, took the girls inside, and rather than stay and watch them go through their routine, she drove to the service station where the mechanic looked under the hood of the SUV, lifted his grimy hat and scratched his head.

"Beats me," he admitted, shifting a toothpick from one side of his mouth to the other. An elderly man with a barrel body and silver beard stubble, he frowned and wiped the oil from his hands. "Seems to be working just fine. Why don't you bring it in next week and leave it—can you? We'll run diagnostics on it."

She made an appointment, mentally crossed her fingers, rounded up the girls and managed to stop at the grocery store and ice-cream parlor before they had a total meltdown.

"Why doesn't Daddy live with us?" Mindy asked as they pulled into the driveway of their house.

Nicole parked and pocketed her keys. "Because Mommy and Daddy are divorced, you know that. Come on, let's get out of the car."

"And Daddy lives far away," Molly said, drips of bubble-gum ice cream falling from her chin.

"He don't come and see us. Bobbi Martin's daddy comes and visits her."

"Would you like for your father to visit?" Nicole had opened the back door and was unsnapping the straps to Mindy's car seat.

"Yeth."

"Nope." Molly shook her head. "He don't like us."

"Oh, Molly—" Nicole was about to argue and then saw no reason to defend Paul. He'd had no interest in the twins since the divorce. Sending Nicole child support payments seemed to fulfill all his requirements as a father; at least in his opinion. "You just don't know your father."

"Is he going to come see us?" Mindy asked, her eyes bright, her ice-cream cone forgotten. The single scoop of cookies-'n'-cream was melting into her fingers.

"I don't know. He doesn't have any plans to, not yet. But, if you like, I could call him."

"Call him!" Mindy swiped at the top of her cone with her tongue.

"He won't come." Molly didn't seem upset about it; she was just stating a fact. "You can have the rest," she said, handing her mother the cone and bolting from the rig. She tore off across the wet grass to the swing set.

"Can't you undo this yourself?" Nicole asked lifting the safety bar of the car seat.

"You do it." Mindy smiled impishly, then, still clutching her cone, slid out of the car.

You're spoiling her, Nicole told herself as she juggled the grocery sacks and carried them into the house. *You're spoiling them both, trying to be father and mother, feeling sorry for them because, they, like you, are growing up without their father.*

Was it her fault? She had a lot of reasons for moving

away from San Francisco, for wanting to start over. But maybe in so doing, she was robbing her daughters of a vital part of their lives, of the chance to know the man who'd sired them.

Not that he'd shown any interest when they still lived in the city. He'd never seen the girls for more than a couple of hours at a time and his new wife had been pretty clear that she saw his twins as "baggage" she didn't want or need.

So Nicole wasn't going to beat herself up about it. The twins were doing fine. Just fine.

Patches, who had been washing his face on the windowsill, hopped lithely to the floor. "Naughty boy," Nicole whispered, but added some dry food to his dish, unpacked the groceries and watched her girls through the back window. They were playing on the teeter-totter, laughing in the crisp air as clouds began to gather again. Nicole pressed the play button on the answering machine.

The first voice she heard was Thorne McCafferty's.

"Hi. It's Thorne. Call me." He rattled off his phone number and Nicole's stomach did a flip at the sound of it. Why he got to her after all these years she didn't understand, but he did. There was no doubt about it. She knew that he'd been her first love, but it had been years, *years* since then. So why did he still affect her? She glanced to the windowsill where she'd placed the bud vase with its single white rose—a peace offering, nothing more.

Sighing, she wished she understood why she couldn't shake Thorne from her thoughts. She wasn't a lonely woman. She wasn't a needy woman. She *didn't* want a man in her life—at least not yet. So why was it that every time she heard his voice those old memories that she'd tucked away escaped to run and play havoc through her mind?

"Because you're an idiot," she said and finished unloading the car. She remembered seeing him for the first time, the summer before her senior year in high school. He'd been alone, dusk was settling, the sky still glowing pink over the western hills, the first stars beginning to sparkle in the night. The heat of the day hung heavy in the air with only a breath of a breeze to lift her hair or brush her cheeks. She was sitting on a blanket, alone, her best friend having ditched her at the last minute to be with her boyfriend and suddenly Thorne had appeared, tall, strapping, wearing a T-shirt that stretched over his shoulders and faded jeans that hung low on his hips.

"Is this spot taken?" he'd asked and she hadn't responded, thinking he had to be talking to someone else.

"Excuse me," he'd said again and she'd twisted her face up to stare into intense gray eyes that took hold of her and wouldn't let go. "Would it be all right if I sat here?"

She couldn't believe her ears. There were dozens of blankets tossed upon the bent grass of the hillside, hundreds of people gathered and picnicking as they waited for the show. And he wanted to sit *here?* Next to her? "Oh, well…sure," she'd managed to reply, feeling like an utter fool, her face burning with embarrassment.

He'd taken a spot next to her on her blanket, his arms draped over half-bent knees, his spine curved, his body so close to hers she could smell some kind of cologne or soap, barely an inch between his shoulder and hers. Suddenly she found it impossible to breathe. "Thanks," he said, his voice low, his smile a flash of white against a strong, beard-shadowed chin. "I'm Thorne. McCafferty."

She'd recognized the name, of course, had heard the rumors and gossip swirling about his family. She had even met his younger brothers upon an occasion or two, but she'd never been face-to-face with the oldest McCafferty son. Never in her life had she felt the wild drumming of her heart just because a man—and that was it, he wasn't a boy—was regarding her with assessing steely eyes.

Five or six years older than she, he seemed light-years ahead of her in sophistication. He'd been off to college somewhere on the East Coast, she thought, an Ivy League school, though she couldn't really remember which one.

"I imagine you do have a name." His lips twitched and she felt even a bigger fool.

"Oh...yes. I'm Nicole Sanders." She started to offer him her hand, then let it drop.

"Is that what you go by? Nicole?"

"Yeah." She swallowed hard and glanced away. Clearing her throat she nodded. "Sometimes Nikki." She felt like a little girl in her ponytail and cutoff jeans and sleeveless blouse with the shirttails tied around her waist.

"Nikki, I like that." Plucking a long piece of dry grass from the hillside he shoved it into his mouth and as Nicole surreptitiously watched, he moved it from one sexy corner to the other. And he was sexy. More purely male and raw than any boy she'd ever been with. "You live around here?"

"Yeah. In town. Alder Street."

"I'll remember that," he promised and her silly heart took flight. "Alder."

Dear God, she thought she'd die. Right then and there. He winked at her, stretched out and leaned back on his elbows while taking in the back of her head and the darkening heavens.

As the fireworks had started that night, bursting in the sky in brilliant flashes of green, yellow and blue, Nicole Frances Sanders spent the evening in exquisite teenage torment and, without a thought to the consequences, began to fall in love.

It seemed eons ago—a magical point in time that was long past. But, like it or not, even now, while standing in her cozy little kitchen, she felt the tingle of excitement, the lilt, she'd always experienced when she'd been with Thorne.

"Don't go there," she warned herself, her hands gripping the edge of the counter so hard her fingers ached. "That was a long, long time ago." A time Thorne, no doubt, didn't remember.

She waited until she'd fed and bathed the girls, read them stories, and then, dreading talking to him, punched out the number for the Flying M Ranch.

Thorne picked up on the second ring. "Flying M. Thorne McCafferty."

"Hi, it's Nicole. You called?" she asked while the twins ran pell-mell through the house.

"Yeah. I thought we should get together."

She nearly dropped the phone. "Get together? For?"

"Dinner."

A *date?* He was asking her out? Her heart began to thud and in the peripheral vision she saw the rose with its soft white petals beginning to open. "Was there a reason?"

"More than one, actually. I want to talk to you about Randi and the baby, of course. Their treatment, what happens if we can't find the baby's father, convalescent care and rehabilitation when Randi's finally released. That kind of thing."

"Oh." She felt strangely deflated. "Sure, I suppose, but her doctors will go over all this with you."

"But they're not you." His voice was low and her pulse elevated again.

"They're professionals."

"But I don't know them. I don't trust them."

"And you trust me?" she said, unable to stop herself.

"Yes."

The twins roared into the room. "Mommy, Mommy—she hit me!" Molly cried, outraged, while Mindy, eyes round, shook her head solemnly.

"Not me."

"Yes, she did."

"You hit me first." Molly began to wail.

"Thorne, would you excuse me. My daughters are in the middle of their own little war."

"Oh, I didn't realize." He paused for a second as she bent on one knee, stretching the phone cord and giving Molly a hug. "I didn't know you had children."

"Two girls, dynamos. I'm divorced," she added quickly. "Nearly two years now."

Was there a sigh of relief on his end of the conversation, or did she imagine it over Molly's sobs?

"I'll talk to you later," he said.

"Yes. Do." She hung up and threw her arms around both girls, but her thoughts were already rushing forward to thoughts of Thorne and being alone with him. She couldn't do it. Even though he'd tried to apologize for leaving her and she'd spent years fantasizing about just such a scenario, she wouldn't risk being with him again. It wasn't just herself and her heart she had to worry about now, she had the girls to consider. And yet…a part of her would love to see him again, to smile into his eyes, to kiss him… She pulled herself up short. What was she thinking? The kiss in the parking lot had been passionate, wild and evoked memories of their lovemaking so long ago, but it was the kiss on her cheek that had really gotten to her, the soft featherlike caress of his lips against her skin that made her want more.

"Stop it," she told herself.

"Stop what?" Mindy looked at her mother with wounded, teary eyes. "I didn't do it!"

"I know, sweetie, I know," Nicole said, determined not to let Thorne McCafferty bulldoze his way into her life... or her heart.

Thorne walked into the barn and shoved thoughts of Nicole out of his mind. He had too many other problems, pressing issues to deal with. Besides Randi's and the baby's health, there were questions about her accident and, of course, the ever-present responsibilities he'd left behind in Denver—hundreds of miles away but still requiring his attention.

The smells of fresh hay, dusty hides and oiled leather brought back memories of his youth—memories he'd pushed aside long ago. As the first few drops of rain began to pepper the tin roof, Slade was tossing hay bales down from the loft above. Matt carried the bales by their string to the appropriate mangers, then deftly sliced the twine with his jackknife. Thorne grabbed a pitchfork and, as he had every winter day in his youth, began shaking loose hay into the manger.

The cattle were inside lowing and shifting, edging toward the piles of feed. Red, dun, black and gray, their coats were thick with the coming of winter, covered with dust and splattered with mud.

After a day of being on the phone, the physical labor felt good and eased some of the tension from muscles that had been cramped in his father's desk chair. Thorne had called Nicole, his office in Denver, several clients and potential business partners, as well as local retailers as he needed equipment to set up a temporary office here at the ranch. But that had just been the beginning; the rest of the day he'd spent at the hospital, talking with doctors or searching for clues as to what had happened to his sister.

For the most part, he'd come up dry. "So no one's figured out why Randi was back in Montana?" he said, tossing a forkful of hay into the manger. A white-faced heifer plunged her broad nose into the hay.

"I called around this afternoon while you were at the hospital." The three brothers had visited their sister individually and checked in on their new nephew. Thorne had hoped to run into Nicole. He hadn't.

"What did you find out?"

"Diddly-squat." Another bale dropped from above. Slade swung down as well, landing next to Thorne and wincing at the jolt in his bad leg. His limp was still as noticeable as the red line that ran from his temple to his chin, compliments of a skiing accident that had nearly taken his life, though the scars on the outside of his face were far less damaging than those that, Thorne imagined, cut through his soul. "I talked to several people at the *Seattle Clarion* where she wrote her column, whatever the hell it is." Slade yanked a pitchfork from its resting place on the wall.

"Advice to the lovelorn," Thorne supplied. Drops of frigid rain drizzled down the small windows and a wind, screaming of winter, tore through the valley.

"It's a lot more than that," Matt said defensively. "It's general advice to single people. Things like legal issues, divorce settlements, raising kids alone, dealing with grief and new relationships, juggling time around career and kids, budgeting…hell, I don't know."

"Sounds like you do," Thorne said, realizing that Matt had maintained a stronger relationship with their half sister than he had. But then that hadn't been difficult.

"I take a paper that prints her column. It's been syndicated, y'know. Picked up by a few independents as far away as Chicago."

"Is that right?" Thorne felt a sharp jab of guilt. What did he know about his sister? Not much.

"Yeah, she adds her own touch—her quirky humor—and it sells."

"Since when did she become an expert?" Slade wanted to know.

"Beats me." Matt scratched the stubble on his chin. "Looks like she could've used some pearls of wisdom herself."

Thorne kicked at a bale, causing it to split open. Why hadn't Randi come to him, explained about the baby, confided in him if her life wasn't going well? His back teeth ground together and he reminded himself that maybe she didn't know things weren't on track, maybe this baby was planned. "Okay, so what else did you find out?" he asked, refusing to wallow in a sea of guilt.

Slade lifted a shoulder. "Not a hell of a lot. Her co-workers, of course, all figured out she was pregnant. She couldn't really hide it. But none of them admitted to knowing the father's name."

"You think they're lying?" Thorne asked.

"Not that I could tell."

"Great."

"No one even thinks she was dating anyone seriously."

"Looks serious enough to me," Matt grumbled.

Slade reached across the manger and pushed one cow's white face to the side so a smaller animal could wedge her nose into the hay. "Move, there," he commanded, though the beast didn't so much as flick her ears. Wiping his hand on the bleached denim of his jeans, he said, "Randi's editor, Bill Withers, said that she'd planned to take a three-month maternity leave, but he'd assumed she'd stay in town, because she told him that as soon as she was on her feet and she and the baby were settled in, she was going to work out of her condominium. She had enough columns written ahead that they'll run for a few weeks. Then, she'd be back at it again, though she didn't plan to start going into the office until after the first of the year."

"So there was no trouble at work?"

"None that anyone is saying, but I get the feeling that there was more going on than anyone's willing to admit."

"Par for the course. Reporters, they're always ready to snoop into anyone else's business—they've already been calling here, you know. But ask them about what they know and all of a sudden the First Amendment becomes the Bible." Matt snorted and picked up the used strands of baling twine. "Does anyone at her office know anything about her accident?"

"Nope." Slade dusted his hands. "They were shocked. Especially the ones she was supposedly closest to. Sarah Peeples, who writes movie reviews, gasped and nearly fell through the floor, from the sound of her end of the conversation. She couldn't believe that Randi was in the hospital and Dave Delacroix, he's a guy who writes a sports column for the paper, thought I was playing some kind of practical joke. Then once he figured out I was on the level, he got angry. Demanded answers. So, basically, I drew blanks."

"It's a start," Thorne said as they finished up. The wheels had been turning in his mind from the moment he'd heard about Randi's accident; now it was time to put some kind of plan into action. Slade forked the last wisps of hay into the manger. "I'll catch up with you," he said as he traded his pitchfork for a broom. "Pour me a drink."

"Will do." Thorne followed Matt outside and dashed through rain cold enough that he knew winter was in the air.

Once in the house again, Matt built another fire from last night's embers and Thorne poured them each a drink. As they waited for Slade, they sipped their father's Scotch and worried aloud about their headstrong sister and wondering how they would take care of a newborn.

"The problem is, none of us know much about Randi's life," Thorne said as he capped the bottle.

"I think that's the way she wanted it. We can beat ourselves up one side and down the other for not being a part of her life, but that was Randi's choice. Remember?"

How could he forget? At their father's funeral in May, Randi had been inconsolable, refusing any outward show of emotion from her brothers, preferring to stand in an oversize, gauzy black dress apart from the rest of the family, while a young preacher, who knew very little of the man in the coffin, prayed solemnly. Most of the townspeople of Grand Hope came to the service to pay their respects.

She had to have been four months pregnant at the time. Thorne would never have guessed as they paid their last respects on the hillside. But then he'd been lost in his own black thoughts, the ring his father had given him the summer before hidden deep in his pocket.

John Randall hadn't been a churchgoing man. Under the circumstances, the young minister whose eulogy had been from notes he'd taken the day earlier, had done a decent enough job asking that the blackheart's soul be accepted into heaven. Thorne wasn't certain God had made such a huge exception.

"Randi's kept her life pretty private."

"Haven't we all?" Matt remarked.

"Maybe it's time to change all that." Thorne ran a hand

through the thin layer of dust that had collected on the mantel.

"Agreed." Matt lifted his glass and nodded.

The front door banged open. A gust of cold wind blew through the hallway and Slade, wiping the rain from his face, hitched himself into the living room. He shrugged out of his jacket and tossed it over the back of the couch.

"Any word on Randi?" Making his way across the braided rug, Slade found an old-fashioned glass in the cupboard and without much fanfare, poured himself a long drink from the rapidly diminishing bottle of Scotch.

"Not yet. But I'll check the answering machine." Matt crossed the room and disappeared down the hallway leading to the den.

"She'd better pull out of this," Slade said, as if to himself. The youngest of the three brothers, Slade was also the wildest. He'd left a trail of broken hearts from Mexico to Canada, if rumors were to be believed and never had really settled down. While Matt had his own ranch, a small spread near the Idaho border, Slade had put down no roots and probably never would. He'd done everything from race cars, to ride rodeo, and do stunt work in films. The scar running down one side of his face was testament to his hard, reckless lifestyle and Thorne had, at times, wondered if the youngest McCafferty son harbored some kind of death wish.

Slade stood in front of the fire and warmed the backs of his legs. "What're we gonna do about the baby?"

"We take care of him until Randi's able."

"Then we'd better get this place ready," Slade observed.

"The orthopedist called earlier," Matt said, entering the room. "As soon as some of the swelling has gone down and Randi's out of critical condition, he'll take care of her leg."

"Good. I put a call in to Nicole. I want to meet with her so that she can tell me about Randi's doctors and her prognosis, rehab, that sort of thing."

"Nicole?" Matt replied, his eyes narrowing as if struck by a sudden memory. "You know she mentioned that you knew each other, but I'd forgotten that you were an item."

"It was only a few weeks," Thorne clarified.

Slade rubbed the back of his neck. "I hardly remember it."

"Because you were off racing cars and chasing women on the stock car circuit," Matt said. "You weren't around much when Thorne got out of college and was heading to law school. It was that summer, right?"

"Part of the summer."

Slade shook his head. "Let me guess, you dumped her for some other long-legged plaything."

"There was no other woman," Thorne snapped, surprised at the anger surging through his blood.

"No, you just had to go out and prove to Dad and God and anyone else who would listen that you could make it on your own without J. Randall's help."

"It was a long time ago," Thorne muttered. "Right now we've got to concentrate on Randi."

"And that's why you called Dr. Stevenson?" Obviously Matt wasn't buying it.

"Of course." Thorne sat on the arm of the leather couch and knew he was lying, not only to his brothers but to himself. It was more than just wanting to discuss Randi's condition with her; he wanted to see Nicole again, be with her. The strange part of it was, ever since seeing her again, he wanted to see more of her. "Now, listen," he said to his brothers. "Something we'll have to deal with and pronto is finding out who the father is."

"That's gonna be tough considerin' Randi's condition." Slade rested a shoulder against the mantel and folded his arms over his chest. "Just how long you plannin' on stickin' around, city boy?"

"As long as it takes."

"Aren't there some big deals in Denver and Laramie and wherever the hell else you own property—things you need to oversee?"

Thorne resisted being baited and managed a guarded grin, the kind Slade so often gave the rest of the world. "I can oversee them from here."

"How?"

"By the fine art of telecommunication. I'll set up a fax, modem, Internet connection, cell phone and computer in the den."

Matt rubbed his chin. "Thought you hated it here. Except for a few times like that summer after you graduated from college you've avoided this ranch like the plague. Ever since Dad and Mom split, you've spent as little time here as possible."

Thorne couldn't argue the fact. "Randi needs me—us."

Matt added wood to the fire and switched on a lamp. "Okay, I think we need a game plan," Thorne said.

"Let me guess, you'll be the quarterback, just like in high school," Slade said.

Thorne's temper snapped. "Let's just work together, okay? It's not about calling the shots so much as getting the job done."

"Okay." Matt nodded. "I'll be in charge of the ranch. I've already talked to a couple of guys who will help out."

Slade walked to the couch and picked up his jacket. "Good enough. Matt should run the place, he's used to it and I'll pitch in if we need an extra hand. Thorne, why don't you give Juanita a call? Maybe she can help with the baby. She's had some experience raising McCaffertys, after all, she helped Dad with us."

"Good idea, as we'll need round-the-clock help," Thorne decided.

"We'll get it. Now, the way I think I can help best is by concentrating on finding out all I can about what was going on in our sister's life, especially in the past year or so. I have a friend who's a private investigator. For the right price, he'll help us out," Slade said.

"Is he any good?" Thorne asked.

Slade's expression turned dark. "If anyone can find out what's going on, it'll be Kurt Striker. I'd bet my life on it."

"You're sure?"

Slade's gaze could've cut through steel. "I said, I'd bet my life on it. I meant that. Literally."

"Call him," Thorne said, persuaded by his usually cynical brother's conviction.

"Already have."

Thorne was surprised that Slade had already started the ball rolling. "I want to talk to him."

"You will."

"I'll keep on top of the doctors at the hospital," Thorne said. "I can do most of my business here by phone, fax and e-mail, so I won't have to go back to Denver for a while."

Matt held his gaze for a long second and for the first time in his life Thorne realized that his middle brother didn't approve of his lifestyle. Not that it really mattered. "Then let's just get through this," Matt finally said, as if he suddenly trusted Thorne again, as he had a long time before.

"We will."

"As long as Randi cooperates," Slade said.

"She's a fighter." Thorne's reaction was swift and he recognized the irony of his words. Phrases such as *she's really strong, she'll make it,* or *she's too ornery to die,* or *she's a fighter,* were hollow words, expressed by people who usually doubted their meaning. They were uttered to chase away the person's own fears.

"Look, I'm going to take inventory of the feed," Matt said.

"I'll check the gas pump, see what's in the tank." Slade snagged his jacket with one finger and the two younger brothers headed for the front door.

Thorne watched them through the window. Slade paused to light a cigarette on the porch while Matt jogged across the lot, disappearing into the barn again.

As kids they'd been through a lot together; depended upon each other, but as men, they'd gone about their own lives. Thorne had become the businessman, first law school and a stint with a firm before branching out on his own. His father had been right. He'd wanted to prove himself and the measure of a man's success, he'd always thought, was the size of his bank account.

For the first time in his life he wondered if he'd been wrong. Thinking of Randi battling death and her newborn son just starting his life gave him pause as he walked down the hallway where family portraits graced the walls. There were pictures of his father and mother, his stepmother and all four McCafferty children. Thorne in his high school football uniform and his graduation cap and gown, Matt riding a bucking bronco in a local rodeo, Slade skiing down a steep mountain and Randi in her prom dress, standing next to some boy Thorne couldn't begin to name. He stopped, touched that framed photo and silently vowed that he'd do anything, *anything* to make sure she was healthy again. He'd heat a cup of coffee, then call Nicole. She might have more news on his sister. That was the only reason he was calling her, he reminded himself as he walked into the kitchen and snapped on the lights. From the corner of his eye, he caught sight of his reflection in the windows. For a split second he imagined a mite of a woman with wide gold eyes and a fleeting smile at his side, then pulled himself up short.

What was he thinking? Nicole was Randi's ER admitting physician and that was it. Nothing more. Yet, ever since he'd first seen her in her office at the hospital, her heels propped on her desk, and her chair leaned back as she cradled the phone between her ear and shoulder, he hadn't been able to force her from his mind. It hadn't helped that when he'd caught up with her in the parking lot, he'd seen her not as Randi's doctor, but as a woman—a beautiful, bright and articulate woman. He hadn't been able to stop himself from kissing her and he'd been thinking about it off and on ever since. Nicole Sanders Stevenson was all grown-up, educated and self-confident—more intriguing now than she had been as a girl of seventeen. Despite her small stature she was a force to be reckoned with—way too much trouble for any man.

And yet…

The wall phone jangled. Snapped out of the ridiculous path of his thoughts, he grabbed the receiver on the second ring. "McCafferty ranch," he said. "Thorne McCafferty."

"So you are there!" a sharp female voice accused, and Thorne envisioned Annette's pretty face in a scowl. He'd dated her for a few months, but had never really connected with her. "What in the world happened? We were supposed to meet the mayor last night!" Annette's tone brought him up sharp and he gave himself a quick mental shake. He'd never called her. Never once thought of her after leaving his office yesterday.

"There was a family emergency."

"So you couldn't pick up a phone? You have a cell phone and you're on one right now…oh, listen, I don't mean to go off on you." She took in a deep, audible breath. "Your secretary told me that your half sister was in some kind of wreck and I'm sorry for her, I really am. I hope she's okay…?"

"She's in a coma."

"Oh, God." There was another long, weighty pause. "Well, I, um, understand, I really do. Dear Lord, how awful. I know you had to get back there in a hurry, Thorne. That's understandable and I made your apologies to my father and the mayor, but it seems to me that you could have called me yourself."

"I should have."

"Yeah…oh, well." She sighed. "Dad was disappointed."

"Was he?" Thorne drawled, imagining Kent Williams's reaction. The shrewd old man was probably in a stew as he'd wanted to invest with Thorne and was hoping they could cozy up with members of the city council and get an edge on a zoning ordinance that was up for review. "Thanks for giving him my apologies. You didn't have to do that. I would have called him."

"And me, would you have called me?"

"Yes."

"Eventually."

"Right." No reason to lie. "Eventually."

"Oh, Thorne." She let out a world-weary sigh and some of the shrewishness in her voice disappeared. "I miss you."

Did she? He doubted it and their relationship had always left him feeling alone. "It looks like I'm going to be in Montana a while."

"Oh." There was hesitation in her voice. "How long?"

"A few weeks, maybe months. It all depends on Randi."

"But what about your work?"

"What about it?"

"It's—it's your life."

Was my life, he wanted to say. Instead, added, "Things have changed."

"Have they?" Silent accusations sizzled over the wires.

"Afraid so."

"What does that mean?" But she knew. It was obvious. "You know, there are other men who are interested in me. I've put them on hold because of you."

"I'm sorry."

She waited and the silence ticked between them. "So, what're you telling me, Thorne?" she asked. "That it's over? Just like that? Because your sister is in the hospital?"

"No, Annette," he admitted, "it's not because of Randi. You and I both know that this wasn't going anywhere. I was up front about that at the beginning."

"I thought you'd change your mind."

"It didn't happen."

"So I should start seeing other men."

"It wouldn't be a bad idea."

"Okay." Again a frosty pause. "I'll think about it," she said.

"Do."

"And you, too, Thorne," she said with a renewed amount of spunk. "You think about what you're giving up." She hung up with a click and he replaced the receiver slowly, wondering why he didn't feel any sense of loss. But then he never had; not with any woman. Not even with Nikki way back when, and she'd been the most difficult. But he hadn't trusted her with his heart and when it came time to take off for law school, he'd left Grand Hope, his family and Nicole Sanders and never once looked back. Until now. While away at school, whenever he'd thought of her, which was often at first, he steadfastly turned his mind to other things. Eventually he'd quit thinking about her altogether and he'd lived by the axiom that women weren't a priority in his life.

But now, as he stared out the window into the dark, wet night, he felt a change inside him, a new kind of need. He reached for the phone as it rang again sharply.

Annette. He should have known she wouldn't give up without a fight.

"Hello," he said, as the receiver reached his ear.

"Thorne? This is Nicole." Her voice was cold and professional.

He knew in a heartbeat that Randi's condition had worsened. Fear clutched his heart and for the first time in his life he felt absolutely helpless. Oh, God. "It's my sister," he stated.

"No. Randi's still stable, but I just got a call from the hospital because they couldn't get through to you—your line was busy." Nicole hesitated a beat and before she got the words out, Thorne experienced an anguish the like of which he'd never felt before. He sagged against the wall as she said, "It's the baby."

Chapter 5

"What about him?" Thorne clutched the receiver in a death grip. His heart thudded in dread. For the love of Mike, how could one little baby, Randi's son whom he'd never even held, make such a difference in his life?

He heard the back door open and Matt, unbuttoning his sheepskin jacket, strode in. "Slade's still—"

Thorne silenced his brother with a killing glance and a finger to his lips.

"What about the baby?" he repeated, bracing himself and he saw Matt's dark complexion pale.

"He's lethargic, experiencing feeding problems and respiratory distress, his abdomen is distended, his temp has spiked—"

"Just cut to the chase, Nicole. What's he got? What went wrong?" Thorne was pacing now, stretching the telephone cord as Matt's eyes followed his every move.

Nicole hesitated a beat and Thorne found it hard to breathe. "Dr. Arnold thinks the baby might have bacterial meningitis. He's going to call you later and—"

"Meningitis?" Thorne repeated.

"No way!" Matt broke his silence.

"How the hell did that happen?"

"When Randi came into the hospital, her membranes had already ruptured—"

"What? Ruptured?"

Matt swore under his breath, then looked up, his gaze locking with that of his older brother. "Let's go," Matt said. "Right now. To the damned hospital!" Thorne cut him off with a quick shake of his head. He had to concentrate.

Nicole was talking again—her voice calm, though he sensed an urgency to her. "Her water had broken in the accident and there's a chance that there was contamination, the baby was exposed to some source of bacteria."

"This Dr. Arnold? Is he there? At the hospital now?"

"Yes. He'll call you with more information—"

"We're on our way."

"I'll meet you there," she said as he slammed the receiver down.

"What the hell's going on?" Matt demanded.

"The baby's in trouble. It doesn't sound good." Thorne was already striding to the front hall where he yanked his coat from a hook and shoved his arms down the sleeves. Matt was right on his heels. The two men half ran to Thorne's truck, but before he climbed into the passenger side, Matt said, "Wait a minute, I'd better tell Slade that we're on our way to the hospital—"

"Make it fast," Thorne ordered, but Matt was already running toward the barn. He disappeared inside. Thorne jabbed his key into the ignition, the truck roared to life and he glared at the barn, willing his brother to return.

Less than a minute later Matt, head ducked, holding on to the brim of his Stetson, dashed through the rain. Thorne was already throwing the pickup into gear by the time Matt opened the door and slid inside.

"He's gonna follow us."

"Good."

Thorne stepped hard on the accelerator, though he didn't know why. The urge to get to the hospital, to do *something* pounded through him. What had gone wrong?

Rain poured from the sky and the twin ruts of the lane glistened in the glow of the headlights as water spun beneath the tires.

"Okay, now what happened?" Matt demanded, his face tense in the dark interior.

"Something went wrong."

"What?"

"Everything." Thorne squinted against oncoming headlights, shifted down and turned onto the main road cutting through the pine-forested canyons and rolling acres of farmland surrounding the Flying M. In clipped words, Thorne repeated his conversation with Nicole.

Matt's jaw clenched. "Why was Nicole the one who called? Why not the pediatrician?"

"He couldn't get through, but I'll have more phone lines installed. Tomorrow. And I'd asked Nicole to phone me if there was any change. She said Dr. Arnold would call us, but I'm not going to hang around and wait. I want answers and I want them now."

The ranch was nearly twenty miles from town. Thorne pushed the speed limit and the truck's tires sang against the wet pavement.

They arrived at the hospital in record time. Thorne was out of the truck like a shot. Matt kept up with him, stride for stride. They sprinted across the dark parking lot, flew through the automatic doors of the lobby, then took the stairs two at a time to the second floor.

This time, Thorne didn't allow any nurse to tell him what to do. The poor woman, a slight blonde with a tentative smile tried to ward them off. "Excuse me, you can't come in here," she said, pointing to a sign that read Authorized Personnel Only.

"Where's the McCafferty baby?" Thorne demanded.

"Who are you?"

"I'm the baby's uncle and so is he," Matt said, hooking a thumb toward Thorne. "We're Randi McCafferty's brothers."

"The only family the baby has right now," Thorne explained, "as our sister is in Intensive Care and we haven't located the child's father." That wasn't a lie. Not really. He just didn't bother to add that they had no idea who the father was. Slicing Matt a look warning him not to elaborate, Thorne continued. "I want to see my nephew."

"He's in his crib," the nurse said patiently. "And he's being monitored closely." Her lips pursed and she motioned toward the glassed-in room where the baby, lying seemingly peacefully under a warm lamp, with a monitor strapped to him, was sleeping. Tubes were inserted into his small body and he breathed with his tiny mouth open. Another nurse hovered near his plastic bed. The blonde nurse continued, "Dr. Arnold has seen him and should be right back—oh, here he is now." She was obviously relieved to pass the responsibility of dealing with Thorne and Matt to a small man with wire-rimmed glasses, slightly stooped shoulders and a ring of wild white hair.

"Dr. Arnold?" Thorne asked, pinning the shorter man with his gaze.

"Yes."

"I'm Thorne McCafferty. This is my brother, Matt. The baby's mother is our sister. What the hell's going on?"

"That's what we're trying to find out," Dr. Arnold said calmly, obviously not offended by Thorne's sharp words and demanding attitude. "The baby's suffering from bacterial meningitis, probably contracted at the site of the accident as your sister's amniotic sac had already ruptured." Thorne's chest tightened. He felt a muscle in his jaw work as the doctor explained in finer detail what Nicole had already told him on the phone. Slade, white-faced, jaw set, fists coiled, arrived and was introduced quickly and brought up to speed.

"So how dangerous is this?" Thorne demanded.

"Very." The doctor was solemn. "We're a small hospital but luckily, we've got a state-of-the-art intensive pediatric unit."

Matt got straight to the point. "Is the baby going to make it?"

"I wish I could tell you that he's out of the woods, but I can't." The doctor's eyes, behind his glasses, were solemn. "The mortality rate for this kind of meningitis is high, somewhere between twenty to fifty percent—"

"Oh, God," Matt whispered.

"However, your nephew's survival chances are good here because of the staff and equipment. Already the baby's on antibiotic therapy and a mechanical ventilator along with compulsive fluid management."

"What?"

"An IV to minimize the effects of cerebral edema. Even if the baby is to survive, there's a chance that he might be deaf, blind or have some retardation."

"Damn," Slade mumbled and ran a hand over his chin and was suddenly pale as death, his scar more visible.

Thorne was thunderstruck. He stared at Randi's baby and felt, for the first time in his life, impotent. Frustration burned through his bloodstream.

"Isn't there anything else you can do?" Matt asked, lines of worry sketching his brow.

"There must be," Thorne added.

"Believe me, we're doing everything possible." Dr. Arnold's voice was steady.

"If there's anything he needs, anything at all—equipment, specialists, whatever—we'll pay for it." Thorne was adamant. "Money isn't an issue here."

The doctor's lips pulled together just a fraction. His spine seemed to stiffen and his voice was clipped. "Money isn't the problem right now, Mr. McCafferty. As I said we have the best equipment available, but this hospital is always looking for endowments and benefactors. I'll see that your name is on the list. Now, if you'll excuse me, I want to check on my patient."

He punched a code into a keypad and the doors marked Authorized Personnel Only opened. Dr. Arnold disappeared for an instant before he stepped into the neonatal nursery and was visible through the thick glass of the viewing window. Thorne's teeth clenched, anger and impotence burned in his brain. There had to be something he could do to help Randi's boy. There had to be! He stared at the pediatrician hard, but if Dr. Arnold felt Thorne's eyes upon him, he didn't so much as flinch or glance up. Instead he focused on the baby, carefully examining the fragile little boy who was Randi's only child—John Randall McCafferty's sole grandchild.

"He's got to pull through," Matt said, his fists balling in determination. "If he doesn't and Randi wakes up to find out that he didn't make it—"

"Don't say it! Don't even think it! He's gonna be fine. He's got to!" Slade slashed Matt a harsh glance filled with his own private hell. Not too long ago he'd lost a girlfriend and an unborn child. "He'll make it."

"Will he?" Matt wasn't convinced. "Here? I mean, I know this is a good hospital—the best around—but maybe he needs specialists, the kind that you find in bigger cities at teaching hospitals in L.A. or Denver or Seattle."

"We'll check it out," Thorne agreed. "I'll find out the best in the country."

"Right now it would be a mistake to move him." Nicole's voice came from somewhere down the hallway.

Thorne hadn't heard her approach but saw her reflection in the glass, a pale ghost in jeans and ski jacket, a filmy image that pulled strangely on his heartstrings. "Trust me on this one, Thorne, the baby's in good hands."

He turned and stared into a face devoid of makeup except for a bit of lipstick, her hair falling freely to her shoulders, her gold eyes quietly reassuring. She looked younger than she had before, more like the girl he remembered, the one he'd thought he'd loved, the one he'd so callously left behind. "Sorry it took me a while to get here, I had to round up a babysitter."

"You have a child?" Matt asked.

"Two. Twin girls. Four years old." Her serious face brightened at the mention of her daughters and Thorne tried to ignore the ridiculous spurt of jealousy that ran through his blood that another man had fathered her daughters, then he gave himself a swift mental shake. What the hell was he thinking? "And I'd trust them to Geoff—er, Dr. Arnold."

"Good enough for me," Matt allowed, though his face was still tense.

"Nothin' else we can do but have some faith in the guy," Slade agreed, then cursed softly in frustration.

"There are always other options," Thorne disagreed.

"None better." Nicole's voice brooked no argument. Her face was a mask of certainty. She had absolute trust in this man and again, ludicrously, Thorne felt a prick of jealousy that she would have such unflagging confidence in another male. "Let me talk to Geoff and see what's up." Nicole punched a code into the door lock. "I'll just be a minute." The electronic doors opened. Nicole slipped through.

Slade shifted from one foot to the other. Scowling through the glass, he eyed the two doctors and finally said, "I think I'll go check on Randi, then head back. You can fill me in when you get home."

Matt nodded curtly. "I'll come with you." He glanced at Thorne. "I'll catch a ride back to the ranch with Slade."

"Fine," Thorne said. "Call Striker again. Tell him I want to talk to him. ASAP."

"What about?" Slade asked.

"The kid's father for starters."

"Okay, I'll try to find Kurt."

"Don't try. Do it."

Slade's eyes flared and he slanted Thorne a condescending, don't-push-me-around smile. "Don't worry, brother. I'll handle it." With that he turned and walked away.

"Hell, you can be an insufferable bastard," Matt growled. "You might be used to barking orders at your office and everyone hustles to do what you want, but back off a bit, okay? We're all in this together. Slade'll call Striker."

"Will he?" Thorne's eyes narrowed. "It seems to me he's made a lot of promises in his life that he somehow managed to forget."

"He's straightening out."

"Good, 'cause he sure as hell has messed up his life."

"Not all of us are blessed with the Midas touch," Matt reminded him. "And, as far as I can see, you're not in much of a position to start slinging arrows." Matt glanced through the glass to Nicole. "Somethin' about the lady doctor that's got you riled?"

Thorne didn't respond.

"Thought so." Matt's smile was positively irritating. "Well, good luck. She doesn't much look like a filly that's easy to tame."

"This has nothing to do with her."

"Right. I forgot. You never get too involved with a woman, now, do ya?" Matt gave an exaggerated wink, pointed his finger at Thorne's chest, then sauntered down the hall after Slade.

Irritated as hell Thorne waited, watching Nicole and Dr. Arnold through the glass, hating the feeling that he was powerless, that the baby's life was out of his control, and that his brother had seen through his facade of indifference when it came to Nicole Sanders Stevenson. The truth of the matter was that she'd already gotten under his skin. He'd kissed her last night not certain of her marital state, not really giving a damn, then taken a flower to her doorstep like some kind of junior high kid suffering some kind of crush. Afterward he'd called her and manipulated the facts just to get a date with the woman. He'd never acted this way before. Never. Didn't understand it. Yes, she was beautiful and beyond that she was smart. Sassy and clever. But deeper still, he sensed a woman like no other he'd ever met. And he'd lost her once. Given her up all for the sake of making a buck.

He was still mentally kicking himself up one side and down the other when Nicole emerged. Her brow was creased, her eyes shadowed with concern.

"How bad is it?" Thorne asked.

Little lines appeared between her eyebrows and he

braced himself for the worst. "It's not good, Thorne, but Dr. Arnold is doing everything he can here. He's also linked by computer to other neonatologists across the country."

Thorne's jaw was clenched so hard it ached. "What can I do?"

"Be patient and wait."

"Not my strong suit."

"I know." The ghost of a smile crossed her lips as they walked down the stairs and outside together. Nicole flipped up her hood and held it tightly around her chin. They dashed through puddles to her SUV while sleet pelted from the sky in icy needles.

"Thanks for calling me and letting me know about J.R.," he said as they reached the rig.

"J.R.? That's the baby's name?"

"He doesn't really have one. But I've been thinking that he should be named after my father since Randi is still in a coma and well…who knows what she'll call him when she wakes up." *If she wakes up. If the baby survives.* "Anyway, I appreciate the call."

"No problem. I said I would." She fumbled in her purse, found her keys and unlocked the door.

"Yeah, but you didn't have to go to the trouble of getting a babysitter and driving down here." It had touched him.

"I thought it would be best." She flashed him a small grin. "Believe it or not, Thorne, some of the doctors here, including Dr. Arnold and me, really care about our patients. It's not a matter of clocking in and out on a schedule so much as it is about making sure the patient not only survives but receives the best care possible."

"I know that."

"Good." She blinked against the drops of water running

down her face and a twinkle lighted her gold eyes. "Okay, so now you owe me one."

"Name it," he said so softly that she barely heard the words, but when she looked into his face and saw an unspoken message in his eyes, her throat caught and she was suddenly touched in the most dangerous part of her heart. She remembered his kiss, just yesterday in this very parking lot, and she couldn't forget all the passion that was coiled behind the press of his lips against hers. And that was just the start of it. She knew that within the past day and a half her life had changed irrevocably, that she and Thorne had rediscovered each other and it scared the devil out of her, so much that she couldn't think about it. Not now. Not ever. "Careful, McCafferty," she said, clearing her throat. "Giving me carte blanche could be dangerous."

"I've never been one to steer clear of trouble."

"I know." She sighed, remembering how many of her friends had tried to warn her off Thorne way back when. The McCafferty boys were known as everything from rogues to hellions who always managed to find more than their share of trouble. "Look, I've got to go—"

He grabbed the crook of her elbow. "I meant it when I said thank you, Nicole. And I really am sorry."

"For—?"

"For taking off on you way back when."

Her heart jolted a bit when she realized his thoughts had taken the same wayward path as her own. As the wind ripped the hood from her head, she warned herself not to trust him. "That was a long, long time ago, Thorne. We— well, I was a kid. Didn't really know what I wanted. Let's just forget it."

"Maybe I can't."

"Well, you did a damned fine job of it for a lot of years."

"Not as fine as I'd hoped," he said. "Look, I'd just like to set the record straight."

"Now?" She glanced away from him and felt her pulse skyrocketing as the sleet ran down her neck. "How about another time? When we're both not in danger of freezing?"

His fingers gave up their possessive grip and she yanked open the door. Hoisting herself behind the wheel, she pulled the door shut and plunged her key into the ignition. With a flick of her wrist, she tried to start the engine. It ground, then died. She pumped the gas, all too aware that Thorne hadn't moved. He stood outside the driver's door, his bare head soaked, his long coat dripping, as she tried again. The engine turned over slowly, revved a bit and then sputtered out.

Three more flicks of her wrist.

Three more grinding attempts until there was no sound at all. "No," she muttered, but knew it was over. The damned rig wasn't going to move unless she got behind it and started pushing. "Great. Just…great." And Thorne was still standing there, like a man without a lick of sense who wouldn't come in out of the freezing rain.

He opened the door. "Need a ride?"

"What I need is a mechanic—one who knows a piston from a tailpipe!" she grumbled, but reached for her purse and slid to the ground. "Failing that, I suppose a ride would be the next best thing." She locked the SUV, abstained from kicking it and turned. He took her hand in his, linking cold, wet fingers through hers as they dashed to his pickup. She told herself not to make any more of this than what it was, just an old friend offering help. But she knew better.

Once inside the cab, she swiped water from her face and directed him through town as the defroster chased away the condensation on the windows. He drove carefully, negotiating streets that were slick with puddles of ice as the radio played softly.

"So tell me about yourself." Headlights from slowly passing cars illuminated the bladed angles of his face and she reminded herself that he really wasn't all that handsome, that he was a corporate lawyer, for God's sake, the kind of man she wanted to avoid.

"What do you want to know?" she asked.

"How you got to be a doctor."

"Medical school."

He arched a brow and she laughed. "Okay, okay, I know what you mean," she admitted, glad to have broken some of the ice that seemed to exist between them. "Guess I wanted to prove myself. My mother always told me to aim high, that I could achieve whatever I wanted and I believed her. She insisted I have a career where I didn't have to rely on a man." And Nicole knew why. Her own father had taken off when she was barely two and no one had seen or heard from him since. No child support. No birthday cards. Not even a phone call at Christmas. If her mother knew where he was, she'd never said and her answer to all of Nicole's questions had never wavered. *"He's gone. Took off when we needed him most. Well, we don't need him now and never will. Trust me, Nicole, we don't* want *to know what happened to him. It really doesn't matter one way or another if he's dead or alive."* At that point in the speech she'd usually bend on a knee to look her young daughter straight in the eye. Strong maternal fingers had held firm to Nicole's small shoulders. "You can do anything you want, honey. You don't need a deadbeat of a father to prove that. You don't need a husband. No—you'll do it all on your own, I know you will and you can do and be anything, *any*one you want. The sky's the limit."

In the last few years Nicole had wondered secretly if her need to succeed, her driving ambition, her quest to make her mark was some inner need to prove to herself that she could make it on her own and that the reason her father left had nothing to do with her.

Of course at seventeen, after meeting Thorne McCafferty, she'd fallen head over heels in love and been ready to chuck all her plans—her dreams and her mother's hopes— for one man…a man who hadn't cared enough for her to explain what had gone wrong.

Until now.

She sensed it coming. Like the clouds gathering before a storm, the warning signs that Thorne hadn't given up his need to explain himself were evident in the set of his jaw and thin line of his mouth.

He waited until the second light, then slowed the truck and turned down the radio. "I said I wanted to explain what happened."

"And I said I thought it could wait."

"It's been nearly twenty years, Nikki."

She closed her eyes and her heart fluttered stupidly at the nickname she'd carried with her through high school, the only name he'd called her. "So why rush things?" *Don't be taken in, Nicole. He used you once and obviously he thinks he can do it again.*

He let her sarcasm slide by. "I was wrong."

"About?" she said in a voice so low, she thought he might not have heard her.

"Everything. You. Me. What's important in life. I thought I had to go out and prove myself. I thought I couldn't get entangled with anyone or anything—I had to be free. I thought I had to finish law school and make a million dollars. After that I thought I'd better keep at it."

"And now you don't?" She didn't believe him.

"And now I'm not sure," he admitted, his fingers drumming on the steering wheel as the interior of the cab started to fog.

"Sounds like midlife crisis to me."

He shifted down and took a corner a little too fast. "Easy answer."

"Usually right on."

"You really believe that?"

She leaned back in the seat and stared out the window to the neon lights of the old theater, and wondered why she was in this discussion. "Let's just say I've experienced it firsthand."

"Oh."

"And I swore to myself that the next midlife crisis I was going to suffer through was going to be my own."

He parked at the curb in front of her little bungalow and she reached for the door handle. "I suppose I could ask you in for some coffee, or cocoa or tea or something."

"You could."

She hesitated, one hand on the door handle. "Then again, maybe it wouldn't be such a good idea."

"And why's that?"

She tilted up her chin a bit. "Because this is getting a little too personal, I think."

"And you'd rather keep it professional."

"It would be best for everyone. Randi—the baby—"

To her surprise one side of his mouth lifted in a sexy, damnably arrogant slash of white. "Is that the reason, Doctor, or is it that you're scared of me?"

No, Thorne, I'm not scared of you. I'm scared of me. "Don't flatter yourself."

"Why should I stop now?" He reached for her, dragged

her close and started to kiss her, only to stop short, his mouth the barest of whispers from hers. His breath fanned her face. "Good night, Nikki." Then he released her. She opened the door and nearly fell out of the truck. Embarrassment washed up her cheeks as she strode to the door and felt him watching her, waiting until she made it inside. Then he threw his truck into gear and took off, disappearing through the veil of silvery sleet.

Chapter 6

"Damn!" Thorne slammed down the receiver and stared out the window to a winter-crisp day where evidence of last night's storm still glistened on the grass and hung from the eaves in shimmering icicles. A headache pounded behind his eyes. He'd been on the phone all morning, guzzling cups of coffee as bitter as a spinster's heart.

He'd bedded down in his old room, the one that had abutted his folks' suite and his brothers had, by instinct, claimed the bedrooms where they'd been raised. But when he'd awoken this morning he'd been alone in the house.

During the intervening hours, he'd called the hospital, hoping for a report of improvement in Randi and the baby's condition. As far as he could tell, nothing had changed. His sister was still comatose and the baby, though stable, was still in danger. He'd hooked up his laptop computer to the antiquated phone lines and looked up everything he could on little J.R.'s condition. From what he could determine, everything that could be done to counteract the meningitis was being done at St. James. He'd even managed to call the office, check in with Eloise and tell her that he hoped a portable office would be set up here, in his father's den, by the end of the day. He wondered what John Randall would've done in a similar situation and, thinking about his father, removed the gift he'd been given from his pocket. The ring winked in the sunlight and Thorne folded his hand over the silver-and-gold band.

"I want you to marry. Give me grandchildren." John Randall's request seemed to bounce off the walls of this old pine-paneled room that still smelled faintly of the elder Mc-Cafferty's cigars and Nicole's image came to mind, the only woman he'd ever dated that he'd considered as a mother for his children. And that thought had scared him nearly twenty years ago. It still did because nothing had changed. Oh, there had been a lot of women since he'd dated her; Thorne hadn't been celibate by any means, but no one woman had come close to touching his heart.

Until he'd seen Nicole again.

Not that he wanted a wife or mother for his children or—

What was he thinking? Wife? Children? Not him. Not now. Probably not ever…and yet…the reason he was thinking this way was probably because of his father's dying request, his father's wedding ring, and the fact that his own mortality wouldn't go on forever. Randi's situation was proof enough of that.

Oh, for the love of God. Enough with these morbid thoughts. He looked around this room again and wondered how many deals had been concocted here in the past. How many family or business decisions dreamed up while John Randall had puffed on a black market Havana cigar, rested the worn heels of his boots on the scarred maple desk and leaned back in a leather chair that had been worn smooth by years of use?

This damned metal band had been his father's wedding ring, a gift from Larissa, Thorne's mother, on their wedding day. John Randall had worn it proudly until Larissa had found out about Penelope, the younger woman whom her philandering husband had been seeing. The woman who had broken up a marriage that had already been foundering. The woman who had eventually given John Randall his only daughter.

And now Thorne's mother, too, was dead, a heart attack just two years ago taking her life.

Thorne slid the ring into his pocket and reached for the phone again. He dialed Nicole's number and hung up when her answering machine picked up. Drumming his fingers on the desktop he wondered if she'd managed to get her car towed, if she'd found another means of transportation and how, as a single mother of four-year-old twins she was getting along. "Not that it's any of your business," he reminded himself, bothered nonetheless. He wondered about her marital state—about the man who had been her husband, then forced himself to concentrate on the problems at hand—there were certainly enough without borrowing more. Nicole was a professional, a mother, and a level-headed woman. She'd be fine. She had to be.

He heard the sound of the front door opening and the heavy tread of boots. "Anyone here?" Slade yelled, his uneven footsteps becoming louder.

"In the den."

Slade appeared in the doorway. He was wearing beat-up jeans, a flannel shirt and a day's worth of whiskers he hadn't bothered to shave. A denim jacket with frayed cuffs was his only protection against the weather. He held a paper coffee cup in one hand. "Good mornin'."

"Not yet, it isn't."

Slade's countenance turned grim. "Don't tell me there's more bad news. I called the hospital a couple of hours ago. They said there was no change."

"There isn't. Randi's still in critical condition and the

baby's holding his own." Thorne rounded the desk and snapped off his laptop, turning off his link to the outside world—news, weather and stock reports. "I was talking about everything else."

"Such as?"

"To begin with, your friend Striker hasn't returned any of my calls, Randi's editor at the *Clarion* is always 'out' or 'in a meeting.' I think he's avoiding me. I've talked to the sheriff's department, but so far there's nothing new. A detective is supposed to call me back. The good news is that the equipment I ordered for this office is due to arrive today, and the phone company's gonna come in and install a couple of lines. I've talked to an agency specializing in nannies as we'll need one when J.R. gets home—"

"J.R.?" Slade repeated.

"I call the baby that."

"After Dad?" Slade asked, obviously perplexed.

"And Randi."

Slade gave out a long, low whistle. "You have been busy, haven't you?"

Thorne elevated an eyebrow and remembered that this was his youngest brother, the playboy, a man who had never settled down to any kind of responsibility.

"All I've had time for this morning is a call into Striker and a couple of cups of weak coffee down at the Pub'n'Grub. I ran into Larry Todd down there."

"Why does his name sound familiar?"

"Because he was the man who ran this place when Dad became ill."

Thorne settled into his father's chair and leaned back until it squeaked in protest.

"Get this. Randi kept Larry on when she inherited the bulk of this place."

Thorne remembered, though he hadn't paid much attention at the time. He'd been in negotiations for the Canterbury Farms subdivision at the time and had been dealing with land use laws, an environmental group, the city council and an accounting nightmare because one of his bookkeepers had been caught embezzling off the previous project. On top of all that, John Randall had died and Thorne, though he'd known his father was dying, had been stricken by the news and assuaged by grief. He hadn't cared much about the sixth of the ranch he'd inherited and had left Randi, who owned half of the acres and the old ranch house, to run the place as she saw fit.

"But just last week, Randi called Larry up, told him she didn't need him any longer and that she'd pay him a couple of months' severance pay."

Thorne's head snapped up. "Why?"

"Beats me. Larry was really ticked off."

"When did this happen?"

"A day before the accident."

"Did she hire anyone else?"

"Don't know. I just found out about it."

"Someone would have to come and look after the stock."

"You'd think." He saw movement outside the window and watched Matt hiking the collar of his jacket more closely around his neck as he made his way to the back door. Slade frowned. "Guess I'd better help out with the cattle. I told Larry we'd hire him back, but he's pretty mad. I thought Matt might talk to him."

"Let's see."

They convened in the kitchen where Matt had set his hat on the table and had flung his jacket over the back of a ladder-back chair. He was in the process of pouring himself a cup of coffee. "There's nothing to eat around here," he grumbled as he searched in the refrigerator, then the cupboard. He dragged out an old jar of instant creamer and poured in a healthy dose as Slade and Thorne filled him in on everything they'd already discussed.

"We need Larry Todd back on the payroll," Thorne said to Matt. "Slade ran into him today and thought you might talk to him."

Matt studied the contents of his cup and nodded slowly. "I can try. But he called me after Randi let him go, and to say he was a little ticked off is an understatement."

"See what he wants," Thorne suggested.

"I'll give it a shot."

"Convince him."

"I'll try." Matt slowly stirred his coffee. "But Larry's been known to be stubborn."

"We'll deal with that. I've got a call in to Juanita to see if she'll come on board again," Thorne said.

"She might be working for someone else by now. Randi let her go after Dad died." Matt hoisted himself onto the counter and his feet swung free.

"Then we'll have to make it attractive enough that she'll come back."

"Might not be that easy," Slade said, sipping coffee from his paper cup. "Some people feel obligated to stay with their employer."

"Everyone can be bought."

Slade and Matt exchanged glances.

Thorne didn't waver. "Everyone has a price."

"Including you?" Matt asked.

Thorne's jaw hardened. "Yep."

Slade snorted in contempt. "Hell, you're a cynic."

"Aren't we all?" Thorne said, undeterred. "And we'll need a nurse. When Randi and the baby get here, we'll need professional help." He was running through a mental checklist. "I'll call a law firm I used to deal with."

"A law firm?" Slade shook his head. "Why in the world would we need lawyers?"

"For when we find the boy's father—he might want custody."

"He should probably get it, at least partial," Matt allowed.

"Maybe, maybe not. We don't know a thing about this guy."

Slade rolled his eyes and tossed the remains of his coffee into the sink. "For the love of Mike, Thorne, don't you trust anyone?"

"Nope."

"If Randi chose this guy, he might be all right," Matt conceded.

"So then where is he? Assuming he knows that she was pregnant, why the hell hasn't he appeared?" The same old questions that had been plaguing Thorne ever since learning of his sister's accident gnawed at him. "If he's such a peach of a guy, why isn't he with her?"

"Maybe she doesn't want him." Slade lifted a shoulder. "It happens."

"Any way around it, we'll need to see about our rights, the baby's rights, Randi's rights and—"

"And the father's rights," Matt pointed out before taking a long swallow of coffee. "Okay, I've got to run into town and go to the feed store. While I'm there I'll pick up some supplies and hit the grocery store for a few things. When I get back, I'll call Larry."

Slade reached into his pocket for a pack of cigarettes. "I'll ride into town with you," he said to Matt. "I want to talk to the sheriff's department, find out what they know about Randi's accident."

"Good idea," Thorne agreed. "I've called but haven't heard back."

"Figures. Look, I've left a message with Striker, but I'll phone him again," Slade promised, shaking out a cigarette and jabbing the filter tip into the corner of his mouth. "What's your game plan?"

"I'm setting up my office in the den, already scheduled equipment delivery and then I'm going to run into town myself. Visit Randi and the baby." He didn't add that he intended to see Nicole again.

"Yeah. I figured we'd stop by the hospital, too," Matt allowed. "If you get any calls from Mike Kavanaugh, tell him I'll call him back."

"Who's Kavanaugh?" Thorne asked.

"My neighbor. He's looking after my spread while I'm here."

Slade crumpled his empty coffee cup and threw it into the trash. "How long will he take care of it?"

Matt shrugged into his jacket and squared his hat on his head. "As long as it takes." He locked gazes with his brothers. "Randi and the baby come first."

Nicole ground the gears of the rental car and swore under her breath. She wheeled into the parking lot of the hospital and told herself to trust that the mechanics looking at the SUV could find the problem, get the part, fix whatever was wrong, and return it to her soon, without it costing an arm and a leg.

She had half an hour before she was actually on duty and planned to use the time to check on Randi McCafferty and the baby before taking over in the ER.

Setting the emergency brake, she switched off the rental, grabbed her briefcase and told herself that her interest in Randi and the baby was just common courtesy and professional concern, that oftentimes she looked in on patients once they'd been moved from the ER. This wasn't about Thorne. No way. The fact that he was related to Randi was incidental.

She argued with herself all the way through the physicians' entrance and in the elevator to her office.

"Something wrong?" a nurse she'd known since she'd arrived at St. James asked as she passed the nurses' station in the west wing.

"What?"

"You look worried. Are the twins okay?"

"Yes, I mean Molly has a case of the sniffles, but nothing a little TLC and a couple of Disney movies won't cure. I guess I was just thinking."

"Well, smile a little when you think," the nurse said with a wink.

"I'll try."

She made her way to the Intensive Care Unit, where she looked at Randi's chart. "Any change?" she asked.

"Not much," Betty, the ICU nurse, said with a shake of perfectly coiffed red curls. "Still comatose. Unresponsive, but hanging in there. How's the baby?"

"Not good," Nicole admitted as she glanced into Betty's concerned gaze. "I'm on my way to check on him now."

Betty's lips folded in on themselves. The gold cross suspended from her neck winked against her skin. "A shame," she said.

"Where there's life, there's hope." Nicole glanced over Randi's chart, then headed down to Neonatal Pediatrics where little J.R., as Thorne called him, was struggling for his life. As she stared at the tiny baby, hooked up to tubes and monitors, her heart ached. She remembered the birth of her own twins, the elation of seeing each little girl for the first time, the feeling of relief that they were both so perfect and healthy. She'd been jubilant and even Paul, at that time, had seemed happy. He'd looked at her with tears in his eyes and told her, "They're beautiful, Nicole. As beautiful as their mother."

His kind words still haunted her. Were they the last he'd ever spoken to her? Surely not. There had to have been a few more compliments and tender glances before the toll of two high-powered jobs and rambunctious daughters had robbed the marriage of whatever gel had bound it together. Naively Nicole had believed that children would bring Paul and her closer together—of course she'd been wrong. Bitterly so.

"Has Dr. Arnold been in today?" she asked the nurse on duty.

"Twice."

"Good." *Come on, J.R.,* she thought watching the tiny fingers curl into fists. *Fight. You can do it!*

But the baby looked so frail, so small and his vital signs hadn't improved.

"Has the family been in?"

"All three uncles at one time or another."

Nicole had suspected as much. If anything, the McCafferty brothers seemed determined to see that their sister and her son improved, if only by their sheer, collective will. If only it was that easy. "I'll be back later," she said and walked into the hallway, nearly bumping into Thorne in the process. She glanced up to his worried gray eyes and she felt her heart turn over for him as he so obviously loved this little baby.

"How's he doing?"

"The same," she said, turning to look through the glass at the baby. "I thought you'd already been in."

"Couldn't stay away," he said, then cleared his throat. "I had business in town and thought I'd stop by again." He stared at the tiny baby and for an instant Nicole wondered what it would have been like if she and Thorne had had a child together. If things had turned out differently, would they have become parents? Bittersweet were the thoughts, for certainly if she and Thorne had both stayed in Grand Hope, she wouldn't have become a doctor nor would she have her own precious daughters.

"J.R.'s a fighter," she said, touching the back of Thorne's hand. "Try not to worry."

One side of his mouth lifted in a cynical smile. "That seems to be impossible."

"Anything's possible, Thorne," she said and wondered why she felt compelled to comfort him. He turned his hand around and clasped her fingers in his.

"Do you really believe that?"

"With all my heart." Their gazes locked and she thought she might drop right through the floor. The hospital seemed to recede in a fine mist and she felt as if she and he were alone in the universe. Oh, God, this was so wrong....

Her pager buzzed and she dropped his hand. Digging in her pocket, feeling heat wash up her neck, she found the beeper and read the message. "I've got to run." She looked up at him again. "Have faith, Thorne. J.R. will pull through." Why she'd said something she couldn't possibly know as truth, she didn't understand, but she turned quickly on her heel and hurried to the emergency room where she was due to start her shift.

She was immediately accosted by an admitting nurse.

"When it rains it pours. Been quiet here for hours, but now we're swamped. You can start with room three. We've got a seven-year-old girl who fell off her horse. Looks like she might have broken her wrist."

"On my way."

"After that, there's a teenager with a sinus infection, and a toddler with a pea wedged up her nose. An RN tried to help, but the mother wants a doctor to look at it." The nurse rolled her eyes. "New mother. This is her first."

"Reassure her that the nurse can handle the extraction and I'll check it out after I'm done with the others."

"Will do—uh-oh." The nurse frowned as she looked over Nicole's shoulders.

"What?"

"Bad news. It's the press. They've been nosing around here ever since the McCafferty accident, but I thought it would die down by now." From the corner of her eye Nicole saw a van for a local news station roll to a stop just outside the windows of the waiting room. "Someone must've gotten wind that the baby was in distress."

"Great."

The nurse's mouth curved into a pained expression. "It doesn't take much in Grand Hope to cause a stir, does it?"

"Never has," Nicole said. The McCafferty family had always been a subject of interest to the townspeople as John Randall had been a flamboyant, once rich man who had actually run for local politics. His public and private life had been the subject of more than one wagging tongue— and his sons had been wild as teenagers, always getting into trouble; but, as the town had grown and the McCafferty children had become adults and spread like seeds in the wind, they had garnered less interest.

"I'd better go see what's up," the nurse said.

Nicole had more important things to do than worry about the press. She pulled the chart of the girl with the broken wrist from the door, scanned the information and, managing a smile, forced all thoughts of Thorne's family from her mind as she spied a frightened blonde girl with a tearstained face sitting on the edge of the examining table. Dirt and grass stains were ground into her bib overalls and her mother, a petite woman with worried eyes behind thick glasses stood as Nicole entered.

"You're Sally," Nicole said to the girl who nodded slowly.

"Yes, yes. And I'm her mother. Leslie Biggs. She was riding her horse and fell off just as they got back to the barn. I was on the porch when I saw it, heard her cry…." The mother's voice, gruff and soft, fell away.

"I fell off a horse when I was about your age," Nicole told her new patient.

"Did you?" The girl sniffed, her eyes rounded, but there was a hint of suspicion in her words, as if she expected the doctor to try to cajole her into a good mood.

"Yeah, but I was lucky, I didn't hurt anything except my pride. I was showing off for a boy, thought I could make my pony jump over a pile of firewood and he balked. Stopped dead short. I kept going. Landed in a cow pie." She sent the mother a quick glance. "I think a basic law of physics was involved."

"Ick." The new patient giggled then cried out as Nicole gingerly touched her swollen arm.

"Yep. I never landed a date with Teddy Crenshaw after that. Nope. In fact, he told the story all over school."

"What a creep."

"I thought so. Talk about embarrassing. Now, let's see what we've got here. Looks like we're going to need some X rays…"

* * *

Dead tired, Nicole, finished with her shift, rounded the corner to her office and spied Thorne, big as life, leaning one broad shoulder against the frame of her locked door. He was less intimidating in casual slacks and a sweater, a leather coat unzipped and gaping open.

She nearly missed a step and her stupid heart fluttered as she caught the intensity of his silvery gaze. Lord, what was it about the man that always put her on edge? The plain truth of the matter was that the man bothered her. He always had. He reminded her of a runaway train on a downhill track, a locomotive that gathered speed to race headlong toward his destination. "You work here now?" she joked.

"Seems like it."

"Seriously, have you been here the whole time?"

"No." He flashed her the remnant of a smile. "Believe it or not, I do have a life of my own. I came back looking for you."

"For me?" She didn't know whether to be flattered or wary. "So you just waited at my office? How'd you know I'd be showing up here? Sometimes I take off directly from the ER."

"Lucky guess."

She arched an eyebrow as she unlocked her door. "Somehow I don't think you ever rely on luck."

"So I called."

"Mmm." The door opened and she stepped inside. He was right behind her. "I assume you've seen your sister and the baby again."

"Yep."

"Any change?"

"Not that anyone's saying."

"I've got a call in to Dr. Arnold."

"So do I."

Rounding her desk, she slid into her chair and said, "Let me check my messages." Thorne waited, standing in the doorway and she waved him inside as she listened to several quick recordings—one from the mechanic. They'd located a part and would start working on the SUV as soon as it arrived. The second call was from Jenny saying she was taking the twins to the park, two more were from specialists she'd consulted with and finally a quick message from Dr. Arnold, giving her an update. She called him back, got his machine again and left another message.

Hanging up, she shrugged. "Nothing. The baby's stable. His condition hasn't worsened and Dr. Arnold is guardedly optimistic." She noticed Thorne's eyebrows slam together, saw his jaw set in frustration.

"There must be something more you can do."

She bristled slightly. "You know that Dr. Arnold's in contact with other physicians and pediatric units across the country—linked up by computer."

"Maybe it's not enough."

"So what do you suggest?"

"You're the doctor."

"Then trust me. Trust Dr. Arnold."

"I guess I don't have much choice," he admitted, rubbing his jaw and scowling.

"There are always choices, Thorne. Just not good ones. Moving the baby to another hospital would be a big mistake."

"Like I said, no other choices."

Feeling as if he were questioning the integrity of the hospital, she wanted to argue, but she didn't. He was upset, understandably so. A man who was used to being in charge, in control of every facet of his life, reduced to the mere mortal status.

"Have a little faith," she told him.

If only he could. As Thorne gazed into Nicole's amber eyes, he felt only a slight case of well-being. But he told himself not to be seduced into a lull, just because he was starting to care for this woman. He couldn't afford to become complacent, not while his sister was battling for her life and the baby was struggling for his. There had to be something more that he could do. "I'll try," he said and caught a shadow of a smile tug at the corners of her lips.

For a second he thought of the kiss they'd shared so recently, the intimate linking of their hands this afternoon and how it had felt years ago, to make sweet, sensuous love to her. The turn of his thoughts was insane, here in this sterile office, with the sounds of the hospital vibrating behind him, and yet he couldn't keep his mind from straying to a simpler, more innocent time when he and Nicole had made love in the long hay ready to be cut, while the Montana sun had shone on two naked bodies glistening with sweat, flushed from the heat of recent lovemaking and supple with youth. He'd kissed her then and she, giggling, had struggled to her feet, dashed through the waist-high grass and down a soft slope to the creek where she'd splashed through the shallow water and he, chasing after her, had caught her before she'd scrambled up the opposite bank. He'd kissed her again, the cool water swirling and eddying around her knees and then he'd cradled her body, drawn her down and made love to her in the creek, where the sunlight pierced the branches of aspen and pine to sparkle on the clear surface.

Finches and tanagers had fluttered in branches, singing over the babble of the creek and butterflies and water skippers had joined a few bees hovering near the water, but all Thorne really remembered was the silky feel of Nicole's skin against his, the play of her muscles and the taste of her mouth as she kissed him wildly.

Now, staring at her he felt those same male stirrings that had been forever with him when he was near her. No longer a tanned girl running naked through a country field, she was a woman, a doctor dressed in a lab coat, seated in an office that boasted of the professional woman she'd become.

Surrounded by tomes of medical information, a sleek computer, certificates and degrees decorating the walls, Nicole Stevenson had come a long way since she'd been Nikki Sanders, a smart, pretty high school girl with big dreams and little else. As if she, too, in that split second remembered their reckless, jubilant lovemaking, she cleared her throat. "Well, good, then that's that."

"When are you finished here?"

"Just about done," she admitted, and straightened a few files that were scattered over her desk. A forgotten, half-drunk cup of coffee, stained with peach-colored smudges from her lipstick sat unattended near her computer. On a small bookcase, along with medical books, were several picture frames that showed off photos of her daughters smiling and bright-eyed as they posed for the camera.

"So those are your daughters," he guessed, surveying the snapshots of the sprites.

She nodded, her eyes glowing with parental pride. "Molly and Mindy and yes, I can tell them apart."

He laughed. "But no one else can."

"Just their father," she admitted and seemed suddenly uncomfortable. "Or at least he could at one time. It's been a while since he spent much time with them."

"Why?"

She hesitated, sighed and picked up one of the framed photos. "Lots of reasons. Time. Distance. Space…but I'd say the most important was disinterest. Don't quote me, though, I'm just the ex-wife who carries a grudge." She set the picture back on the bookcase, ran her finger over the surface as if checking for dust and straightened. "But I'm sure you didn't come here to hear me complain about my divorce."

"Actually I stopped by to see if you needed a ride. Your rig's not in the lot."

"Towed earlier. And thanks." She was touched that he'd thought of her, then reminded herself not to trust him. He'd left her once before, destroyed all her silly schoolgirl fantasies. "But I've got a rental."

"When will the SUV be ready?"

"That's the sixty-four-thousand-dollar question, I'm afraid. Don't know yet."

"Well, if you need another vehicle we've got more than we need at the ranch and I'd give you a ride anytime."

His eyes held hers for a split second and the back of her throat went dry. Unspoken messages—all male—filled his gaze.

"Thanks. I'll let you know."

"Do. And there's one more thing."

"What?" she asked, looking up.

"Would you have dinner with me?"

"What?" To his amusement, she actually looked shocked.

Thorne's lips curved into a satisfied smile. "I just asked you for a date. For Saturday night. This shouldn't come as a big surprise. I think we talked about it a few days ago." He folded his arms across his wide chest and smiled. "So, Doctor, what do you say?"

Chapter 7

"I just don't want the rug pulled out from under me again," Larry Todd said. He was tall, about six-three or six-four, with straight blond hair that fell over piercing green eyes. Somewhere between forty-five and fifty, he stood military straight on the porch, a thick jacket zipped to his neck as a raw wind chased down the valley.

"I'll draw up a contract for a year," Thorne assured him. "By that time Randi should be in charge again. Then you can deal with her."

Frowning slightly, Larry gave a sharp nod. "Okay." He slid a glance at the three brothers who had spent the day showing him around the place that he already knew like the back of his hand. If anything, Larry had pointed out the flaws in the ranch—the stretches of fence that needed to be repaired, the way the soil was eroding on the north side, why it would be a good idea to sell off some of the timber on the lower slopes of the foothills, pointing out that buying a new bailer wasn't necessary this year, while investing in a larger tractor was a necessity. He knew about a neighbor's bull—a prize-winner that could be traded for one on the ranch to mix up the genes of the herd. Why Randi had seen fit to let him go was beyond Thorne.

"So, how is that sister of yours?" Larry asked and, despite his falling out with Randi, deep grooves of concern stretched across his brow.

"Still in a coma." Slade kicked at a small dirt clod with the toe of his boot.

"But she'll pull through."

"The doctors think so," Thorne replied.

"And the baby?"

The men exchanged glances. Thorne said, "We had a scare. He's still not out of the woods, but he's doin' better."

"Good. Good." Larry tugged at the hem of his gloves, fitting the rough leather more tightly around his fingers as the phone blasted from inside the house. "Draw up that contract and we'll talk again."

He took the steps toward his pickup as Thorne heard Juanita shout his name.

"Mister Thorne. Telephone!" she yelled and all three brothers smiled. It was good to have her back. They'd grown up with her heartfelt convictions, flashing dark eyes and stern sense of right and wrong.

Thorne stepped inside the house. "Boots off!" Juanita's voice rang from the vicinity of the kitchen. She appeared, round-faced, her black hair now shot with strands of wiry gray, wiping her hands on the edge of her apron. "It's your secretary."

"I'll take it in the den." Thorne snapped up the receiver and listened as his secretary gave him an update on his on-going projects. The development he was working on with Annette's dad had hit a snag with the planning commission, there was threat of a framers' strike and a real estate agent he worked with was "frantic" to talk to him.

By the time he got off the phone his brothers had settled into the living room. They stood in stocking feet, warming the backs of their legs against the fire. Their jeans were grimy and they smelled of horses and dirt. A silver belt buckle—the one their father had won at a long-forgotten rodeo—held up Matt's Levi's and the watch John Randall had worn for as long as Thorne could remember was strapped to Slade's wrist. So they all carried mementos of the man who had sired them—personal gifts he'd bestowed upon them with strings attached—just like the ring Thorne had gotten. Thorne wondered what promises John Randall had wrung from his younger brothers, but he didn't bother to ask.

"What's this about you having a date?" Slade asked, a crooked grin slashing through the dark stubble surrounding his chin.

Thorne met his brother's curious gaze steadily. "I thought I'd take Nicole out to dinner. That's all."

"Sure." Slade wasn't convinced.

A cat-who-ate-the-canary smile was pasted to Matt's square jaw and he shifted the toothpick he'd been sucking on from one side of his mouth to the other. "She isn't exactly your type, is she?"

"Meaning?"

"Kinda down-to-earth, for you," Matt said, obviously amused. "A woman with as much brains as beauty."

"The settlin' down kind," Slade added.

Thorne refused to be galled by his brothers' needling. Neither one had much room to talk when it came to affairs of the heart. "It's just a date," he said, but sensed that there was more involved. He'd had hundreds of dates in his life, spent hours with lots of women and yet tonight seemed different—a little more serious. Maybe it was because Nicole worked at the hospital where his sister and her son were still recovering, but that wouldn't explain the slight elevation in his pulse at the sight of her, the restless nights when he dreamed of making love to her or the fact that he was breaking one of his own cardinal rules: Never Go Back.

Never in his life had he dated a person with whom he'd once before been involved. He figured there was just no rhyme or reason to it. If a love affair hadn't worked out in the past, why would a second try guarantee success? The old adage, Once Burned, Twice Shy, said it all. And yet here he was, planning a date with a woman who had been his lover long ago. He frowned for a second, remembering that he'd seduced her—taken her virginity and after a few short, hot-summer weeks, left her to her own devices.

It hadn't been that he'd grown tired of her; quite the opposite. The more he'd been with her, the more he'd wanted to be with her and it had scared the daylights out of him. At that point in his life he'd had too much to do, too many ambitions yet to be fulfilled. He didn't have time for a serious relationship or a girl he could have easily thought of as his wife.

The truth of the matter was that his feelings for Nicole had terrorized him. But then, he'd been little more than a boy at the time. Now, things had changed.

"If it's just a date, then why all the secrecy, and why did you ask me to—"

"Just take care of it, okay?" Thorne snapped.

"Okay, okay," Matt said holding his hands up, palms outward. "You got it. Two horses, saddled and waiting."

"What?" Slade clucked his tongue. "Horses? Have you flipped? You're taking out a *doctor*. One who practiced in *San Francisco* before she came here. She's a classy, sophisticated lady."

"But not the kind I regularly date?" Thorne threw back at him.

"Not the kind to jump on a horse in the middle of the

winter." Slade shook his head as if his brother had gone stark, raving mad.

"Maybe I'm not taking a doctor out," Thorne said, though he didn't feel the need to explain himself. "Maybe I'm taking out an old friend. Nikki Sanders."

"Who's now a mother, divorced and an M.D."

"Well, you boys stay put and hold down the fort, would you? I'll handle Nikki."

"Or she'll handle you," Matt predicted. "Now listen, be careful with her, all right? She doesn't seem to be the love-'em-and-leave-'em type."

"And we might need to get hold of you. If there's any change in Randi or the baby's condition," Slade clarified.

"I'll have the cell phone with me."

Slade nodded. "Good. Just in case there's any trouble."

"There won't be!" Matt was insistent.

"Let's hope not," Slade said, unconsciously running a finger over the scar running down his cheek. "We've all had enough of that to last a lifetime."

Thorne couldn't disagree. For the past few years, it seemed as if bad luck had become a part of the family legacy. John Randall had lived life full, made and lost fortunes, enjoyed good health and believed that it was his God-given right to be good-looking, rich and powerful. He'd stepped on those who'd gotten in his way, cast off a good woman for a younger model, sired three sons and a daughter; but when fate had turned on him, shredding his fortune, stripping him of a fickle woman, robbing him of his health, he'd been shocked, flabbergasted that his luck had eluded him and the gods of fortune had seen fit to turn on him and laugh, mock him for his pitiful arrogance, in the end leaving him a shell of the man he'd once been.

His death hadn't ended the downward spiral. Randi had

lost her mother less than a year earlier. Slade had suffered his own personal loss and Randi's accident, her coma and the illness of her newborn all seemed to be part of a cruel twist of fate.

But it was about to stop. It had to. Randi and little J.R. would recover. The mystery over the boy's paternity and her accident would be solved. Thorne would settle down, marry, have himself some kids.... He pulled up short as he reached the top of the stairs. How had his thoughts gotten so far out of line. Married? Kids?

"Not in this lifetime," he told himself, but felt the pressure of his father's wedding ring deep in the pocket of his slacks and had the vague suspicion that Dr. Nicole Stevenson might change his mind. The truth of the matter was that it was already happening. Even now, he couldn't wait until he saw her again.

Why had she ever agreed to something as foolish as a date? Nicole wondered as she flung on her favorite black dress, then wrinkled her nose in distaste at her reflection in the full-length mirror. The short silk was far too sophisticated for Grand Hope, and yet Thorne was used to big-city women who attended charity balls and gala events.

Her bed was littered with other outfits, everything from black jeans and casual sweaters to this damned dress. "It's just for a few hours," she chided herself as she felt like a damned schoolgirl getting ready for a date with the most popular guy in school. Gritting her teeth, she settled for gray wool slacks, a fitted navy cowl-necked sweater, sterling hoop earrings and black boots. "The everywhere outfit."

"Hey, Mommy. You beau-ti-ful," Mindy said as she slid

into the room in her slipper-footed pajamas and drew up short.

Molly was on her heels, sliding headlong into the bed and sniffing loudly from her cold.

"Thanks," Nicole said. "But you're prejudiced."

"What's that mean?" Molly asked suspiciously.

"That you like me just because I'm your mommy."

"Yeth." Mindy nodded, running in circles around the freestanding mirror and Molly raced ever faster, sliding on the hardwood floor.

"Careful," Nicole said.

"Are they bothering you? Girls, come on into the kitchen," Jenny called. "Let's make some popcorn."

"They're fine," Nicole yelled back.

Molly gave chase to her twin, around and around the mirror. Both girls scampered gaily, laughing and shrieking as Nicole twisted her hair onto her head, applied a few strokes of mascara, a light dusting of eyeshadow and a slash of lipstick, then eyed her reflection again. She was struck by her image. Not because she was drop-dead gorgeous, but because there was a light in her eyes, a bit of anticipation, that startled her. For all intents and purposes, she looked damned close to a woman in love.

"Don't even go there," she told herself as she saw headlights flash through the panes of her bedroom window. *Thorne.* Her stomach did a quick nosedive.

"Go where?" Molly asked.

"You don't want to know."

"Where you going?" Mindy asked.

"Out." Nicole bent down to hug them both, careful not to let Molly's runny nose brush against her sweater.

"Here, let's take care of that," she offered, reaching onto

the bureau for a tissue, but Molly shrieked, shook her head violently and scampered off.

"It's okay."

Nicole caught her in the kitchen where Jenny was popping the corn and the smell of butter and sharp reports of the kernels popping reminded Nicole of a rifle range. There was a hard knock on the door and both twins slipped away and ran into the living room as fast as their little legs would carry them.

"I get it!" Mindy cried.

"No, me!" Molly shoved her out of the way, her springy curls flying wildly. Nicole caught up with her just as Mindy, without looking through the window, threw the door open. Cold air breezed through the house. Thorne stood on the stoop and Nicole, straddling a wiggling Molly, managed to wipe her nose amid violent protests and wails.

"Sorry," she said, looking over her shoulder, her hair falling out of its clasp. "Come on in."

"No! No! Mommy, no!" Molly screamed.

Thorne entered as Nicole straightened, wadded the used tissue and blew her bangs from her eyes. Molly, her pride wounded, ran to her room while Mindy, sucking on a finger, looked up at the tall stranger with wide, suspicious eyes. "My daughter, Mindy," Nicole said, "and the tornado that just screamed down the hall is Molly."

"Am *not* a 'nado!" Molly protested.

Thorne couldn't swallow a smile. "And here I thought you were skinning live cats from the sound of it."

"I *hate* you, Mommy!" Molly screamed and slammed her door.

Nicole ignored the outburst and tucked her hair into place. "I'm so glad you got to see my parenting skills in action."

The door down the hall opened again. "I mean I really, *really* hate you!" Bang! The door slammed shut.

"Excuse me." Nicole's smile was forced. "I have to go deal with my daughter."

"Me, too." Mindy followed after her as Nicole headed down the hallway. She felt Thorne's eyes on her back and wished to God that he would have come at just about any other hour of the day. Why did the girls have to act up now? She tapped softly on the door. Molly's sobs were theatrically loud as Nicole entered and found her four-year-old draped dramatically across one of the twin beds.

Stepping over scattered dolls, clothes and toy cars, Nicole crossed the room. "Oh, honey, come on, it's not that bad."

"Is…is…too," Molly said, hiccuping through her tears.

Nicole gathered her into her arms, straightened and began rocking slowly, cradling her daughter's head into the crook of her neck, mindless of the damage of tears to her sweater. "Shh, shh, sweetheart," she whispered as Mindy, not wanting to be left out, wrapped her chubby little arms around one of her legs and eyed the doorway where Thorne appeared, his shoulders nearly touching each side. An amused smile played upon his lips and he folded his arms across his chest.

"Who he?" Molly asked crossly, her little face drawn into a frown.

"A…a friend. Mr. McCafferty."

"Thorne," he corrected and Molly's expression turned sour.

"Like on roses?"

"Just about."

Mindy giggled. "It's funny."

"Is it?" Thorne's eyes glinted a bit and he bent onto one

knee. "Let's just say it's been a pain in my backside ever since I can remember. Lots of kids used to make fun of me. Now, what's your name?"

Mindy bit her lower lip.

"She's Mindy," Molly said looking down at her sister in disdain, her tears and trauma temporarily forgotten.

"And you're...?"

"Molly." Wriggling she struggled down to the floor and looked up at the stranger with her knowing, imperious four-year-old gaze.

"Mr. McCaff—er, Thorne and I are going out."

"You need any help?" Jenny's voice floated into the room and the top of her head was visible over Thorne's shoulder. He stepped into the room and she appeared, arms outstretched toward the twins.

"Jenny, this is Thorne McCafferty," Nicole said and before she could finish the introductions, the twins raced to Jenny's open arms.

"Popcorn?" Molly asked.

"You want some?"

"Yeth." Mindy nodded frantically.

"Good. Let's go into the kitchen and fix up some bowls." Jenny winked at Nicole, muttered a quick "Nice to meet you," and carried both twins out of the room.

"Welcome to my life," Nicole said, turning her palms upward as if to encompass the entire room. "It's kind of hectic."

He nodded slowly. "Between this and the ER, you're on the go most of the time." One side of his mouth lifted. "My guess is that you wouldn't have it any other way."

"Well, that's where you're wrong, Mr. McCafferty. In my ideal world I'm independently wealthy, living on a private tropical island and my nannies watch my children while I lie around a pool in the sun sipping frozen daiquiris and having a hunk of a pool boy named Ramon rub the kinks from my muscles."

He laughed and she giggled.

"You'd die of boredom in two days."

"Probably," she admitted, rolling her eyes. "Crazy as it is, I kinda like my life." She tried to pass him, but he grabbed her wrist and held fast.

"It's not crazy at all."

"No?" Her pulse skyrocketed and she felt the warmth of his fingertips against the soft skin adjacent to her palm.

"It's good." His gaze lingered on hers and for a split second she thought he would kiss her again, right here in the house with the kids only a few feet away. Her knees went weak at the thought. "Not many people appreciate their lives nor do they realize how lucky they are." His gaze slid to her lips and she swallowed hard.

"How about you? Do you know you're a lucky man?"

One dark brow rose insolently and her pulse fluttered crazily. His fingers tightened around her wrist. "At this moment I feel very lucky." His head lowered and his breath caressed her face. "Very lucky indeed." He brushed a kiss across her cheek and she gasped. Then he released her. "I think we'd better go now."

Dear Lord. She nearly sagged against the wall, but rallied. "Just give me a couple of minutes to change—this sweater has had it." She escaped to her room on weak legs, closed the door and drooped against it for a minute. What was wrong with her? He'd just touched her arm, for Pete's sake. He hadn't even kissed her and yet she'd nearly melted, like some idiotic, naive schoolgirl. *Just like the girl you once were when you dated him.*

"Damn it all anyway!" Suddenly angry at herself, she

ripped off the sweater, looked down, saw that her slacks hadn't escaped their share of damage as well and sighed. From the depths of her closet she found another sweater—a red V neck and threw it over her head and traded the slacks for a long black denim skirt that buttoned up the front. Muttering under her breath, she undid her hair, swiped a brush through it and though it still crackled with electricity, decided she looked fine—good enough for the likes of Thorne McCafferty. She yanked her favorite black leather jacket from a hook on the back of her door and walked into the kitchen where Thorne, still amused, watched Molly throw pieces of popcorn at her sister while Jenny's attention was distracted.

Mindy shrieked. Jenny responded and Nicole couldn't get out of the house fast enough. She slid into her jacket, cinched the belt tight and planted a kiss on each twin's forehead, then did it again when the girls decided to put up a fuss. As she and Thorne walked onto the porch, the twins were wailing loudly, crying, "Mommy...don't go... Mommy, Mommy, Mommmeee—"

"It's nice to be wanted," Thorne observed, holding open the door of his truck as the wind tore at Nicole's hair.

"Always," she agreed, glancing to the house where two little sad faces were pressed against the windowpanes of the kitchen nook. She waved but neither girl responded other than to appear woefully forlorn. "This will last less than two minutes. As soon as the pickup disappears around the corner, they'll be sweetness and light again."

"You're sure?"

"Positive." She leaned back against the seat and eyed him. "Okay, Mr. McCafferty, so where are we going?"

His smile was a slash of white in the darkness. "You'll

see," he said, ramming the truck into reverse and backing down the drive.

"Oh, so now you're being mysterious."

"I'm *always* mysterious."

"In your dreams, McCafferty," she said.

"No, Nikki." He slid a knowing glance in her direction. "In yours."

Chapter 8

"Are you out of your mind?" she asked, shaking her head as Thorne turned into the lane of the Flying M Ranch. The last place on earth she wanted to be was anywhere near the McCafferty home. Too many old memories haunted the spread, too many long-forgotten feelings threatened to jeopardize her emotional stability.

"I've been accused of just that more often than you'd think."

"I thought we were going to a movie or dinner or..." She let her sentence drift off as she wiped the condensation on the glass and stared through the passenger window to the wintry, star-spangled night.

Frost clung to the blades of grass, reflecting in the beams of the headlights. Dried weeds and brambles clung to the fenceposts and in the fields, illuminated by a pearly moon, the dark shapes of cattle and horses moved silently. The ranch house itself loomed in the distance. Warm patches of light glowed from a few of the windows and the security lamps gave the outbuildings an eerie bluish tinge.

Thorne parked near the garage and pocketed the keys.

"Don't tell me, you're doing the cooking," she muttered sarcastically.

"Hell, no. Wouldn't want to poison you." He climbed

out of the cab, rounded the front of the truck and opened the door for her.

"Then what?"

"You'll see."

"Once again the enigmatic soul," she observed, taking the hand he offered and hopping down to the gravel that crunched under her boots as they walked, hand in hand, to the stables. Her heart was drumming by this time, her sense of anticipation spurred by an adrenaline rush that she found difficult to ignore. What the devil did he have in mind?

He threw open the door to the stables and drew Nicole inside. They weren't alone. There, hitched to the top rail of their stalls were two horses, bridled, saddled, liquid eyes watching them approach. "You're crazy," she whispered.

"You think?"

"Certifiably."

"Come on, Doc. Where's your sense of adventure? Take your pick. The General here, is docile as a lamb," Thorne said, indicating the tall chestnut gelding with a crooked blaze. "Or, if you'd prefer, you can have Mrs. Brown, but I've got to warn you, like most women, she's got a temperamental streak."

"Chauvinist," she said.

"Always." His grin was expansive as she, refusing to back down, deftly untied the reins of Mrs. Brown's bridle. The horse's dark eyes appraised her. "It's been a while since I've been in the saddle," Nicole admitted to the high-strung mare as she patted the animal's soft muzzle, "but I think you and I will get along just fine." Mrs. Brown tossed her dark head and the bridle jangled loudly.

"You're sure?" Thorne was skeptical.

"Positive."

"It's your funeral."

"Then be sure to send flowers."

"I think I already did. Well, at least one flower." Thorne laughed as he tied a thick pack and roll to the back of The General's saddle, then clucked his tongue. They led the horses through a back door that opened to a group of paddocks that led to a field crisp with hoarfrost.

"This is absolutely insane," Nicole thought aloud as she undid a few more buttons of her skirt and swung into the saddle. Mrs. Brown sidestepped and fidgeted while the staid General waited patiently as Thorne mounted.

"Where, exactly, are we going?" she asked, holding tight to the reins so that her horse wouldn't immediately spring to the lead. "And don't tell me 'you'll see.'"

"Take a guess."

"I couldn't," she lied because deep in the very most inner part of her she knew the answer, as certainly as if he'd said the words. Through a series of gates they walked, the animals anxious, the moon a shining platter over the dark hills, the creek running through the foothills. Nicole's heart thudded and she bit her lip as, at the final gate, Thorne kneed the gelding and The General broke into a gentle lope. Ever eager, Mrs. Brown bolted, stretching her shorter legs, trying desperately to take the bit in her teeth.

"Take it easy, girl. All in due time." Leaning forward Nicole patted her mount's shoulder but as the words passed her lips she wondered if she was talking to the horse or giving herself some hard but necessary advice. What was this all about, this moonlit ride alone with Thorne?

Wind streamed through her hair. Cold air brushed her cheeks. Her skirt billowed behind her and exhilaration lifted her spirits. Oh, so easily, she could be swept away in the romance, the pure cheeky thrill of this night ride. But she wouldn't.

Because of Thorne. The man wasn't trustworthy. He'd proved it once before and she would be a fool of the highest order if she were ever to give her heart to him again.

"Never," she vowed aloud.

"What?" He turned his head and astride the taller horse, his face thrown into relief, his hair rumpled in the wind, he appeared more dangerous and dark than ever. No longer a corporate big shot, but a forceful man, as wild and unbending as this sweep of harsh Montana land.

"Nothing. It—it's nothing," she said and, in an effort to get away from the questions he might hurl at her, kicked her little mare and gave the animal her head.

Mrs. Brown exploded forward. Her hooves pounded. Her legs stretched and retracted. Faster and faster, flying past the larger horse as if he were plodding.

Nicole laughed out loud and cast all caution to the wind. The moonlit night played with her heart and mind. The wind brought tears to her eyes and tangled her hair. She felt freer and younger than she had in years—a girl in the rush of love. Over the rise she rode with the gelding bearing down on them. She cast one glance over her shoulder and spied Thorne, hunched forward, his eyes drawn like a rifle bead on her, his mouth a line of satisfied determination.

"Oh, God," she whispered, then shouted, "hi-ya!" and slapped Mrs. Brown's shoulder with the reins. The little horse shot forward even faster, the ground whirling by in a rush. Over the flat land, across a rise, onward until the trees surrounding the creek appeared— great, black towers bordering the field and looming ever closer. Nicole drew back on the reins and heard The General snorting and blowing as Thorne, too, pulled his mount to a stop.

Nicole tried to catch her breath.

How long had it been since she'd been here? Seventeen

years? Eighteen? But it had been summer then, a time of youth and hot, breathless days, when the touch of Thorne's lips against the nape of her neck was as sensual and welcome as a cool breeze.

Her throat swelled at the thought of their lovemaking, so hot, so uninhibited, so long ago. Why had he brought her here now, in this shadowy night with winter as close at hand as summer had been years before?

He climbed off his horse and stood on the frozen ground looking up at her. "Need help?"

"No... I..." She cleared her throat and gave herself a swift mental shake. For God's sake, she wasn't the tongue-tied teenager she once had been. She was a grown woman, a mother, a doctor for crying out loud! "I'm fine," she said, inwardly cringing at the lie because the truth of the matter was that she wasn't fine at all. In fact she was far from it, but she swung down from the saddle and landed on the hard ground only inches from him and determined not to show one sign that any part of him intimidated her. Dusting her hands, she hoped to appear more collected than she felt. "So...why did you bring me here? Just for old times' sake?"

"Something like that."

"Gee, and I didn't think you were nostalgic."

"Maybe you were wrong about me."

Her throat tightened. "I... I, uh, don't think so." She offered him a smile filled with a bravado she didn't really feel. Her skirt was tugged by a gust of wind that rattled through the leafless trees and shivered the longer blades of grass. "I'm just surprised that you seem to feel a need for a trip down memory lane."

"Don't you want to sometimes?" His voice was low, his eyes silver with the moonlight and her breath was suddenly trapped in the back of her throat.

"No." She shook her head. "As a matter of fact, I think it would be a bad idea."

"Oh?" His arms surrounded her and he drew her close, his nose touching hers. "Well I think it's a damned fine one." His lips found hers and she gasped, her mouth opening and granting his tongue easy access. She told herself that she was being foolish, that being with him was emotional suicide, that getting involved with a man named McCafferty was sure to break her heart all over again and yet she couldn't stop herself. Emotions old and new enveloped her and desire swept through her veins. As if of their own accord her traitorous arms wound around his neck, her eyes closed and she sank against him.

Oh, Thorne...it's been so long....

His lips were sweet warm pressure, his hands big and strong as they splayed against her back, and the combination of the cold starry night and his hot skin was seductively erotic. A small moan escaped her throat only to be answered by his own husky groan.

Don't do this, Nicole, she told herself to no avail. She sensed the horses wandering off, heard, over the ever increasing drumming of her heart, the soft plop of their hooves and the chink of their bridles as they tried to pluck at the frozen blades of grass. Somewhere in the distance an owl hooted and a gentle breeze rushed through the dry leaves of the aspen trees guarding the creek.

"I've wanted to do this from the first time I saw you again," Thorne admitted, his fingers catching in her hair. He tugged, pulling her face away so that he could stare at her. His features were shadowed, his eyes a silver reflection of the moonlight.

"From the first time you saw me again."

"Yes."

"At the hospital?"

"At the hospital."

"Liar." Her breath fogged in the air.

"Never." He kissed her again and this time she responded without the shackles of the past. She kissed him with the same abandon she had as a young girl. It felt so right to have his strong arms drag her to the ground, so natural to turn her head so that his lips and tongue found that spot in the curve of her neck that caused her entire body to convulse.

Warm, liquid sensations streamed through her. Her blood heated, her heart thudded and he kissed her as if he would never stop.

She felt the knot of her belt loosen, noticed when her jacket opened and his hands reached beneath the hem of her sweater. Her back arched as his skin brushed against hers and as he kissed her he scaled her ribs with warm-tipped fingers.

A dozen reasons to deny him screamed through her mind.

Twice as many silenced her doubts. Why not make love to this man? What would it hurt? It wasn't as if she'd never lain with him before, never felt the seduction of his kiss or the power of his body joining with hers.

His tongue was sweet persuasion as his fingers found the few buttons that were still holding her skirt closed. She gasped as his fingers brushed the bare skin of her thighs. *Stop him, Nicole! Are you nuts? You can't make love to him. You can't!* And yet as certain as it was that the sun would rise over the eastern horizon, she knew that she would love him again.

Within minutes both her skirt and sweater were disposed of, dropped in a pool on the ground and Thorne was lying above her, kissing her, touching her, causing the blood in her veins to tingle and dance. When she opened her eyes, she looked into a face she'd once loved, a face etched by the years, a face of bladed angles and hard edges, yet in the depths of his eyes and the set of his mouth she saw re- gret—the tiniest hint of remorse. .

The ice around her heart cracked and she blinked against the sting of sudden unwanted tears. Through their soft sheen she saw the moon above him, a bright, frigid disk surrounded by thousands of twinkling stars and she heard the soft babble of the creek.

"I never said I was sorry." His voice was a hoarse whis- per.

"Shh." She placed a finger to his lips. "You don't have to say—ooh."

He drew her finger into the warmth of his mouth.

"Oh, no—"

But she didn't pull away as his hot, wet tongue drew anxious circles on her skin as he sucked.

"Thorne—please—"

She intended to deny him but didn't get that chance.

In a heartbeat he released her finger and kissed her hard. Any thoughts of refusal were suddenly stripped away. Her hands found the zipper of his jacket and the buttons of his wool shirt underneath. Her skin tingled, her blood was on fire.

They kissed and touched. Callused fingers caressed her bare skin and she, too, touched him intimately, kissing him and tugging at his clothes, touching him as his jacket and pants fell away. Her fingers traced the deep ridges of his muscles, thrilling to the hard, tight flesh beneath his skin. She kissed the thatch of springy hair upon his chest and was rewarded with the same heart-stopping sensuality as he traced the fragile bones at the hollow of her throat with his tongue, then lowered himself to her breasts where he caressed one button-hard nipple and suckled at the other.

"You're more beautiful than I remembered," he claimed, his breath cool against her hot flesh.

Don't listen to this, don't believe him.... But already she was lost.

Heat burned through her and her mind spun in delicious circles of lovemaking. Deep in the most private part of her she tingled and became moist. Desire thrummed in her blood and seemed to shimmer in the crisp winter air. His breathing was as heavy as her own, his skilled hands rubbing and touching and creating a maelstrom that caused her to gasp.

"I've dreamed of this," he said, lowering his face and kissing her abdomen.

Deep inside she convulsed. Her fingers shot through his hair. Lower still he slid, his tongue rimming her navel. She bucked upward, then quivered with the want of him and bit her lower lip as he kissed the inside of her thigh. Her eyes were closed but as his fingers found the feminine folds of her womanhood and he touched the most sensitive spot within her, she groaned. His fingers were bold, his breath feather soft and seductive, his tongue quick. She arched again and cried out, her fingers digging into the cold, hard dirt as the first spasm hit. Her eyes flew open and the sky seemed to blur—stars and moon blending in pearlescent shards as sensation after sensation rocked her. She was dragging in each breath, spiraling downward, floating....

His fingers dug into her buttocks. He held her close and assailed her again and again, his tongue working exquisite magic, sending her soaring again and again until she was certain her heart and lungs would burst.

"Thorne..."

He came to her. While she was gasping, barely able to move, the sweat of her body drying in the cold night air, he moved upward, spreading her bare legs with his own, kissing her abdomen, her breasts, her throat.

"Now?" she whispered, her blood stirring again.

"Mmm." He kissed her and she responded, felt the male hardness of him pressed against her mound.

"But—"

"Now. You can do it, Nikki." His mouth cut off any further protest. With one quick thrust he claimed her. "We can do it."

She stared up at him and as their gazes locked, he moved, slowly at first, taking his time as the fires within her stoked all over again. Her skin broke out with perspiration and liquid heat seared her. She heard a roaring in her ears, felt the pressure build again. Her mind spun in endless circles and she caught his rhythm, meeting each of his thrusts, opening to him, clinging to him.

Faster and faster. She closed her eyes, thought she was dreaming, cried out and heard his own answering scream as with one final stroke he fell against her, flattening her breasts, his face buried in the crook of her neck. "Oh, Nikki. Sweet, sweet Nikki."

The old ache in her heart reopened at the sound of his breathless voice. She held tight to him, feeling afterglow seep through her bones.

Finally her heart slowed and she could breathe again.

She'd never felt like this—never with Paul, only with Thorne.

"Well, well, well," he whispered. "That was—" he looked down at her "—worth the wait."

"Oh, was it?" She cocked an insolent eyebrow and imagined that her eyes glowed with a wicked light. "Was it good for you—"

"Don't!" He shook his head and laughed, the deep timbre of his voice ringing in the hills. "Just don't, okay?"

"Just checking."

"Or being a wise guy." He kissed her on the lips then and rubbed her arms. "Cold?"

"Not yet."

"You will be, but I've got something for that." Without bothering with his clothes, he rolled off her, climbed to his feet and whistled to the horses. The General's head shot up and he came close enough that Thorne loosened the saddlebag. From its depths he withdrew a thermos, a bottle and an insulated pack. "I'm afraid to ask what you're doing." Shivering a bit, Nicole slipped into her sweater and skirt.

"You're getting dressed?"

"If you haven't noticed, it's subfreezing out here." She glanced at the creek where ice glinted between the exposed roots of the trees at the water's edge.

"You're tough. You can take it."

"You be the macho one, okay?"

"Always." She tried not to stare at his nakedness, refused to notice the play of his shoulder muscles, or the expanse of his chest or the dark juncture of his legs. Instead she concentrated on his actions which included spreading a small tablecloth, handing her a foil-wrapped package and opening the thermos.

"What is this?"

"Juanita's speciality. Soft tacos and Spanish coffee."

"What? Are you crazy?"

"You keep bringing up my sanity, but believe me, I'm as sane as you are. Eat." He sat on the bare ground and she shifted her eyes away from his long, muscular thighs to accept a speckled enamel cup with steaming coffee laced with alcohol.

"I don't believe this." She unwrapped her soft taco and took a bite. A delicious blend of flavors exploded in her mouth. She sipped from her cup and felt the hot liquid slide down her throat. "Tell me this isn't how you treat all the women in your life."

"Nope. Only one." He stared at her for a long minute and she, avoiding looking into his eyes, buried her nose in her cup and drank a long sip.

"So I guess I'm special?" she teased.

"Very." He was still looking at her.

Another long swallow and bite. She wanted to believe him with all the naivete of her lost youth, but didn't dare. "So special it took eighteen years and a tragedy to force you to face me again?"

He was about to take a drink, but stopped short, his cup halfway to his lips. Somewhere nearby one of the horses snorted. "Maybe I didn't make myself clear earlier," he said. "I started to apologize for the past, but you stopped me."

"I know, you don't have to—"

"Sure I do, Nikki. I've got a lot of excuses, but that's all they are and not very good ones at that. This is the here and now. I would hope that you would take me at face value."

"Well that's damned hard to do when you're sitting there naked as a jaybird and I'm having one devil of a time concentrating on your face, if you know what I mean."

"I know exactly," he said, setting his cup aside. Her heart stopped for she knew what was coming. In a split second, he'd grabbed her again, kissed her as if he never intended to stop and, stripping her of her clothes, made love to her all over again.

Nikki, the romantic young girl who still resided deep in

the most hidden parts of her, was in heaven at the thought of a love affair with Thorne McCafferty.

But Nicole, the grown woman, knew she'd just crossed a threshold into certain emotional hell.

Chapter 9

"Barring any unforeseen complications, the baby's going to pull through." Dr. Arnold's voice was a balm but Thorne, in his relief, wanted to jump right through the ceiling of the den where he'd taken the call. For hours he'd been trying to concentrate on alterations to a contract he'd been faxed by Eloise, or playing phone tag with his real estate agent and tax attorney, but all the while he'd been worried about his sister and the baby.

Then there was Nicole. Always at the edges of his mind. It had been two days since their first night together by the creek and he'd had to rein himself in rather than chase her down, but he had too much to think about to rush headlong into a passionate love affair.

"...so as long as he continues to improve, I would guess that he can come home in about three days. Since your sister isn't ready to be moved yet, I assume that you've made arrangements for his care."

"Absolutely," Thorne said, though the truth of the matter was that he hadn't made much headway in finding a suitable nanny and the upstairs room that he planned to become the nursery was a long way from being ready for a newborn.

"Well, if you have any questions, give me a call. I'll be checking in on the baby every few hours, just to make sure that he's turned the corner and the nursing staff will notify me of any change."

"Thanks," Thorne said and felt as if a weight as heavy as any he'd ever felt in his life had been lifted from his shoulders. "Thank God," he whispered and leaned his head on the desk. He couldn't imagine what would have happened if little J.R. hadn't survived; he'd never allowed his thoughts to wander down that dark and painful path.

Maybe things were finally turning around. He shoved his paperwork aside and walked in stocking feet out of the den. In the past week he'd changed his habits, giving up the strict regimen he'd adhered to in Denver and loosening up. Randi's condition and the baby's tenuous hold on life had turned his thoughts away from corporate takeovers, mergers, land deals and developments. He'd had less interest in oil leases and start-up software companies than he'd had on this ranch—the land he'd once disdained.

What about Nicole? Isn't she one of the reasons you've found life here idyllic?

Rubbing his jaw, he realized that he hadn't shaved this morning and that it didn't bother him. As he walked down the hall to the kitchen he wondered if he was getting soft or getting smart.

"I tell you I don't want any strangers in this house!" Juanita's voice was firm.

"Thorne's interviewing nannies…they're all referred by an agency I think."

"One that only wants to make money. And what does he know about taking care of babies?"

"Good point."

"My ears are burning," Thorne said as he strode into the kitchen and caught Slade's eye.

Juanita was elbow deep in flour, throwing her weight

into a rolling pin that was stretching a disk of dough. Every once in a while she stopped to sprinkle the dough with cornmeal or flour and her expression was thunderous. "That baby, he needs his mother and Señorita Randi—she would not want someone she does not know or trust taking care of her son!" Juanita took off a few seconds and made the sign of the cross. "I have told you this before."

"I haven't hired anyone yet."

"Good." Juanita rattled off a stream of rapid-fire Spanish that Thorne was grateful he didn't understand.

Slade chuckled and shook his head. He reached into the pocket of his shirt and withdrew a folded piece of paper. "Larry Todd's signed on," he said. "I'm goin' to meet him in about—" he checked his watch "—half an hour."

"Good."

"Later this afternoon Kurt Striker is gonna pay us a visit. Will you be around?"

Thorne's head snapped up. "You bet I will. Has he found out anything else?"

"Nothing that I know of, but we'll see." Slade wandered to the back door where his boots were waiting. Nearby Harold, their father's half-crippled dog, lay on a rag rug. Harold thumped his tail and Slade rewarded him by scratching him behind the ears while Juanita slid a warning glance toward dog and man.

"I just washed the floors."

"I know, I know."

Harold, suitably abashed, rested his head between his paws and stared up at her with sorrowful eyes.

"Stay." Juanita pointed at the dog with her rolling pin.

"He's not moving," Slade said.

"Good news," Thorne said and caught Juanita's and Slade's attention.

"Señorita Randi?"

"The baby. He's pulling out of it."

Slade let up a whoop and Juanita prayed and crossed herself, her dark eyes filling with tears of relief. "I knew it," she said.

"Does Matt know?" Slade asked, unable to stop grinning, his eyes rimmed in red.

"Don't think so. I just got the call. Why don't you tell him?"

"Damned straight, I will."

"Good." Thorne ran a hand over his chin. "I'll run into town—got to talk to some local attorneys about Randi, then I'm gonna stop by the hospital. I'll meet you and Striker back here later," Thorne said.

"Fair enough." With a nod and a crisp salute to Juanita, the "warden" as he sometimes called her, Slade disappeared through the back door.

"Thank goodness for the baby," Juanita said as she turned back to her dough. "As for that one." She hitched her head toward the door that was closing behind Slade. "He is too…*irrespetuoso*…too—" She waved one hand frantically in the air, sending a cloud of flour around her head.

"Too irreverent."

"*Sí. Irrespetuoso* for his own good."

"You're the one who once referred to Randi's mother as a witch."

"That was years ago and is irreverent—"

"Irrelevant."

"It is fact."

"If you say so."

"I do."

"He's had his own demons to deal with."

"*Sí.*" Her lips pursed and she plunged her hands into the

bowl of cornmeal and went about her task, though both she and Thorne considered his youngest brother and the personal pain that Slade had endured.

His thoughts dark, Thorne slipped back to the office, called Eloise and checked in. Her voice was professional and bright, but Thorne didn't miss the stress of the office.

"Buzz Branson's been calling twice a day," Eloise informed him. "Your accountant would like to go over the projected profit and loss on the Hillside View development and Annette Williams left her number twice." His conscience twinged at the mention of Annette's name, though he thought they'd reached an understanding the last time they'd spoken. Obviously not.

"If anyone calls back, give him—or her—the number here," Thorne said. "If I'm not in they can leave a message on the answering machine."

"Will do. Now you probably want to know that there's still talk of a strike by the local carpenters' union. It could involve one of the framing crews, and one of the partners in Tech-Link is under investigation by the IRS."

Thorne let out a long whistle. "You're just full of good news, aren't you?"

"Wouldn't want you to feel unloved," Eloise said wryly.

"Don't worry. As I said, give them the new number—it's connected to two lines and an answering machine, so I'll get any messages. You've got it."

"Will do," she promised and he hung up feeling more dispassionate about his business than he had in years. He looked out the window to the gleaming acres of raw land where he'd grown up. Hooking his thumbs into the belt loops of his jeans, he leaned a shoulder against the window frame and watched a herd of cattle lumber across the winter-dry acres. Shaggy red, black and mottled gray coats moved slowly and every once in a while a lonesome calf bawled.

Thorne had loved it here as a kid, turned his back on it disdainfully when he'd approached adulthood and spent the next twenty years avoiding the place. Now, it got to him. Just as a certain lady doctor did. *You're losing it, McCafferty,* he thought without a trace of despair. *Whatever that edge was that separated you from your brothers and your old man, it's getting dull with age.*

And he couldn't let that happen.

Rather than dwell on his changing attitude, he strode to the stairs and climbed upward to his room. Some of his clothes had arrived and he thought he'd best shake himself out of this maudlin nostalgia that had gripped him ever since seeing Nicole again. He unpacked his favorite gray suit, starched white shirt and burgundy tie, then he headed to the bathroom to shower and shave.

"She hasn't responded yet?" Nicole asked the RN on duty in ICU. Randi McCafferty lay still, unmoving, her monitors in place, the bandages removed from her face. She was healing slowly, at least externally, but she looked worse than ever. Her skin was discolored and scabbed over, her cheeks still swollen.

"No. We even talked to her and one of the brothers—the one with the dark eyes—"

"Matt."

"Yes, he stopped by earlier and talked to her for fifteen minutes, but there wasn't the slightest bit of response." She held Nicole's gaze. "Sometimes it takes a while. Dr. Nimmo isn't concerned yet and he's the best neurosurgeon around."

That much was true, and the other doctors who were attending to Randi, Dr. Oliverio, an orthopedist and an OB-

GYN, were outstanding as well. "I know, but I was just hoping. Since the baby's doing better, it would be nice…"

Again she looked down at Thorne's sister. *Wake up, Randi! You've got so much to live for!*

"Unfortunately the press keeps snooping around. Several people from the local paper have called and one woman tried to get in here. She posed as the patient's sister."

"Randi doesn't have a sister," Nicole said, irritated.

"We knew that." The nurse smiled. "Security took care of her."

Nicole wished the reporters would leave Randi and her baby alone. She realized the mystery surrounding Randi's accident and pregnancy was a big deal in this small town, but it seemed blown out of proportion. The patients needed to recover—without the eagle eye of the press scrutinizing them.

"Well, let me know if there's any change." Nicole touched Randi's fingers with her own. "Come on," she encouraged, "you can do this. You've got a little baby who needs you and three brothers who are worried sick."

She made her way down to her office and sighed. It had been a long night in the ER, made more difficult because of her lack of sleep from a few nights before.

After making love by the creek and eating the cold meal, she and Thorne had ridden the ridge at midnight then returned to the ranch. She hadn't gotten home until well after one and then had slept poorly, thinking of Thorne, tossing, turning and pounding her pillow in frustration.

The next day hadn't been any better and last night Molly, complaining of bad dreams and a sore throat, had crawled into bed with her. Again, she'd slept poorly and one of the main reasons was Thorne. She'd remembered kissing him, touching him and making love to him in the cold winter air. Worst of all she thought she might be falling in love with him all over again.

"Foolish, foolish woman," she said, skirting a janitor's cart and rounding a corner of the corridor. She didn't have time to fall in love with any man, much less one who had walked away from her in the past. No, she couldn't fall in love with Thorne. Wouldn't! Gritting her teeth, she forced her mind away from the sexy eldest McCafferty brother and concentrated on the tasks at hand. Her shift in the ER didn't start for nearly two hours, but she had catch-up work to do, patient notes to write on her computer, some calls to make to colleagues, and, as always, she wanted to check on the twins.

At the thought of her girls she smiled though she was concerned as Molly had developed a cough and this morning had been barking up a storm. The trouble with being a doctor was that she knew what complications might develop and she was always worried sick whenever either one of them showed the least sign of illness. "Get a grip," she told herself as she entered her office and shed her lab coat, hanging it over the back of her chair.

To ease her mind she put a quick call in to Jenny and the twins, then switched on her computer and checked her e-mail before writing her patient notes and returning the patient and colleague calls that she retrieved from her voice mail. Her stomach rumbled as she hadn't eaten for hours, but she ignored the hunger pangs and kept working.

Over an hour later she took a break and stopped by the neonatal care unit where little J.R. blinked up at her under the warm lights. "How 'ya doin', little guy?" she whispered as he focused on her. Carefully she picked the baby up and held him to her chest. Tears came to her eyes as she smelled the baby scent of him, felt him snuggle against her, his tiny body swaddled and warm. "You just hang in there, sweetie. Your momma's gonna be so glad to see you when she wakes up."

Soft little coos hung in the air and Nicole thought her heart would break for the poor child whose mother was struggling for life and whose father was nowhere to be found—completely unknown. But J.R. did have his uncles, three rugged men who loved him dearly.

"Got time to feed him?" one of the nurses asked and Nicole couldn't resist. With practiced hands she held baby and bottle and smiled as she watched him suckle hungrily. It felt so right to hold him and she realized how much she wanted another child.

Thorne's child? her wayward mind taunted. *Is that what you want? Isn't he the man you think you're falling in love with? The confirmed bachelor who left you before?*

She blinked hard and fought a powerful wave of emotions as she slowly rocked and cradled little J.R. Was it so wrong to want another baby?

Forget it, you've got the twins; that's enough for a single parent. Would you really want to raise another one without a father?

But Molly and Mindy did have a father, though Paul didn't really seem to give a damn. He rarely called them, never came to visit, wasn't interested in hearing about them. He was remarried now to a professional woman like himself, one who swore she didn't want to be tied down with children. But she was young. Nicole expected she might change her mind.

"There you go," she said softly as the baby quit drinking to stare up at her. "You are precious." She kissed the top of his downy curls and glanced through the plate glass window. Thorne was on the other side, his gaze centered on her, his expression unreadable. Dressed in a business suit, crisp white shirt and perfectly knotted tie, he appeared more unapproachable than he had been, more hard-edged. The terms *shark* and *corporate raider* slid through her mind and she reminded herself he wasn't her kind of man; she'd learned that lesson well.

Nonetheless she felt a flush of scarlet climb up the back of her neck at being caught in such a tender moment. Managing a weak smile she laid the baby back into his crib and hesitated when he began to cry. "Shh. You're all right," she assured the infant.

The nurse stepped forward. "I'll take it from here," she said as Nicole slipped through the door and joined Thorne in the hallway.

"Didn't expect you here," she said, stuffing her hands into the pockets of her white coat.

"Had business in town. Thought I'd check on Randi and the baby."

"He's much better."

Thorne managed a smile. "I see that. I just wish my sister would respond."

"She will. In time."

"I hope." He didn't seem convinced. "Can I buy you lunch?"

She thought about the work in her office. She'd finished most of it and she was hungry. Why not? *Because it would be best if you gave him up right now. He's not in love with you—you're just a convenient distraction while he's in town. But he's going to leave, Nicole. You know it. His life is in Denver.*

"I have to be in the ER in a few minutes."

"So how about a cup of coffee in the cafeteria?" His smile was irresistible.

"Okay. You've twisted my arm," she said with a laugh. Together they walked through the hallways, passing nurses with medication carts, aides helping patients walk and an assortment of visitors looking for loved ones.

The cafeteria was a madhouse, and over Thorne's protests that she should eat something more substantial, she grabbed a carton of vanilla yogurt, a cranberry-pecan muffin and a cup of black coffee while he ordered a turkey sandwich and cup of soup.

Once served, Thorne carried the tray to the end of a Formica-topped table where a few pages of the morning newspaper were scattered. Several nurses were talking at the next table—one of them had obviously just gotten engaged and the others were gushing; clusters of visitors had gathered in several groups and several of her colleagues were debating the addition of another wing and trauma unit.

Nicole slid into a seat near a shedding ficus tree and Thorne sat opposite her. A few of her colleagues cast curious glances in her direction, but for the most part they were left alone. "I was hoping you could help me," he said, unwrapping his sandwich.

"How?" She bit into her muffin.

"As I said before, when J.R.'s released we'll need a nanny."

She swallowed and grinned up at him. "Don't tell me the three McCafferty brothers can't handle one baby."

"We're all busy."

"Mmm." She dipped her spoon into her yogurt.

"I don't think it's gonna be like the movie *Three Men and a Baby* at the Flying M."

"No?" She laughed. "The thought conjures up some interesting scenarios. Thorne McCafferty, CEO, president of the Chamber of Commerce and...diaper changer. Matt

McCafferty, calf roper, horse brander and…baby burper. Slade McCafferty, daredevil and—"

"Okay, okay, I get the idea." His lips twitched and his gray eyes sparkled.

"Good." She winked at him.

"So you've had your fun," he said around a bite of sandwich.

"It's just nice to be with a man of sooo many talents," she teased.

"Only you would know."

The laughter died from his eyes and Nicole nearly dropped her spoon. Thoughts of making love to him flitted through her mind. Heat climbed up the back of her neck and she swallowed hard at the thought of their recent lovemaking.

"If I recall—"

"Enough, okay? I get it," she whispered, not wanting anyone to overhear the conversation. "Truce."

"Then you'll help me find a nanny."

"I guess I don't have much choice."

"Good. I accept your white flag."

"I didn't surrender, just suggested a truce!"

His eyes glittered with wicked mischief. "Whatever you say."

Still flushed, she managed to change the subject and make small talk through the rest of the meal. Why did she let him get to her? Bait her? Tease her? Flirt outrageously with her? What was it about him that she found downright irritating and incredibly sexual? Good lord, she was becoming one of those foolish, man-crazy women she abhorred! Glancing at her watch, she realized she was running out of time. "Duty calls," she said, standing.

He scraped his chair back. As she discarded the remains

of her lunch in the trash bin, he walked with her stride for stride and she was aware how distinctive he looked, a tall man in a long black coat amidst doctors and nurses in white lab coats or green scrubs, or visitors in an array of cotton, denim, rawhide or flannel. There were a few business types as well, salesmen, for the most part, but none were as tall or as arrogantly self-important as was Thorne McCafferty in his crisp white shirt, silk tie and expensive suit. His presence demanded notice and noticed he got.

At the table where the nurses sat, more than one pair of interested eyes watched him as he held open one of the double doors leading to the hallway, while his other palm rested against the small of her back, as if he needed to guide her through. It was a simple gesture, maybe even a polite, automatic movement on his part, but she stepped away from him as they entered the corridor and was thankful that he dropped his arm to his side. The less personal contact they had, the better.

And yet...

"Has anyone located J.R.'s father?" she asked. "He might have a say in what kind of care the baby gets."

"Not yet." His eyes turned as cold as a blast of winter. "But I'll find him." She didn't doubt it for a moment. Thorne McCafferty was an intimidating force, a man who, if he chose to hunt someone down, would leave no stone unturned in his quest. As she pushed the elevator call button, he touched her shoulder.

She started to step inside, but he took hold of the crook of her arm and pulled her against him. To her surprise he kissed her. Hard. So hard, her knees nearly gave way.

"What was that all about?" she asked, as he finally released her.

"Just something to remember me by."

As if I don't have enough.

Thrusting his hands into the pockets of his coat, he turned and walked toward the front of the building. Nicole, stripped of her breath and dignity in one fell swoop, entered the elevator car. Gratefully, the doors whispered shut and she was alone. *So she wouldn't forget him?*

Well, he needn't worry. Sighing, Nicole leaned against the back wall of the car. Thorne McCafferty was impossible to forget.

Chapter 10

Kurt Striker looked like the television version of an ex-cop turned private detective—hard features, deep-set eyes that, when they weren't pinning you in his cold, green glare, moved restlessly, his gaze taking in everything.

He shook Thorne's hand in a strong grip that he released quickly. In a jean jacket, matching Levi's, scratched boots and collarless shirt, he stood on the back porch, watching the clouds roll across the western hills. Slade smoked. Kurt didn't seem to mind as he squinted into the distance. Growling deep in his throat, Harold rounded the end of the porch and with a wag of his tail, slowly climbed the steps to settle at Slade's feet.

"Good to finally meet you," Thorne said.

Kurt nodded and Thorne noticed a few flecks of gray in his otherwise brown hair. "Thought you'd want to know what I've found out."

So there was some information. Good. "Anything." Thorne hitched his head toward the kitchen. "Let's go inside and talk." Slade took last one pull on his cigarette, then flipped it into an empty metal can that rested on a weathered bench. Together they walked into the house where the sharp scent of pine from some kind of cleanser mixed with the aroma of roasting pork.

"Boots off! Muddy boots on the porch," Juanita called from deep in the recesses of the pantry.

"Eyes in the back of her head," Slade grumbled, checking the scuffed leather of his hiking boots. "Forget it."

"Mine're clean," Kurt said.

Juanita was on a new subject as she emerged from the pantry. Carrying two plastic bags of small onions and red potatoes, she kicked the pantry door shut, then dropped both sacks onto the butcher block and shook her head. Pointing an accusing finger at Thorne, she said, "That woman—that Annette. She called again. Insists you phone her, today." With a roll of her expressive eyes, she muttered something in Spanish.

Thorne couldn't hide his irritation. "Next time let the machine answer."

"I did. But I heard it record. I was dusting." Juanita's back was as stiff as an ironing board, her chin elevated a fraction as if she expected Thorne to reprimand her for eavesdropping. "And that is not the worst of it, another reporter called today. Wants to talk to you. *Dios!*" She clucked her tongue, threw up her hands and shook her head as if she couldn't understand the folly of it all.

"I'll talk to them later," Thorne said. Then he turned to Kurt. "Let's go into the living room."

Juanita opened the bag of onions and began peeling them deftly. "Would you like something to eat? A *bocado?* Something to drink?"

"Snacks would be fine. And beer," Thorne said as they walked down the hall. While Slade and Striker made their way to the living room, Thorne shed his jacket, rolled up the sleeves of his shirt and followed.

"So, what've you got?" he asked once they were all in the living room.

Striker stood near the windows. His forehead was creased, his eyes serious. "I don't think your sister was involved in a single-car accident." Thorne's eyes narrowed on the other man. "I suspect another car or truck or some kind of rig was involved."

"Wait a minute. Doesn't this go against everything the police have told us?" Thorne was thunderstruck. He glanced at Slade to back him up.

"That's what I heard." Slade was kneeling at the fireplace, striking a match to the paper and dry kindling.

"It's only a theory at this point," Striker admitted. "But there does seem to be a discrepancy. A few paint scratches on her back fender. No skid marks, no other evidence, but I think it's a distinct possibility another vehicle was involved."

The fire crackled to life and Slade tossed a thick chunk of oak onto the hungry flames. Juanita carried in a tray of three long-necked bottles of beer and a basket of chips. As soon as she disappeared, Striker crossed the room and settled into a corner of the worn leather couch facing the fireplace. Both he and Slade picked up bottles. Thorne didn't. He wasn't interested in anything other than the story the detective was concocting.

"What does the sheriff's department have to say?" he asked, ignoring the fact that his gut was clenching hard, his head pounding. Striker's hypothesis wasn't good news. Not at all. If someone had run Randi off the road or even hit her accidentally, it meant hit-and-run was involved—or worse. It could have been intentional.

"They're not saying much. Though they're still considering all the possibilities. The trouble is, they don't have any eyewitnesses and as Randi's in no condition to tell them what happened, they're not jumping to any conclusions."

"But you seem sure."

Green eyes found his and held. "I said it was just a theory. I'm not sure about anything."

"What about the baby's father?"

"Got a few leads, but haven't talked to the guys yet."

"Who are they?"

"Men she was seen with about a year ago. Seems your sis didn't have a steady boyfriend, at least not recently. She hung out with people she worked with at the paper, and friends she knew from school, but no one she knew realized she was in any serious romance. She never told any of her friends about the guy, whoever he is." He took a long swallow from his beer. "But there are some men who dated her that I'm trying to track down, one's a guy named Joe Paterno, a photojournalist who did some freelance stuff for the *Clarion.* Then there was a lawyer by the name of Brodie Clanton—he's connected to big money in Seattle. His grandfather was a judge at one time. The last guy's a cowboy type she met while helping someone with an interview."

"His name?"

"Sam Donahue."

"I knew a Sam Donahue," Slade said as he took up a position near the bookcase, leaned his hips against the liquor cupboard and crossed his ankles. "When I rode the circuit a while. Matt knows him, too, if he's the guy I'm thinking of. Big. Blond. Tough as nails."

"That's the one."

"*He* was involved with Randi?" Thorne couldn't believe his ears.

"Appears so. Haven't quite caught up with him yet."

Slade scowled and took a long swallow from his bottle. "Donahue was bad news. In and out of jail, I think."

"You're right."

"Hell," Thorne snarled.

"The more I learn about little sis, the more I feel like I didn't know her at all." Slade shook his head.

"None of us did," Thorne said as the front door opened and slammed shut. Matt, bringing in a rush of cold wind, strode into the living room and caught the tail end of the conversation.

"None of us did what?" he asked, yanking off his gloves and looking from one man to the next. His face was ruddy with the cold and he tossed his hat onto the cushion of a vacant armchair.

Slade introduced him to Kurt Striker and caught him up with the conversation as he grabbed the last bottle of beer and twisted off the cap. "Sam Donahue?" He snorted. "No way. The guy's not Randi's type."

"Oh, so you're the expert now. Tell us, who is Randi's kind of guy?" Thorne demanded, more frustrated than ever.

"I wish I knew," Matt admitted. "Hell."

"What else have you got?" Thorne asked the private detective.

"Not much more, except that your sister wasn't having such a great time at her job, either. Though everyone at the paper's been tight-lipped, some of her co-workers thought she'd gotten into some hot water with the editors."

"How?" Thorne asked, his eyebrows slamming together.

"Good question. I've got copies of all the columns she wrote for the past six months, but those are only the ones that were in print. According to her friend Sarah Peeples who writes movie reviews, Randi had about two weeks' worth of columns that she'd written but hadn't yet been printed. No one has seen them. And there was talk of some kind of project she was working on, though the paper denies it. Again, no one's seen any copies of it."

"Except maybe Randi."

"And she's not talkin'," Matt observed, his mouth a grave line as he leaned against the bookcase and the fire crackled and hissed.

"She writes advice to the heartbroken for God's sake!" Slade interrupted.

"And what else?" Striker thought aloud.

Matt frowned down at his beer. "Now wait a minute. You said that Randi's vehicle *might* have been struck, but no one knows if it was intentional or not. It's a pretty big leap to go from a single-car accident because the driver hit black ice to some kind of…what? Attempted murder?"

"All I'm saying is that there might have been another vehicle involved and if there was, the driver is, at the very least, guilty of hit-and-run. From there it only gets worse."

"*If* she was hit." Matt's gaze fastened on the private investigator. He was obviously skeptical.

"Right."

"I think we're making big assumptions here."

"Just checkin' out all the possibilities," Slade argued. "We owe it to Randi."

"God, I wish she'd wake up." Matt straightened and shoved a hand through his hair in frustration.

"We all do." Thorne looked from one brother to the other. "But until she does, we've got to keep trying to figure this out." To Striker, he said, "Keep at it. Talk to anyone you can. We need to find the father of Randi's baby. If there's any way you can find out the blood type of the men she was involved with, we could at least eliminate some of the possibilities."

"Already doin' it," Striker admitted.

"How do you do that?" Matt said.

Kurt sent him a look silently telling him he didn't want to know.

"Just handle it." Thorne wasn't sure he liked Kurt Striker, but he believed the man would do what had to be done to dig up the truth. That was all that mattered. He didn't even care if the law was bent a little, not if Randi's life was truly endangered by someone with a grudge. But *who?*

Striker nodded. "Will do. And I'm gonna try to find those missing columns. I don't suppose any of you know if she had a laptop computer?"

Slade lifted a shoulder, Matt shook his head and Thorne frowned.

"Nothin's on her desktop."

"How do you know that?" Matt asked.

"I checked."

"You broke into her apartment?" Matt looked from one of his brothers to the next. "Hey—isn't that illegal? Randi'll kill us if she ever finds out."

"Or someone doesn't take care of that first." Striker took a long, final tug on his long-necked bottle.

"Wait a minute. . . ." Matt stared at Thorne incredulously. "Don't you think we're leaping to conclusions, here? I mean she had a wreck, she got hurt, but I don't see that there's any hint of foul play."

"You don't know there isn't."

"But why? Everyone she ever met liked her and as Slade said, she gave advice to the lovelorn for crying out loud. Not exactly cloak and dagger stuff. It's not like she was writing scandal sheets or political exposes."

"It was more than just lovelorn cra—stuff," Slade clarified. "Her column was about single people—"

"Right. I know," Matt snapped.

"But the point of it is that none of us really knew what

she was doing with her life, did we?" Thorne pushed up his sleeves. "She didn't even tell us she was pregnant. Now, there's a chance someone, either by accident or intent, was involved in her accident. We just have to find out who."

"And *why*." Matt threw up a hand in exasperation. "Don't we need a motive?"

"Not if it was an accident and someone was just scared to come forward." Slade drained his bottle.

Matt's back was up. "Well then, looking into her computer records and breaking into her apartment wouldn't be necessary, would they?"

"Hey! Anything's worth a try!" Slade shot to his feet and walked up to his brother. "Don't you think we should look into everything?" Slade's color was high, his jaw set, just the way it had been when they'd been kids growing up and were about to start throwing punches.

Matt held his ground. Even managed that slow, go-ahead-and-try-it smile that both his brothers found so damned irritating.

"We don't know a lot," Slade said through clenched teeth. "Kurt's gonna help us get to the bottom of it. You got a problem with that?"

A muscle worked in Matt's jaw and his brown eyes narrowed on his younger brother. "No problem. I just want what's best for Randi and J.R., you know that. And some son of a bitch is responsible for her condition. I want him found and nailed. You bet I do. But that's what the sheriff's department is for."

"Unless they're sittin' on their butts," Slade said.

"Right. But I don't think we should go on a witch hunt until we're sure there's a witch."

Kurt stood. "Don't worry. If there is one, I'll find him... or her."

"Good." Slade took a step back.

"That settles it. Do what you have to," Thorne said, then walked Striker to the door where they shook hands again. The phone rang as the door shut behind the investigator. "I'll get it," Thorne said, striding to the den. He had work to do and couldn't let his brothers' tempers deter him.

"Hello?" he nearly shouted.

"Boy, are you in a bad mood." Annette's voice sang through the wires.

He felt instantly weary. "Just busy."

"When are you coming back to Denver?" Good old Annette. She didn't beat around the bush.

"Don't know," he admitted, resting one hip on the corner of his father's desk and letting his leg swing free. The thought of returning to his office and the penthouse and the whirl that was his life in the Mile-High City held little appeal right now.

"So you like being a cowboy again?" she asked and laughed without a trace of acrimony—as if nothing had changed between them.

"Believe it or not, I do like it here," he said with complete honesty. "Don't think I'm much of a cowboy."

"Oh, darn, and I was just pressing my denim skirt and checked blouse."

"Was there something you wanted?"

"Mmm. Actually there was. Daddy's forgiven you."
Thorne doubted it.

"And he still wants to work with you."

"So, why didn't he call me?"

"Because I wanted to. To make sure there were no hard feelings."

"None on this end." And yet he didn't trust her.

"Good. And don't worry, Daddy will call you himself.

Let me know when you're in town. Oh, and Thorne—take off the bolo, it's not your style."

"I'm not wearing a tie of any kind."

"Oh, dear. That's worse yet. Well, so long, pardner," she said with a laugh. There was a click on the other end of the line and he was left holding the receiver and wondering why she'd bothered to call.

"Doesn't matter," he reminded himself because he didn't feel a thing for her; never had. Nor had he experienced any special bond with the women he'd dated in the past few years. Until he'd seen Nicole again. From the moment he'd first laid eyes on her in the hospital, he'd been taken with her. He wondered what she was doing right now, considered dialing the number he'd already committed to memory, then reminded himself that he had other things that had to be done.

For the next two hours he returned phone calls, e-mails and faxes, but his concentration wasn't as focused as it usually was and thoughts of his sister and her baby kept sneaking into his mind.

When he'd finally hung up from a call with his attorney Thorne leaned the desk chair back so far it protested. Drumming his fingers on the curved arm, he stared through the window into the night. A dozen questions burned through his brain. Why was Randi in Montana? Who was the baby's father? Did the accident involve another vehicle? Would Randi and the baby be okay? When would she come out of the coma?

He had no answers to any of those and another thought, one he'd kept steadfastly at bay, burrowed into his brain. He wondered what Nicole was doing tonight. "Forget it," he growled at himself, but his mind kept wandering back to the night they'd made love, their bodies glistening with sweat under the cold winter stars. When could he see her again? He glanced at the phone, mentally cursed and wondered how she'd managed to get under his skin.

He remembered taking her into his arms in the parking lot of the hospital and her small gasp of surprise as he'd kissed her; he remembered the way she'd moaned when he'd made love to her by the creek; and he remembered seeing her hold the baby in the nursery, looking down at the child's tiny face, smiling and whispering to the infant, so naturally as if she were his mother. The effect on Thorne had been immediate and heart stopping.

If he didn't know better, he'd think he was falling in love. But that was ridiculous. He wasn't the kind of man to fall into that kind of trap.

He wasn't ready to tie himself up with one woman, not yet. He had too much to do.

Oh, yeah? And what's that? Make another million or two? Turn a losing company into a winning corporation? Develop another subdivision? Go back to an empty penthouse in a city where your only friends are business associates?

Standing, he raised his arms over his head and stretched, his spine popping a bit. Of course he'd return to Denver and resume his life. What was the other option? Stay here? Marry Nicole?

He froze. *Marry Nicole?* Dr. Stevenson? Impossible! No way!

And yet the thought held a seductive and dangerous appeal.

"This is ridiculous," Nicole told herself as her shift ended and she opened the door to her office. Thankfully it had been a slow day in the emergency room, with only a broken hip, an asthma attack, a dog bite, a case of severe appendicitis and two kids with contusions and concussions in a bicycle-car mishap. In the lulls between patients she'd been able to catch up on her notes, check on some of the patients she'd admitted earlier including Randi and J.R., and think about Thorne McCafferty.

She'd been thinking about him a lot lately. Too much. She sat in her desk chair and twiddled a pen. They'd talked on the phone a couple of times since they'd made love near the creek and, of course, he'd come for lunch that day and run into her at the hospital time and again when he'd been visiting his sister. He'd always stopped by to see her and consequently a few rumors had already started and some of her co-workers had winked at her whenever he'd appeared.

"Forget him," she told herself, knowing it was impossible. He was getting to her all over again, even though he'd taken off on her once before. He'd given no excuses, just taken off and bailed out to chase after dreams of making his mark in the world, leaving her heartbroken. In spite of this, she was fascinated by the man. Stupidly fascinated, she reminded herself. She couldn't take a chance on letting him hurt her again.

She finished her paperwork, then perused photocopies of a few of Randi McCafferty's columns that Clare Santiago, Randi's OB-GYN, had given her. Out of curiosity about her new patient and the hoopla created by the local press, Clare had found some of the articles on the Internet and printed them out.

Now, as Nicole scanned the columns, she smiled. Randi gave advice freehandedly. With tones of irony and sarcasm, she dished out levelheaded counsel to single people who had written to her concerning their love lives, work problems, past relationships, or troubles juggling hectic schedules. Randi borrowed literary clichés, old adages and peppered the column with hip slang; but most of the advice was given tongue-in-cheek and showed off her clever, if sometimes cutting, wit. Nicole actually laughed at a few of the passages, and wondered if any of Randi's headstrong older brothers had ever been on the receiving end of her razor-sharp tongue.

If only the woman lying in ICU could talk. Tucking the articles into a file, Nicole decided to call it a day. She snapped off her computer and desk lamp, then stretched and walked into the hallway. Before she'd go home, she would look in on Thorne's sister—the silent, comatose woman whose advice had touched millions.

Outside the doors of ICU, Nicole found Slade and Matt McCafferty waiting impatiently.

"Hi." Matt was standing near a post and quickly removed his hat.

Slade, seated in a chair in the small waiting area, quickly tossed aside a battered magazine and climbed to his feet.

"I thought I'd check on your sister before I went home."

"There's no change," Slade grumbled. "I was just in there and the doctors are talking about setting her broken bones now that the swelling's gone down." He looked down at his hands as they worked the brim of his hat. "She looks like hell."

"But improving," Nicole countered. "These things take time."

"Well, I wish she'd wake up." Matt's brow was furrowed with deep lines of worry. He motioned toward the closed doors. "Thorne's with her now."

"He is?" Why did her heart do a stupid little flip at the mention of his name?

"Yep." Slade checked his watch, stared at the face a second and his lips rolled in on themselves. "He should be out soon if you want to talk to him."

One side of Matt's lips curved upward. "So what is the deal with you and Thorne?"

"Is there a deal?" she said, matching his grin.

"I'd say so." Slade gave a quick nod. "Never seen Thorne so…content."

"He's not content," Matt said, shaking his head. "Hell, that guy doesn't know the meaning of the word. But he is less restless. Not as quick to jump down someone's throat. Distracted."

"Is that right—"

The doors flew open and Thorne, in jeans and a leather bomber jacket, burst through. His face was a thundercloud, his jaw set, his eyes narrowed until his gaze landed full force on Nicole.

"Something wrong?" she asked.

"Yeah, there's something wrong." He hitched a thumb toward the doors swinging shut behind him. "She's still in a coma and looks like hell. The doctors keep saying she's doing as well as can be expected, but I don't know if I can believe them. It's been over a week since she was brought in here."

"Everything that can be done is being—"

"Is it?" he demanded and she was aware of how much taller he was than she. "How do I know that?"

"I thought we'd been through this—the competency of the staff, the efficiency of the hospital, the time it takes the body to heal—"

"Enough." He glared down at her, then rammed his hands through his hair in frustration. "Hell!"

"What is it you want?" she demanded.

"You mean other than my sister and her child to be well,

the baby's father located, the truth about her accident figured out, and world peace?"

"Is that all?" She lifted an imperious eyebrow and held his arrogant, demanding and ultimately irresistible gaze fast.

"No. I could use a cup of coffee, too!"

"Well, I'll find one for you, just as soon as I heal your sister and finish the last-minute details on the world peace thing," she snapped, hearing a snicker behind her. Turning on her heel, she found Slade trying and failing to swallow a smile. "Something funny?"

"Nothin' at all. In fact I'm enjoyin' the show. Not often someone puts ol' Thorne in his place."

"Is that what she's doing?" Thorne asked, then before Nicole could protest, grabbed her by the crook of the elbow and propelled her down the hallway. "You two," he called over his shoulder, "can leave. I'll catch up with you later."

"Wait a minute. What do you think you're doing?" she demanded as he forced her around a corner to a tiny alcove with a window seat and two potted plants.

"This." He didn't waste time, just lowered his head and kissed her so hard she couldn't breathe.

Her bones began to melt and she told herself this was insane, that he had no right to manhandle her anywhere, but especially not here, in the hospital where she was working. Yet there was a part of her that responded to his spontaneity, the thrill of a man wanting her enough to drag her into the comparative privacy of the alcove.

His mouth was pure magic—warm, insistent pressure. She kissed him back, her lips parting to accept his tongue, her heart pounding a wild, frantic cadence as her beeper went off.

She jerked back and saw the amusement in his eyes.

"Couldn't resist," he said by way of explanation as she reached into her pocket for her pager.

"Maybe you should learn to exercise some control." She checked out the digital display of numbers and recognized Dr. Oliverio's extension.

"Ha." He let out a short laugh. "I don't have a helluva lot of that around you," he admitted. "Nor, *Doctor,* do you."

"You surprised me, that's all. Look, I have to go."

"Emergency?"

"I don't know," she admitted, "but I'd better check it out."

His grin was pure mischief as he pulled her to him and kissed her soundly again. "I'll call you later."

"Fine." She turned and found two aides walking down the hallway and pretending they hadn't seen anything, but the smiles they tried to disguise and the twinkle in their eyes as they exchanged knowing glances convinced her otherwise.

Clearing her throat she marched down the corridor toward her office and reminded herself, for what seemed the fiftieth time, she wasn't going to get involved with Thorne McCafferty.

But a little voice inside her head had the audacity to insinuate that it was too late. She was already more involved than any sane woman would allow herself to be.

Chapter 11

"I'll let you know," Thorne said, raining what he hoped appeared to be a patient smile on the woman seated in his father's favorite recliner. Her name was Peggy, she'd moved to Missoula from Las Vegas this past year and was now in Grand Hope. As far as he could tell her experience with young babies had been limited to raising her own children, who were now grown, and spending a few years as an aide in a day-care center. Her other jobs had included working as a supervisor in a cannery in California and as a maid for a hotel while she'd lived in Nevada. She was pleasant enough, he supposed, but he wasn't convinced she was the woman for the job of living at the ranch and taking care of little J.R. "I'm still interviewing."

She smiled as she stood and tossed her shaggy graying hair over her shoulders. "Well, let me know. You've got my number."

"It's on the résumé."

She stuck out her hand and he clasped it, noticing that she wore a ring on every finger. Her makeup was thick, her fingernails long and polished a deep maroon. "Thanks." She strolled out of the living room, her slim hips rolling beneath tight jeans. At the door front, he handed her a battered suede coat and a heavy fringed purse. She slung the strap over her shoulder and headed out the door.

Boots pounded on the stairs. "Well?" Matt asked as he appeared from the second story. He looked expectantly at his brother. "Found someone?"

"Not yet." Thorne glanced through the window and watched Peggy climb into a huge station wagon that had enough grime on it that some wise guy had written Wash Me on the back windshield. She paused to light a cigarette and blow out a geyser of smoke before putting the car into gear and gunning the engine. No, Peggy Sentra wouldn't do. Nor would the other two women he'd already met.

"You interviewed three people."

"And I'll probably have to talk to a dozen or so more." The three women he'd seen, Peggy and the two others, had barely made an impression on him other than they were entirely unsuitable to take care of his newborn nephew and were a far cry from what he'd expected. "I've already left a call on the voice mail of the agency."

"Little J.R.'s coming home tomorrow."

"I know, I know," Thorne snapped. "And I guess the four of us, you, Slade, Juanita and I will just have to juggle the duties until we find someone."

"Hey, whoa there," Matt said, holding up both hands palms outward. "I'm gonna be out tomorrow—got to fix the fence on the north end of the property before we move the herd. Slade, Adam Zolander and Larry Todd are supposed to help me. The day after that I've got to run back to my own spread, so you'd better count me out until I get back."

Thorne frowned, but didn't argue. Matt owned a ranch near the Idaho border, a place he'd barely been able to afford, and yet he'd scraped together enough money for a down payment and talked the previous owner into taking a contract on the rest. Matt was known to work sixteen- or eighteen-hour days—all for that scrap of hilly land and a small run-down farmhouse. Thorne had never understood Matt's connection with the land, his need to ranch his own place, but there it was. Whereas Thorne had learned at an early age that acreage was valuable because it held its worth or could be developed and sold for a profit, Matt seemed to believe that he was somehow linked to the soil.

"All right. You're out."

"And so is Slade tomorrow, so, unless you can con Juanita into changing diapers and burping the baby, looks like you're the chosen one, the nanny." Chuckling, he grabbed his hat. "And the nursery's just about ready. I got the crib and changing table and bureau together, but we still need some staples—formula, diapers, baby powder and sleepers."

"Already ordered," Thorne said.

"Good."

Laughing to himself, Matt threw on his jacket, then walked outside. Thorne headed back to the den. Time for Plan B.

The phone rang and Nicole, already reaching for her keys, grabbed the receiver instead. "Hello?"

"Hi." Recognizing Thorne's voice she leaned against the window and smiled to herself. Why her lips curved upward, she didn't understand, but she didn't fight it as she stared into the night-darkened backyard. The girls clamored around her and to quiet them she pressed the index finger of her free hand to her lips.

"I need your help."

"*You* need *my* help?" She smothered a smile. There was

something amusing about the CEO of McCafferty International asking for any kind of advice or aid.

"Absolutely. J.R.'s being released from the hospital tomorrow and that'll be quite a change around here."

She eyed her two dynamos. "You have no idea."

"I thought maybe you could give me some pointers."

"Oh, sure." She laughed as she watched Molly chase after Mindy with a rubber snake. Mindy shrieked in mock horror. "Don't you know that I do this motherhood thing day by day?"

"Can we discuss it over dinner?"

"I have the girls."

"Bring 'em."

She laughed out loud. "I don't think you understand what you're asking."

"Probably not, but maybe it's time I learned. I could pick you up and—"

"No, we'd better meet. I finally got the SUV back and it's ready to go *and* equipped with safety seats. Besides that I have been known to cut out early if the twins—" she was eyeing the girls as they streaked by with her I'm-the-mom-and-you'd-better-listen-to-me scowl "—make the mistake of acting up, which I'm *sure* won't happen tonight. They wouldn't dare."

Mindy bit her lower lip, but Molly ignored the warning and wriggled the fake-looking snake in her sister's face. "I already told the girls I'd take them to the Burger Corral. It's on the corner of Third and Pine."

"I know where it is," he said dryly. "I grew up here. But I was thinking of something a little quieter."

"Believe me, when you've got four-year-olds, you don't want quiet."

Molly was tugging at the edge of her jacket. "Come *on,* Mommy."

"Look, if you want to meet us, do," she invited. "We're on our way right now."

"I'll be there in half an hour."

Nicole hung up and told herself she wasn't thinking clearly. Hadn't she already told herself not to get involved with Thorne, that just because they'd shared a few kisses and quiet conversations and made love wasn't any reason to put on her old pair of rose-colored glasses again—the ones with the cracked lenses from trusting Thorne Mc-Cafferty before? But there was something about the man she found so damned irresistible it was dangerous. More than dangerous—emotional suicide. "Come on, kids, put your jackets on."

The phone rang again almost instantly and Nicole picked up thinking that Thorne had changed his mind. "Want to back out?" she teased.

"I think it's a little too late for that now, isn't it?" Paul's voice was a damper on her good mood and she steeled herself for what was certain to be a tense conversation.

"I was expecting someone else to call."

"Then I'll make it short." His voice had all the warmth of a blue norther and Nicole wondered how she'd ever once thought she'd loved the man.

"Okay."

"It's about visitation rights."

"What about them?" she asked, her fingers clenching the receiver in a death grip, the knot in her stomach tightening as it always did when she and Paul began to argue—which was nearly every time they spoke.

"I know that I'm supposed to have the girls every other Christmas and each summer."

"That's right." Her heart began to pound. She couldn't believe it but thought he might actually be angling for custody. Oh, Lord, what would she do if she lost the twins?

"But Carrie and I are going to visit her folks in Boston over the holidays and this summer we've planned a trip to Europe. Her company is sending her to a convention in Madrid and we thought we'd take the opportunity to see France, Portugal and England while we're there. So, there would be four weeks right in the middle of summer where we couldn't take the twins."

As if parental responsibility were an option.

She glanced at her daughters, now struggling into their jackets and her heart broke when she thought about them growing up without a father.

"You know we'd *love* to have them if it were possible, but Carrie's got to think of her career."

"Of course she does."

"Just like you do, Nicole. Like you always have." There it was: the inevitable dig. What was deemed noble for Carrie was somehow disgraceful for Nicole because she was a mother. She let the little barb slide. No reason to reduce the conversation to hot words at this point.

"Don't worry about it," she said, though her throat was thick. "It would probably be best if they stayed with me."

"Actually, I think so. It would be hard on Molly and Mindy to uproot them and drag them here to the apartment. They're not used to a big city or being confined to a few rooms. With both our jobs it would make it really difficult and—"

"Look, I understand, but I've got to run. Do you, uh, want to speak to the girls?" She couldn't stand to hear one more minute of his rationalizations for giving up his children. They were his daughters, for God's sake! So precious. So wonderful. And they deserved better.

"Oh." A pause. "Sure."

Without much enthusiasm, she put each of the twins on the phone, let them speak to the stranger who had sired them and within three minutes was back on the phone. "I'm already late and I've really got to run now, but we'll work the visitations out."

"I knew I could count on you." The words echoed through her mind and she toyed with the question of what he would do if he couldn't rely on her.

"I'm glad you understand." Relief was heavy in his voice.

"Goodbye, Paul." She hung up incensed and helped Mindy zip up her jacket. "Come on, kids, let's roll."

"You mad, Mommy?" Mindy asked as Nicole slung the strap of her purse over her shoulder. Catching sight of her reflection in the window, she understood her daughter's concern. Her eyebrows were slammed together, her mouth pursed tight at the corners.

"Not anymore. Come on, let's get into the car." She opened the door and the twins swarmed through, their chubby legs flashing, their shoes pounding on the back porch, their laughter and giggles ringing through the night air.

"I get shotgun!" Molly cried.

"No, me—" Mindy started to pout.

"You're both in the back seat, in your car seats and you know it," Nicole said. "Remember?"

"But Billy Johnson gets to ride in the front seat," Molly said. Billy was a wild-haired boy in their preschool.

"So does Beth Anne."

Another friend.

"Well, you don't." Nicole helped strap them into their respective seats, then climbed behind the wheel. She paused long enough to reapply her lipstick, then twisted on the ignition and grinned as the SUV roared to life. As she put the rig into reverse she felt a twinge of apprehension about meeting Thorne again. Whether she liked it or not she was in some kind of relationship with him and that thought worried her.

"It's not a date," she told herself.

"What?" Molly demanded.

"Nothing, sweetie, now you girls figure out what you want to get for dinner," she said and silently added, *and I'll try to figure out what to do with Thorne McCafferty.*

Within fifteen minutes she'd driven to the small restaurant, parked in the crowded lot, then shepherded her girls to a corner booth near the soda fountain. With the efficiency of the mother of twins, Nicole helped the girls out of their jackets and let them wander to the video games where a group of boys who looked about eight or nine were trying to best each other and the sounds of bells, whistles and simulated gun reports punctuated the buzz of conversation, clatter of flatware and rattle of ice cubes from the self-serve soda machine.

Somewhere, above it all, there was the hint of music, some old Elvis Presley hit, she thought, but couldn't remember. She recognized some of the customers—the couple who owned a small market around the corner, a boy she'd stitched up when he'd cracked his head inline skating, a young mother who worked at the preschool where her twins were enrolled.

She ordered a diet cola for herself and milk shakes for the girls, then waited nervously until she spied Thorne push open one of the double glass doors. Tall, broad-shouldered, a determined expression on his bladed features, he glanced around the interior until his gaze landed full force on her. Her breath caught as if she were a silly schoolgirl and she mentally chided herself. *Get over it. He's just a man.* What was it about him that caused her idiotic heart to turn over at the sight of him? She waved and he strode through the maze of tables and booths.

"Where are—?" he started to ask before he spied the twins standing on chairs and peering over the shoulders of the boys working the video games. "Oh."

"They'll be back. I'm just lucky they don't understand they need money to work the machines."

"Then they'll break you."

"Exactly."

Hanging his leather jacket on a peg already holding one of the twins' coats, he glanced around the open restaurant, then slid onto the bench opposite her. "Not exactly what I had in mind when I called," he admitted, "but it'll do."

"Oh, will it?" she mocked.

"I haven't been here since high school."

"Fond memories?" She managed to keep her tone light though there had been times when she'd sat in this very booth hoping that Thorne McCafferty would call or return to Grand Hope. It hadn't happened.

"Some fonder than others." His gaze touched hers for a second. Picking up a plastic-coated menu, he elaborated, "I had the first date of my life here with Mary Lou Bennett when I was a freshman in high school. I was scared to death and then another time—" his eyes narrowed a fraction "—I got into a fight with a kid a couple of years older than me. What was his name? A real tough... Mike something or other... Wilkins...that was it. Mike Wilkins. He beat the tar out of me in the parking lot."

"He beat you up?"

"Yep. But I hate to admit it." He lifted an eyebrow. "Oh, yes, Dr. Stevenson, I wasn't always the tough guy you see before you."

"What happened?" she asked, fascinated. She'd never heard this story before.

"The police came and hauled us both in. Took our statements and those from the kids that had collected around the fight. My dad had to come down and claim me and I was nearly kicked out of school and thrown off the football team, but, as usual, John Randall managed to pull some strings. The worst punishment I ended up with was a black eye, a couple of loose teeth and some pretty bad damage to my ego."

"Which you probably deserved."

"Probably." One side of his mouth lifted in a self-deprecating grin. "I was a little cocky."

"Was?"

He snorted a laugh.

"What was the fight about?" she asked, surprised at his candor.

"What else? A girl. I was hitting on his girlfriend and for the life of me I can't remember her name, but she had red hair, a cute little smile and a few other attributes as well."

"And that's what attracted you—her 'attributes'?"

"And the fact that she was Mike Wilkins's girlfriend." His gray eyes twinkled. "I've always liked a challenge and a little competition never hurt, either."

At that moment Molly came running up. "I want a quarter."

"Why?"

"'Cause that kid—" she pointed an accusatory finger at

a boy of eight or nine with spiky blond hair and freckles "—he says I need one to play the games."

Nicole shot Thorne a knowing look. "Well, we don't have any time right now. Go and get your sister and let's order."

"No!" Molly's lower lip stuck out petulantly. "I want a quarter."

"Listen, not tonight, okay? Now, come on—" Nicole glanced up at Thorne and sighed. "Excuse me for a second, would you?" She climbed out of the booth, made her way to the video machines and peeled Mindy from the chair on which she'd been standing. Mindy put up her kind of low-keyed fuss while Molly, ever more vocal, was bordering on being obnoxious.

"I want a quarter!" she demanded, stomping her little foot imperiously.

"And I told you that we couldn't come here unless you behaved." Nicole managed to get both girls onto booster chairs, one on her side of the booth, the other next to Thorne.

"I want French fries," Molly stated.

"Oh, do you? Now there's a surprise."

"And a hot dog."

"Me, too," Mindy agreed. They managed to stay in their seats until the waitress, a slim teenaged girl in black slacks, crisp white shirt and red bow tie took their order. Then they were off again, making a beeline for the video machines as the restaurant filled up and conversation buzzed through the air.

"See what you're in for?" Nicole's gaze followed her children. "I might have two the same age, but you'll have a newborn to deal with."

"Just until Randi can take over." He frowned and then settled back.

"I take it no one's been able to locate the baby's father?"

"Not yet. But we will." Determination pulled at the corners of his mouth.

She was disappointed that he seemed so anxious to cast off his responsibility of temporary father, but, as the waitress returned with their drink order, she reminded herself that he was, after all, a confirmed bachelor, a man more interested in making money than making babies.

Thorne noticed the play of emotions that crossed her face and the way her teasing smile suddenly disappeared.

"The reason I called you was that I need your help," he admitted. "We need a babysitter until Randi's well enough to take care of J.R."

"Oh."

He tried not to notice the sexy way her front teeth settled against her lower lip as she watched her girls, or the seductive way her blouse gaped at her neckline, showing off just the hint of cleavage. She glanced at him and in that second, when her gold eyes met his, he felt the incredible urge to kiss her again—just as he always did.

"It shouldn't be that hard to find someone suitable. I'm willing to pay whatever it takes."

"Money isn't the issue."

"Of course it is."

She rolled those expressive eyes and unwrapped her straw. "You still don't get it, do you? It's not about money." Taking a long sip from her soda she thought for a minute. "That's always been your problem, you know. Don't you understand that you can't go out and *buy* love? You can't expect to find the most loving, caring babysitter just by offering her a few more dollars. People are who they are. They don't change when you wave a check in front of their faces."

"I know that, but most people perform for money."

"You don't want someone to perform, you want some-one who cares. There's a big difference. I'm not saying you don't pay them well, of course you do. But first you find the caring, warm, loving person. Then you pay them what they're worth to you."

"Is that what you did?"

"Absolutely. I located Jenny through an advertisement I ran in the local paper. After interviewing a dozen or so women and looking at day-care centers, she called, we met and the rest is history. She's a part-time college stu-dent and the nicest woman you'd ever want to meet. She's warm, affectionate, wholesome and has a great sense of humor, which you need with kids. We work it out so that our schedules mesh. It takes some doing, but it can be ac-complished." The waitress came with their trays of food and Thorne helped Nicole round up the girls. Just as they sat down, Nicole's pager went off. She glanced at the readout and frowned. "Look, I've got to make a call," she said. "I've got a cell phone out in the car—would you mind watching the girls just a minute?"

Thorne lifted a shoulder.

"No, Mommy," one of the twins cried.

"I'll be right back. Promise. Mr. McCafferty will help you open the ketchup packets for your French fries."

"Sure," Thorne said, though the thought of being with two four-year-old dynamos was a trifle daunting. Nicole slid out of the booth, then clipped across the tile floor. The twins looked ready to bolt after her, but Thorne distracted them with their milk shakes. He unwrapped their plastic straws then pushed them deep into their cups.

While one twin tried to suck up the milk shake the other was busy trying to open ketchup packages. Again he assisted and then squirted the red sauce over the fries. "Nooo!" the little girl wailed. "I want to dip!"

"What?"

"I want to dip. I don't want it on the top." Her little face was screwed up in a scowl as she glared at her basket. The other twin was sucking like crazy, trying to draw the too thick milk shake up her straw.

"It don't come," she complained.

"Just try harder."

"I am!"

"I don't like it," the first one insisted and Thorne seeing no other answer, took her hot dog, put it in his basket, then placed his cheeseburger in her basket and switched them. He handed her an opened packet of ketchup.

"You do it any way you want. Now—" he took the milk shake from the other girl's hands and opening in the lid, used the straw to swirl the chocolatey goo "—that should help," he said, replacing the lid and straw. "If it doesn't work, just give it a little time, it'll melt."

"Where's Mommy?" number one asked as she plopped a French fry into a pool of ketchup that she'd created.

"In the car making a call."

"Is she coming back?"

"I think so," he said and winked. The pixies tore into their food, pulling off the buns and squeezing more mustard and ketchup onto their hot dogs than was necessary but Thorne, not used to being around children of any age, decided to let them do what they wanted. By the time Nicole returned, they had condiments on their faces, hands, clothes and even in their hair.

"Everything all right?" he asked.

"Minor emergency—nothing serious. I handled it. Oh, what happened?" she asked, eyeing her daughters.

"They ate."

"Didn't they give you bibs?" Her eyes fell to the tray where two plastic bibs were tucked.

"Didn't see 'em."

Sighing, she wiped one face, then the other before finally turning her attention to her own dinner. "You have a lot to learn," she said, biting into her hamburger.

"That's why I need a nanny."

"Or two," she said.

"As I mentioned, I was hoping you could help me out in that department."

"How?"

"Either you or your sitter might be able to give me the names of people who would be interested in a part-time or full-time job taking care of the baby. At least until Randi's on her feet and able to care for him."

"It's a possibility," she said, touching a napkin to the corner of her lips, then automatically wiping a smudge from one of her daughter's cheeks.

"Don't!" the little girl cried.

"Oh, Molly, don't be such a grump." Nicole was undeterred and soon, despite much cringing and grumbling, the little girl's face was condiment-free and they were all digging into their food again.

Thorne watched Nicole with her daughters, how she joked with them and played with them even when she was disciplining them. She didn't raise her voice, always paid attention when they spoke and pointed out their mistakes with a wink and a smile. It didn't always work. The precocious one challenged her mother and the shier little girl sometimes didn't speak and offered Nicole a cold shoulder, but throughout the meal one thing was clear—Nicole Sanders Stevenson, M.D., was one helluva mother.

Not that it mattered. He wasn't looking for a woman who could raise children. Hell, he wasn't even looking for a woman period.

Yet, for a reason he couldn't name he still carried that damned ring his father had given him in his pocket.

Chapter 12

Thorne had never felt so awkward in his life. He'd just fed the baby and burped him and heard soft little sighs against his shoulder as he walked from the den to the living room and wondered how the hell he was going to get J.R. into his crib without waking him. The baby, bright-eyed and healthy, seemed the most content while being held, which was a worry.

A natural athlete, Thorne had been able to handle a wet football, rope a calf, ride a horse, or crack a baseball over the fence, but when it came to holding, feeding, burping and diapering a tiny infant, he was all thumbs.

Not that his brothers were any better at it. Matt had spent his life on the ranch and had dealt with everything from newly hatched chicks to orphaned lambs and foals who were rejected by the mares that gave them birth. He'd helped bring litters of puppies and kittens into this world. But when it came to helpless human babies, he, too, seemed out of place and incompetent. Slade was the worst. Although fascinated beyond belief with the baby, he seemed terrified to hold J.R. That part was downright ridiculous in Thorne's estimation, though Matt was amused that his daredevil of a brother was frightened of the infant.

J.R.'s eyes blinked open.

Uh-oh.

Within seconds he started to put up a fuss and Thorne tried not to panic. "You're all right," he said, wondering how it was that mothers seemed to have some kind of natural rhythm while holding and swaying slightly as they held a child. He'd seen that same natural reaction through the glass window of the hospital when Nicole had cradled and fed the baby.

He tried to sway, felt like an ass and the baby started crying in earnest, wailing and turning red in the face. "Now, it's okay," Thorne reassured the child when he had no idea whatsoever was wrong with him. "Hang in there."

Juanita's footsteps echoed down the stairs. "I'm coming, I'm coming," she said to Thorne's utter relief.

A second later she appeared. "He is tired."

"He *was* asleep."

"Then why didn't you put him in his *cuna?*"

"Because I couldn't get to his *cuna*," Thorne said, emphasizing the Spanish word, "without waking him up."

"But you woke him up anyway." She lifted a graying eyebrow as the baby cried louder than Thorne thought was possible.

"Believe me, I wasn't trying to."

"Here, let me have him. Come on, little one," she said softly, prying him from Thorne's stiff fingers. She began to murmur softly in Spanish as she carried the infant from the room and to Thorne's mortification the baby started to quiet. Within minutes silence prevailed and Juanita, walking softly, returned.

"How do you do that?"

"Practice," she said and smiled.

"Maybe I need lessons."

"*Dios,* all you brothers do. And probably Señorita Randi

as well. How is she going to take care of the baby, write her columns, finish her book and get well?" She shook her head as she headed to the kitchen.

"There is no book," Thorne said, following her down the hallway. "Remember, that was always just her dream. Nothing ever came of it."

"But she said that she would write one. I believed it. She will be rich and famous one day. You will see." She scrounged in the refrigerator, muttered something under her breath and reached inside where she found a package, opened it and looked at Harold who lay on a rag rug near the back door. "I saved this soup bone for you," she told him as the crippled dog climbed to his feet and wagged his tail. "But you take it outside." She tossed the bone to the dog and looked over her shoulder at Thorne. "There is a book."

"I hope so," Thorne said, but nearly dismissed the idea. Randi had talked about writing the Great American Novel ever since she was fifteen. To his knowledge she hadn't written the first sentence much less a chapter or two. There was nothing to it, he told himself, but made a mental note to mention Randi's pipe dream to Striker. Why not? It certainly wouldn't hurt.

Nicole climbed out of the bathtub and stepped into her robe. The twins were asleep, the house quiet. Cinching the belt, she padded to the kitchen and heated a cup of cocoa. Patches, curled on a cushion of one of the café chairs at the table, opened one eye and yawned, showing off needle-sharp teeth before resting his chin on his paws again. The microwave dinged and Nicole picked up her cup to carry into the living room where a fire still burned in the grate. Scarlet coals glowed brightly and the fire popped and hissed.

Sipping from her cup, Nicole settled into a corner of her love seat and flipped through a parenting magazine. She'd just started reading an article on a toddler's stages of life when she noticed the column—advice for the single parent, written by R. J. McKay. Why it caught her eye, she didn't know, but she began reading the text and an eerie sensation crawled up her spine. It was written with a light hand and ironic style that was identical to that in the columns she'd read by Randi McCafferty. But no one had ever mentioned that Randi had expanded her column from newspapers to magazines. Not that it wasn't common.

She sipped her cocoa and started rereading the article when she heard a vehicle ease down the street. The engine slowed, then died in front of her house and when she twisted to peek through the blinds she spied Thorne striding up her front walk.

Her pulse leaped at the sight of him and then she remembered that she was wearing only her robe. On her feet in an instant, she started for the bedroom just as she heard the doorbell ring.

"Damn." She hesitated then walked back to the door and swung it open. Wind ruffled his hair and billowed her skirt as it swept into the room. "Well, Mr. McCafferty, this is a surprise."

A cocksure smile stretched across his lips as his gaze traveled the length of her. "A good one, I hope."

"That depends," she teased, unable to stop herself.

"On?"

"You, of course."

He didn't wait. In half a heartbeat he crossed the threshold, his arms were around her and his cold lips found hers. Icy wind swirled around them and just before she closed her eyes and he kicked the door shut, she saw the first few snowflakes fall from the night-dark heavens.

But the snowfall was instantly forgotten. The pressure of his lips was insistent and her heart went wild, pounding out of control, thundering in her ears.

Warmth invaded her limbs and desire slowly uncoiled deep within her. He backed her against the foyer's wall and she willingly complied, winding her arms around his neck, parting her lips, thrilling to the cool, welcome touch of his skin against hers. He smelled of the outdoors—pine laced with the traces of some musky cologne. His body was hard, tense muscles strong as they pressed intimately against hers. This was a mistake. She knew it, but couldn't resist the sweet seduction of his touch, the tingle his lips evoked.

His hands found her belt and as if he had all the time in the world he continued to kiss her as he loosened the knot. His tongue touched hers, flicking and tasting, causing her head to swim. She could barely breathe as her robe parted and with cold, callused fingers he lifted one breast in his hand. Her nipple puckered expectantly and deep inside she turned liquid.

"Oh, Nicole," he murmured against the shell of her ear. Desire was throbbing through her and emotions she didn't pause to understand raced through her mind. "We're alone?" His voice was low and husky.

"No." She shook her head and had trouble finding her voice. Lust pulsed through her veins. "The twins are here."

"Asleep?"

She nodded as his fingers scraped along the front lapel of her robe, touching her skin so lightly she wanted to scream. "It's…it's all right," she said though she wasn't thinking clearly, couldn't concentrate on anything but the want of him.

"Good." He kissed her again and reaching down, placed an arm beneath her knees and lifted her from her feet. As if she were nearly weightless he carried her down the short hallway past the girls' room to her bedroom—a private sanctuary where, heretofore, no man had ever been allowed to enter.

Somehow he managed to close and lock the door before placing her on the bed. Beneath her old hand-pieced quilt, the mattress sagged under their combined weight. "Wh-what's got into you?" she asked as he pushed the robe off her shoulders.

He stopped, his hands unmoving for a second as his silvery gaze found hers. "You, Doctor." He leaned forward and kissed her slowly on the lips. "You've gotten into me and I can't seem to do anything about it but this."

"Would you want to?" she asked and smiled.

"No." He parted the robe and took both her breasts in his hands. Holding them together he kissed the tops of each before guiding her fingers to his shirt. She needed no further instruction and began to remove his jacket, sweater and jeans while he never stopped kissing her, touching her, or causing her blood to heat and the yearning deep within her most private of regions to become ever more insistent.

Don't do this, that nagging little voice in her head screamed, but she ignored it.

His fingers tangled in her hair, then moved down her back, kneading and probing. His body molded to hers. He tasted of salt and desire and she wanted him as she'd never wanted another man.

Only he could satisfy her.

Only he could send her soaring to heights she'd only imagined. She kissed him and dug her fingers into his shoulders.

Anxious, strident muscles rubbed against her softer, yielding flesh. His tongue found and rimmed the hollow of her throat before seeking darker, deeper clefts that made her bite her lip to keep from screaming out. Intimate spasms erupted deep inside before he came to her, parting her legs, kissing her and holding her close. She arched upward, wanting more, needing release. "Thorne—" she whispered when she thought she'd go mad with desire "—Thorne, for the love of—oh, oooh."

With one forceful thrust he began to make love to her then and didn't stop. As her breathing became shallow and her body sheened with a layer of perspiration, he kissed her, loved her. Over and over he claimed her until the first streaks of daylight pierced through the window shades and she, exhausted, still holding him close, finally drifted off.

The girls awakened a few hours later and the bed was cold and empty, only the faint scent of sex lingering with the sweet, sensual memories of lovemaking stealing through her mind. She glanced at the bureau where the rose he'd given her had faded and died, the petals falling onto the old wood. She hadn't thrown the flower out; couldn't.

She was tired, yes, but felt better than she had in years. She sang in the shower, laughed when the girls fought, dressed with a smile on her face. It was only when she was yanking a brush through her hair that she caught a glimpse of her reflection, and she noticed the curve of her lips and the sparkle in her eyes. "Oh, no," she said, disbelieving.

But she couldn't deny the plain truth that stared her squarely in the face: she was, despite all her warnings to herself, falling head over heels in love with Thorne McCafferty.

Denver held no appeal to him. His apartment seemed as cold and empty as an ice cave and though it was clean, every surface shining, fresh towels hung over the brass towel bars, a lit fire at his fingertips, he felt no sense of homecoming. His closet was filled with suits, sport coats, slacks and three tuxedos; the view from his living room and master bedroom, a spectacular array of the lights of the city. And yet he felt as if he were in a foreign land, an alien in a penthouse that he'd called home for more years than he wanted to count.

He'd arrived in town in the morning and gone straight to the office. Somehow he'd survived four meetings before driving here where he intended to change and attend the black-tie affair hosted by Kent Williams. The dinner was for a charitable cause but the business behind the scenes was all about turning a profit. Not that he minded. Thorne was the first man to admit to being interested in making money.

And yet...

He poured himself a glass of Scotch and stared out the panorama of windows. Snow was falling and the lights of the city winked through the veil of flakes. He saw his own reflection in the glass, a tall man in a slightly wrinkled suit, holding a drink he didn't want and feeling more alone than he ever had in his life.

He'd never been one to dislike his own company; in fact, he'd silently laughed at men who needed a woman on their arms, showpieces, accessories, or even wives they adored. It had all seemed so weak and cowardly; but now, as he looked at that pale, distorted, ghostlike image of himself in the window, he imagined Nicole with him. Whether dressed in a sequined evening gown, or a pair of jeans and tennis shoes, or a lab coat over slacks and a blouse, her image seemed perfect at his side.

"Idiot," he muttered and tossed back his drink. He'd go to the damned party, do his business and drive to the airport tonight. The weather service was predicting two feet of snow to be dumped on the Denver area in the next couple of days, but Thorne intended to return to Grand Hope as soon as he could escape the obligations of his position.

There were too many pressing problems in Montana for him to tarry in this soulless suite he'd once considered home.

Home. Ha!

What were all the old sayings?

Home sweet home?

There's no place like home?

Home is where the heart is?

He took one final look around the living room as he strode to the bedroom to dig out one of his tuxedos. One thing was for certain: his heart wasn't here. Nope—it was currently residing in the hallways of St. James Hospital with the stubborn, bright, beautiful emergency room physician he'd once turned his back on—a divorced woman with two children already and no apparent desire to settle down again.

Well, all that was about to change. Thorne was used to taking charge of a situation, of getting what he wanted, and right now as he pulled out the designer tux with the forest-green cummerbund, he wanted Dr. Nicole Stevenson. One way or another he'd have her.

Nicole was dead on her feet. She'd worked overtime as there was a horrible accident involving two cars and a pickup. The wreck had occurred just two miles outside the city limits of Grand Hope. An eighty-year-old man and a teenager hadn't survived; the man's wife and three other teenagers were fighting for their lives. All were in critical condition with head injuries, punctured lungs, cracked ribs, ruptured spleens and all manner of contusions. A middle-aged housewife and her two children that were in the pickup had survived with only minor injuries, but the ER had been a madhouse and every available doctor, nurse, aid and anesthesiologist had been called in. Only now, ten hours after the first ambulance had arrived and they'd dealt with the severely injured, were things finally settling down. The rest of the patients, a woman who had scalded herself, an eight-year-old who had slammed his finger in a car door, three flu cases and a man complaining of dizzy spells had been forced to wait.

But the worst of the chaos was over, the patients stabilized, and relief physicians had arrived. Finally, Nicole could go home. She poured herself a fresh cup of coffee and quickly wrote some notes on her computer before grabbing her jacket, laptop and briefcase and leaving St. James.

The parking lot was a blanket of white as snow had fallen all day long. Six inches had piled in the parking lot and ice and snow had collected on the SUV's windshield. She waited for the defroster and wipers to clear the glass, then drove carefully into town.

She hadn't heard from Thorne since yesterday morning and she was beginning to miss him, though she didn't want to admit how deeply and emotionally entangled she'd become with him and his entire family.

"Oh, don't be a fool," she told herself as she stopped to ease the rig into four-wheel drive. She decided to call Thorne when she got home, tell him about a friend of Jenny's who was interested in the nanny job and just reconnect. After all, in these days of women's liberation, why couldn't she call him rather than sit by the phone or wonder what he was doing?

She made her way home and found her girls already

dressed in their pajamas and ready for bed. "Sorry I'm late," she apologized to Jenny after hugging each twin and listening to them babble on about what they'd done during the day. There was talk of a snowman in the backyard and Mindy complained that Molly had hit her with a snowball.

"Did not!" Molly cried, but guilt contorted her little face and she called her sister a tattletale when she finally confessed without a drop of remorse.

"They've been pretty good," Jenny admitted and hugged each girl before leaving. With the twins standing on the love seat, their noses pressed to the window, Nicole watched as Jenny drove off through the storm, the taillights of her battle-scarred station wagon winking bright red against a shower of snowflakes.

It was nearly two hours later, once Molly and Mindy were fast asleep, that she dialed the number of the Flying M. The phone was answered by a woman with a thick Spanish accent.

"McCafferty Ranch."

"This is Nicole Stevenson. I'm looking for—"

"The doctor. *Dios!* Has something happened to Señorita Randi?"

"No, I just wanted to talk to Thorne."

"But Randi, she is the same?"

"Yes. As far as I know."

There was a heavy sigh on the other end of the line. "Thorne, he is not here, but you can speak to Slade."

Disappointment pierced her soul. "No, that's all right. Have Thorne give me a call when he returns."

"He is not coming back for a while," the woman said, then holding her hand over the receiver spoke to someone else and within a few seconds Slade's voice boomed over the wires.

"Is this Nicole?"

"Yes."

There was a moment's hesitation. "Oh. Well, I thought you knew. Thorne's in Denver. We don't expect him back for a few days. We're not really sure but the storm's hit hard there and it looks like he won't be back for a while—uh-oh." In the background she heard a baby start to put up a fuss. "Was there a message I could pass along to him?"

"No, not really," she said, feeling deflated somehow. "I thought he was looking for a nanny and I have the number of a woman who might be a possibility."

The baby was really wailing by this time. "Great. The job hasn't been filled yet. Why don't you give me the information?"

"Sure. The woman's name is Christina Foster." She gave Slade Christina's number and was about to hang up when she remembered something she'd wanted to tell Thorne but hadn't had the chance. "You know, Slade, I was reading an article in a magazine the other night. It was about single parenting and the byline was for an R. J. McKay. I know this sounds crazy, but it sure read like something your sister might have written."

"Is that so?" Slade was all ears. "You still got a copy of it?"

"Yes."

"I'd like to see it."

"Sure, but as I said, I'm not certain it was written by Randi."

"Nonetheless."

"I'll make you a copy and send it to you."

"Thanks."

She hung up and felt a big case of the blues threatening to overtake her. So Thorne was in Denver. So what?

Why didn't he mention that he was going? Why hasn't he called?

"Stop it," she told herself. She *wasn't* going to be one of those women who sat around and stewed over a man. No way, no how. And yet, as she pulled the blinds and saw one last view of the snowy night, she couldn't help wish that Thorne was here with her, holding her in his arms and making love to her as if he would never stop.

Cradling a cup of coffee, Thorne glowered out the window to the gray morning. Snow was still falling as if it would never stop and the airport was a mess. At another time in his life, he would have kept busy, gone to the office, buried himself in his work, managed his life around the natural disaster that seemed hell-bent on causing him problems. But now he wanted to return to Grand Hope, Montana—to the ranch, to Randi, to little J.R. and especially to Nicole. Grand Hope was where he belonged. With his brothers and sister. With his nephew. With the woman he loved.

Silently he sipped his black coffee and laughed at himself. Thorne McCafferty, once upon a time a confirmed bachelor, now contemplating not just living with a woman for the rest of his life, but marrying her.

Matt and Slade would needle him mercilessly when they found out. But he didn't mind.

His head still ached from the buzz of last night's party. Kent Williams had been attentive and brought several ideas to him—a condominium project in Aspen, single-family courtyard homes in a development just outside of Denver, and an apartment complex in Boulder. He'd been certain they could work something out and all the while Annette had hovered near him, touching him, smiling up at him, showing off her sleek body in a low-cut gown of mauve silk while he spoke to other businessmen and reporters who were covering the event. She'd even managed to loop her arm through his while a society page reporter had spoken with him and a photographer had flashed his picture.

Thorne hadn't been interested in her advances, but had managed to smile and accept her attentions throughout the night. Only when he was leaving and she suggested that she was available to come to his place for drinks did he pull her into a private alcove of the hotel and tell her in no uncertain terms that it was over. When she'd pouted, he'd had to tell her that he was involved with another woman. She hadn't believed him and had thrown her arms around his neck and tried to kiss him. Only then, when he hadn't responded, had she realized that he was serious.

"I just hope whoever she is she knows what she's got in you," she'd said icily. "No woman with any heart wants a man married to his work."

He hadn't responded but had silently thought that Nicole didn't even know he loved her; would probably reject him when he proposed. At that thought he smiled for the first time in twenty-four hours. The memory of making love to her had lingered in his mind, but that wasn't all of it. Their lovemaking was wild, raw and passionate, but sex wasn't the driving force. No, he loved Nicole the concerned physician, Nicole the tenderhearted mother, Nicole the brassy woman who stood up to him and joked with him as well as Nicole the sexy lady he wanted to forever warm his bed.

So he was stuck in Denver. Great. He might as well make the most of it. He decided to go into the office, do as much work as he could while he was here and then as soon as the weather broke, he would fly back to the pine-forested slopes of Montana where he belonged.

He showered, changed into a business suit that felt strangely uncomfortable, then he walked the few blocks through the snow-crusted streets to the office. He spent the next hour with Eloise who brought him up to date on his projects. "You know," she said, checking off another item on her list as she sat on one side of his desk and he on the other. "This is working better than I thought."

"What is?"

"You being at the ranch in Montana. I have to admit that I thought it was a crazy scheme when you came up with it."

"The art of telecommunications."

"I suppose."

"Or maybe you just like being in charge when I'm gone."

"Oh, yeah, that's it." A twinkle lit her eyes. "Okay, is there anything else?"

"Yes, get me a florist on the line, would you?"

"You want me to send flowers for you?"

Thorne leaned back in his chair. "No, this time I'll handle it personally."

"Uh-oh. Someone special?"

"Very." He leaned back in his chair and noticed the shocked expression on his secretary's face. "Very special to me."

"Will do." She left his office, buzzed him a few minutes later and told him the florist was on line two. Thorne pulled at his collar and told the man on the other end of the line what he wanted and when he was finished, he grinned widely. That should knock the lady doc's socks off.

The intercom buzzed insistently and when he picked up, Eloise told him that a man named Kurt Striker was on hold.

"Put him through." There was a click. "Striker?"

"Yep. Listen, you told me to let you know if I found out anything about your sister's accident."

All the muscles in the back of Thorne's neck contracted. "I remember."

"Well, I've done some pokin' around."

"And?"

"I think that your sister's accident involved another vehicle—a maroon Ford product, from the looks of it. Either that rig edged her off the road on purpose or clipped her fender, sent her reeling and the driver got so scared he didn't bother to stop. The least it could be is a hit-and-run accident, the worst-case scenario is attempted murder."

Thorne's heart turned to stone. A tic developed over his eye.

"You're sure about this?"

"Yep," Striker said, his voice as strong as steel. "I'd be willing to bet my life on it."

Chapter 13

"I guess when your name is McCafferty, there's no way you can keep it away from the press." Maureen Oliverio slapped a copy of the newspaper down on the table and slid into a chair in the cafeteria where Nicole was finishing her lunch.

"Don't tell me, some reporter is writing about Randi again."

"Not just Randi, but the whole damned family." Maureen opened a packet of nondairy creamer and poured the white powder into her cup of coffee. "Page three."

Nicole pushed her cup of soup aside and spread the paper open. As she did, her heart nearly stopped. Yes, there was an article about the McCaffertys and Randi's accident, but the text was more in-depth and gave an overview of John Randall McCafferty, who had once been so influential in the area surrounding Grand Hope. There was also a sketchy story of what his children were doing. There were old snapshots of the McCafferty brothers playing football, a picture of Slade after his skiing accident, a shot of Matt riding rodeo and another picture, one taken just the day before, if the date was to be believed, of Thorne at a charitable fund-raiser in Denver. On his arm was a striking woman who positively glowed in her designer gown and diamonds.

Nicole's world spun for a second. Her throat closed and she tried to deny what was so obvious. Then, gritting her teeth and finding a scrap of her self-esteem she scanned the article before lifting her eyes and reading the concern in Maureen's gaze. "I don't know what possessed me to buy this," the emergency room team leader said, "but I thought you'd like to see it."

"Yes. Thank you." No words were spoken but a moment of understanding passed between them. Maureen wouldn't embarrass her by stating the obvious: that Thorne was dating other women while he was seeing Nicole, and Nicole didn't have to make excuses or defend him. The thread of friendship—the woman-bond—between Maureen and Nicole ran too deep for that kind of false pride. They were more than colleagues, more than friends. They belonged to an unspoken sisterhood of single women raising families.

"You can have it."

"Good."

Her pager went off and Nicole read the message—a code that she needed to be in the ER. At the same time Maureen's beeper caught her attention.

"Gotta run," Nicole said.

"Me, too. I'll meet you in the ER."

On her feet in an instant, Nicole tucked the damning newspaper under her arm. What did she expect? Of course Thorne dated other women. He probably had one in every city where he did work. The thought made her stomach turn over. Why, oh, for the love of God, why did she let herself fall in love with him?

At the elevators Nicole gave herself a quick mental shake. She couldn't be worrying about Thorne or wondering about him or pining over him. She had work to do. Important work. She climbed onto the elevator car, pushed the button for the main floor and once on ground level, swept through the doors to the ER.

"What've we got?" she asked, pulling on a pair of disposable gloves as Maureen appeared through a side door. Tension crackled in the air.

"Plane crash, just outside of town. Some idiot was trying to fly a private jet in this mess," a nurse said as she hung up the phone. "Close enough that he's coming in by ambulance."

"How many injured?" Nicole asked.

"Just the pilot, I think."

"And he's alive?"

"As far as I know."

"Lucky stiff."

At that moment the sound of sirens split the air. "Okay, people, let's get to work!"

The ambulance, siren screaming, roared into the parking lot. Tires and chains squealed. Two paramedics flew out of the back. A police car—lights flashing in red and blue—skidded in behind the ambulance. As the patient was wheeled inside, two deputies from the sheriff's department stormed in.

"What have we got here?" Nicole asked.

"Thirty-nine-year-old man, unconscious, head injuries, broken femur, blood pressure stable at…"

The paramedic rambled on and Nicole heard the vital signs, but her heart was thundering, her legs weak as she stared into the mangled face of the patient and knew, before anyone said a word, that this was Thorne. The overhead lights seemed brighter and started to swim in her eyes. Her heart pounded in her ears and she couldn't breathe. Her legs threatened to give out and she braced herself against the wall.

"Who is he?"

"Thorne McCafferty," she heard through her fog and forced her eyes into the serious gaze of a woman deputy from the sheriff's department. Her name tag read Detective Kelly Dillinger.

"Oh, God," she whispered. "No. No. Oh, God, no—"

"I'll take over," Maureen said from somewhere behind her and the room began to go dark. "Nicole. I said—"

"No, I'll be all right." Her fingers wrapped around the cold metal railing of the gurney as she turned to face Maureen.

"I'll handle it, *Doctor*." Behind the understanding in Maureen's eyes, was an insistence that warned Nicole she would hear of no argument. Several nurses were staring. All the while Thorne lay still, needing assistance. "You're too involved emotionally, and I'm the team leader," Maureen pointed out.

"All right." Nicole had no choice but to back down. She was shaking and needed to pull herself together. "But as soon as you've examined him, let me know. I'll be in my office and I'll call his family."

"Fine." All business, Maureen Oliverio nodded. "Talk to the detective and I'll see to the patient. Let's go!"

As she watched helplessly, Thorne was wheeled into an examining room.

"What did she mean you were too involved?" the detective asked.

With pale skin and piercing brown eyes she stared at Nicole from beneath the brim of her hat. A few wisps of red hair feathered around her face.

"I—I know the family."

"And Thorne McCafferty specifically?"

"Yes. He and I have dated," she admitted, finally coming to grips with the situation. Her spine found some starch and she was no longer quivering inside but she suspected her face was pale as death. "He's a friend of mine. What happened?" As she talked she peeled off her gloves and tossed them into a waste receptacle.

"His plane went down in the storm and we're investigating the cause of the accident. Probably just the weather, but we have to be sure." Detective Dillinger's lips pursed a bit. "He's lucky to be alive."

Nicole glanced to the examining room and nodded. To think that Thorne might have lost his life. Oh, God. What then? Her heart ached at the thought of it. She cleared her throat and saw a news van wheel into the lot. "Uh-oh."

Looking over her shoulder, the detective recognized the van. Her lips tightened into a frown of disapproval. She nodded to her partner and ordered, "Handle the vultures. And don't tell them the name of the pilot until we talk to his family."

"Got it." The other officer, a lanky man in his early twenties, blocked the entrance. The reporter, a petite woman in a bright-blue coat, argued as a wiry cameraman stared through the glass.

"Can we talk somewhere a little more private?" Detective Dillinger asked and for the first time Nicole was aware of the curious stares that were cast in her direction.

"Yeah—my office, just let me tell the staff where to reach me." Another doctor agreed to take over for the next half hour while Nicole managed to rein in her wild emotions and escorted the detective upstairs to her office.

"Have a seat," Nicole offered, snatching a stack of books off the chair. She set the books on an empty corner of her desk and settled into her own seat.

"I know this is tough on you right now, and I wouldn't

bother you, but since you're close to the McCafferty family maybe you can give me some information."

"As soon as I alert his brothers," Nicole said, her head finally clear again. Somehow she had to put her own emotions aside and don her facade of professionalism, not only for herself, but for Thorne as well. Her fingers were still slightly unsteady, but she picked up the phone. "Matt and Slade need to know that their brother's been in an accident and admitted to St. James." She didn't wait for a response, just dialed the ranch and gave the message to Slade, who shocked, didn't say a word until she was finished.

Then he swore a blue streak. "Damn it all, how can this happen? What kind of a fool gets into a plane in the middle of a blizzard?" he asked, then sighed loudly. "I guess it doesn't matter. Just tell me. Is he gonna make it?"

"Yes—I think so." The thought of Thorne giving up his life was too painful to consider. She cleared her throat and was aware of the detective's eyes silently assessing her and her reaction. "A team of our best doctors is working to stabilize him in the emergency room. From there he'll see specialists."

"Son of a—" Slade began, and then shouted in another direction. "Juanita, can you watch the baby for a while? Thorne's been in an accident and he's at the hospital."

"Dios!" the woman cried. "This family, it has a *maldición!"*

"There is no curse, Juanita." Slade's voice was muffled but firm. "Will you watch—"

"Sí, sí! I will stay."

"I'll round up Matt," Slade said into the mouthpiece. "We'll be there as soon as we can." He hung up and Nicole, still shaken, slowly set down the receiver. Once again, she found herself staring into the scrutinizing gaze of Detective Kelly Dillinger.

"They're on their way?" she asked.

"Both Matt and Slade."

"Good."

"What is it you want to know?"

"Just a little family history," the detective said, pulling out a notepad. "The reason is simple. First the sister is nearly killed in an accident, has a baby who nearly doesn't make it, remains comatose and leaves a lot of questions unanswered. We can't contact the baby's father as no one seems to know who he is, and we can't talk to her and find out why her car went out of control."

"I thought she hit ice," Nicole said, a needle of dread piercing her heart.

"She did. But the family's insistent that there was another vehicle involved. They hired an independent investigator who's determined to prove that there was some kind of foul play." She took off her hat and red hair spilled around her face in soft layers. "Okay, that's what some families do. It makes them feel better—to pay someone to dig deeper than the police. Or so they think."

"But—was there? Foul play?"

"We don't know," the detective said, her face without expression, her eyes serious. "But I'm trying to find out." She clicked her pen a couple of times, then jotted a quick note. "I wasn't convinced that there was anything to go on, but now there's been another accident involving another member of the family, so I guess I'm just covering all bases."

"But the plane crash, it was an accident." It had to have been. No one would try to harm Thorne—to *murder* him!

"Most likely it was an accident. The storm was bad and those light planes…well…" She cocked her head to one side. "But if it's all just coincidence, then this McCafferty family is having one string of bad luck. If not...then maybe that P.I. knows something the sheriff's department doesn't. I'm here to figure it out."

Nicole's head pounded. Was this possible? Someone out to hurt the McCafferty clan? She swallowed hard and refused to give in to that kind of fear. So far no one had proved anything other than the fact that there had been some accidents. Bad luck, that was it. It had to be.

She checked her watch. Thorne had been in the ER for over thirty minutes. Surely someone knew the extent of his injuries by now. Yet no one had called and she was edgy, her nerves strung tight as piano wires. What if something had gone wrong? Distracted, she tried to answer as many questions as possible and talked with the detective for a few more minutes before she explained that she really had to go back to work.

"That's fine. I'll need to speak to the patient when he wakes up," Kelly Dillinger said, "and I'll want to talk to his brothers." She scraped her chair back, grabbed her hat and together they took the elevator down to the emergency room. The detective hurried out to her police car and Nicole was immediately immersed in her work.

Nicole saw three more patients, a seven-year-old girl who needed five stitches to her forehead after being hit by the end of a twirling baton that had lost its rubber tip and had been wielded by her younger brother, a septuagenarian with a mild case of bronchitis, and an ashen-faced teenager who thought she had a bad case of the flu and showed shock, then horror when tests confirmed that she was nearly three months' pregnant.

By the time Nicole had finished the examinations, the ER was clear. She talked to the nurses and found out that

Thorne had been admitted. He was stable and aside from a few contusions and a broken leg that would require surgery once the swelling had gone down, he was healthy.

"Thank God," she whispered as she made her way to his private room. Matt and Slade were camped out at his bedside. Both men wore deep frowns and their eyes were dark with worry.

"I can't believe it," Slade muttered as he walked to the hallway and reached into the inside pocket of his jacket for a crumpled pack of cigarettes. He retrieved the pack, then realized what he was doing and returned it to his pocket. "What in the hell is going on?" He shot an angry glance at Nicole. "Now we got two in this hospital again! The baby just got home and Thorne winds up here!"

"He's going to make it, though. Okay?" Matt muttered. "That's something."

"Damned fool! What was he doin' flyin' in that storm?" Slade closed his eyes and pinched the bridge of his nose as if trying to stave off a headache.

"He thought he should get back—"

Slade's eyes flew open and he dropped his hand only to raise a finger and jab it at Matt's chest. "Because he doesn't have any faith that we can handle the ranch, or the baby or Randi's situation, ourselves. He's got no faith in anyone but himself! A control freak. That's what he is. A damned, corporate control freak."

"Enough!" Matt's face had turned a deep shade of scarlet. "This isn't getting us anywhere."

"I'm going to tell Striker." Slade rammed his fingers through his hair and as if a sudden thought had struck him, turned all of his attention in Nicole's direction. "You said you had some article that Randi might have written?"

"I took a copy and sent it to you."

"Hell, I didn't even think of the mail today." He rubbed the back of his neck in frustration.

"Have you talked to anyone from the sheriff's department?" Nicole asked.

"The sheriff's department?" Matt's eyes narrowed. "Why?"

"They're investigating the accident. I spoke with a Detective Dillinger and she said she wants to talk to you."

"Because—?" Matt asked, but the look in his eyes convinced Nicole that he already knew the answer.

"Because finally someone's starting to believe what Kurt Striker has been saying all along," Slade answered. "I'm going to call him right now."

"And I'll talk to the police." Matt's jaw was hard as granite. "If this isn't just an accident, I'm going to find out who's behind it." He squared his hat onto his head. "You'll call me if there's a change in Thorne's condition?"

"Of course."

As the brothers strode down the hall together, Nicole entered Thorne's darkened room. She told herself that she saw injured people all the time, victims who had suffered horrid accidents and disfigurements, that she could stomach anything. But seeing Thorne lying inert beneath the crisp bedsheets, with an IV running into the back of his hand, his leg elevated in a temporary cast, his face cut and swollen beyond recognition, each breath seeming labored, her heart nearly broke.

"Oh, honey," she whispered, her throat closing in on itself. She loved him. God, how she loved him and he'd betrayed her; been with another woman. She licked her lips and fought tears. There he lay, a broken leg, a concussion, his head bandaged, his features barely recognizable. "I'm sorry it didn't work out," she said, her voice a rasp, her fingers touching the tips of his. "I did love you. Oh, Thorne, if you only knew how much." Sniffing a bit, she cleared her throat. "But then I always was a fool over you. I suppose I always will be." His eyelids didn't so much as flutter. "You get better, y'hear? I'll be back and, damn it, if you do something foolish like take a turn for the worse, I swear, I'll kill you myself." She laughed a bit at her own stupid joke and realized that tears were falling from her eyes. "Oh, look at this. I'm such a moron. *You* make me a moron. I, uh, I've got to go check on the girls." She dabbed at her eyes with a tissue she found near the bedside. "But I'll be back. I promise." She leaned over the bed and placed a kiss on his forehead, leaving a lipstick smudge and a tearstain that she quickly brushed aside. "You know, Thorne," she confided, "I was foolish enough to want to spend the rest of my life with you."

She waited, half expecting him to respond, silently praying there would be a squeeze on her fingers, rapid eye movement behind his closed lids, even the barest change in his breathing, but she was disappointed. Like his sister in ICU, Thorne heard nothing and didn't so much as flinch.

Nicole left the room with a weight as heavy as all Montana pressing down her shoulders. She wrote her notes in a daze, then grabbed her coat, changed into boots and headed home. Outside the snow was still flurrying, swirling and dancing across the frozen landscape. In gloves and a down ski jacket, she turned the radio and heater on full blast, but couldn't thaw the ice in her soul at the thought of Thorne's plane crash and how close he'd come to losing his life.

And how would you feel then? If he'd died or was in serious risk of losing his life? Or paralyzed for the rest of his life?

She shuddered and tried to concentrate on a song playing

through the speakers, but the lyrics of false love scraped too close to the bone. Angrily, she snapped off the radio. She was no longer involved with Thorne. He wanted it that way. It had been a mistake to get involved with him again but it was over. Over, over, over! His choice. She braked for a stoplight and waited impatiently, gloved fingers tapping on the steering wheel as a few brave souls bundled in scarves, boots and thick winter coats hurried along the snow-covered streets of Grand Hope. Barren trees lifted naked arms to a night sky where millions of snowflakes caught in the neon lights of the city continued to fall.

So what did you expect from him? A marriage proposal? Her wayward mind taunted as the light changed to green and she stepped on the accelerator.

The thought made her laugh without a grain of humor. Then minutes later, still lost in her own thoughts, she turned onto the street where she lived, and promised herself that she would get over Thorne McCafferty once and for all. She had her girls. She had her work. She had a life. Without Thorne. She didn't need him.

The SUV's wheels slid a bit as she pulled into the driveway but she managed to park in front of the garage. Hauling her briefcase and laptop computer with her, she dashed through the short drifts and climbed up the back porch. Stomping the snow from her boots and pulling off her gloves with her teeth, she opened the back door and heard squeals of delight.

"Mommy! Mommy! Come see." Two sets of feet pounded the floor as the girls raced into the kitchen.

Nicole was unzipping her coat, but leaned down to hug each of the twins. Yes, her life was full. She didn't need a man and certainly not Thorne McCafferty.

Patches hopped lithely onto the counter.

"The flowers. Bunches and bunches and bunches of flowers," Molly said, holding her arms as wide as she could.

"Flowers?" Nicole asked and noticed the fragrance of roses that seemed to permeate the air.

"Yeth." Mindy was pulling on one hand, dragging her to the living room. Molly gripped her other.

"You get down!" Nicole ordered the precocious feline as they passed the counter. The cat hopped to the floor as Nicole stepped into the living room and gasped. Jenny was standing near the fireplace and the grate was lit, several logs burning brightly, and all around the room, on every table, in the corners and on the floor, were dozens and dozens of roses. Red, white, pink, yellow—it didn't matter, bouquet after bouquet. "What in the world…?" she whispered.

"There's a card." Jenny pointed to a bouquet of three dozen white long-stemmed roses.

"Read it! Read it!" both girls chimed.

With shaking fingers she opened the small white envelope. It read simply: "Marry me."

Tears burned behind her eyelids. "Do you know who sent these?" she asked.

Jenny smiled. "Don't you?"

Knees suddenly weak, Nicole dropped into a side chair. "Dear Lord…"

"What, Mommy? What?" Mindy asked, her little eyebrows knotting in concern.

"Thorne's in the hospital."

"What?" Jenny's smile fell away and haltingly Nicole told her about the plane crash.

"Oh, my God, well you've got to go back there. You've got to be with him."

"But the girls…"

"Don't worry about them. I can handle them." The twins' faces fell and Jenny added, "We'll have pizza delivered and make popcorn balls and…and a surprise for your mommy."

"But I don't want Mommy to leave," Mindy said.

"Baby!" Molly accused, pointing a tiny finger at her sister.

"Am not!"

"Shh…shh…no one's a baby."

Touched by the dazzling array of flowers, Nicole stared at the soft petals and long stems and her heart pounded with a love she so recently tried to deny. "I—I do have to go back to the hospital," she said, "but I'll be back soon."

Mindy's face began to crumple. "Promise?"

Nicole kissed her daughter's forehead and stood on legs that threatened to give out again. She plucked one crimson rose from its vase and winked at her daughters. "Promise."

Through a veil of pain, he heard the door open and expected that it was the nurse bringing much needed medication.

"Thorne?"

Nicole's voice. His heart leaped, but he didn't move. Nor did she turn on the light as she walked to his bedside. Carefully she laid a long-stemmed rose on his chest. "I—I don't know what to say."

He didn't respond. Didn't move. In his semiconscious state a few hours ago, he'd heard her claims of loving him yet not wanting him, of saying it would never work out, so he'd thought she'd gotten the flowers and had rejected him. He hadn't been able to respond then, didn't know if he could now. He barely remembered the accident. There had been a problem, an engine had died and he'd been forced to land in a field, nearly made it when the plane had crashed into a copse of trees...he was lucky...

"I got the flowers. Dozens and dozens of them. You shouldn't have...oh, Thorne," she whispered, dragging him back to the present, to Nicole. Beautiful, sexy Nicole. "I wish you could hear me. I want to explain...."

Here it comes again. She was going to repeat what she'd said earlier. Without moving he braced himself for the worst.

"I was—am—overwhelmed." She cleared her throat and he felt her fingers find his. "I read the card."

He felt like an idiot. Why had he bared his soul to her? She didn't want him, she'd made that clear enough. He braced himself against the pain.

"And I wish I could make you hear me, that you'd understand just how much I love you. Marry you? Oh, Lord, if you only knew how much I wanted to do just that, but I saw your picture with that woman at the fund-raiser in Denver and I—I thought you weren't ready to settle down, that you never will be and so, I don't know what to do. If there was any chance that we could be together, you and I and the girls, believe me I'd—"

Despite the pain, he forced his hand to move. His head felt as if it might explode, but he grabbed her hand then, held on to it fiercely. The rose dropped to the floor.

"Oh! Dear God—"

"Marry me," he rasped, forcing the words through lips that felt cracked and swollen. Pain screamed through his body but he didn't care.

"But—what? Can you—"

"Marry me." He squeezed her fingers so tightly that she gasped again.

"You can hear me?"

He forced his eyes open, blinked against the fragile light that seemed to blind. "Nicole—would you please just answer?" Somehow he managed to focus on her face—God, it was a great face. "Will you marry me?"

"But what about the other woman, the one in the paper?"

"There is no other woman. Just you." He stared at her hard, willing her to believe him. "And there will always only be you in my life. I swear it."

He watched her swallow hard, bite her lip, fight the indecision.

"I will love you forever," he vowed and then the tears came, slowly at first and then more rapidly, falling from her gorgeous amber eyes. "Marry me, Nicole. Be my wife."

With her free hand, she dashed the tears away. "Yes," she whispered, her voice cracking. "Yes." He yanked hard, pulled her over him and when his lips found hers some of the pain disappeared and he knew that from this day forward he would gladly give up whatever possessions he had, that nothing else came close to the love he felt for her and he would cherish this woman until he gave up his very last breath.

"I love you, Doctor," he vowed as she lifted her head and laughed. "And this time, believe me, I'll never leave you and I'll never let you go."

"Oh, I bet you say that to all the women physicians," she teased, her eyes bright with tears as she picked up the rose and laid it next to him on the bed.

"Nope. Only one."

"Lucky me," she sniffed, leaning down and brushing her lips against his.

"No." Of this he was certain. "Lucky me."

Epilogue

"You're sure you want to live here?" Nicole asked, her gaze roving around the snow-covered acres as she and Thorne sat on the porch while the twins, in matching snowsuits, frolicked in the yard. The old dog, Harold, barked and joined them, acting like a pup, and cattle and horses dotted the landscape. Slade, dressed in a thick buckskin jacket, was walking near the barn, checking the pipes and watering troughs along with the stock.

It was beautiful here and Nicole's heart was full. Though Thorne's leg was casted, there was no keeping him down and they'd planned as soon as he was on his feet again to marry.

"I'll live here as long as Randi lets me."

Randi was the one worry. It had been nearly a month since her accident and she was still unconscious. Though Kurt Striker was still looking into the possibility of a hit-and-run driver forcing her off the road, he hadn't found any suspects and Thorne's plane crash was still under investigation. Was it foul play? Thorne hadn't thought so, or so he'd insisted, citing the fact that he should have had the plane checked out before flying off in the snowstorm. But he'd been anxious to return to Montana. "By the way," he said, "I have something for you."

"What's that?" she asked.

"Something to make our engagement official."

"Oh?" She lifted a wary eyebrow as he winced and dug into a front pocket of his jeans. Slowly he extracted a ring, a band of silver and gold.

"It was my father's, from his marriage to my mom," he explained and Nicole was touched, her throat clogging suddenly as he slipped it onto her finger. "For some sentimental reason, the old man kept it even after the divorce and while he was married to Randi's mother. He gave it to me before he died and now…because of tradition, I guess, I want you to have it." His smile was crooked. "I think we'll have it sized to fit." The ring, an intricate band of gold and silver, was much too big for her finger but she clutched it tight, knowing that it meant so much to Thorne. That he would share it with her said more than words.

"It's beautiful."

"And special."

"Oh, Thorne, thank you," she whispered, then kissed him as he held her close and the old porch swing swayed.

"And you're special to me, Nicole, you and the girls."

She had trouble swallowing over the lump in her throat. Never in her wildest dreams had she thought she'd ever hear those words from Thorne McCafferty, the man who had so callously used her and then walked away.

As if he could read her thoughts, he placed a kiss upon her head. "I know I made a mistake with you and I've kicked myself a dozen times over, but I want to make it up to you, to the twins. I… I never thought I'd want to settle down, to have a family of my own to…" he struggled for a moment, looked across the snow-crusted fields "…to share my life here. On the Flying M. But I do. Because of you." His eyes found hers. "You're the one, Nicole. The only one."

She sighed against him and looked at the ring. God, she loved him. Blinking back tears of joy, she whispered, "I love you."

"Oh, you do, do you?" he said, a slow, sexy smile creeping from one side of his mouth to the other.

"Scout's honor," she said. His grin was infectious and she tossed a sassy smile back his way. "You don't believe me?"

"Maybe…"

"But maybe not?"

"You could prove it."

She laughed and rose to the bait. "And how would I do that?"

His eyes gleamed wickedly. "Oh, I can think of a dozen or two different ways."

"And I can think of a hundred."

He rose awkwardly to his feet and pulled her to hers. "Then let's start, shall we? As my father would say, 'time's a wastin',' and he did say he wanted some grandchildren."

"What about J.R. and the twins?"

"A start, lady, just a start."

"Slow down, Romeo," she said giggling.

"No way, lady. We've only got the rest of our lives."

She threw back her head and laughed huskily. "I do love you, Thorne McCafferty, but if anyone's going to have to do the proving it's you."

"All right." He swept her off her feet and she squealed.

"Thorne, don't! Your leg! For crying out loud, let me go! Put me down!"

He held her tight, his shoulder braced against the side of the house, his strong arms holding her close. "Never," he vowed, then kissed her hard. She closed her eyes, kissed him back and wondered if anyone had the right to feel this happy. As he lifted his head and stared into her eyes, he said again, "I will never let you go, Nicole. Never again."

And she believed him.

* * * * *

Also by B.J. Daniels

HQN

Buckhorn, Montana

Out of the Storm
From the Shadows

Montana Justice

Restless Hearts
Heartbreaker
Heart of Gold

Harlequin Intrigue

Cardwell Ranch: Montana Legacy

Steel Resolve
Iron Will
Ambush Before Sunrise
Double Action Deputy
Trouble in Big Timber
Cold Case at Cardwell Ranch

Visit her Author Profile page at Harlequin.com,
or bjdaniels.com, for more titles!

SECOND CHANCE
COWBOY

B.J. Daniels

Many thanks to my good friend Lynn Kinnaman
for not only encouraging me to write this book,
but for giving me the ending and making us both cry.

Chapter 1

Charlotte Evans was already late for her doctor's appointment when she looked up and saw a silver SUV blocking the narrow road into town.

The hood of the SUV was up. No sign of the driver.

"Great," Charlotte muttered as she braked to a stop. She should have taken the main road. But, as was her habit, she preferred taking the shortcut into town even though it was more rugged. Normally it was faster. Less chance of getting behind a tractor or a doddering old farmer in a beat-up pickup or cowboys moving a herd of cattle.

She considered turning around. But the barrow pits on both sides of the road were deep and muddy from last night's rain, the road too narrow and steep here above the creek—and, in her condition, an insane idea. There were enough crazy people in her family as it was.

She waited for a moment, motor running. It was one of those hot July days, the Montana sky wide and blue, only a few clouds dotting the horizon. She had her window down, since her old car didn't have air-conditioning. The hot summer air was making her sweat. She hated to sweat.

Still no sign of the driver. She beeped her horn.

A hand waved a hello from under the hood.

"Terrific," Charlotte said under her breath and shut off her engine. How long was this going to take?

It was hard enough living so far from town, let alone getting herself behind the wheel eight months pregnant.

She really didn't need this. To make matters worse, on the way to Whitehorse she'd started having contractions.

It would be just her luck to have this baby beside the road. Somehow that might be fitting, she thought. She just hoped the driver of the SUV knew how to deliver a baby.

Opening her car door, she maneuvered her ungainly belly from behind the steering wheel and got out. She told herself she would never have gotten pregnant if she'd known even half of the things that were going to happen to her body. If only.

Slamming her car door, she waddled toward the SUV, cursing under her breath.

A head appeared as the driver leaned out from the front of the car. "Sorry, didn't hear you drive up," the female driver called. "Had my head stuck under the hood." The head disappeared again.

Charlotte wondered how things could get worse. She just hoped this woman knew what she was doing under there.

At least if the driver had been a man, there might be a chance he could get the car moved out of the way so she could get to town.

She stopped for a moment as another contraction took her breath away. She remembered her doctor saying something about false labor. She hoped that was what this was. Maybe she should have read even one of the books her mother kept buying her about labor and delivery, Lamaze, breast feeding and child rearing.

The last book really was a kick, since her mother had done such a bang-up job with her three, Charlotte thought uncharitably. Actually, being pregnant had made her wonder how her mother had gone through it three times much less raised three kids alone.

As Charlotte waddled the rest of the way up to the front of the SUV, she saw that the woman was teetering on the bumper as she leaned under the hood to work on the engine—wearing a pair of latex gloves, of all things.

"It just quit running," the woman said, looking up. She was at least fifteen years older than Charlotte, with brown hair and eyes and a look of privilege about her. Charlotte would have hated her on sight except that the woman had a smudge of grease on her cheek and she was almost as pregnant as Charlotte herself.

The woman smiled. "Know anything about cars?"

She'd taken an auto mechanics course last year in high school, but she hadn't paid any attention. She shook her head with a silent groan. Apparently this *could* get worse. "Did you call AAA or one of the local garages in town?"

"No cell phone coverage out here."

"I really need to get to my doctor's appointment," Charlotte said. "If we could just move your car over a little, I think I can squeeze mine past. I can drive you into town and you can get someone to come back out with you to work on it."

"I think I've got it fixed. Would you mind getting in and trying to start it while I jiggle this cable?"

Charlotte sighed. Just the thought of trying to climb into the huge SUV— She bent over a little, grimacing as she was hit with another contraction.

The woman was giving her a worried look. "Tell me you aren't in labor."

Charlotte held up her hand and breathed through the

contraction. It felt so good when it stopped. "False labor." She hoped.

"How far along·are you?" the woman asked, studying her.

"Eight months." The lie came so naturally. "You?"

"Seven. So how close are your contractions?"

Charlotte shrugged. "Not that close."

"Your first baby?"

Charlotte nodded and felt the woman looking at her ring finger. "I'm separated from the father." That was actually kind of true. "I'm older than I look." Another lie.

"Must be difficult. Having a baby all by yourself."

She had her mother and her worthless brother, but she didn't mention that. She knew how pathetic it would sound. Even more pathetic if the woman knew the half of it.

"You can understand why I need to get into town to the doctor," Charlotte said.

"Yes. We definitely need to see to you. But I don't think it's going to be a problem. Just pop behind the wheel and try to start the engine. This should at least allow us to get the car out of the way if nothing else. Neither of us is up to pushing it."

The woman had a point. Although arguing was second nature to Charlotte, who'd been arguing for years. With her older sister. With her mother. With her brother. With herself.

But she wasn't up to it right now, and the woman was right. She didn't want to have to push the SUV out of the way and she doubted she could get past it anyway, as steep and unstable as the edge of the road was.

She opened the door of the pricey SUV and, with great effort, pulled herself up to slide behind the wheel. Her feet were a mile from the gas pedal.

"I need to move the seat forward," she called as she bent over as best she could to look for a handle.

She felt the cool metal the moment it was jammed against her throat.

The pregnant thirtysomething driver of the SUV held a gun in her hand. It was so incongruous: this obviously wealthy pregnant woman with the expensive clothes, salon haircut and freshly manicured nails beneath latex gloves holding a gun on *her*.

It made no sense. That was probably why it didn't register that she was in serious trouble until it was too late.

Chapter 2

At the Whitehorse Sewing Circle, the women gathered around the quilting frame were unusually quiet on this hot summer afternoon.

Normally they would have been abuzz with chatter. Instead they were sipping lemonade, eating the dainty little cookies Laci Cavanaugh had sent over, and smiling a lot—while busting at the seams to share the latest gossip the moment Pearl Cavanaugh left.

Pearl, whose mother had started the group too many years ago for most to remember, had a strict rule about gossip.

But Pearl hadn't been coming for months since her stroke, and the group had taken to gossiping and quilting with a relish. Pearl had been living at the nursing home until recently. Now that she was better and mobile in her wheelchair, Titus had brought her home to stay.

She hadn't quite gotten the knack of sewing with her left hand, but she tried hard. And there wasn't anyone in the group who was going to say she couldn't sew if she wanted to.

To a lot of people Pearl and Titus Cavanaugh were Old

Town Whitehorse royalty. Both were feared—if not respected.

"Well, isn't Pearl looking well," said Alice Miller the moment Titus had wheeled his wife out the door.

It wasn't until they heard the crunch of gravel as Titus left with his wife that Helene Merchant gave out a relieved sigh accompanied by a laugh and said, "I thought we were never going to get to visit."

A few of the women laughed with her. Alice Miller, who always sided against gossip, pursed her lips but said nothing. She had tried since Pearl left to keep the women in line, but she was ninety and had given up, saving her energy for quilting.

The problem was, in Old Town Whitehorse there was always something to talk about. Even on a slow day there was always the Evans family.

Old Town was the site of the original Whitehorse. But when the railroad came through five miles to the north, by the Milk River, the town had moved and taken the name with it.

Some of the more hearty homesteaders had stayed in what was now called Old Town. They'd kept the original Whitehorse Cemetery—the name forged in a wrought-iron arch over the entrance—where many of their kin rested for eternity.

The Whitehorse Community Center, the one-room schoolhouse and a few houses were all that was left of the town. Titus Cavanaugh, Pearl's husband, still performed church services at the center on Sundays and took care of hiring a schoolteacher for the school. He was as close to a mayor as Old Town had.

"Have you heard any more about Violet Evans?" Pamela Chambers asked in a whisper, as if the walls had ears.

"That crazy place she's in gave her a job," Helene said. "She's working at a nurses' station. The word is they're going to let her out of the nuthouse and back on the streets. *Doctors*."

"It scares me," Muriel Brown said. "We all know how dangerous she is. Remember the summer all the cats disappeared? Violet always had that look in her eye from the time she was little."

Even Alice Miller couldn't argue the point.

"The other daughter—Charlotte? She's about to have a baby any day," Corky Mathews said. "How old is she anyway?"

"Eighteen, nineteen at the oldest," Helene said. "Anyone heard who was responsible for fathering the baby?"

There was a general shake of heads. This had been a popular topic for months. "Could be anyone," Helene said. "But you know what I heard at the Cut and Curl?"

The women all leaned in. Except for Alice Miller, who sometimes wished her hearing wasn't as good as it was.

"It was some older man from out of town." Helene nodded and went back to her stitching.

"Poor Arlene. You have to feel for her," Muriel said. "Look how her children have turned out. Violet crazy, Charlotte in the family way and Bo, well, is he the most worthless young man you've ever seen? I wonder if Arlene will ever come back to the group."

Looks were exchanged around the table, along with shrugs. Arlene did always have the latest gossip, but with Pearl returning now…

"Eve Bailey's marrying the sheriff," Alice Miller threw in, hoping to give the poor Evans family a break.

The conversation turned to weddings and the possibility of more babies. The Whitehorse Sewing Circle was famous for its quilts. For years the circle had made a quilt for every newborn.

"I saw the cutest pattern," Pamela said, and the afternoon passed in a blur of talk of quilt patterns, material and—always a good standby—food and the latest recipe one of them had tried, as the group stitched away just as it had done for years.

Friday, 6:38 p.m.

Arlene Evans stared at the image in the mirror and felt like crying. She'd changed clothes four times already. If she didn't make up her mind and quickly, she was going to be late. Why had she accepted a date in the first place? She was too old to date.

When Hank Monroe had asked her out, she'd been so excited and surprised she hadn't thought about the actual *date* part. But the reality set in the moment she went to buy something to wear.

For years she hadn't given a thought to the way she looked. No one else had, either. Floyd, her former husband of too many years to count, had hardly given her a sideways glance. So she'd worn what any working ranch woman wore: an oversize long-sleeved Western shirt, jeans and boots. She couldn't remember the last time she'd worn a dress—and she'd bet neither could anyone else in the county.

Her brown hair was long, thick and straight as a stick—the same haircut she'd had in high school, which she trimmed herself when she remembered. Usually her hair was either swept up in a ponytail or thrust under a hat, so she paid little attention to it. She couldn't remember the last time she'd worn her hair down, let alone curled it.

"Stop acting foolish," she snapped at her image in the mirror as she snatched up an elastic band and pulled her drooping curls up into a ponytail.

She took off the dress she'd spent too much money on, tears welling in her eyes as she recalled how cute it had looked on the hanger.

"What did you expect?" she asked herself, sounding just like her mother. Her mother, even dead for years, was right. "Can't make a silk purse out of a sow's ear."

Arlene hurriedly washed the makeup she'd experimented with from her face and changed into a shirt, jeans and boots. She was what she was, and this date with Hank Monroe was a one-time shot.

She thought about the first time she'd seen him and couldn't help but smile. He'd called about signing up for her rural Internet dating service. His voice had been deep and soft and had a strange thrilling effect on her.

They'd agreed to meet at a local café so she could get him signed up. She'd been nervous about meeting him because he wasn't like most of her clients—twenty- to thirty-something. He was forty-eight—mature, like herself.

The minute she'd walked into the café, she'd spotted him. He'd looked up and their eyes had met.

It sounded ridiculous, she knew, but her heart had begun to pound wildly. Hank Monroe wasn't handsome, but there was a masculine strength in his features and in the broad shoulders, slim hips and long legs cased in denim. He looked like a man who could wrestle grizzly bears if he had a mind to.

And, her smile growing as she remembered the first time he'd laughed, he'd made *her* laugh, surprising them both since hers resembled a donkey's bray.

Hank Monroe had made her feel young and beautiful—all the things she wasn't.

Which should be a clue.

Her mother again. But it was true. Hank had signed up for her dating service to meet *women,* not date the owner of the service. Who knows why he'd asked *her* out? Just being polite, she could only assume, suddenly glad she hadn't dressed up. No reason to act like this was a real date after all.

As she came out of her bedroom, she found her son Bo sitting on the couch, watching television, a huge bag of potato chips in his lap, his bare feet up on her coffee table.

With a frown, she brushed his feet off the table and took the bag of chips from him even as he protested.

"Hey! What am I supposed to eat for dinner?" he groused.

"There are leftovers in the fridge," she said, putting a clip on the chips and taking a cloth back to the living room to wipe the smudges from the coffee table.

"Leftovers?" he demanded indignantly.

She turned down the television volume and straightened to look at her twenty-three-year-old son. He'd been her pride and joy. In her eyes he could do no wrong. She shuddered as she recalled when that had changed.

"Where is your sister?" she asked, determined not to get into an argument with him. Not before her date, anyway.

He shrugged.

Arlene realized she hadn't seen Charlotte since her almost-nineteen-year-old had left for her doctor's appointment earlier that afternoon. Charlotte's old blue sedan wasn't parked out front, and Arlene realized she hadn't heard Bo and Charlotte arguing for hours.

"She should be back from her doctor's appointment by now. Did she call?"

Bo's attention was back on the television. "Nope."

Arlene frowned, hoping the appointment had gone well. Charlotte had been more irritable than usual before she'd left. Arlene remembered how uncomfortable it was being pregnant the last few months. She wondered if Charlotte wasn't having second thoughts about keeping the baby. She could only hope.

"Well, when your sister gets home, make sure she eats something besides potato chips and candy bars. Remind her she's feeding a baby who needs something nutritious to eat."

For a moment Arlene thought about canceling her date. If she didn't cook something, she was afraid neither Bo nor Charlotte would eat properly.

"Promise me you'll eat and make sure Charlotte does."

Bo rolled his eyes. He'd heard this enough times. For months she'd harped on Charlotte to take care of herself for the baby's sake. Not that Charlotte had any business being pregnant, Arlene thought as she headed for her car—and her date.

Her date. What *had* she been thinking? Dating was for people half her age who still had the stamina—and the optimism. She had neither.

She'd made a point of insisting she would meet Hank Monroe at the restaurant. He'd wanted to pick her up at her house, but the last thing she wanted was for him to meet her family. She knew that once he did, it would be the kiss of death, and she just wanted to enjoy this moment in time knowing it couldn't last anyway.

Why shoot herself in the foot before she even got out of the starting gate?

* * *

Hank Monroe looked up as his date came through the restaurant door. He smiled, recalling the first time he'd laid eyes on her. What was it about Arlene that had resonated with his own life? He couldn't be sure. Something in her soft brown eyes. In the determined set of her shoulders. In her hesitant, shy smile.

And that laugh…

Now, as he watched her tug her shirt down over her slim jeans and saw how uncomfortable she looked as she glanced around the restaurant, he felt his heart go out to her again.

Arlene was tall and rangy like a lot of Montana ranch women. Nothing like his petite, classically pretty ex-wife Bitsy. He tried not to see Arlene through Bitsy's eyes. Bitsy took everything at face value. She would never have understood what he saw in this woman. But then, Bitsy had never understood him, had she?

Nor would Bitsy appreciate a woman like Arlene Evans. Few people would, he realized. Bitsy had always been comfortable in her skin. Arlene, he suspected, never had.

He rose quickly, his smile broadening, hoping to reassure her. "You look wonderful." It was true, although he saw she didn't believe it.

Her cheeks flared. "I didn't know what to wear."

"Your choice was perfect." He pulled out the chair for her and mentally kicked himself. He shouldn't have picked a fancy restaurant for their first date.

As he took the chair across from her, he watched her try to relax. Something else that didn't come easy for Arlene. The woman had an energy that was like being close to a live electrical wire.

"I haven't been on a date in a while," she said.

He smiled. "Me either. Feels odd, huh?"

"Yes. But...nice."

It did feel nice. "So tell me how the matchmaking business is going," he said, leaning toward her.

She brightened and told him she had a half dozen new clients just this week alone. "I still can't believe it."

"You had a great idea and you've made it happen. You should be very proud of yourself."

"Knock on wood," she said, lightly tapping the table.

She didn't seem the superstitious type. He wondered what had her worried. Or if, like him, she was leery when things seemed to be going too well.

Later that night, after their date, Hank had that exact feeling as he checked the perimeter of the ranch house, as he always did before he entered the house. Old habits died hard. Other people would have thought it paranoid. For him it was merely prudent and part of his life. The life he'd once chosen and had only recently escaped from.

He'd had a great time tonight. That alone worried him. He'd signed up for the dating service on a whim. Once he'd met Arlene, he hadn't wanted to meet any other women. He wasn't even sure he was ready to date. It felt too dangerous. But he'd asked Arlene out. And he couldn't say he was sorry. Just worried.

There were some things that were inescapable. Guilt. Regret. And his old life. It dwarfed the other two in comparison.

That was the reason he never bothered to lock his house. He knew from experience how easy it was to get into any house, even those with expensive security systems. He had bought the ranch from a corporation that had used the house for conferences.

Because of that, the place was way too large for him.

But he'd fallen in love with the view of the Little Rockies and he'd told himself that with all the land surrounding the place he would be as safe here as anywhere.

As he stepped into the house, he found himself whistling. He couldn't remember a night he'd enjoyed more. Arlene was a fun date—once she relaxed.

They'd had dinner, then gone to the movie—the only one in Whitehorse. A comedy had been showing. That was something else he had in common with Arlene—the way they laughed.

"You bray like a donkey," Bitsy had told him when they'd first gotten together. "You really need to do something about that."

He'd quit laughing around her.

During the movie, he'd found himself simply enjoying the sound of Arlene's laugh. It had felt so good, so natural.

Later, he'd thought about kissing her good-night but had chickened out. *Coward.* The desire had been there. He'd told himself he was just afraid of scaring her off. Clearly this dating thing was as alien to her as it was to him.

But he knew that he was the one who wanted to take it slow. That was another thing they shared—the feeling that when things were going too well, something was bound to happen to jinx it.

As he passed his office, he saw that the message light on his answering machine was flashing. He preferred an answering machine with small disposable tapes over voice mail. Just as he'd always periodically checked his house and car for listening devices. Even here on the ranch in Montana.

He would have liked to believe he'd dropped off his former associates' radar. But he'd worked for the agency too long to pretend that was even possible.

Still, as he pushed the play button, he was startled to hear a familiar voice.

"Hank, it's Cameron. Call me. We need to catch up. It's been too long."

He stared down at the machine, shaken. By the unexpected sound of his old friend and former boss's voice as much as by the calmness of the words—and the underlying threat. Code words. They brought it all back, and for a moment it was as if he'd never left the agency.

He didn't need to replay the message. He quickly deleted it, knowing it was futile to think that would be the end of it. The words echoed in his head. Code words that informed him there's been a breach in security. He was in danger.

Arlene Evans woke smiling. That alone shocked her. Normally the blare of Bo's music down the hall or the sound of Charlotte clamoring around in the kitchen started her day off wrong.

But this morning, after her date with Hank Monroe, nothing could ruin her good mood. They'd had a nice dinner. He'd been easy to talk to. The movie had been enjoyable. They'd stood out in the moonlight and talked afterward.

She been afraid he'd kiss her. And afraid he wouldn't. He didn't. But he'd asked her out again. She felt like a schoolgirl.

Just the thought seemed…foolish. She was too old to be having these feelings. Especially the ones Hank Monroe had sparked with just the brush of his fingers when they'd both reached for the popcorn at the same time. Or when he'd put his arm around her. Or touched her back with the palm of his hand as they'd left the theater. Desire after all these years of feeling nothing?

She rose and dressed, wrapped in the memory of the night before and the prospect of another date tonight. He'd also invited her to the county fair this coming weekend— his first county fair, he'd said.

She hadn't told him, but she planned to enter in the baking division and almost always took blue ribbons. It was the one thing she excelled in, and normally she would be a nervous wreck worrying that she might not win this year. That she'd lost her touch.

But Hank Monroe had taken her mind off the fair this year.

Which, she reminded herself sternly, wasn't good. Baking lasted. Men didn't. "Stick to what you're good at," her mother had always said. "It's little enough."

Arlene felt her smile slip. She was making too much of one date with the man. Getting her hopes up was always a mistake.

She'd learned that the hard way, she thought, remembering high school dates that never showed while she waited by the window and her mother berated her for opening herself up to that kind of humiliation.

By the time Arlene reached the kitchen, she was no longer smiling. She yelled down the hall for Bo to turn down the music. He didn't. She started to tell Charlotte to go down the hall and tell him when she noticed her daughter wasn't lying on the couch, where she usually was this time of the morning. Nor was the television on or the kitchen counter a mess from where Charlotte had made herself a snack before breakfast.

More puzzled than worried, Arlene walked down the hall to her daughter's bedroom and pushed open the door. The bed was just as it had been when Arlene made it the previous morning.

Charlotte hadn't come home last night.

Stepping across the hall, she opened her son's bedroom door. The room was bedlam—just the way he apparently liked it. He'd barred her from cleaning it, which she should have been grateful for. Instead the room was an embarrassment, a reflection on her.

"What if someone comes by and sees this mess?" she'd demanded time after time.

"No one comes by," he'd said.

"Well, if anyone did, they'd think I was a terrible mother."

Bo had laughed at that.

"Have you seen your sister?" she mouthed now over the horrible music blasting from his stereo.

He was sprawled on his bed, frowning at her and motioning for her to go away and close the door.

She reached over and grabbed the cord on the stereo and pulled hard. The music stopped, filling the room with an abrupt deafening silence.

"What?" he demanded.

"Your sister. She didn't come home last night."

"So?"

"She's eight months pregnant."

"I noticed. But I'm not my sister's keeper." He reached to plug the stereo back in, but she still held the cord and jerked it back out of his grasp.

"I want you to clean your room."

He looked at her as if she'd lost her mind.

"I'm serious, Bo."

He mugged a face at her.

"I also want you to get a job."

He let out a surprised laugh. "I have a job. I help you with your Internet dating service."

"No, you don't." She tossed him the end of the cord and closed the door behind her, telling herself she shouldn't be worried about Charlotte.

Actually, this was just like her daughter. Charlotte had been cranky yesterday and late for her doctor's appointment. Arlene had tried to talk to her again about putting the baby up for adoption. Charlotte hadn't come home just to punish her.

Arlene told herself she wasn't going to rise to Charlotte's bait. Not this time. But she worried about the baby. That poor, innocent baby was going to need a mother—and soon.

The phone rang. "Hello." She just assumed it would be Charlotte making ultimatums before she came home.

"Arlene?"

Just the sound of Hank Monroe's deep voice buoyed her spirits instantly. "Hank," she said a little breathlessly.

"Is everything all right?"

"Fine," she said too cheerfully, hoping he didn't hear the slight catch in her throat.

"Arlene, you can be honest with me. What's wrong?"

She took a deep breath and let it out slowly. He was going to find out sooner or later anyway. Wouldn't it be better if it came from her? "It's my daughter. My youngest daughter. She's pregnant. Not married. And she didn't come home last night."

"Maybe she's with her boyfriend."

"I don't think there *is* a boyfriend. At least not one who's free."

"I see," he said. "How about her friends? Have you tried them?"

"She doesn't have a lot in common with her old friends anymore." Arlene felt her throat close and fought back the tears. Most of the time she could stand what her life had become. But revealing the truth to Hank made it more real, more sad and tragic.

"I was just getting ready to call the doctor's office and see if anything unusual happened during her visit yesterday."

"All right. Let me know what you find out."

She promised she would and called the doctor's office, only to get a recording. It was too early. She'd have to wait. And the one thing she really wasn't good at was waiting. Grabbing her purse, she headed for the door.

The moment she walked into the sheriff's office Arlene knew it was a mistake.

"Arlene," Sheriff Carter Jackson said as he got to his feet. He didn't look happy to see her. But then, who could blame him given the other times she'd come in raging in defense of her children over whatever trouble they'd gotten into?

"It's Charlotte," she said, hating that her voice broke. She always tried so hard to be strong, believing a woman alone had to be strong or the world would crush her in an instant. "She's missing."

"Missing," he repeated, then motioned to the chair opposite his desk as he dropped back into his. "When was the last time you saw her?"

Arlene took the chair but teetered on the edge, too nervous to relax. She hated being forced to come here.

"Yesterday afternoon, when she left for her doctor's appointment. She didn't come home last night and she never made her doctor's appointment. I just stopped by the doctor's house. No one has seen her."

He leaned back in his chair and rubbed his jaw as he studied her. "Is it possible she's run away?"

"No. I mean, I can't imagine. She's eight months pregnant."

He nodded. "Maybe she left with the baby's father."

Arlene felt sick. "I think he's married."

The sheriff picked up his pen and tapped it on a stack of papers on his desk. "You realize I can't file a missing-persons report until she's been gone for at least twenty-four hours, but I'll tell the deputies to keep an eye out for her."

"I'm afraid something has happened to her."

"I can understand your concern."

"Can you?" She hated the edge to her voice.

"I'll admit, Arlene, that I can't help but be skeptical. It isn't like we haven't been here before."

She rose. "Well, thank you for your time," she said, turning and stiffening her back, head high, as she headed for the door.

"Keep me apprised of the situation," he called after her. "I'm sure you'll hear from her soon."

As she left, fighting tears of frustration, she passed Eve Bailey coming in. She hadn't seen her neighbor for a while and was surprised how happy Eve looked, then recalled that Eve and the sheriff were to be married in the coming week.

Arlene nodded at Eve as they passed, not trusting her voice. She'd always wanted that for her daughters. A handsome, eligible man. A wedding where everyone in the county came to celebrate. A white wedding dress and the mother-daughter talk.

She'd wanted that desperately because she'd never had it.

She fought the tears all the way to her pickup. What had she done wrong? At the rate things were going, she'd never have to worry about buying a mother-of-the-bride dress or fussing over last-minute details with the caterer.

* * *

Eve Bailey wasn't getting cold feet. She was marrying the man she loved—had loved since she was a girl.

But now that the Fourth of July was coming up so quickly, she was anxious. She wanted this wedding to be perfect.

Her mother, with her new husband Loren Jackson, would be flying in. Her father, Chester Bailey, would be giving her away. He would be attending the wedding with his girlfriend Susie.

How did other families handle all this extended-family stuff? She just hoped there wouldn't be any trouble. But that wasn't what bothered her. Here she was with all this extra family and she wasn't related by blood to any of them except for her twin, Bridger Duvall.

She had hoped by the time she married Sheriff Carter Jackson that she would know who she was. For years she'd yearned for someone who looked like her. Bridger had her coloring, but it wasn't like being able to look at your mother and father and see yourself.

She had tried to accept that she would never have that because of the circumstances of her adoption. But still she wondered what her birth mother was like. Was she even still alive? On her wedding day, Eve would have loved to have her "other" family in the pews as well as her adopted family.

Unfortunately she and her adoptive mother had never been close. Eve blamed herself. She knew she had been a difficult child. From early on she'd known Lila wasn't her "real" mother even though Lila had sworn differently. It didn't seem to matter that Lila loved her and considered Eve her own.

Eve hoped to make up for that somehow. But looking

for her birth mother had only made the chasm between her and Lila grow wider—and brought light to the illegal adoption ring.

"Is everything all right?" Carter asked as she stopped in his office doorway, hands on her slim hips, dressed in Western attire with a straw hat pulled low over her long dark hair.

"Yes. No. I think so."

He laughed and came around his desk to take her in his arms. "Just a little longer," he whispered against her ear.

She nodded, sick of thinking about nothing but the wedding. "Was that Arlene Evans I just saw leaving? She looked different somehow."

"Charlotte seems to be missing," he said as he motioned Eve into a chair and took one opposite her.

"The girl is about to have a baby any day, isn't she?"

He nodded.

"Poor Arlene, those kids have put her through hell," Eve said. "What if our kids turn out like that?"

"I'll lock them up down here in the cells until they straighten up."

Her eyes widened even though she knew he was kidding. "Seriously, there could be some bad gene in Bridger's and my blood that we don't know about."

Carter's face softened. "There is no bad gene. Look how well both of you turned out."

"Right." But Eve couldn't help but worry. Soon they would be having children. The sooner, the better, since she was now thirty-four. At least their kids would be able to look at their parents and know who they were, even though their mother still probably wouldn't have a clue who she was or where she'd come from.

"I'm okay," she said, seeing the worry in her soon-to-be

husband's face. "Really. It's just the wedding and every-thing." She reached across to squeeze his hand.

She had one constant she could hang on to: she knew she belonged with Sheriff Carter Jackson. Now, if they could just get through the wedding without anything like sheriff business keeping him from the altar...

As Arlene climbed behind the wheel of her pickup, she didn't blame Sheriff Carter Jackson for being skeptical about Charlotte's disappearing act. Arlene herself couldn't help but believe he might be right.

She blamed herself. She'd failed miserably as a mother. It was the only explanation for the way her three had turned out. And even now she had no idea what she'd done wrong. Floyd had always been too busy farming—until recently, when he'd bailed out completely.

Drying her tears, she pulled herself together as she drove home. She had to believe that Charlotte would come back and that that innocent little baby was all right.

"Arlene?" Hank's voice sounded like heaven when he answered the phone. "Any news on your daughter?"

She swallowed the lump in her throat and turned her back to Bo, who was sprawled on the couch, watching tele-vision. "She never went to her doctor's appointment yes-terday, and I still haven't heard a word. I'm worried sick."

"I'll come right out and help you look for her."

She glanced over her shoulder at Bo. "I don't think that's a good idea."

"Arlene, I want to help."

She'd hoped to put this off. She took the phone outside to the porch and closed the door firmly behind her.

"The truth is, I haven't been honest with you about my family." The tears that burned her eyes surprised her. She hadn't cried for years, and now all of a sudden she was a waterworks. "I've made a horrible mess of my life. Of my children's lives. I have one daughter in a mental institution, another one pregnant and a son—" Her voice broke and she couldn't continue.

"I haven't told you about my family either," Hank said. "I've made my share of mistakes, as well, Arlene. You know I told you I was widowed? It's true. My wife and I never divorced but we hadn't lived together for years. I'm walking out the door now. I can be at your place in fifteen minutes. Just give me the directions. We'll find your daughter."

Arlene cupped her hand over her mouth for a moment to keep from sobbing, her relief overwhelming her. She'd been handling things on her own for so many years, just the thought of someone wanting to help her… When there were problems, Floyd had always left it up to her to take care of them, blaming her no matter what the trouble was or the outcome.

"You need to drive south toward Old Town," she finally managed to say.

"I'll be right there."

Chapter 3

Hank drove down the narrow dirt road, flying over the small rises, dropping down to creek bottoms and cattle crossings.

He hadn't seen another vehicle since he'd left White-horse. Nor was there a house or fence in sight. The land rolled in waves of green grasses toward the badlands of the Missouri Breaks.

Of all the places he'd been in the world, none seemed as desolate as this right now. He'd heard this called one of the loneliest places in America. One hundred and fifty miles of country with only a few roads, none of them passable when wet, scores of townships without a town or even a house and, ripping a deep, twisted canyon through it all was the Missouri River, where the badlands rose up from the canyon floor in pre-glacial cliffs.

This country of purple-shadowed coulees filled with stands of scrub pine, spruce and cedar was what had brought him here. The river bottom was cloaked in thick stands of cottonwoods that reached for the big sky, and the prairie let him see for miles.

Montana was said to have a population density of six people per square mile. Out here that number dropped to zero-point-three people.

He had yearned for isolation. For open spaces. For freedom. Here in this part of Montana, one of the last lawless places, he had found it.

Had he blinked, he would have missed Old Town Whitehorse. A weathered sign was barely visible in the tall weeds beside the road. Whitehorse. Someone had added *Old Town* above the faded lettering in black paint.

Hank slowed as he passed a one-room schoolhouse, the Whitehorse Community Center, a few more old houses, the cemetery with its wrought-iron arch.

The railroad might have lured the first residents to the north, but a lot of Whitehorse apparently had remained right here.

He turned down the road as Arlene had instructed. Not far along he spotted the farmhouse. It was big and white with a wide screened-in porch. Behind it, a faded red barn with a horse weather vane that moved restlessly in the breeze.

He pulled in, parked. As he got out of his SUV, he saw Arlene waiting for him, on the front porch. Her face lit at the sight of him and he felt that pull inside him, his heart beating a little faster, the sky a little bluer.

What was it about this woman? She was far from beautiful. But there was a strength to her. An inner beauty that seemed to radiate from her face when he looked at her.

His grandmother would have said she came from good stock. A woman who'd never been pampered. A woman who he suspected had never been loved—at least not enough. And that, he thought, explained the vulnerability that she tried so hard to hide.

After the phone call from Cameron last night, he knew he shouldn't be here. He didn't want to bring his old life anywhere near this woman, who he suspected had enough problems without him becoming one of them.

But as he walked toward her and saw the determined set of her shoulders under the oversize shirt, the way she stood in boots and slim jeans that emphasized her height, there wasn't a chance in hell that he could turn his back on her.

He'd help her find her daughter, then he'd make some excuse not to see her anymore until he knew what the hell Cameron wanted. A breach in security? That had nothing to do with him any longer. Even if his former enemies had learned who he was, he'd suspected long before he'd quit that all the bad guys knew the other bad guys. That's why he hadn't returned the call. He didn't want any more to do with that spook stuff.

"I shouldn't have called you," Arlene said, coming down the porch steps toward him. "I'm sure this is just Charlotte being Charlotte. I don't want you bothered with it. She likes to worry me."

He smiled ruefully, thinking of his own daughter. "Kids do that."

"Really, I shouldn't have involved you in this," she said nervously.

"Arlene, I want to help. I wouldn't have offered if I didn't."

Tears welled in her eyes. She made a swipe at them. "I made some lemonade."

He didn't need any lemonade, but he had a feeling she needed to keep busy. "Lemonade sounds wonderful."

She glanced toward the house. "My son is home."

"I look forward to meeting him."

Her skeptical glance almost made him laugh as she angled back up onto the porch to open the front door.

He followed her inside. The place was immaculate right

down to the plastic covers on the couch and chairs. The floors looked freshly scrubbed, and there wasn't even a dust mote in the air.

The only thing out of place was the young man sprawled on the couch watching TV. He frowned when he saw Hank but didn't move.

"Bo, this is Hank Monroe," she said, biting off each word as she gave a jerk of her head that indicated her son should stand.

Bo ignored the gesture. "So you're dating my mom?" he asked, his tone incredulous as he gave Hank the once-over.

"Bo," Arlene snapped as she stepped into the living room to shut off the television.

Hank said nothing, his gaze locking with Bo's. Bo looked away first, and Hank followed Arlene into the kitchen. He heard the television come back on, but Bo turned it down, obviously not wanting to miss what was going on in the adjacent room.

"I did teach him manners. He just refuses to use them. I'm sorry," Arlene said as she poured Hank a glass of lemonade from a sweating glass pitcher.

"Don't be." He took a sip. The lemonade was wonderful and he said as much.

She beamed and offered him some gingersnaps she'd made. "They take first place at the fair every year." She glanced toward the living room, clearly anxious.

Hank motioned to the chair across from him. "Why don't you tell me when you last saw Charlotte."

Arlene pulled out the chair, brushing at nonexistent crumbs on the seat, and sat down. She took a deep breath and let it out slowly. "I saw her just before she left for her doctor's appointment. Her appointment was for three, but as usual she was running late. I was worried about her driving too fast on the road into Whitehorse. I offered to take her, but…" Her voice broke.

"You said you talked to the doctor and she didn't make her appointment?"

Arlene nodded.

"Had she missed an appointment before?" he asked, pretty sure he already knew the answer.

"Yes, but she was getting so close to her due date I can't imagine her just blowing this one off."

"Okay. There is only one road into Whitehorse, right?"

Arlene's eyes widened as she shifted her gaze to the living room. Bo was caught watching them and instantly got a don't-look-at-me expression.

"Charlotte wouldn't have taken the shortcut would she?" Arlene asked her son.

"Why do you keep asking me what Charlotte would do?" Bo demanded, raising his voice. "I have no idea. It's not like we ever talk. You should know that."

"I should know a lot of things," Arlene snapped.

Bo shot to his feet, angrily snapped off the television and stalked down the hallway. A door slammed, and a few moments later Hank heard a stereo come on.

"Can you show me this shortcut?" Hank said, getting to his feet.

She glanced down the hallway for a moment, and he could see how badly she wanted to go down there and yell at her son. Slowly her gaze came back to him and she rose from her chair as if she was an old woman. Her children were killing her, he thought as they went outside to his vehicle.

"What was Charlotte driving?" he asked.

"A small, dark blue Chevy. I can't remember what year. It's an older-model sedan."

He nodded. "And what was she wearing?"

Arlene shook her head. "I don't remember exactly. She's so big and she refuses to wear maternity clothes, so whatever she had on was stretched over her stomach."

"I think that's the style now."

Arlene looked mystified by that.

"What about the baby's father?" he asked. "Is it possible she's with him?"

"I doubt it. She wouldn't tell me who the man is, but from what I could gather he's involved with someone else. I'm not even sure he knows about the baby."

Hank took that in, wondering how the man couldn't know in a town the size of Whitehorse. From what little time he'd lived in the county he'd discovered there were no secrets. Everyone seemed to know his name even though he spent little time in town and had met only a few people.

"I tried her cell phone," Arlene was saying. "It goes straight to voice mail. I left a message...."

"Maybe you should call the sheriff," he suggested as they drove out of town.

"No." She softened her expression and her words as she continued. "I already spoke to the sheriff. He can't file a missing-persons report yet. The thing is, Charlotte has had some problems with the law. The sheriff thinks this is just one of her stunts—and, you know, he's probably right."

The shortcut was narrow, with deep barrow pits on each side—much like the main road to Old Town Whitehorse.

But the road was closer to the Evanses' farmhouse, and since Hank hadn't seen Charlotte's car on his way to Arlene's, this would be the next place to check.

He found himself taking in the land that ran toward

the Missouri Breaks, fascinated this untamed country was right out Arlene's back door. Who couldn't get lost in this?

"I'm sure Charlotte probably just stayed in town," Arlene said, drumming her fingers on the armrest. "It's just that I can't imagine who she might have stayed with." When she looked at him, he saw the pain.

He realized he had never known the names of his daughter's friends. There'd been a stream of them in and out of the house over the years, but he'd never been home enough to keep track of them.

His daughter had grown up without him being around. He'd told himself that she was fine, Bitsy was doing a great job raising her. That he wasn't needed. His job was to provide for his family. Only now could he admit what bull that had been.

"What was your husband like?" he asked.

"Absent," she said and craned her neck to look out as the road dipped down to a creek crowded with thick stands of chokecherries and dogwood. "Wait. Back up. I think I saw something."

He stopped the SUV and reversed back up the hill.

"There!" she cried.

He pulled over to the edge of the road as best he could although it wasn't wide enough for another car to pass and put on the emergency flashers even though he doubted any other cars would be coming along. Arlene was already out of the car and running to the edge of the road.

He joined her as she pointed down the slope and saw the patch of blue through the dense, tall brush along the creek.

Closer, he could see the tracks in the soft earth where a car had gone off, some of the sagebrush limbs broken or uprooted.

"Oh, God," Arlene said beside him. She took a step toward the ravine, but he stopped her.

"Stay here. I'll go check."

Arlene looked stricken. "If she went off the road... The baby—"

"Let's not jump to conclusions before we know if that's even her car down there, okay?"

She nodded, although they both knew it had to be.

He walked down the road to a spot where the slope wasn't so steep and worked his way down to where he'd seen the patch of blue from above.

The chokecherries and dogwood were thick and hard to navigate, but he hadn't gone far when he caught the glint of a chrome bumper.

Forcing his way closer, he glanced into the rear window. The car was covered in dust but he could see that there was no one in the backseat.

Working his way along the passenger side of the car, he covered his hand with the tail of his shirt to open the door. If this was a crime scene, he didn't want to destroy any more evidence than necessary.

The door opened and he peered in. No eight-months-pregnant woman inside. The keys were in the ignition, he noted. The car appeared to be in Neutral.

He glanced around. No sign of a struggle. No blood. No indication anything had been taken, since there were a couple dollars in change in the drink holder and the glove box was still closed.

He glanced at the driver-side door. It was closed, a dense wall of brush against it—just as there had been against the passenger-side door. Just to be sure the car was Charlotte's, he checked the registration in the glove box.

Then, reaching across, he pulled on the trunk lever. The lid groaned open.

Closing the door, he straightened and moved to the rear of the car. He was relieved to find the trunk empty except for the usual junk most people carried there.

He closed the lid, careful not to leave his prints.

"Hank?" Arlene called down, sounding scared.

"She's not here," he called back. "I'll be right up." He climbed out of the ravine to find her standing on the road where he'd left her. She'd worn a path in the dirt, though, where she had paced.

"It's her car, isn't it?"

He nodded. "But she wasn't in it when the car went off the road."

She didn't seem to hear him. "Oh, my God, she could be out there anywhere, wandering around, maybe having her baby."

"Arlene." He touched her arm. "She *wasn't* in the car when it went off the road."

She stared at him. *"What?"*

"Come here." He walked her over to the spot where the car tracks left the road. "See. Someone walked around here, then walked to the edge of the road. See how deep the footprints are?"

"What are you saying?"

"The car was pushed off the road. The keys were in it and the car was in Neutral."

"Why would Charlotte do that?"

"The prints would indicate the size and shape of a woman's shoe."

Arlene met his gaze. "How do you know so much about this kind of stuff?"

"I like murder mysteries," he said truthfully.

She looked sickened as she glanced back down into the ravine. "She's run off, hasn't she?"

"It would appear that way. Her purse isn't in the car. There was no sign of a struggle. Did she take a suitcase or an overnight bag when she left for her doctor's appointment?"

Arlene shook her head. "I don't know. She could have put one in the car the night before."

"We'll know more once we get the car out of the ravine. Who should I call?" He pulled out his cell phone but quickly realized he couldn't get any coverage out here. "I'll call from town."

She nodded and gave him a name of a tow truck operator. "Thank you."

He wished there was something he could say to relieve her worry. "She isn't alone. Someone met her here." He pointed to another set of tire tracks on the opposite side of the road.

"I can't imagine who it could have been." She frowned as if she remembered something.

"What?"

"Just that I've seen a car I didn't recognize drive by the house numerous times over the past few months," she said. "A silver SUV."

"Did you happen to notice the license plate?"

She shook her head. "I didn't pay much attention to it. I wouldn't have noticed it at all except that we get so little traffic out our way."

"You didn't see the driver?"

"No. I can't be sure if it was a man or a woman."

"You don't know of anyone who drives a car like it?" he asked.

She shook her head again. "I wish I was of more help."

"Don't worry. She'll turn up."

"Only if she wants to be found. You don't know Charlotte."

Hank smiled and put his arm around Arlene as he walked her back to his car. "Charlotte doesn't know me."

Hank waited until the tow truck operator unhooked Charlotte's car in the front yard of the farmhouse before opening the car.

Arlene came out of the house and stood on the porch, watching.

Hank slid behind the wheel, careful not to touch anything. He heard Arlene come up to the side of the car.

"You still aren't convinced she ran away," Arlene said.

"Better to be safe than sorry," he said as he tilted his head to study the steering wheel. "How tall did you say your daughter was?"

"Five-four."

"Someone taller drove her car last," he said. "She work on her own car?"

Arlene's laugh had an edge to it. "And ruin her nails?"

He sniffed the steering wheel, then got out and checked the hood latch.

"What is it?" she asked.

"Engine grease on the steering wheel. Whoever drove the car had it on their hands, but it apparently didn't come from this car."

"So it came from the other car," Bo said, coming out of the house to join them. "You already suspected she met someone out there and rode with them. So what's the big deal about the engine grease?"

"Nothing maybe," Hank said. "I guess it would depend on who picked her up out there."

"Seems pretty clear to me," Bo said. "No one uses that shortcut, so it couldn't have been just someone passing by. Charlotte had obviously set it up. No one would see her get into the other car. Seems to me she was buying time by ditching hers." He looked at his mother as if she was the reason Charlotte had run away.

"That's one theory," Hank admitted. "So who *did* pick her up?"

"Don't look at me," Bo said. "I don't know anything about it." He turned to head back into the house.

"But you know who fathered her baby," Hank said to the young man's retreating back.

It was only a slight movement of the shoulders, a telltale sign. "What does it matter anyway? The guy obviously doesn't want anything to do with her."

Arlene looked as if she wanted to trail after her son. "Bo doesn't know anything. He's just talking."

Bo *knew* something. And if he knew, then Hank figured it wouldn't be that hard to find out. There was nothing Hank loved more than a challenge. "I'll see if I can find anything out."

"I've tried for months without any luck."

"Don't worry," he said, giving her a reassuring smile. "I have a way with people."

Arlene returned his smile, thinking he certainly did. She'd tried for months to find out who the father of the baby was without any luck at all. "I'm not sure it's going to do any good, though. If she's run off with him..."

"Then at least you'll know who she's with."

"Why are you doing this?" she had to ask.

Hank moved to her and took both of her hands in his. "Because I like you and you need help."

She tried to pull away, hating the fact that she needed anyone's help but maybe especially Hank's. That wasn't the relationship she wanted with him. "I don't want you dragged into my problems."

"Arlene, this doesn't change how I feel about you."

How could it not? And how *did* he feel about her? "I'm a terrible mother."

He laughed. "No, you're not."

"Oh, you have no idea. The mistakes I've made…"

"Believe me, my mistakes are legendary."

"I wish I could do it over," she said with heat. "I would do things so differently."

He chuckled. "Wouldn't we all." He let go of her hands to step to the car. She watched him lock it. "For the time being, don't drive the car. Let me see what I can find out."

She nodded numbly. She couldn't help being worried about Charlotte and the baby. "I didn't realize how much I wanted to be there when my first grandbaby was born. I had wanted Charlotte to put the baby up for adoption. But still I thought I could be there for my daughter and at least see the baby…."

She turned away, not wanting him to see her cry. Hank's kindness had turned her into a fountain.

This wasn't the way she'd wanted things to be between them. She didn't want him to know this side of her. Not the woman with all this baggage. How could he even stand to look at her?

"Arlene," he said.

She turned to find him directly behind her.

He cupped her cheek. His thumb pad brushed the corner of her mouth. "Try not to worry," he said softly. "I'll see you tonight."

She looked into his eyes. He still wanted to go out with her tonight? She nodded numbly.

He smiled. "Leave it to me."

She watched him walk to his vehicle, still stunned not only that he'd come into her life, but also that he was still there.

Won't be for long.

Her mother's voice. But Arlene didn't argue with the sentiment. Wait until Hank learned about her daughter Violet.

Violet Evans peered out the hospital window, past the pathetic array of patients, to the fence that had become her prison.

Just a few more weeks.

It had been her mantra for months, and lately it hadn't been working—and that worried her more than she wanted to admit.

She'd been doing so well, pretending for months to be catatonic before miraculously coming out of it with no apparent memory of the bad things she'd done in the past. How many people could pull something like that off? Very few if any, she would wager.

She'd always known she was smart, but lately she'd come to realize she might be a genius.

Of course, she had to hide that fact from the doctors. Clearly they weren't half as intelligent as she was, since they had no idea what she was up to.

Just a few more weeks.

And she would be free.

So why couldn't she relax and just do what they were asking of her? Why did she feel as if her insides were starting to show through her skin?

The doctors had insisted she do an in-patient work program to prepare her for when she got out. Which meant she filed for hours at the nurses' station. She thought she would go crazy for sure if she had to do it much longer.

And then there were the nightmares. She'd never told anyone about them. These doctors would have a field day with even one of her dreams. She shuddered to think of what they would make of them. What she herself made of them if she let herself delve too deeply.

Just a few more weeks.

But it was getting harder and harder to remember that, and just the thought of never getting out of here—

She shoved that thought away and concentrated on revenge. But even the revenge she'd planned against her mother had lost some of its power.

Maybe worse than the nightmares was the voice she kept hearing in her head. She'd thought it was her mother's but lately she couldn't be sure it wasn't her grandmother's.

It was distracting and confusing, and she wasn't sure how much longer she could keep this up. The place was literally driving her crazy, making her question things.

Like her mother's culpability in all this.

She shook her head, trying to banish the confusion. Of course it was her mother's fault. Everything was always the mother's fault.

Chapter 4

Bo Evans disliked Hank Monroe even before he'd met the man. He would have disliked any man his mother dated. Not that he felt any loyalty to his father. Floyd Evans was a spineless bastard who'd abandoned them the moment there was trouble. Hell, Floyd Evans had abandoned them long before that.

"What did I tell you?"

He looked up to find his mother standing in front of him. She had the remote in her hand. He swore as she muted his show. "Tell me about what?"

"Getting a job."

He shook his head. It had just been a threat. At least he hoped that's all it had been. "If I got a job, I'd have to be in town all day. Maybe even have to work nights. You'd be here by yourself. You don't want that. You need me around."

His mother laughed and he realized this was a new reaction. "Nice try. I want you to find a job. And then I want you to find a place to live."

He stared at her as if he'd never seen her before. He suspected he hadn't. This was Hank Monroe's doing, the bastard. He'd put this into her head.

"This is about Hank, isn't it? You think he's going to always be around?" Bo scoffed at that. "Once he gets what he's after, he'll be gone. The guy's playing you. He's going to break your heart."

"Well, I've been played before and certainly had my heart broken by those closest to me, haven't I?" she said, shutting off the television. "You have until the end of the week."

"And then what?" he demanded. "You're not going to put me out on the street. Not your favorite son."

To his surprise, she said nothing. Instead she walked over to the garbage can and dropped the remote into it.

Bo told himself she was bluffing, that she was just upset about Charlotte. Once Charlotte was back here and the baby was born, things would get back to normal. Well, as normal as life here had ever been.

"What's the point of throwing away the remote?" he called after her as she headed for her bedroom down the hall.

"Don't worry, you won't need it," she said, stopping to look back at him. "You'll be at work. Anyway, I've had the cable service canceled. Out here we might be able to get *one* of the local stations clear enough for you to watch. So you won't need the remote, because what would be the point of changing the station?" Without another word, she turned and continued to her bedroom, closing the door behind her.

Bo swore and kicked the coffee table over. The one thing he didn't want was anything to change. He was happy with his life. He slept till noon most days, hung out either watching television or listening to music until it was time to go out with his friends.

He'd had jobs before, but his mother had always been all right when he'd quit them and offered to help her. The only thing that had changed that he could see was Hank. Who was this guy anyway?

The good news was that Hank wouldn't be around long, Bo told himself. Not once he got to know Arlene. But Bo feared he couldn't wait that long. He was going to have to take matters into his own hands.

Either he had to find Charlotte and get her butt back here, or he was going to have to sabotage this little romance between his mother and Hank Monroe.

He called his friend Cody, since his car was in the shop and his mother had refused to let him drive hers. "Pick me up tonight. My mom has a date and there's something we need to do. Bring a crowbar. And if you have a ski mask, bring that, too."

Arlene was getting ready for her date with Hank when the phone rang. She hurriedly reached for it, praying it was Charlotte.

The voice on the other end of the line was authoritative, and she knew from experience whoever was calling was going to give her bad news.

"Is it Charlotte?" she cried, just wanting to get the worst over with.

"I beg your pardon? This is Dr. Ray Hamilton calling from the state hospital in regard to your daughter Violet."

Violet? Had she been released? Was she on her way here? Arlene glanced toward the dark windows and thought Bo was right. She didn't want to be here alone.

"Is she…?" Arlene couldn't form the words.

"We are required by law to let you know that Violet will be leaving our facility in a few weeks."

"Leaving for where?"

"She is being released on her own since she is an adult, Mrs. Evans. I'm sure you were told about your daughter's medical breakthrough."

"No. You're wrong. You don't know Violet. If you let her out—"

"I'm sorry you feel that way, but I'm afraid the evaluation of her mental health isn't up to you. We are just required to let you know. Good day, Mrs. Evans."

"No," Arlene said into the phone even though she knew the doctor had hung up.

Violet was getting out.

She stood in her bedroom too stunned to move. Hadn't she known that her life had been going too well? The business? And Hank?

Hank. She felt her heart sink. For just a few hours she'd let herself believe she could be happy.

Not that she'd ever thought she deserved it.

She reached for the phone and dialed Hank's number, telling herself it was for the best. Better to end it before it was started. Better to end it before he did.

She glanced toward the chair where her mother had sat for years.

You're right, Mother. It's all my fault. You told me I would end up alone. You were right. That must make you very happy.

She made a swipe at her tears. Hank's line was busy. She'd have to try again in a few minutes.

Facing the mirror, she straightened her shoulders and lifted her chin. She would face this alone. It wasn't as if she hadn't been here before.

"Who is this guy anyway?" Cody asked as he and Bo drove into Hank Monroe's ranch.

"We're about to find out." Bo had waited until he'd seen Hank drive out before he'd instructed Cody to drive down the hill to the huge ranch house. No one should live in such a large house. Especially some dude living by himself, Bo thought angrily.

"You sure he doesn't have someone working for him?" Cody asked, sounding nervous.

"I asked around," Bo said. "Hank has a bunch of land, but the only animals on the place are a couple of horses. He has Claudia Nicholson come out twice a week and clean. There's no security system."

Cody pulled up in front of the house, cut the engine and sat for a moment, staring at the house. "Is the guy crazy?"

"Apparently so, since he's dating my mother," Bo quipped. "Come on." He opened his door and climbed out.

"What exactly are we looking for?" Cody asked.

"Whatever we can find." Something incriminating. So he could tell his mother what he suspected she already suspected: Hank Monroe *was* too good to be true. Bo was counting on it as he picked up a rock to bust a window.

"This guy *is* a fool," Cody said as he tried the front door and it swung open. "The door wasn't even locked." His friend made a face as Bo dropped the rock. "I don't like this. Seems a little too easy, you know?"

Bo knew. "The guy is clueless. Don't worry about it." He shoved past Cody and entered the cool, dim, massive living room. Hank Monroe apparently had money. But how had he made it?

"Where do we start?" Cody asked as they took in the place. "Nice. Maybe it wouldn't be so bad if he married your mother."

"He's not going to marry her," Bo snapped. "No one marries someone like her unless he has to." He'd heard how she'd come to marry Floyd Evans; he'd overheard his grandmother Evans talking about it. Floyd Evans wouldn't have married her except that she'd been pregnant with Violet.

"Still, what does it hurt having a guy like this dating your mother?"

Bo ignored the question. He didn't like talking about his mother's love life. He couldn't imagine what Hank saw in her. The guy had to be up to something.

Cody followed him down the hallway.

"You check the bedroom," Bo ordered. "Look for drugs or anything weird." He stepped into what was obviously a home office and went straight to the file cabinet first. He had no idea what he was looking for, but he didn't find anything interesting and turned to the computer.

The computer appeared to be brand-new, state-of-the-art, and it didn't have anything on it except the software it had come with.

Discouraged, he glanced around the room, his gaze falling on the answering machine—and the flashing red light.

He reached over and hit the play button.

Hank felt his cell phone vibrate when he was not two miles from the ranch. While he didn't lock the doors at the ranch, he did have a security system of sorts: when a door was opened, he got a call on his cell. And since this wasn't the day that Claudia Nicholson cleaned, he turned around and sped back toward the ranch.

He took the back way in and, as he came over a hill, met with a road full of cattle and two cowboys on horses herding the slow-moving cows to another pasture.

That cost him valuable time.

He parked just over the hill from the house and took out the gun he kept taped on the underside of the SUV seat.

Crickets chirped in the tall green grass as he made his way toward the house. The evening breeze stirred the stand of ponderosas, sending the scent of pine wafting through the warm air. In the distance, the Little Rockies range slowly turned from violet to black against the midnight-blue sky.

Hank could feel the air grow heavy around him, the heft of the gun too familiar in his hand. He'd been here before, too many times, and had thought he'd put this part of his life behind him.

Right. That's why you keep guns stashed in places easy to get to should you need them.

The back door was unlocked. He turned the knob without making a sound and stepped in. The air inside felt cool and smelled of the orange-scented cleaner Claudia used.

The back door opened into the laundry room. He stepped from it to the doorway to the kitchen. Empty.

He moved quickly through the large commercial kitchen, into the open living area with its huge fireplace and assorted leather furniture. The ranch house had come furnished. He had yet to sit in every chair.

Shoving away the thought of how ridiculous that was, he glanced down the hallway, pretty sure whoever had been here was gone.

But he gripped the gun as he moved down the hallway, not willing to take the chance he was wrong. He wasn't a man who took chances. That's how he'd managed to live this long.

At his office, he looked in and saw that his chair had been moved and one of the file cabinets wasn't closed all the way.

As he moved down the hallway, he noted that there were tracks in the thick, recently vacuumed carpet. He checked each room, which took him some time. Another problem with having a house this size.

Finding nothing, he returned to the office. What had the intruder been looking for?

Nothing appeared to be missing. Not his expensive stereo equipment, wide-screen televisions or artwork. But then, his intruders—from the tracks in the thick carpet, there had been two of them—hadn't had enough time to do much damage.

All of it could have been replaced. None of it had any sentimental value. He liked it that way. He'd already lost the important things in his life.

He checked the file cabinet first. Nothing missing. He didn't bother with the computer, since there was nothing on it to steal.

Sitting down at his desk, he considered who might have been here. He glanced at the answering machine. No messages.

The phone rang, startling him. He let the machine pick up.

"Hank?" Arlene's voice, worry in her tone. "I'm not going to be able to make our date tonight. I'm sorry. I… Something's come up."

He started to reach for the phone, but she hung up too quickly. He was worrying that she'd heard something about Charlotte. He hit rewind to play her message again to gauge how much worry he'd heard.

The machine seemed to rewind a little too long, and then he realized why. There'd been another new message.

"Hank. It's Cameron. Call me. Something has come up of grave importance. It concerns you, I'm afraid, and could be dire."

There was a pause, then Arlene's message. The answering machine shut off, throwing the room into a dense silence that was almost palpable.

Hank swore. Cam wasn't leaving his messages in code any longer. What the hell had happened that Cam would be calling? Grave importance? Something concerning him that could be dire?

Hank swore again. They weren't going to draw him back in. He didn't care what the problem was. He was done with that life.

As he reached over to erase the tape, he realized that whoever had been in the house had played the message. That's why the light hadn't been flashing. His intruders had listened to Cam's message.

"That was too close, man," Cody said as they sped down the road. "If you hadn't looked out the back way and seen him coming… He had a *gun*."

"Yeah, what was that about?" Bo was still panting. They'd pushed Cody's car out of the drive so Hank couldn't hear them start up the engine and come hauling ass after them. "What's the guy doing with a gun?"

Cody shot him a look. "Who cares? He's dangerous. And if he finds out we were in his house—"

"He won't," Bo snapped, not sure of that at all. How had the dude known in the first place? And who was this guy anyway? he thought, remembering what he'd heard on the answering machine. And what kind of crap was Hank Monroe involved in?

Unfortunately Bo hadn't a clue. The house was expensive as all hell and impersonal, as if Hank Monroe wasn't staying long. He was hiding something, that was a given. The question was how to find out what.

"Let's stop by your place. I need to use your computer," Bo said.

"Tell me why I had to bring along a crowbar and a ski

mask so you could call up a porn site on my computer?"
Cody said belligerently. "I thought we were going to do
something fun?"

"I'm not after porn," Bo snapped. "I'm trying to find
out more about Hank Monroe. Look," he said, "after I'm
done, we'll go buy some beer and see if we can find those
girls we saw the other night. What do you say?"

Hank called Arlene from his cell. "Sorry, I'm running
a little late. They're moving cattle out by me."

"You didn't get my message?" she asked. "No, I guess
you'd already left."

"Did you hear from Charlotte?" he asked, hoping that's
all it had been: Charlotte had come home and Arlene
needed to stay with her daughter tonight.

"No, nothing."

"Are you all right?" he asked.

"Sure. That is, I'll be fine."

He didn't doubt that. She was strong. She wouldn't have
gotten this far if she wasn't. From the moment he'd met her
he'd known her life had been hell. Maybe that was why
he'd asked her out.

He'd seen himself in her.

"You can tell me what's happened when I pick you up,"
he said. "Get dressed. I made reservations for the play at
the theater in Fort Peck. I haven't been there yet, but I hear
the building is something to see and the performances are
wonderful."

"I don't think that's a good idea." Arlene hesitated. "I
got a call about my oldest daughter. I haven't told you about
Violet."

"You can tell me about her on the way."

"And ruin a perfectly good date?" Arlene said with a humorless laugh.

"Nothing could ruin our date. Trust me, you'd be surprised what it takes to shock me. Get dressed, wear something casual. I'm on my way."

Arlene hung up the phone, so touched by Hank's understanding and kindness that her eyes were swimming again in tears. She made an irritated swipe at them. She acted as if no one had ever been kind to her.

You don't deserve this.

Her mother again. So maybe it was true that she hadn't gotten a lot of compassion. The thought made her laugh. Her mother and compassion had never crossed paths.

But how *had* Arlene gotten so lucky to have Hank Monroe in her life? Even for a while?

He wants something from you. He'll hurt you just like all men.

Arlene turned on the radio to drown out her mother's voice and dressed quickly, not wanting to be late. As she dabbed on a little lip gloss, she caught her reflection in the mirror. For a moment she was taken aback. She didn't recognize the woman looking back at her.

There was color in her cheeks, and her eyes seemed to twinkle. She smiled at her reflection, almost embarrassed by what she saw—because she hadn't seen it in so long she had trouble even putting a name to it. Joy.

Instantly she turned from the mirror. How could she go on a date as if Charlotte wasn't missing and eight months pregnant? As if Violet wasn't getting out of the mental hospital and homicidal? As if Bo wasn't somewhere getting in trouble instead of looking for a job?

The phone rang, and for an instant her heart sank. It

would be Hank canceling. He would have had time to re-think their date. He would make some lame excuse.

She braced herself for the worst. It wasn't as if she hadn't been here before. "Hello?"

"It's me."

"Charlotte? Oh, my God, you have had me worried out of my mind. Where are you? Are you all right?"

"I'm fine. I just called to tell you that the father of my baby and I are going away to make a life for ourselves. Don't come looking for me. I'll write as soon as we get settled."

"The *baby?*" Arlene cried.

"It hasn't come yet. I had some false labor, but I'm fine. I'll call you when the baby comes."

"Charlotte, wait. I…" But the line had gone dead.

Arlene stood for a moment holding the phone. All her worry, and Charlotte was fine. She felt anger well inside her at her youngest daughter for scaring her so and waited for the relief to sink in as she hung up the phone.

Her children were no longer children. She'd protected them for years when she should have made them take re-sponsibility for their own actions. But she'd wanted so badly to be a good mother. A perfect mother. And she'd gotten it all wrong.

She'd become her mother.

There was a horrible thought.

She replayed Charlotte's words in her head, still waiting for the relief to wash over her. Charlotte was fine. And yet Arlene had no idea where she was or who she was with or when she would hear from her again. Nor would she get to see her first grandbaby born.

She straightened and met her gaze in the mirror again, determination burning in her eyes.

She didn't deserve a second chance, not with the mess she'd made of her life. But if Hank was giving her one, damned if she wasn't going to take it.

"Thank you for tonight," Arlene said when he parked in front of her house later that evening. "I had a wonderful time."

"My pleasure. I'm glad you heard from Charlotte. I still might try to find out who she left town with, if you don't mind."

"No, I appreciate it. But are you sure you want to do that?"

He laughed. "I've always been a big fan of mysteries. I can't stand it when I can't figure out the ending. I never cheat, though," he said quickly, making her smile. "But I am also seldom wrong about who did it."

"You would have made a good cop," she said. "You would have been the one who never gave up until he caught the bad guys."

She didn't know how close she'd come to the truth. Or maybe she did. Arlene was a lot sharper than he guessed people had ever given her credit for.

"That would have been me, all right." He'd always loved the chase. It had gotten into his blood—and cost him dearly. Cost him his family. And for a while he'd been afraid it would cost him his soul. He still wasn't sure it hadn't.

Leaning toward her, he kissed her gently on the lips. It felt so good he drew her to him. She felt stiff in his arms at first. He took his time, kissing her slowly, gently, teasing her lips and the tip of her tongue with his own.

He felt her shock the first time his tongue ran over the tip of her own. A soft chuckle emanated from him. A pleased chuckle as he drew her even closer.

He could feel her pulse pounding as he cupped her jaw, his thumb caressing her skin. She sighed against his lips.

Pulling back to look into her eyes, he could see that her cheeks were flushed with pleasure, her eyes bright. He smiled at her, wanting to brush his fingers along her collarbone to unhook the top button of her shirt and reveal the swell of her full breasts.

He wanted to make love to her, slowly and tenderly. To arouse what he sensed in her was a passion that she kept tightly reined in.

"I should get in the house," she said, sounding out of breath.

He nodded as he started to get out to walk her to the door.

"No, please," she said, opening her door and quickly slipping out. She bent to look in at him. "Thank you again. Good night."

"Good night." He sighed as she hurriedly closed the door and strode up the steps to disappear inside the dark house. Apparently Bo wasn't home.

Hank hesitated a moment, not liking the idea of her being out here all alone. Then he reminded himself that Arlene was probably as capable as anyone of surviving in this part of the country. It wasn't as if her children had ever been there for her.

He recalled what she'd told him about Violet, her oldest.

"I didn't know what to do," Arlene had said in tears. "I wanted to get her help when I'd seen that something was wrong with her when she was just a girl. But my mother, my mother-in-law and Floyd forbade it. I should have done it anyway. I should—"

Hank had touched her lips with a finger. "You have to

stop blaming yourself. She's getting the help she needs now at the state mental hospital, right?"

Arlene had looked over at him and he'd seen the fear in her eyes. "She has everyone fooled. They're going to let her out, and I'm just terrified of what she'll do."

As he drove away now, he feared Arlene had reason to be afraid.

Chapter 5

The next morning Hank asked himself what he was doing as he parked in front of the Cut and Curl beauty shop where Charlotte Evans had worked.

Charlotte had called her mother and said she was with the father of her baby and making a new life somewhere else. So why didn't he just let it go?

Because of Arlene. She should have been relieved, but he'd known that something had been bothering her last night and, finally, on the way home he'd asked her what it was.

"Don't you realize just the thought of Violet getting out of the mental hospital is enough to have me worried?" she'd asked. "She hates me, blames me for everything. Not that I'm *not* to blame."

"You didn't make Violet into an attempted murderer," he'd assured her. "A lot of kids grow up in horrible environments where they don't get enough food and are beaten every day and they don't become killers. You aren't responsible for what Violet did."

"She tried to kill me. Her own mother." Arlene's voice had broken. "She even got her brother and sister involved."

He'd reached over and taken her hand. "They failed. That should tell you something."

Arlene had laughed and made a swipe at her tears. "That my children fail at everything? No," she'd said, sobering, "*I* failed *them*."

He'd chuckled at that. "Don't you think a lot of parents feel that way? My daughter won't even talk to me. She hates me—and rightfully so. I wasn't there for her. I was busy with my job, but I told myself that she was better off being raised by her mother than me."

"I'm sorry."

"It's my own fault. We all make choices. At the time we think they're the best ones. It isn't until later, hindsight being twenty-twenty, that we wish we'd done it differently."

Arlene had nodded. "There are no second chances."

"I'm not so sure about that." He'd glanced over at her, her face silhouetted against the night prairie. The Larb Hills had been a deep purple as they paralleled Highway 2. The sky overhead had been a dense dark canopy except for the twinkling lights of a zillion stars. Hank had never seen so many stars.

"It isn't just Violet," Arlene had said after a few moments. "It's Charlotte. She sounded so...matter-of-fact on the phone. So distant."

That, Hank realized now, was what had his instincts telling him that something was wrong. If the girl really had run off with the father of her baby, wouldn't she be triumphant? Especially if the man was married. It would mean she'd won him. And she'd be gloating, knowing all of this would hurt her mother. Relieving her mother's mind was the last thing Charlotte Evans would do, from what he could gather.

He hesitated before getting out of the SUV. What he was about to do was more than illegal, impersonating an FBI agent.

And, possibly worse, he would call attention to himself. Enough people in town wondered who he was, what he did for a living and why he'd picked Whitehorse, Montana. He didn't need any more rumors circulating.

Once he went into the beauty shop and impersonated an FBI agent, word would get out. Word might even get back to the agency where he'd really worked, and that was the last thing he needed, since Cameron was already trying to get in touch with him. He hadn't returned the calls, telling himself Cam would do anything to draw him back in.

But wasn't what he was doing right now just as bad?

He could just imagine what Bitsy would have to say. *You just can't help yourself, can you?*

He thought of the times he'd promised her he was going to get out of the business, spend more time at home.

While he doubted Bitsy had really believed it, he told himself he'd meant it at the time. Maybe he'd been lying to himself about that—just as he had everything else.

He'd been good at what he did. So was it any surprise a part of him missed it? Maybe just a little?

The bell over the door jangled as he stepped inside. All heads turned. A middle-aged stylist was giving an elderly woman a perm. A twentysomething was bent over another twentysomething's hand, giving her a manicure. All except the elderly woman getting her hair done wore pale pink shop smocks indicating they worked there, including the teenager sitting behind a small desk, doodling on a scratch pad. Business was obviously slow.

He saw at once that everyone except the elderly woman knew who he was. Having always lived in a big city, this small-town lack of anonymity continued to amaze him. How could there ever be any secrets?

"Hello," he said as he entered the room. The smell of

perm solution was strong, but not as strong as the nail products.

"If you're looking for a haircut—" the middle-aged woman began.

"Just information," he said, garnering everyone's attention again as he pulled what could have been law-enforcement credentials from his wallet. What he flashed them, was, in fact a medical insurance card.

He'd discovered a long time ago that attitude was the key. "I'm trying to find Charlotte Evans."

"What's she done?" the teenager asked, no longer doodling.

"Can you tell me the last time you saw her?" he asked, ignoring the teen and directing his questions to the older of the bunch. "I'm sorry, I didn't catch your name."

"Tamara Lawson. I own the place. But Charlotte doesn't work here anymore. She hasn't for months."

"But she worked here when she became pregnant," he said.

"That wasn't our fault," the teen said with a giggle.

Tamara shot her a look. He saw the resemblance between the two and guessed the teen must be her daughter.

"What's going on?" the elderly woman demanded loudly. He saw that her hearing aid was sitting on the counter.

"It's nothing to concern yourself with, Mabel," Tamara shouted back at the woman.

The dark-haired twentysomething getting her nails done laughed at what the teen had said.

Hank smiled. "But you knew about the pregnancy. And you are…?"

"Jana. Charlotte was barfing all the time. How could we not know about it?"

"She tell you who the father was?" Hank asked.

They all shared a look, and the manicurist went back to work on Jana's nails.

"She tell you something, miss?" he asked the young woman doing her coworker's nails.

"Linsey," she said.

"Charlotte got knocked up on purpose," the teen said, obviously hating being ignored. "At least that's what she told us."

"Sahara," her mother chastised.

"I wouldn't be asking if it wasn't important," Hank said. "Charlotte seems to have disappeared."

Jana made a disbelieving sound.

"Anything you tell me will be held in the strictest of confidence," he added.

"What does he want?" the elderly woman shouted.

"A haircut," Tamara shouted back as she finished Mabel's last curl and stuck her under the dryer.

"Do you know Charlotte?" Tamara asked him as she walked away from the client and the noisy dryer.

He shook his head. "She could be in trouble."

"She's always in trouble," Tamara said with a shake of her head.

It felt like old times. He waited a beat, then said quietly, "Tell me about the father of the baby."

"All we know is what she told us. It was some man she met one night at the café. She worked here and at the Northern Lights restaurant for a while. I got the impression he was a lot older and married."

"She said she put something in his drink," the teen interjected.

"She drugged him?" Hank asked, no surprise in his voice.

"She wanted a baby," the teen said.

"At least at that moment," Tamara said, seeming to have given up on shutting up the teen.

"Does the father know about the baby?" he asked.

Tamara shook her head. "I'm not even sure she knew his name."

"Do you know where he was staying?"

Silence. Then Sahara said, "She took him to the Shady Rest Motel." The teen looked indignant. "I know because Charlotte said he was so out of it she charged the room to his credit card."

Hank nodded. A credit card. Perfect. "And you say he was married?" he asked Linsey.

Clearly she didn't want to be the one to tell him anything. Had she and Charlotte been friends?

"He told Charlotte he was separated and getting a divorce, but I think that was just a line," Linsey finally confided.

Smart girl.

"She doesn't want the baby, you know," the teen said. "But she won't give it up for adoption because her mother wants her to."

Everyone shot the girl a look.

"Well, it's true," the teen said.

Arlene had never missed entering her baked goods in a county fair since the age of eleven. She loved to bake and prided herself on her pie crusts, her moist yet light-as-air cakes and her cookies, especially her gingersnaps.

For years she'd used baking as a way to relax. It was something she could do well—one of the few things.

That's why it surprised her the morning after her date with Hank that she didn't feel like baking.

"So how was your date?" Bo asked as he came into the kitchen.

"Fine. How is your job hunt going?" she asked.

"I thought you'd be baking by now. Where's your rejects?"

Her "rejects" were cookies that weren't quite perfect. She'd never realized before that Bo paid any attention to fair time. Apparently he did. For a while she'd had all her blue ribbons displayed in the living room. Since she met Hank, she'd moved them into her sewing room. Funny how she didn't feel the need to validate herself with blue ribbons with him.

"I don't think I'm going to enter after all this year," she said. "With Charlotte gone and—"

"I don't believe this," Bo snapped. "You're changing your whole life over a man."

"That's not true. Maybe it's just that I have enough blue ribbons. I don't need any more. I *know* I'm a good cook."

He stared at her. "You're going to let one of the Cavanaughs take your blue ribbons?"

Bo knew exactly what to say to get her worked up. She'd always been envious of the Cavanaughs. Pearl and her husband Titus were like royalty in Old Town Whitehorse. And their granddaughters, Laci and Laney, were princesses. Same with the Baileys. Eve, Faith and McKenna Bailey were beauties.

Since Arlene married Floyd Evans, she'd felt she'd needed to prove something to the elite families of Old Town.

Bo's words brought back that familiar insecurity. Maybe she *should* enter. She didn't want the whole county speculating on why she hadn't.

But as quickly as the feeling came, it passed. Was she

tired of trying to prove herself to people who had never accepted her anyway?

"Laci Cavanaugh is a great cook," she said. "I'll be interested to see what she enters. I'm sure she'll do well."

"You're starting to scare me," Bo mumbled as he left the room.

Arlene didn't even hear the blare of his stereo down the hall. She was thinking about last night at the play. And Hank.

Hank couldn't help worrying as he left the beauty shop. It had almost been too easy. Charlotte was young, indiscreet and, he suspected, liked to shock people. Her blatant disregard for social mores had apparently disavowed any loyalty her coworkers might have had for her.

Except Linsey, who had made an effort not to talk about Charlotte. She had one friend, anyway.

The ease of getting the information wasn't what bothered him. It was Charlotte sharing it with everyone. Being a suspicious person, Hank felt as if the girl had tried to sell her story a little too hard.

Had she just been trying to cover up the identity of the man who had really fathered her baby? A local man she'd now run off with?

Whoever he was, the man didn't live in Whitehorse or Hank suspected it would be all over town that he'd left. Unless no one knew yet that he'd left with Charlotte.

Still, Hank couldn't shed the feeling that something wasn't right. Charlotte wasn't the kind of young woman who felt the need to come up with an elaborate plan just so she could run away.

The car stashed in the ravine worried him. Why hide the car? She had no reason to think anyone would come after her, so she didn't need to buy time. She could have left the car parked in town somewhere. Or even left it beside the road. Why go to the trouble, eight months pregnant, of ditching her car that way?

The engine grease on the steering wheel also bothered him. He wondered if he could get a clear print. It was worth a try. He'd love to narrow down who'd been with Charlotte that day on the road.

But it meant calling on a few old friends. It wasn't like they didn't know where he was, he thought, reminded of Cam's calls. So why not see if he could track down this mystery man of Charlotte's?

By late afternoon, Hank had the name of the man Charlotte Evans had checked into the Shady Rest Motel with eight months before. But, Hank reminded himself, this might not even be the father of Charlotte's baby. There was more than a good chance the girl had lied to the women she'd worked with, for whatever reason.

He called Arlene. "I have a possible lead. According to her coworkers, Charlotte told them the man was from out of town."

"Her coworkers told you that? They wouldn't give me the time of day."

"I was very persuasive and they don't know me," he said. It also helped that he'd let them believe he was a lawman of some sort.

"The man lives in Billings, was just in town for a couple of nights and apparently met Charlotte at the restaurant where she was working," Hank said. "It seems Charlotte was determined to get pregnant and may have picked him because he was from out of town."

"Oh, my God," Arlene said. "Do you think Charlotte is with him?"

"Maybe, although I doubt it. He told her he was separated from his wife and getting a divorce, but more than likely he lied about that. But he could have heard from her." Hank wondered, though, what the man would have done if Charlotte had gone to him for help. Especially if he had later realized that she'd drugged him and set him up. Most men wouldn't have taken that well.

"The man's name is John Foster," Hank said. "I thought we might take a road trip and have a little talk with him."

The Fosters lived in a house on the rims—a unique geological feature of Montana's largest city, Billings.

The house was large and expensive, the landscaping extensive with a picturesque view of the Yellowstone River valley.

Hank rang the bell and glanced over at Arlene. "You all right?"

She nodded.

"Keep in mind, he might not be the father of Charlotte's baby."

"I know."

"Would you rather wait in the car?"

She smiled. "Are you worried I'm going to make a scene?"

"I wouldn't blame you."

"No," she said and touched his cheek. "You wouldn't."

The door opened. A Hispanic woman of indeterminate age asked in broken English, "May I help you?"

"We're here to see Mr. Foster. John Foster," Hank said.

Before the woman could answer, a tall, thin, thirtysomething man appeared behind her. "I'll take care of this, Delores."

Delores quickly disappeared down a hallway.

John Foster frowned as he came forward. "What is this about?"

"We need to speak to you about a missing person," Hank said.

"Are you...police?" he asked, shifting his gaze to Arlene.

"Do you mind if we step inside, Mr. Foster? I'm sure we can clear this up quickly if you'll just answer a few questions about your stay in Whitehorse, Montana."

John Foster's already pale face blanched bone-white. He looked as if he might pass out.

"I don't know what you're talking about," he said.

"Maybe your wife can help us," Hank suggested.

"She isn't here." His voice broke. "Please. My wife doesn't know. She's shopping, but she could come home at any moment."

"Then I suggest you answer our questions before she gets back," Hank said, surprised Arlene was letting him handle this. He knew that wasn't her nature. She'd had to handle everything for years without any help. Maybe that's why she was being so quiet now.

"Come in, then," John Foster said and quickly led them down the hallway to what appeared to the den and home office. He closed the door behind them, but didn't offer them a chair.

Hank produced the photograph Arlene had given him of Charlotte and watched the man's expression. He knew now where the phrase *guilty as sin* came from.

"When was the last time you saw her?" Hank asked.

"I only saw her that one time. In Whitehorse. I swear." His eyes were wide with fear. "She told me she was twenty-one."

"And you believed her?" Arlene asked sarcastically.

"Oh, God, don't tell me she's—"

"No, she's not a minor," Hank said. "She's eighteen. And pregnant."

They had been standing in a large den furnished in lush carpet and deep leather chairs around a massive cherry-wood desk.

John Foster dropped into one of the chairs like a puppet whose strings had just been severed. "*Pregnant?* No."

"You didn't think to use protection?" Arlene asked.

"Look, I don't even remember what happened. I swear to you I didn't think I had that much to drink. I woke up the next morning and she was gone. I thought I'd dreamed it."

"Sure you did," Arlene said.

"The girl hasn't contacted you since?" Hank asked, although from John Foster's reaction, Hank would have sworn the man hadn't known about the pregnancy. If Charlotte had contacted him, it would probably have been for money. The baby would have been the leverage.

"I swear I never saw or heard from her again. You have to believe me. Please, my wife hasn't been well. I don't want her—"

Following a soft tap, the office door swung open and a woman in her early thirties peered in. "Oh, I'm sorry. I heard voices. I didn't realize we had company."

Between her dress and her composure, Hank guessed she was Mrs. Foster. What took him by surprise was the fact that the woman was very pregnant.

John was on his feet and practically wringing his hands. "Meredith, this is—"

"We're here as part of an investigation involving a missing young woman from Whitehorse, Montana," Hank said, interrupting him. Her hand was cool to the touch as cool as the lady herself.

Meredith Foster lifted one perfect eyebrow. *"White-horse?"*

"Your husband spent a couple of nights in Whitehorse about eight months ago," Hank said. Out of the corner of his eye he saw that John Foster looked about to hyperventilate.

"I don't understand," Meredith said.

"The young woman in question waited on your husband at a restaurant called Northern Lights," Hank said.

Meredith Foster laughed. "You're questioning everyone who this woman waited on eight months ago?"

"Just those individuals who might have felt sorry for her and offered to help her," Hank said.

Meredith finally looked at her husband. "My husband is a kind man. If the woman was in some sort of trouble…"

"Your husband was seen consoling her after she dropped one of the patron's meals," Hank said.

"Well, that explains it, doesn't it?" she said. "I'm willing to bet he also left her a large tip. John is very generous."

"Yes, he did leave a *very* large tip," Hank said.

Meredith's laugh reminded him of wind chimes as she stepped to her husband. She wrapped long, manicured fingers around his forearm as if to hug him. Or steady him.

"I'm sorry this young woman ran away," she said as she placed her other hand on her protruding belly. "Her mother must be worried sick." Her gaze flicked to Arlene.

Hank took a notepad from the desk and a pen. "This is my cell phone number. If you think of anything else or happen to see or hear from her—"

"Why would she contact my husband?" Meredith asked, seeming to lose a little of her cool.

"He was kind to her. She could have gotten his name from his credit card. If she was in trouble, she might reach out to him," Hank said, then tipped his Western hat. "I'm sorry if I upset you. Your husband mentioned you hadn't been well…?"

"I've had a difficult pregnancy," she said, her hand again going to her stomach.

"When are you due?" Arlene asked.

"Next month," Meredith said and smiled up at her husband. "We can't wait for the baby to be born."

"You don't know if it's a girl or a boy?" Arlene asked.

"No," Meredith said, cutting her gaze to Arlene. "I want to be surprised."

"They're lying," Arlene said the moment they were in Hank's SUV. "At least she is. She knows about her husband and Charlotte."

Hank looked over at Arlene as he started the engine, admiring her instincts, especially since they so closely coincided with his own. "She's covering for him, I agree. But I don't think he knew Charlotte was pregnant—or that his wife was onto him."

"So you think he's the father of Charlotte's baby?" Arlene asked. "He's obviously been quite busy."

"Hard to say until Charlotte's baby is born and a DNA test can be administered," Hank said. "But I'd say he's afraid he is. And so is his wife."

"That doesn't help us find Charlotte," Arlene said. "Maybe he isn't the father. Maybe Charlotte is with the father of her baby right now, safe somewhere."

Maybe. "Well, the one thing I think we can count on is that Charlotte isn't being kept locked in the basement of the Foster house."

"No," she agreed distractedly. "You didn't tell me about what happened at the restaurant."

He looked straight ahead as he pulled out into the street.

He hadn't told her, either, that a woman matching Meredith Foster's description had been to the restaurant asking about Charlotte. "I should have told you, but you already had enough to worry about."

"Well, you're wrong. I can take it."

He smiled over at her. "I never doubted that. That's one of the things I admire about it. You're a survivor, Arlene."

Arlene laughed at that, shaking her head as she studied him. She'd quit asking herself why he was doing this. Clearly he was enjoying it. And he was very good at this intrigue business. Maybe too good at it?

"You never told me what kind of business you were in before you retired," she said, watching his reaction to her question.

He kept his gaze on the road. "Corporation stuff, not very interesting."

She said nothing, hearing the lie and feeling a little ill. She turned away to stare out her side window. Just when she was starting to trust him. Was even trusting him with Charlotte's and her grandbaby's lives.

Suddenly he pulled off the road, cut the engine and turned to her. "I worked for the government. I don't want to lie to you. But I also can't tell you exactly who I worked for or what I did. Let's just say it was in security."

"Thank you," she said, looking into his eyes. They were a deep, rich brown. "Don't worry. I won't say anything to anyone, if that's what you're worried about."

"My wife got sick of the secrecy," he said, chewing at his cheek as he looked thoughtful. "So did I. But that life is behind me now."

The way he said it, she wondered whether he was trying to convince her or himself.

"We all right?" he asked.

She nodded and smiled over at him. "What do we do now?"

"We hope we hear from Charlotte," he said. "If John Foster is the father, then she hasn't contacted him."

"What about Meredith Foster?"

"I doubt Charlotte would try to run a blackmail scam on her," Hank said. "Even in her condition, difficult pregnancy and all, Meredith Foster isn't the pushover her husband apparently was. Charlotte wouldn't get anywhere with that woman."

Arlene couldn't argue that. Still, she wondered what a woman like that would do if she found out about her husband's affair—and the subsequent pregnancy.

Chapter 6

"It's all a horrible mistake," John Foster said the moment the two had left.

"Of course it is," Meredith agreed. "Why don't you make us both a drink and I'll tell you about my day."

John didn't move. "You aren't upset with me?"

"John," she said, cupping his cheek, "we agreed not to ever discuss those days you were gone. It doesn't matter. I know that whatever problems that waitress has, they have nothing to do with us. Now—that drink?"

He nodded quickly. "I just don't want you upset. The baby…"

She placed a hand over her stomach. "The baby is fine. Now, please, make yourself a martini. I'll take a mineral water with a wedge of lime."

He scurried away to the bar. Meredith Foster watched him go, wishing she didn't know her husband so well.

She had sensed something was wrong the moment John came in the front door eight months ago, suitcase in hand, hangdog look on his face after being gone for three days.

At the time she'd thought, *He's damned lucky I haven't had the locks changed yet.*

"Back to get the rest of your things?" she'd asked as disinterestedly as she could sound.

"I made a mistake," John had said, looking like a whipped puppy. "I haven't been myself lately. I don't really want a divorce. I don't even know why I said I did. I want to make our marriage work."

Meredith had been more startled and upset by this than when he'd asked for the divorce, packed a small suitcase and left, saying he'd be back for the rest of his things.

What had happened in the three days he'd been gone? Suddenly she'd been scared.

"I don't understand," she'd managed to say.

"I belong here with you," he'd said, sounding as if the words were very difficult for him.

She'd thought her father must have gotten to him. Or her father-in-law. The two older men were best friends, successful business partners and John's bosses.

"If that's what you're sure you want," she'd said graciously. "We won't ever speak of this again."

"Thank you, Meredith," he'd said quickly and given her an awkward hug and an even more awkward kiss. "I'll go up and unpack."

"No," she'd said. "Let me do that for you, John. Why don't you make us both a drink?"

He'd glanced at his suitcase, and she'd seen that he would have preferred to unpack it himself. Why was that?

She'd reached for the small suitcase. "I'll take a martini. You make such wonderful martinis."

He'd nodded and handed her the suitcase with obvious reluctance.

Upstairs, she'd placed the suitcase on the bed, taken a bracing breath, opened it. He hadn't taken much with him. Two casual shirts, jeans and some underwear.

She'd lifted out the wrinkled, obviously worn shirt on

top. She'd been able to smell his scent on it—and another scent that had made her gag. Cheap perfume.

Repulsed, she'd leaned down to sniff the rest of the clothing in the suitcase. The cloying perfume had permeated everything, even those items he hadn't worn. The woman must have been all over him.

Meredith had dropped the shirt back into the suitcase and tried to get control of herself. It wasn't jealousy. She'd never loved John enough for that.

But she refused to let him jeopardize their lifestyle. She was content with John. She'd known what she was getting when she'd married him. She'd always believed that her father and father-in-law would keep John in line. What she hadn't seen coming was some midlife crisis at thirty-five.

She'd taken a couple of deep breaths as she'd heard John call up the stairs to her. Hurriedly she'd closed the suitcase and shoved it into the back of the closet.

She'd told herself she would deal with it later. Right then she'd needed to just make all of it go away. Her mother had taught her that the best way to deal with this sort of thing was to pretend it had never happened.

She'd checked herself in the mirror, brushed a lock of her hair back from her face, straightened to her full height and gone downstairs to have a pleasant evening with her husband.

The next morning, after a restless, sleepless night, she'd called her father. "John is back."

"I'm glad to hear he came to his senses."

Had he? Is that what had happened?

"I assume he will be back to work today, then?"

"He's on his way now. I'd prefer you not say anything to him."

Her father had grunted. "Fine, I guess. No reason to beat a dead horse."

She'd winced at his words. That morning John had seemed so cowed, so beaten down.

"Everything is back to normal, then?"

Normal. "Yes."

"I really wish you would reconsider having a baby," her mother had said when Meredith called her.

"You aren't suggesting that the only way I can hold on to my husband is to have a child, are you?"

Her mother hadn't been fazed. "A man is less likely to leave if there are children. Once men get restless, they need something to settle them down. John wouldn't dream of leaving you again if you were pregnant. And if the worst came to pass, a baby insures that a judge would make sure you can take the son of a bitch for everything. Without a baby, you might be forced to get a job."

She'd known her mother was right. The problem was that she didn't want a child, never had. Especially with John. "I like my life exactly as it is."

"Well," her mother had said, "I hope you get to keep it. But once they start asking for a divorce—"

"I have to go, Mother. I just wanted to tell you that John is back. Back to stay." She'd hung up more scared than angry, since she'd suspected her mother had already been down this rocky path. It would explain Meredith's four siblings, she feared.

When the credit card bills had come a month later, Meredith couldn't help but check the charges for the days when John had gone astray. Gas. She'd noted the Montana towns. Apparently he'd driven north out of Billings, buying gas at Roundup, Grass Range and Whitehorse. Twice in Whitehorse.

She'd glossed over the meal charges. Two charges on two separate nights at Northern Lights restaurant in Whitehorse. One almost double the cost of the first night. Apparently he hadn't eaten alone. Then she'd seen that he'd left a huge tip.

Alarms had begun to go off. She felt it had to be a mistake.

Her pulse had thundered as she'd checked the accommodation charges. Two nights in Whitehorse at the Milk River Lodge. Nothing odd about that, since he'd returned on the third night.

But...there'd been an additional room charge at the Shady Rest Motel for the same night he'd already paid for at the Milk River Lodge.

The evidence had been overwhelming.

The perfume on his clothing—she'd washed his clothing twice and aired out the suitcase, but she swore she could still smell that nauseating scent sometimes.

The room charges.

And John's guilt-ridden, shamed face when he'd returned home to her.

There'd been a woman.

A faceless, nameless woman in another town.

The man was an idiot. Didn't he realize he'd left a trail?

As she'd carefully refolded the credit card bill and put it in the bills-to-be-paid file, she'd known the best thing she could do was forget it. Men strayed.

Her own father had over the years. She remembered the way he'd return from a business trip with expensive presents for her mother—and herself. He'd always seemed a little cowed and contrite after one of those trips. Just as John had been.

Meredith had told herself that nothing could be gained by confronting her husband. The deed had been done. The best thing she could do was forget it had ever happened, just as she was sure John was trying to do.

But she'd been unable to shake the memory of that horrible perfume. Or the feeling that her marriage depended on knowing what had happened in Whitehorse.

"I'm going to go visit my friend Debra," she'd told John one morning at breakfast. Debra lived in Big Timber to the west. Nowhere near Whitehorse. "I'll be gone a few days."

"Don't worry about me," John had said distractedly. "I have a lot of work to do for your father."

"Delores will be here to make your meals."

"Fine." He'd been distracted since his return from Whitehorse. Polite. And preoccupied.

Meredith had known she had to find out if this other woman was a threat. She had to know for sure what had happened in Whitehorse—and with whom.

She'd packed a small bag. Her friend Debra had been in Europe for three weeks. Not that John would call to confirm where his wife had really gone. He would wait for Meredith to call him. She would use her cell phone and she would use cash. Unlike John, she was too smart to leave a trail.

Not that John would ever suspect her of anything. His mind didn't work that way. Or maybe he just didn't care enough to bother.

The thought had made her a little sad and she'd wondered why she was going to so much trouble. John wasn't worth fighting for. But her marriage and her position in the community *was,* she had reminded herself.

She was Mrs. John Foster and she was determined to remain so no matter what she had to do, she thought now as John handed her the glass of mineral water with a wedge of fresh lime and she took a drink, watching him over the rim of her glass, hating him more than he could imagine.

* * *

"I've been thinking," Hank said on the drive back to Whitehorse. "I'll do some checking on Mr. and Mrs. Foster and see what I can come up with."

Arlene let out a silent sigh of relief. "Thank you. There is something about that woman…"

"Yeah," he said and let out an oath as he came over a hill. "What the…?"

Below them was the Milk River valley, the trees along the river black compared to the lighter green hillsides. But it wasn't the valley or the few lights of town that could be seen that had caught his attention.

It was the northern horizon. Gigantic shafts of light shot up from it. Glowing white light, red, yellow, like a dozen colossal searchlights.

"It's the aurora borealis—the northern lights," Arlene said, smiling at their effect on Hank. "I take it you've never seen them before?"

"I've heard of them, but I've never seen anything like this." There was awe in his voice, and he pulled over to the side of the road and got out. Arlene followed him as the luminous bands undulated, changing in color and brightness.

"They're believed to be electrical discharges in the ionized air," she said.

He smiled at that and put his arm around her as they watched. She loved that Hank Monroe could appreciate the simple things that Montana offered. He'd obviously seen the world, been places and seen and done things that other people couldn't even imagine. And yet he was standing here tonight with her, transfixed by something that to her was commonplace.

"I saw the lights once in the middle of the night when I

was a girl," she said as they leaned back against the front of the SUV. "The sky was turquoise and bright as daylight."

"It's amazing," Hank said as he pulled her closer. She snuggled against him, and they stood like that watching the northern lights until the sky darkened again, the lights fading and finally disappearing.

"I'll never forget tonight," Hank said quietly as he turned her in his arms. His gaze locked with hers, and she knew even before he leaned toward her that he was going to kiss her.

The kiss rocked her. Not that she wasn't already on unstable ground just being in the man's arms. He cupped her face in his large hands, his touch gentle as he lowered his mouth to hers.

The kiss was soft and sweet as the summer night. A friendly kiss like a cool breeze. And then he pulled her closer, their bodies fitting together like puzzle pieces, and he turned up the heat. A scorching heat that warmed her to her toes and melted something inside her.

She let out a low moan as his fingers moved down the long column of her throat to stop on her throbbing pulse. And for just a moment his lips drew back. Their eyes met, a silent understanding passing between them, and then his mouth was on hers again, hot and demanding, and she was clutching at his shirt, balling the material in her fist as she opened to him.

Arlene knew what would have happened if the semitruck hadn't come along when it did. She hardly noticed the glare of lights or the rumble of the engine as it came over the hill. But the blare of the horn definitely registered. She and Hank jumped apart as if stuck with a cattle prod.

The truck roared past, the driver giving the air horn

another toot as he passed, his grinning face ghostly in the dim cab lights.

Hank laughed, the semi kicking up a small dust devil as it blew on by and down the hill into town.

Arlene watched the truck's taillights until it disappeared over a rise, too shaken to move. Darkness settled in around them, the northern lights long gone. She smoothed her shirt over her hips, feeling a little embarrassed—and disappointed.

Her heart was still pounding and as she touched her tongue to her lips, she could still feel him, still taste him on her.

"Well, that was one way to end a kiss," Hank said, sounding as taken aback as she felt. "I suppose I'd better get you home. It's later than I thought."

She nodded and walked around to climb back into his SUV. Neither said anything on the way to her house. He put a country-western station on the radio, and she settled into the seat. It felt so right being here with him. Just as the kiss had felt so right. And yet scary. She couldn't remember her heart ever pounding that hard. Certainly not when Floyd had made love to her. If that's what you called what he did to her.

"I'll call you tomorrow," Hank said as he walked her to the door. "Try not to worry about Charlotte. I'll continue doing what I can to find her."

"Thank you. Thank you for everything." She hurried inside, afraid what would happen if he kissed her again.

She stood just inside the door for a moment, listening to the quiet house. She could hear crickets outside the open windows, smell the freshly cut hay from the fields across the road, feel her own pulse thundering through her veins.

Hank had her heart pounding. She stood there, her

whole body seeming to vibrate with the remembered feel of his mouth, his arms, the solid wall of his chest pressed against her breasts. Her nipples were still hard and painful beneath her bra. She'd felt Hank's kiss clear to her now-aching center.

As she moved down the hall without turning on a light, she was just thankful that neither Bo nor Charlotte was there right now. She knew even before she turned on the light in her bedroom, what she must look like.

It was an odd thing to stand before the large mirror and see herself with her face aglow, eyes bright and shiny as stars. She stood looking at the stranger in the mirror, enjoying this woman. How long had it been since she'd felt like a woman? Or had she ever?

Don't get too up on yourself.

That's mom talking, she warned herself.

She imagined her mother's pursed lips, the narrowed eyes and could almost see her sitting in that old rocker now reflected in the mirror.

Believe me, you have no reason to think you're anybody, little girl. Take a look in that mirror and tell me what you see. Nobody. So don't go getting on your high horse with me.

Arlene shook her head as she met her own eyes in the mirror and tried to shut out her mother's hurtful, horrible words.

"Just get home?" Bo asked behind her from the open doorway of her bedroom, making her jump.

She hadn't heard him come in and wondered why that was. Or had he been here all along? Waiting for her in the dark? Watching her and Hank? He'd wrecked his car some months back, and she'd told him he had to pay to have it repaired. Of course he hadn't. He'd just bummed rides off friends.

"How was your date?"

"Fine." No reason to correct him. Maybe it hadn't started out as a date, but it had surely ended as one, she thought, remembering Hank's arm around her as they'd watched the northern lights as if the show had been just for them. Not to mention the kiss.

"Is something wrong with you?" he asked. "You seem a little odder than usual."

His tone irritated her. "Did you want something?"

He shrugged. "I stopped by the mailbox on my way in." He handed her the stack of mail. Most of it, she knew, would be bills. "Just wanted to let you know I was home."

Home. The word grated on her. She knew Bo. He would push her to the max. "Bo?"

With obvious impatience, he turned back to her. *"What?"*

"How is the job hunting coming along?" she asked.

"Are you going to tell me to get a job every time you see me?" he snapped.

"If that's what it takes. I'll pick up some boxes in town tomorrow so you can start packing up your things."

He stared at her for a full minute, then shook his head. "You're making a mistake."

"The end of the week."

He shook his head again. "I guess this means I'm not your favorite anymore, huh." At one time she'd found it cute when he said things like that. She had played favorites with him. With Charlotte, too. It made her sick to admit it.

She thought of her brother. According to her mother, Carl could do no wrong. Unlike Arlene. The son was prized in the rural family. He was the male who would take over the place one day. He would build his bride a house on the property. His family would come over for dinner on Sundays. He was the one who stayed.

Daughters married and often moved away with their husbands. But sons in rural Montana stayed and worked the place with their fathers.

At least that was what Arlene had been raised to believe. Her brother had inherited the family farm in Chinook. And as awful as he'd treated their mother, he was still her favorite right up until the day she died.

After Floyd had left, Arlene had leased out this farm, since it had been clear Bo would never work it. If he got his hands on the place, he'd sell it and blow the money.

As she closed the door on her son and leaned against it, she understood that old expression, "This is hurting me more than it is you." She didn't want to lose her son. But the truth was, she'd lost all three of her children a long time ago.

She was through making excuses for them—and for herself. She couldn't change the past. But she could quit making the same mistakes.

As she thumbed through the mail—most of it just as she suspected: bills—she found the envelope addressed to her in Charlotte's feminine script and her heart leaped in her chest.

Hurriedly, she tore it open.

Mom, I'm fine. Sorry to leave the way I did. Don't worry about me or the baby. We'll be fine. Charlotte.

Arlene checked for a return address. None. The postmark was Whitehorse. Had Charlotte mailed this before she'd left? Or was she still in town?

Arlene reread it, finding a little peace in the words. It

was so unlike Charlotte to write her a note of reassurance. But it was definitely Charlotte's handwriting.

She sat down on the bed, relief making her weak. Bo was banging around in his room, obviously angry.

"Hank put this into your head, didn't he?" Bo yelled from the other side of the door. "What do you know about this guy, anyway? Him and his big house, his nice car. You have any idea how he came by any of that? Or maybe what kind of past he has? He could be a criminal, for all you know."

She didn't answer as she carefully folded Charlotte's note, put it back in the envelope and placed it on the night-stand next to her bed. As she climbed into her bed, though, Bo's words echoed in her head.

What did she really know about Hank Monroe? He was kind, caring, generous, fun to be with, loving. And he'd reminded her what desire felt like. What more was there to know?

She thought about what he'd told her today in Billings. He'd worked for the government, some undercover-type agency.

What if he'd lied? Men do that all the time. Especially to get a woman in the sack.

To her surprise, it wasn't her mother's voice this time that she heard, but her own.

Hank drove to the ranch in a daze, his thoughts on Arlene and the night they'd just spent together watching the northern lights.

He was all the way across the porch, almost to his front door, when he realized he wasn't alone. He'd been so lost in his thoughts that he hadn't taken the usual precautions.

He turned quickly, coming face-to-face with his former boss. "Cameron?" Startled, Hank wondered if he had lost his edge. In the old days he would have known Cameron was there.

"You don't answer your messages."

"What the hell are you doing here?"

"You didn't return my phone calls. What was I supposed to do?"

"Leave me alone?"

Cameron shook his head. "I couldn't do that, Hank. I need your help."

Hank stepped back, still upset that he'd been so careless. He'd been thinking about Arlene. "I'm done with the agency."

"Come on, Hank. You can't run from this."

"Like hell I can't. I have enough money I can just keep right on going."

Cameron laughed and looked up at the stars. "As if you could find anywhere more remote than this. How the hell did you find this place?"

Hank didn't answer. He knew Cam was right. There was no place safe.

"I had no idea there were so many stars up there," Cameron said. "Or that you knew how to ride a horse," he said shifting his gaze to Hank. "I like the hat."

Hank swore under his breath.

"I could use a drink," Cameron said.

Knowing there was no way around this, Hank headed for the door. Best to get it over with and send Cameron on his way.

Hank went straight to the bar and poured them each a drink. He handed Cam one, knowing how his old friend and boss took his scotch. Neat. He motioned to one of the leather chairs and took his drink to a chair, as well.

"You're looking well," Hank said as he studied Cameron.

"Thanks. You're not looking so bad yourself. Not that you weren't always an ugly son of a bitch."

Hank smiled and took a slug of his drink. He was no beauty, that was for sure. His early years growing up in a rough mining town had left him with a repeatedly broken nose and more scars than he liked to count. If Cam hadn't taken him under his wing, Hank hated to think where he would have ended up. Probably in prison.

Instead Cameron Harris had taken all Hank's anger and aggression and turned him loose to play cops and robbers on a worldwide scale. While that meant Hank wouldn't see prison, it had certainly twisted his then already warped ideas of right and wrong.

"Now that we've covered the pleasantries, what the hell do you want?" Hank asked, knowing he was wrong for blaming Cameron for the way his life had turned out.

Cam didn't answer right away. He took a sip of his drink. "I didn't come here to screw up your new life."

Hank lifted a brow. "Oh, yeah?"

"I need you to look at some photographs."

Hank felt his belly tighten. *"Photographs?"*

Cameron nodded. "Twenty minutes, tops. Then I'm out of here and you won't be seeing me again."

"Me not seeing you doesn't means you won't be around," he said. "So let's see the photos." It was the last thing he wanted to do, but it was also the only way to get this over with.

Cam studied his drink for a moment, then finished it, set the glass on the table by his chair and rose. "I'll get them."

Hank finished his own drink and stood, too nervous to sit. He started to pour himself another drink, then thought better of it. He needed his wits about him.

Cam came back into the house a few minutes later with a black leather folder. He took it over to the breakfast bar. "You got a better light over here?"

Hank snapped on the overhead and Cam opened the folder.

The photographs were black-and-white, shot with a telephoto and a little grainy. Surveillance photos.

He studied the face at the center. The one in focus. And was relieved that he didn't recognize the man. He scanned the rest. All were of the same man.

"Don't know him," Hank said, pushing the photos away, relieved.

"Not the man," Cam said.

Hank shot him a look, that sick feeling back.

Cam reopened the folder to the first photograph. "The *woman.*"

Hank looked down at the photograph again. He'd missed her the first time. She stood in the shadows, barely visible.

His heart began to pound. It *couldn't* be her.

Cam took a magnifying glass from his jacket pocket and slid it across the counter to him.

Hank didn't take it. Not until he'd flipped through all the photographs, stopping on one of the later shots.

His insides shaking, he picked up the magnifying glass and focused on the woman in the shadows—and felt his new world crumble around him.

A shaft of light from a street lamp had pierced the deep shadows and illuminated part of her face, more than enough to make a positive ID even if he hadn't been able to make out her trademark weapon she held at her side.

He followed her gaze across the photograph to the man at its center and knew even before he asked. "The man was the hit? He's dead?"

Cam nodded. "It's her, isn't it?"

Unable to look at the photograph any longer, Hank put down the magnifying glass and closed the folder.

It wasn't possible. And yet the photographs...

"When were these taken?"

"Last week in Prague," Cam said.

Hank walked over to the bar and poured himself a stiff drink, hating the fact that he needed it badly.

"You were the best," Cameron said, joining him. "Hell, you're a damned legend." He refilled his glass. "But, unfortunately, you're only as good as your last kill. People are asking questions."

"People?"

"This is from the top, Hank."

"Then why isn't one of them here? Why send you?"

"It's a courtesy call. I asked for the job."

Hank looked over at him and frowned. The past lay between them like a minefield.

"People are wondering. You quitting so soon after the job, a job that apparently you didn't want. Or complete," Cameron said. "There's talk that you might have been seeing her. Romantically."

Hank let out a curse.

"How else, they say, can you explain the fact that she's alive after you were told to kill her?"

Hank laughed and downed his drink. He couldn't explain it. But there was no doubt in his mind that the woman in the photograph was Rena. "What is it you want me to say?"

Cameron shook his head. "The agency just wants clarification that it is Rena—and an explanation of why she is still alive and working again for the other side."

Chapter 7

The first time Meredith Foster saw Whitehorse, Montana, she wondered what had possessed her husband to go there of all places.

He could have gone anywhere in the world when he took off with his suitcase and his dreams of freedom. It showed a distinct lack of imagination on John's part that he would come to this little isolated town in the middle of nowhere.

Had he lost his mind?

Considering what had forced her to drive to Whitehorse she had assumed he had. And yet she'd been thankful the town was small. It had certainly made her job easier.

She'd gone straight to the Shady Rest Motel.

The bell over the door had jangled as she'd entered. The air conditioner had hummed in the window while a television droned somewhere in the back. There'd been a crash, loud words and then a child crying, another whining.

Impatiently Meredith had gone over to the door, opened and closed it again. This time when the bell jangled a fifty-something woman had appeared. "May I help you?"

"I certainly hope so," Meredith had said and considered the woman and the best approach—money or tears—to get what she wanted.

Tears had worked like a charm. The poor betrayed wife could always get the sympathy—and the help.

The motel manager had seen John Foster with a local young blond woman from a questionable family in Old Town.

"Her name?" Meredith had asked. "I just want to talk to her. Make sure she leaves my husband alone."

The woman behind the desk had nodded. "Charlotte. Charlotte Evans."

To Meredith's surprise, it had been harder to get information at the restaurant where her husband had gone for dinner.

Charlotte Evans had been a waitress there. No one remembered a guest named John Foster. Charlotte might have waited on him. But the owner, a woman named Laci Cavanaugh, hadn't been willing to provide any information.

"I just want to know why my husband *doubled* his bill as a tip?" Meredith had demanded.

"I wouldn't know, Mrs. Foster. Why don't you ask your husband?"

Meredith had left in a huff. Neither money nor tears had swayed the indomitable Laci Cavanaugh.

Meredith had left shocked that Charlotte Evans was only eighteen. The fool. No wonder John had come home with his tail tucked between his legs. He was damned lucky the girl hadn't lied about her age—or he'd be in jail right now.

She'd felt such a wave of disgust for her husband that for a few moments, she'd thought about returning home and tossing his butt out.

But common sense had reigned. Charlotte Evans was a nobody and certainly not a threat to Meredith's marriage.

And yet Meredith had known she couldn't leave town—

all ten blocks square of it—without seeing this young woman.

The downtown sat adjacent to the railroad tracks, like a lot of towns along the Hi-Line, from what she could gather.

As Meredith had waited in her car along the quiet street outside the Cut and Curl, where she'd been told Charlotte Evans worked, she hadn't been able to imagine living in such a small town.

At quitting time, several women—who obviously all worked there, since they wore matching pink smocks—had come out of the shop. Finally Charlotte Evans had emerged alone and walked to an old blue car parked at the curb.

From what Meredith had heard about the girl, she would have known Charlotte anywhere. What had shocked her was that Charlotte looked younger than eighteen.

What *had* John been thinking? He could have had a daughter her age.

It made Meredith sick to think of John with the blonde, and she'd wondered if waking up next to the girl and realizing how young she was wasn't what had sent John running home.

Disgusted, but not worried about this eighteen-year-old taking her husband, Meredith had hurriedly driven through town, anxious to get home. But on the edge of town she'd noticed that she needed gas.

In this part of Montana, the towns were so far apart she'd had to take advantage of stations along the way or run out of gas in the middle of nowhere on a highway with little traffic.

She'd pulled into a convenience store called Packy's, filled up and gone in for a cup of coffee to keep her awake for the three-hour drive home.

As she'd been waiting to pay, she'd recognized the two women she'd seen coming out of the beauty shop only minutes before Charlotte Evans. The two had their heads together as they waited in line.

Meredith moved closer when she heard one of the women mention Charlotte. She'd listened to the two discuss some big announcement Charlotte had made that day at work.

"Do you think she really did it on purpose?" the one had whispered to the other.

"That's what she said. It's just disgusting even if she didn't, getting knocked up by some old married guy from out of town. She says they were both drunk and that all she remembers is that his name was John."

The one young woman had broken up in giggles. "She got pregnant by a *john*."

Meredith had stood rooted to the floor until finally she heard the clerk call, "Ma'am, can I help you?" She didn't remember paying for her gas and coffee or walking out into the hot afternoon sun to her car.

John. The asinine girl had told these women that she had purposely gotten pregnant by a man from out of town named John?

Meredith had driven a few miles out of town before she'd had to pull over and, physically ill, had retched beside the road. She'd tried to still the panic. The girl had set John up, purposely getting pregnant by the fool so she could…what?

The realization had hit her like a fist, and she'd had to clutch the side of the car as she'd bent over again with another spasm.

There was only one reason: extortion. Soon Charlotte Evans would be contacting John, telling him about the baby, demanding money. Or, worse, marriage?

If John found out, he would do the "right" thing. He'd

always wanted children. Meredith hadn't. Even her father and father-in-law would support John, at least in making sure he took care of his child—especially if the child was a son.

She abhorred the thought of money that belonged to her going to some bastard child and his whore mother. But she knew there was nothing she could do if the foolish girl decided to contact John. The one thing she could not let happen was lose anything that belonged to her because of this mess.

Meredith had left Whitehorse frantic with worry. By the time she'd reached home, she'd calmed down enough to think rationally. There was only one thing to do.

She would have to get pregnant—and right away.

"Clarification?" Hank demanded as he watched Cameron take a drink to one of the leather chairs.

"You can't blame them, Hank."

Like hell he couldn't. He tried to calm down. "What is it they want me to do?" Hank asked, fearing the answer.

"Nothing. We just needed confirmation."

"And clarification."

Cameron shrugged. "They'll take what they get."

He stared at Cameron, too shocked to speak for a moment. "That's it? They aren't demanding I fix this? Or, hell, putting out a hit on me?"

Cameron laughed and shook his head. "Like I said, there's talk. They'd like to know how this happened, but as far as taking any action…" He shook his head again.

Hank glanced toward the darkened window and felt a sudden chill. He remembered another dark night and what he'd thought was a confirmed kill.

He could pretty much guess how it had happened. Rena

had expected the hit. Someone had leaked that the agency was onto her. She had set him up. It was that simple. And that complex.

Hank said as much to Cameron, who simply nodded.

"That's the way I figured it. I'll be sure I put that in my report," Cam said. He finished his drink and reached for the folder with the photographers inside. "My job is done, then."

Hank had been so surprised by Cam's visit he hadn't been thinking clearly. But he was now. "You could have sent the photographs electronically and saved yourself the trip."

"And missed being verbally abused by you?" Cam shook his head. "Don't worry. You're still a legend with the agency. This doesn't change that."

Hank let out a curse. "I wasn't worried about my legend status, and you know it." He had to admit it was good to see Cam. He studied his once best friend and realized maybe he hadn't lost his edge. "You think she's going to come after me. That's why you came here yourself."

"It crossed my mind and a few other minds," Cam said.

Hank began to laugh. "You were *worried* about me."

"Don't let it go to your head."

Even with their difference in age, there'd been a time they were closer than brothers. But that was before Rena, before she went to the other side, before Hank was ordered to kill her.

"Just watch your back," Cameron said as he tucked the folder under his arm and pocketed the magnifying glass.

"Where are you staying?"

"I'm not. I'm driving back to Billings tonight so I can catch an early flight out. If you didn't live in such a God-forsaken place…"

It was three hours to the closest large airport, with miles between towns.

"That's what I love about it up here," Hank said. "They call it 'the big open.' Have you ever seen a bigger sky or felt as small and insignificant?"

Cameron laughed. "You actually *like* it here."

He nodded. "Just one question," he said as Cam got ready to leave. "They aren't hoping to use me as bait to catch her, are they?"

Cameron shook his head almost sadly. "You wanted it that way when you quit the agency. Said you didn't want to see any spooks for any reason."

Hank laughed again. He didn't buy it for a minute. "I know what they're up to. They think my pride will force me to track her down and finish the job. My last job. My perfect record. They think I miss this crap?" He sobered. "I'm done with that life, Cam. I can't kill anymore."

Cameron smiled. "Take care, Hank. I have no idea what you're doing out here in the middle of nowhere, but it really was great seeing you again."

"I wish I could say the same," Hank said, but he reached for his friend's hand and pulled him into a quick hug. "Watch for deer along the highway. That's the biggest threat we have up here."

"You just keep telling yourself that," Cameron said.

Hank watched him hike down the back road to where he must have stashed his vehicle and felt sorry about the way things had turned out. But then, that wasn't anything new, was it? Cameron had saved his life—and taken it from him by getting him into the agency.

Closing the blinds, Hank walked back to the bar and thought about Rena, wondering how long it would be before he saw her again.

With Rena on the loose, he was a walking target. The last thing he wanted was Arlene to be anywhere near those crosshairs.

Meredith threw a surprise dinner party not long after her return from Whitehorse to announce her good news.

She'd waited until everyone was seated and, in the glow of the candles and fine china, announced, "I'm pregnant."

In the shocked silence, it was John's expression that she'd wanted to see the most. He knew that she'd never wanted children, abhorred the idea.

He'd gone deathly pale, his dark eyes wide as the charger under his dinner plate. Then he'd met her gaze and held it, the look in his eyes hardening to flint.

Then they'd both known that she had him right where she wanted him.

"Congratulations!" her father had boomed into the stunned silence. "I, for one, couldn't be happier."

Her mother had smiled over at her, a triumphant twinkle in her eye as she gave her daughter a slight nod.

Meredith had kept a happy smile on her face all through dinner, but she'd worried that this would backfire on her and she would end up with a child she didn't want and John gone.

When she'd mentioned this to her mother later in the kitchen, her mother had given her a rueful smile. "You know John. He has the spine of a jellyfish. That's why you married him to begin with. He might leave you, but never if there is a child. John is brought to tears at the sight of kittens."

"I hope you're right, Mother."

"A woman does what she has to do. Haven't you learned that yet?"

Back in the dining room after dessert, her father-in-law had raised his glass in another toast. Meredith had noticed that her mother-in-law had been watching John from the stony expression on her face, her sentiments had been with her son—and didn't include a grandchild. At least not with Meredith.

She'd once overheard John's mother tell a friend, "I worry for John. Meredith is so…headstrong."

The friend had laughed and said, "Headstrong? And as warm as a glacier. I can't for the life of me understand what John sees in her."

"I tried to talk him out of marrying her, but his father…" That's when Fran Foster had looked up and seen Meredith and known that she'd heard *every* word. Their eyes had locked, and Meredith had let her know with just one look that she would always hate her.

After her announcement, Meredith had raised her water glass, wishing it were wine, and tried her best to look demure. Her hatred of Fran Foster was nothing compared to what she felt for John. He'd forced her into this. She planned to make his life a living hell.

"Thank you," Meredith had said after John senior's toast. "John and I couldn't be happier. Isn't that right, sweetheart?"

John being John had nodded. "We couldn't be happier."

Arlene was getting ready for bed when she noticed there was a message from Sheriff Carter Jackson.

She dialed his home number at once, fearing the worst.

He answered on the second ring. "Arlene, I just wanted to ask if you'd heard from Charlotte."

She had to sit on her bed, her legs were so weak. "Yes. That is, she called and sent a note. We found her car in a gully not far from here. She says she's with the father of her baby."

If the sheriff heard the hesitation in her voice, he didn't react to it. "Good," he said. "I'd hoped that was all it was. I'm going to be out of the office for the rest of the week, then two weeks on my honeymoon...."

"Your wedding. Yes."

"But if you need me—"

"No. I'm fine."

He seemed to hesitate. "Well, one of the deputies will be here, should anything arise."

"Yes." She thanked him for his call and hung up.

Exhausted, she crawled into bed and was almost asleep when she heard the deep throb of a motorcycle. She sat up as the noise grew louder, then died away to the chirp of crickets again.

Charlotte?

She jumped out of bed, pulling her robe around her as she headed for the front door. She stopped abruptly at the sound of a heavy tread on the porch steps.

Peering out the window, she saw the large shape of a man stop at the door and raise his hand to knock.

She opened the door to Charlotte's former boyfriend, bracing herself for the worst.

"Don't go off on me," Lucas Bronson said, holding up both hands. He wore black leather pants and jacket, a red bandanna tied around his dark hair. "I come in peace."

Arlene glared at him. "I thought we saw the last of you." Lucas had been in and out of Charlotte's life since she was fourteen. In and out of trouble during that same time, Lucas was the last person Arlene wanted to see, especially now. "Do you realize how late it is?"

Lucas smiled. He was a good-looking young man a year

older than Bo. He came from a broken family—but then, few families weren't broken, Arlene thought.

"I know it's late," he said. "I just need to see Charlotte. It's important."

"Yo, Lucas, my man!" Bo said from behind her as he pushed past to shake hands with the biker. "Hey, it's good to see you."

"Bo, please go back to bed. I need to speak to Lucas," Arlene said.

Bo shot her a look, no doubt surprised by the calmness he heard in her tone. "What brings you back, man?"

"I need to see Charlotte," Lucas said, craning to look past them into the house. "I hate to wake her, but it really is important."

"I'm afraid—" Arlene began, but Bo cut her off.

"She took off, Luke. Nobody knows where she is."

Lucas looked as if he'd been punched. "No way! She's got to be really pregnant by now."

"Eight months," Arlene said, realizing as she said it that Charlotte had originally lied to her about how far along she was. She hadn't been but a couple of months when she'd told Arlene she was four months along.

Lucas was shaking his head. "She's got to be closer to nine months, since she's carrying my kid."

"What?" Arlene demanded.

"Didn't she tell you?" Then he seemed to realize how ridiculous that was. "Sorry, I guess she probably didn't. It's *my* baby."

"How do you know that?" Arlene demanded.

"She told me she was pregnant before I left."

"But you left *anyway?*"

He had the good sense to look ashamed. "But I'm back *now*. I'm going to marry her."

Arlene groaned. "Did Charlotte know this?"

"We talked about it. She wasn't real keen on it. But I know I can talk her into it."

Arlene tried to shake away the cobwebs in her brain. This didn't make any sense. "I got a call from her saying she was with the baby's father and they were making a new life for themselves."

Lucas shook his head. "No way. Unless it's that old guy she said she was going to get to pay for all her medical expenses."

"Old guy?" Arlene echoed. Old as in *thirty*something John Foster?

Lucas ducked his head, realizing he'd said too much.

"Tell me. My daughter is missing. If you know anything…"

"She bedded some old guy. They didn't…you know. She drugged him and made him think—"

"I get the picture," Arlene snapped thinking if Charlotte was here, she'd ring her neck.

"Wow," Bo said, sounding impressed by his sister's antics.

"I thought I told you to go back to bed," Arlene snapped at her son. "Lucas, you go wherever it is you go. But if you hear anything from Charlotte—"

"I'll let you know. It's weird. I haven't heard from her in several days. I thought maybe she already had the baby."

Several days? Charlotte had been in contact with him? Why, Arlene groaned, was this news to her? "Was she threatening to run away the last time you heard from her?"

"No. She said she'd changed her mind about, you know, hitting the old man up for money," Lucas said. "She was thinking about giving the baby up for adoption. That's when I realized I had to get back here and stop her."

Great, Arlene thought. Charlotte actually had been listening to reason. Maybe there was cause for hope. Or not, she thought, remembering that Lucas had come home to stop her. And knowing Charlotte…

Back in the house, Arlene waited until the sound of the motorcycle faded before she picked up the phone and started to dial Hank's number.

She put the phone back. She wasn't going to be able to get back to sleep and she desperately needed someone to talk to, but she didn't want to do this over the phone. With luck, Hank would still be up. He'd told her once that he was a night owl.

She quickly dressed and drove to his ranch. While she'd never been inside, she'd seen the house from the road when it had belonged to some corporation that only used it a couple of weeks a year.

The lights were on, she saw with relief.

By the time she'd parked her pickup in front of the huge house and gotten out, Hank was standing on the porch, a dark, large silhouette against the lights inside.

The way he stood made her hesitate. Maybe this hadn't been such a good idea after all. It had been impulsive. Hadn't she learned in the past where that kind of behavior got her? Maybe her children had inherited this behavior from her.

She stopped partway to the house. "Hank?"

"What's going on?" he asked. He sounded as if he'd been drinking. Yes, this had been a bad idea.

"I…that is, I thought you might still be up. I hope you don't mind me coming over." She moved toward the porch. "Charlotte's old boyfriend just stopped by. It seems she told him *he* is the baby's father."

"Do you believe him?" Hank asked as she climbed the

wide steps to where he stood. She saw that he had a half-finished drink in his hand.

"I think it's possible." She told Hank about Charlotte's plan. "Apparently she drugged John Foster and made him think they slept together so she could later get money out of him. At least that's the story she told Lucas, her biker boyfriend."

Hank nodded but said nothing. He hadn't invited her inside, either. Clearly he wasn't happy to see her.

"I shouldn't have come by so late," she said. "I'm sorry."

"No," he said. "It's just a lot to take in."

She'd warned him that her family was a train wreck, but it just got worse each day. Hank hadn't signed on for this. She felt guilty. Worse, she'd known it was only a matter of time before he tired of the drama. She certainly had.

When he'd signed up for her rural Meet-A-Mate Internet dating service, he'd said he was retired, looking for someone to spend quality time with, like traveling around the world. He'd just wanted someone to date a few times, have some fun with—not to get roped into their problems.

"I should go," she said and turned to leave.

"Arlene." He seemed at a loss for words as she turned back, and suddenly she was scared of what he would say when he found them.

"I was going to call you," he said finally. "I think we need to take a step back. It's just that things have been happening so fast with us…."

She felt her heart drop. "You don't have to explain. I understand."

"It's not *you*."

Her smile hurt.

"Arlene, when I met you I thought I was ready to start dating, but—"

"My service will find you someone more compatible," she said quickly. "Unless you want to cancel your membership. I'll be happy to refund your money."

"No. That is, I don't want to date anyone else. But I don't want you to lose money on me. I won't break my contract."

"I don't need your money." She warned herself not to say any more, but the words came out sounding as painful as they felt. "Or your sympathy. Isn't that what these have been—pity dates?"

"You're wrong. I thought I could do this, but…"

She turned to leave.

"Arlene!" He swore. "I've handled this so damned poorly. Won't you at least hear me out?"

"I hear you just fine," she called back to him as she hurried to her pickup. She started the engine and backed up, fighting the pain, the disappointment, the hurt.

He was still standing on the porch as she drove away.

She wouldn't cry.

She.

Would.

Not.

Cry.

Chapter 8

The next morning Arlene Evans did something completely out of character. She got up, showered, dressed and drove into Whitehorse without making her bed, without making her son breakfast, without cleaning up her house or starting a load or two of clothes in the washer.

Twenty minutes later she was sitting in the Cut and Curl, so nervous she could barely contain herself.

"You're sure?" Linsey asked, looking more worried than Arlene felt. Clearly all the women in the shop had been shocked to see Arlene walk in—and nervous. "I could just trim a little—"

"No. Cut it off." Arlene closed her eyes at the sound of the scissors. She felt the slight tug at the end of her long, thick hair. She squeezed her eyes shut tighter, feeling as if she was losing more than hair. There was a literal attachment to her hair, a familiarity, a constant that she wasn't sure she could part with.

Too late.

She felt the brush of fingers next to her ear, the cool feel of her wet hair, the whisper of the comb, then the snap of the scissors again and again.

She kept her eyes closed, let her thoughts run. The anger she'd felt at Hank seemed to leave her like the long strands of her hair. She felt herself changing and realized it had been gradual for some time now.

Ever since he'd walked into her life. It was as if he'd started something that couldn't be stopped. He'd been the catalyst. But even with him gone from her life, she couldn't stop what was happening to her.

What's more, she didn't hear her mother's voice in her head, berating her, anymore.

And was it just her imagination or did her head feel almost weightless?

She heard Linsey sweeping up the hair around the chair, then finally a timid question, "Want to take a look, Mrs. Evans?"

"Arlene," she said. "Please call me Arlene." Slowly she opened her eyes. Her hair was still damp, chin-length but layered so it fell in soft curls around her face.

She stared at herself in the mirror. A stranger. No, she thought, tears welling in her eyes. She *knew* this woman. This was the woman she could have been. Should have been. This woman had something the old Arlene never had—a glimmer of hope in her eyes.

"You hate it," Linsey said, taking a step back.

"No," Arlene said quickly. "I love it." She smiled, surprised how the cut seemed to soften her face, even her voice. "I *love* it."

Linsey breathed a relieved sigh and smiled. "It looks good on you. You look so...different."

The other women in the shop added their approval, as well.

Arlene nodded. She felt different. "Thank you."

Linsey beamed. Clearly she'd been worried.

Arlene paid her, giving her a nice tip, and stepped out of the shop, lighter, freer somehow. Amazing what a haircut could do. If she'd known this, she would have gotten one a lot sooner.

She smiled at the thought because it was so unlikely. That old Arlene Evans would have hated this haircut. That Arlene had spent years hiding behind her hair.

She listened for her mother's two cents worth.

Not a word.

She smiled, feeling freer than she had ever imagined she could feel…except for that little ache in her heart where Hank had been.

A warm dry wind blew across the rolling hills keeling over the tall green grass. Hank rode his horse toward the horizon, dust churning up behind him.

In the distance the Little Rockies met the sky in a ragged dark line of deep purple. Above him a hawk soared in all that blue, and only a wisp of clouds scudded along high overhead.

As he rode, he could almost imagine the endless herds of buffalo that had rumbled over this land before him. Before barbed wire. Before the white man.

As a boy, he'd never dreamed of anything like this. Not the land. Nor the ranch. Or even the horse beneath him.

Hell, he'd never dreamed at all. As young as he'd been, he'd seen his future in the dirty streets, in the faces of the poor and disheartened. Cameron had rescued him from that urban squalor. And Hank had blamed him ever since.

You're not angry at Cameron. You're furious with yourself and you know damned well why.

He'd been mentally kicking himself all morning. Usually he could lose himself on horseback as if transported to another time, another life in this immense country.

But not today.

All he could think about was Arlene. He hated the way he'd left things last night.

All his fault. He should never have signed up for the dating service, let alone asked her out. Had he really thought he could put his past behind him? A past like his?

There were no second chances.

And yet, even as he thought it, he rebelled at the idea. The moment he'd seen Arlene that day in the café he'd been filled with a desire to start over. Maybe he had asked her out on impulse. Certainly she had tugged at his heartstrings.

And maybe it had originally been a pity date, just as she'd accused him. He'd seen himself in her and felt sorry for them both. How pitiful was that?

He'd been lonely. He'd wanted someone to share this part of his life with. He'd sensed that Arlene needed a second chance as much as he did.

What had he thought? That he'd find an uncomplicated woman? As if there was such a thing. But Arlene definitely wasn't that.

She was the most complex woman he'd ever met. Maybe that had been part of the fascination, as well. He'd never met anyone like her. She'd *lived*. Just as he had. And they both had the scars to prove it.

The difference was, his old baggage could get him killed. Arlene thought she'd messed up her life? She had no idea the kind of trouble he could bring to her.

He did what he had to do. Walked away. For her sake.

You always were so full of bull, Hank Monroe.

He swore under his breath. Okay, maybe Arlene did scare him. Being with her would be complicated. She made him feel things he'd hoped never to feel again. He'd wanted someone to spend time with, not someone he might fall in love with.

Arlene made him want to step up and be a better man. When he was with her he felt so deeply....

He drew his horse up as a spooked herd of antelope thundered down a sandy-bluffed draw, their color blending perfectly with their surroundings.

"So what the hell are you going to do?" Hank asked himself, his words sailing off on the wind.

He could try to outrun his past. Or he could stay and fight. It was ironic, in a way, that he had moved to a part of Montana that had been lawless until as late as the early 1900s. At least back then you could tell the good guys from the bad even when they weren't wearing their hats.

His horse shuddered under him and took an impatient step as if to say, *Make a decision.*

It wasn't that he hadn't known until that moment what he wanted. He just hadn't admitted it.

With a curse, he turned his horse back toward the ranch. He'd lived by one rule his whole life: There were some things worth fighting for even against the odds.

This life here in this part of Montana was worth fighting for. So was Arlene.

Not that it didn't scare the hell out of him. But he'd made up his mind. He'd tell Arlene everything. He'd understand if she wanted nothing to do with him given his past—and the fact that a hired killer might be coming after him.

After taking care of his horse, he hurried into the house from the barn to answer his ringing phone, thinking it might be Arlene.

He didn't reach his office in time. The answering machine picked up.

"Hank." Cameron's voice.

He felt a chill shudder through him.

"Good news. You've been approved for digital TV. And

that little problem we had with your credit—that's been taken care of. So it's all locked up. Nothing to worry about. Hope that makes your day." There was a click on the line. The answering machine hummed a while longer and then fell silent.

Rena. They'd caught her.

Now all he had to do was find Arlene and hope she'd give him another chance.

Arlene caught her reflection in the window as she headed for her pickup and felt a jolt as it took her a moment to even recognize herself.

She heard a car door open and close and saw Hank coming toward her from across the street.

She didn't know what to feel after last night. But as hard as she tried, she couldn't crush the pleasure that sprang up inside her at just the sight of him.

He smiled, taking in her hair, her face. The tenderness of his gaze was almost her undoing. "Hello, beautiful," he said.

She couldn't help but laugh. Not her usual donkey laugh, this one soft, throaty. His good mood was contagious. So different from the man on his porch last night. What had brought about this change?

She'd promised herself that when she saw him again she wouldn't allow herself to feel anything. That she would go back to being impervious, back to the woman who wouldn't show her hurt even if it killed her.

But there was no going back. Her pleasure showed in her face. She could feel it. Just like her vulnerability. She had no defenses against this man.

"I'm sorry about last night," Hank said quickly. "I need

to tell you what's been going on with me if you'll give me the chance. I came to find you. Mind taking a ride?"

"You really don't need to explain," Arlene said, fearing the explanation could be more painful than even what had been said last night.

He stepped to her so quickly she didn't have a chance to react. His arm encircled her waist. He pulled her to him, his mouth dropping to hers.

The kiss took her even more by surprise. It was filled with passion and yearning and possession.

And when it ended, he pulled back to look in her eyes. "Please give me a second chance."

She could do nothing more than nod, her heart a thunder in her chest as he slipped her hand into his large one and they walked across the street like that. She knew that Linsey and the others would be watching from the window, speculating, but she didn't care. His kiss had warmed her all over, and his hand felt so good, warm, lightly callused, strong.

He drove her out to his ranch, touching her cheek or her hand or her arm occasionally on the way, as if afraid she might bolt.

She'd heard about the house on the rumor mill, but the only local she knew who'd been inside since Hank had bought it was Claudia Nicholson, who cleaned for him.

"I know it's too big," he said as he shoved open the door and stepped back to let her enter. "I'm not sure what I was thinking."

She looked around the massive living room and kitchen and thought about what Bo had said to her. Hank definitely had money. Did the government pay this well?

"Would you like something to drink?" he offered.

She shook her head, concentrating on breathing. Difficult this close to him. She could smell his clean, freshly showered scent. He wore jeans that on him looked sexier than any cowboy's south forty she'd ever seen.

"I want to be honest with you," he said, stepping to her. "I'm crazy about you. Last night I panicked because there was a problem with my former occupation, a loose end that— Oh, hell, a rogue agent I thought was dead who apparently isn't. But I just found out that she's been caught."

"She?" Arlene had to ask.

He nodded. "It's a long story and I don't want to talk about the past. I want…" His gaze locked with hers. "I want you." He let out a small laugh. "Hell, Arlene, you're all I think about. I'm asking you to take a risk here."

A shiver skated the length of her spine at his words. Take a risk? She smiled at that. He had no idea how much of a risk she was taking. Her heart, her hope, the chance of losing this woman she felt herself becoming before she even had a chance to know her.

She was scared. Not of this man's past. But of the future. Especially the immediate future.

I want you.

If she stayed here, she knew they would end up making love. Or at least she hoped so.

Had she ever made love? She had three grown children, but she knew what Floyd had done to her certainly was nothing like in books or movies. Not only that, she hadn't been with a man in… She couldn't even remember the last time Floyd had touched her.

"I'm not afraid," she lied, her voice breaking.

He smiled. "I can see that."

She touched his cheek with the tips of her fingers. That first step, she thought, is always the hardest. But she took it, closing the distance between them. Her pulse thrummed as she cupped his face in her palms and kissed him. He drew her close and she melted into him, knowing there was no turning back now.

Hank could feel Arlene trembling and warned himself to take it slow. He couldn't remember the last time he'd been with a woman. But, fortunately, it was a lot like riding a bike. And this woman made his desire flare and burst into flame. He brushed a lock of her hair back from her cheek. "I like your haircut. It suits you."

Her smile was shy. "I don't know myself anymore."

"I do," he said and kissed her. She came to him, her body softening against his. He saw her arousal in the warm brown of her eyes, flickering heat that flashed and fired as he touched her. A brush of fingers along her slim throat. The glimmer of a touch to her lips with his tongue. The gentle press of his palm hot against her back as he drew her in.

She moaned softly at his touch, fanning his own desire. He slipped the top button on her shirt, his fingers brushing the tender skin at her throat. She shivered as he slipped the next button free, exposing the top of her bra. He saw her throat work as she swallowed. In her eyes, fear mixed with excitement, with desire, with raw need.

The bra was white, the rounded curves of her breasts just as white. His fingertips skimmed over her tender bare skin, the flesh rippling with goose bumps ahead of his touch.

Slowly he opened her shirt and slipped it off her shoulders, letting it fall to the floor. She swallowed again. His gaze locked with hers as he ran his hands over her bare shoulders and down her arms. He could see the hardened nipples of her breasts pressed against the white fabric of her bra.

He reached behind her, unhooked the bra and freed her

breasts. As the fabric brushed the hard tips, she made a sound deep in her throat that skyrocketed his own need. He'd never wanted a woman as badly as he wanted this one.

Arlene felt weak, her legs like water as Hank took her full breasts in his big hands, branding her flesh with heat. Her nipples hardened to aching peaks as his gaze traveled over the swell of her breasts.

She let out a moan, her head falling back as he lowered his mouth to lathe the dark nipples with his tongue. Heat shot to her center. Her insides felt molten and she thought she would die if he didn't take her—and soon.

"Hank," she said on a breath. "Please."

He cupped her bottom with his hands, lifting her off the floor as he carried her to the couch of soft, deep leather. She sank into it, Hank beside her. At the touch of a button, blinds dropped over the windows in a whisper.

His kisses were slow and sensuous. She felt the heat begin to build even higher, a slow, steady flame that licked along her nerve endings.

In the cool, dim light, her fingers worked quickly to remove his shirt, her palms itching to feel the warmth of his chest. With each button freed she discovered tanned, smooth flesh lightly sprinkled with honey-brown hair that narrowed to a vee at the top of his jeans.

As she spread his shirt wide, he dragged her on top of him, her breasts pressed into his hard chest. She heard his sharp intake of breath, felt the hardness of him, the soft tenderness of his mouth as he kissed her.

They wriggled out of their jeans as they rolled around on the huge couch like teenagers, grappling and groping.

Hank let out a chuckle as, finally naked, he pulled her

against him so they were lying side by side, facing each other. "You feel so damned good, Arlene Evans."

She felt his fingers slip between her thighs. She let out a small surprised, pleased cry as he touched her. Her heart began to pound, her breasts ached from her hardened nipples and, against her will, her hips began to move with the motion of his fingers.

"Hank." The word came out on a gasp. "Hank!"

The feeling rocked through her, blinding her, shocking her, liberating her.

He rolled on top of her, his breath tickling her neck as he trailed kisses over her jawline to her mouth. His eyes locked with hers and she saw recognition in his gaze. His look softened, and she felt embarrassed and ashamed that this was the first time she'd ever felt this. All those wasted years.

But almost at once the feeling vanished. She had a lot of years to make up for. Starting right now. He raised himself over her and she wrapped her arms around his neck.

She lifted her hips to meet him, wanting him inside her, needing him inside her.

And then he filled her, making her catch her breath. She rocked against him, caught up in the rhythm of lovemaking for the first time.

That building inside her started again. The beginning of a roller-coaster ride, the climbing up, up, up until she thought she couldn't go any higher or she would start screaming. And then she reached the top, Hank right there with her, and they plummeted down the other side in a breathtaking release of pleasure beyond her wildest dreams.

They lay together, locked in each other's arms, panting and laughing and gazing longingly at one another.

"Wow," he said as he rose up on one elbow to look down at her.

And suddenly she felt shy and a little embarrassed as his gaze took in the length of her. She froze as she saw him focus on her cesarean scar and quickly tried to cover it with her arm, but he stopped her, moving her arm aside as he sat up.

Then, to her amazement, he leaned down and trailed a line of kisses across the ridge of the scar.

When he raised his head, his eyes locked with hers. She reached for him, cradling his head in her hands as she pulled him onto her and kissed him.

She'd suspected she was falling in love with Hank Monroe. Now she knew she was.

Chapter 9

Arlene woke in Hank's big bed to the smell of bacon. For a moment she just lay there, luxuriating in the cool, silken feel of the sheets and in the small homey sounds coming from the kitchen, reliving the long afternoon.

Her cheeks flushed at the memory. The man had been insatiable—and the things he'd done to her! Floyd had never! During their marriage, he would come in from the field, lie down beside her in bed at night and, after a chaste kiss on her cheek, climb on her and huff and puff until he was sated, then he would roll over and go to sleep, and she would lie there until he began to snore.

She would rise, wash up, put on a clean nightgown and go back to bed, where it would take her forever to get to sleep.

She'd never imagined the kind of responses a man like Hank could elicit from her body. *Her* body! She'd never been so wanton. Or so satisfied. Her body felt molten inside, reshaped by fire.

"Hello."

She looked up to see Hank standing in the doorway. He smiled at her and strode over to the bed to lean down and kiss her.

"What time is it?" she asked, glancing toward the window. The sky was still light.

"A little after four in the afternoon. I hope you're hungry. I'm making us bacon cheeseburgers."

"Oh, that sounds heavenly." She sat up, the sheets falling away from her bare breasts.

"If you keep that up, I'll burn the bacon," he warned, his voice low and laced with fresh longing.

Her own desire sparked, but she pulled the sheet over her breasts, feeling the need for a shower. She glanced toward the bathroom.

"Help yourself to whatever you need," he called over his shoulder as he left the room to get back to the kitchen and the bacon.

In the bathroom, she turned on the shower and stepped in. The warm water washed over her skin, reminding her of Hank's hands, his mouth, his body. She shuddered and hurriedly showered.

As she stepped out, her skin flushed, she caught her reflection in the mirror—and was taken aback. She'd completely forgotten about her haircut.

Smiling at her reflection, she fluffed up the wet curls, pleased with the look. Just plain pleased. It felt strange to feel this way, and for just an instant she almost let worry suck the life back out of her. She'd worried about everything under the sun all her life. It felt good to just feel good for a while.

When she opened the bathroom door, she saw that Hank had left her one of his clean shirts and a pair of his shorts. She put them on and, enticed by the smell of bacon cheeseburgers, padded barefoot down the hall feeling decadent.

She found Hank in the kitchen. He looked surprisingly at

home even in such a large commercial kitchen. He handed her a beer and motioned to the table by the window.

Arlene had never had a man cook for her before. She realized as she sat down across from him that he'd provided her with a lot of firsts since they'd met. It amazed her that a woman her age, with three grown children, could have experienced so little. Until now.

They talked and laughed and ate as if they were both starving after their morning and most of the afternoon. She was just getting up to clear the table when the phone rang down the hall.

"I need to get that. Just leave those dishes," Hank called back to her as he hurried down the hall.

She couldn't just leave the dirty dishes. Carrying them over to the sink, she rinsed them and put them in the dishwasher. She had just finished when he came back into the room.

One look at his face and she knew it was bad news.

"What?" she asked on a breath.

"You know I've been looking into Charlotte's disappearance—"

"I forgot to tell you. I got a note from her saying she was fine." Arlene rushed to where she'd dropped her shoulder bag, driven by a need to believe her daughter was all right. She quickly dug through and brought out the envelope. "It's her handwriting. She's fine. She…" Arlene stopped, halted by the look on his face. *"No."*

"As far as I know, Charlotte is still fine," he said, coming to her and drawing her into him. "But I don't think she left of her own free will."

Arlene pulled back. "Why would you say—"

"There were no fingerprints on the steering wheel of Charlotte's car," he said.

She stared at him. "But the motor grease…"

"Whoever pushed the car into the ravine was wearing gloves. Latex gloves. The lab was able to pick up some of the residue from the gloves."

Arlene was shaking her head. "Why would they…?" She turned from him, biting down on her lip. "But Charlotte called, sent me a note…"

"From what you've told me about Charlotte, letting you know so you won't worry isn't like her," he said quietly behind her. "Am I wrong?"

"No." The word came out on a sob.

"The good news is that someone got her to make the call and write the note so she is all right," he said. "But there is something else. After you told me about her boyfriend Lucas?"

She turned. "Yes?"

"I did some checking. If Lucas is telling the truth, based on when you said he left town and what he told you, then Charlotte is closer to nine months pregnant."

"Yes, but…" She understood before he said the words.

"If the person who took her doesn't realize that, they won't be expecting her to give birth yet. They might not be ready when the baby comes."

"The baby? They want the baby?" Arlene cried breaking free to pace around the kitchen. "But Charlotte…what about—" The words died in her throat as she turned to look at him. "We have to find her."

He reached for Arlene, dragging her into his arms, holding her tight. "We'll find her. Get dressed. We need to get going."

She pulled back. "Where…?"

"Let's start with the local gas stations. There's a chance that if Meredith was in Whitehorse, someone will remember her. If they saw her with Charlotte, then we will have something to take to the sheriff."

Hank drove them into town and hit the three gas stations. At the first two, no one recalled a woman matching Meredith Foster's description. Fortunately Meredith Foster would have stood out in Whitehorse.

They hit pay dirt at the gas station on the road south out of town, Packy's.

"I remember a woman like you described," said the cute blond clerk. "I could tell she wanted to pay at the pump and was put out that she had to come inside."

"Was there anyone with her?" Arlene asked hopefully.

"Not that I know of."

Hank tried to hide his disappointment. "What time of the day was it?"

The blonde thought for a moment then started to shake her head but stopped. "No, wait a minute. I *do* remember. I was eating a piece of pizza for lunch behind the counter when she came in. I put it down to wait on her, but I remember her glancing at it as if I was committing a national offense."

That sounded like Meredith.

"Other than gas, did she purchase anything else?"

"Nope. That was it."

Meredith had gotten gas on Friday *before* Charlotte had left home for her doctor's appointment and had not been seen again. So there was no way Charlotte would have been in the SUV. No eyewitnesses. No evidence except circumstantial.

"I forgot to ask you what she was driving," Hank said.

The clerk thought for a moment. "Silver. Can't tell you what make, but it was one of those fancy SUVs."

A silver SUV. Like the one Arlene had seen drive by the house on more than one occasion.

As they were leaving Packy's, Arlene let out a cry. "I forgot to tell you. The doctor told me that someone called to confirm Charlotte's appointment a few days prior to that. The doctor thought it was me. But it wasn't."

"Meredith? It makes sense. She'd been watching your house. She must have known which road Charlotte always took. If she was the one who'd called to confirm the doctor's appointment, then she would have known when Charlotte would be on the road that day."

"If only Charlotte would have let me drive her to the doctor that day," Arlene said after she joined him in his vehicle, "this wouldn't have happened."

"I wouldn't bet on that. I doubt anything would have stopped Meredith."

"We can go to the sheriff," Arlene said. "We have proof Meredith was in town."

Hank shook his head. "We have a witness who *might* have seen Meredith. Even if we could prove Meredith Foster was in Whitehorse, it doesn't prove she took Charlotte."

"It makes no sense," Arlene said. "Why would Meredith Foster want Charlotte's baby?"

He shook his head. He definitely didn't want to speculate. But if Meredith Foster believed Charlotte was carrying her husband's baby, she might not want another baby out there who had any claim to her husband's attention or his money.

Arlene had paled. She shook her head, tears welling in her brown eyes. "She'll hurt the baby. Hurt it and Charlotte, won't she?"

"No," he said quickly. "If she was going to do that, she

would have done it right away. She had Charlotte call you and send the note. She needs Charlotte."

Hank knew his argument had holes in it. But he also knew that he had to give Arlene some hope. "Right now we just have to focus on what we know."

"But if Lucas is the father of Charlotte's baby..." Her voice broke. "Charlotte's lie she was spreading about the older man from out of town being the father got back to Meredith Foster. Don't you see? We have to let Meredith know that the baby is Lucas's. Then she will let Charlotte go."

He wished it were that simple.

Arlene seemed to realize what she was saying. "She can't let Charlotte go, can she? Charlotte can identify her."

"Don't worry. I have a plan." One he hoped to hell would work. He would have to sell Meredith Foster on the idea that a pregnant woman high on hormones could get off easier for kidnapping her husband's supposed pregnant mistress than for a double murder.

He just prayed it wasn't too late.

Meredith Foster was in her private bedroom, getting dressed to go out, when the call came in. She'd moved into the spare room at her doctor's insistence. At least that's the story she'd told John. He had appeared relieved when she'd told him. Apparently he didn't want to be around her any more than she did him.

But she knew he would do anything for the baby. *His* baby.

"The doctor says I need bed rest and no stress if I hope to carry this baby to term," Meredith had said. "She suggested separate bedrooms until the baby is born."

"Whatever you need, Mer," he'd said.

She hated being called Mer, but she'd bitten her tongue. It was hard not to show how angry she was with him. All of this was his fault. But she suspected he knew that. Just as he knew she would make him pay the rest of his life for it. And once they had their baby, he could damn well take care of it.

She picked up the phone after the third ring, already irritated. John was downstairs, but he wouldn't remember that Delores had been called away on a family emergency so there was no one to cook or clean or do the things they'd been accustomed to her doing for them. Including answering the phone. "Hello?"

"Mrs. Foster. We met the other day at your house. My partner and I were investigating the disappearance of a young pregnant woman? Charlotte Evans?"

"Yes, I recall, although I don't believe I got your name or your partner's."

"I just wanted to apologize."

That surprised her enough that it derailed her before she could insist he answer her question. "Apologize?"

"Yes. We had suspected that the baby Charlotte Evans was carrying might have been your husband's. That was when we believed she was eight months pregnant. We have since come across evidence that Ms. Evans was pregnant *before* she met your husband—by an old boyfriend. In fact, she is *nine* months pregnant."

Meredith slumped down on the edge of the bed, trying to take all this in as quickly as possible. "So," she said slowly, "you're telling me that my husband has been cleared, is that right?"

"Yes. So I apologize for upsetting either of you. The problem we've run across is Ms. Evans's lack of credibility because of all the lies she's told. Apparently her only intimate contact was with the boyfriend."

Meredith felt her head swim.

"It's been difficult because of her past with the law and, like I said, all the lies. At this point it's a wonder anyone believes anything she says. Also, her mother has had word from her. Now if she just finds her way to a hospital so she can have this baby, we can close our investigation for good. Again my apologies." He hung up.

Meredith sat holding the receiver. She could not believe this. The stupid girl had *lied?* Meredith wanted to scream. All of this had been for nothing. And now there was no getting out of having a baby she didn't want—and all because of some lying little whore?

She threw the phone against the wall. It shattered, plastic flying in every direction.

"Meredith?" John's concerned voice outside in the hall.

She knew she had to gain control of herself. She couldn't let him see her like this. Especially since she feared what she would do to him.

"It's all right, dear. Just one of those telemarketers who wouldn't take no for an answer." She heard him try her door to find it locked. Swearing under her breath, she went to the door and opened it. "I didn't realize I'd locked the door."

He was looking past her to the phone debris on the floor, no doubt wondering why it was necessary for her to lock her door. Especially since this was the first time he'd ever tried to come into her room.

"It's the hormones," she said quickly. "My temper is worse than usual. I really am terrible company tonight. Would you mind giving my apologies to our hostess? I'm not up to going to anyone's house for dinner."

"Of course. Are you sure I shouldn't stay home with

you? I don't like the idea of you being here alone in your condition."

Yes, her condition. She might have been touched by his concern if it had been for her—or if she didn't hate the bastard so much at this moment.

"That's sweet," she said. "But I insist. I'm just going to bed early. You go. And tomorrow you can tell me what everyone was wearing."

He frowned. Sometimes the man was so dense.

"I'm joking, John. But I will want a report on her caterer. I'm hoping to use that caterer for our next party. Promise me you will try everything she serves at dinner, including the desserts." That should keep him there long enough anyway.

He stepped back, albeit reluctantly, as she closed the door. She didn't lock it until she heard him drive away. Then she hurriedly changed her clothes. She didn't have much time.

Arlene was amazed by how quickly everything fell together the moment they reached Billings. A rented utility van was waiting for them, complete with service uniforms in their sizes, tools, mobile radios and clipboards.

She looked over at Hank. "How did you do all this?"

He smiled. "Let's just say I have a few connections left."

From down the street Hank had called Meredith on a secure cell phone and sewn the seed.

"That's all we can do for now," he'd said after he hung up.

"What if Charlotte is exactly where she said she was— with some man, safe?" Arlene asked. "All of this would be for nothing. Maybe worse. Won't you get in trouble if anyone finds out what you're doing, since you're no longer with the government?"

"Let me worry about that," he said. Just then someone inside the Foster home picked up the phone and began to dial. The number showed up on a readout on the equipment in the back of the van, along with a name. Cara Williamson.

A moment later, a woman answered. "Hello?"

"Cara, it's Meredith. I was hoping we could have lunch tomorrow. I'm going crazy waiting for this baby to come."

"Tomorrow? Let me check. What time were you thinking?"

"Eleven-thirtyish, to avoid the rush. I'm craving that incredible salad they make at Audrey's. Do you mind meeting downtown? I have some errands to run after. Delores, my live-in, had a family emergency, so I'm left high and dry."

"Is everything all right with the baby? I heard the doctor prescribed bed rest."

"For the first few months, but I'm doing so well she's letting me out, thinks I need the fresh air and exercise," Meredith said. "But these cravings..." Both women laughed, discussed the weather and finally got off the line, promising to see each other the next day at 11:30 a.m. at Audrey's.

"You had their phone tapped?" Arlene said, sounding shocked as the van fell silent. She raised a brow. "Is that... legal?'

He smiled at her. "Yes. If you don't get caught. Don't worry. I have immunity for life."

She raised a brow, not sure she believed that. He just didn't want her worrying about him. She had enough to worry about, he knew. "What now?"

"Now we wait."

It didn't take long. The garage door opened. John Foster backed out in his black sports car. He appeared to be dressed for an engagement.

As he drove off, Arlene said, "He's going without his wife?"

"Unless she's taking her own car."

"What if we're wrong?" she asked when Meredith didn't appear. "What if she doesn't have Charlotte?"

The garage door opened again. Two seconds later, a pregnant Meredith Foster drove out in her silver SUV.

Arlene swore. "That's the same color and type of vehicle that I saw driving by my house. We're going to follow her, aren't we?"

Hank started the van, but before he could shift into gear, another car came out of the darkness of a side street.

He let out a curse as John Foster's black sports car began to tail his wife's SUV.

"The son of a bitch is going to blow the whole thing," Hank said as he shifted into gear and joined the parade, staying back a good distance.

They hadn't gone far when he said, "I knew it. She spotted her husband following her. Didn't the dumb SOB realize she would be looking for a tail?"

"Obviously not," Arlene said. "If we're right, he must not know anything."

"But he suspects something if he's tailing her."

Meredith turned into a convenience store. Her husband parked on the street. Hank drove past to circle a block and come back to park far enough away they could watch but not be noticed.

Meredith came out of the convenience store with an ice cream cone and got into her car.

"She doesn't act like she sees him," Arlene said. "Maybe—"

"No, she saw him," Hank said. Meredith turned back the way she'd come. "She's going home. We're not going anywhere tonight."

Hank had wanted to drop Arlene off at a motel, but she wouldn't hear of it.

"I'm staying with you."

"It's not going to be that comfortable in the van all night." He didn't expect Meredith to leave the house again tonight. But he couldn't take the chance she'd leave when her husband, home from wherever he'd gone dressed up like that, was sound asleep.

Hank had known this would put pressure on Meredith. That is, if she had Charlotte. They couldn't be sure of that, and it scared him that while they were killing time in this van Charlotte could be having her baby while being held prisoner by someone else. Someone they couldn't even imagine.

On the way back to the Foster house he'd stopped at a pizza joint, filled up two thermoses with black coffee and bought three large pizzas, loaded.

"Dinner, midnight snack and breakfast," he'd said at Arlene's raised eyebrow.

Every few hours he moved the van. Residents in fancy neighborhoods tended to notice a van parked too long in one spot. Even a utility van. They ate, drank coffee and talked. The van was set up with a monitor, the surveillance camera mounted on the top so they could watch the house from the back and not be seen.

A little after midnight he got a call. He'd set his home phone to forward any calls he got—just in case he heard more on the case.

What he hadn't anticipated was a call from Cameron.

"She's flown."

"What?" he demanded, sitting straight up. "How the hell—"

"Probably the same way she fooled you," Cameron snapped. "I wanted you to know. Just in case."

"Just in case she shows up here?" he demanded.

"Sorry."

Hank swore as he snapped the phone shut. His suspicious mind couldn't help but consider that Rena had been allowed to escape—after she'd been told he was the one who'd identified her from some photographs. They wanted her to come for him. Maybe they hoped he and Rena would kill each other and clean up the mess that way.

Who the hell knew what they wanted? Or if his suspicions weren't just paranoia. It came with the territory.

"What is it?" Arlene asked.

He looked over at her. "It's my old life, the one I tried to protect you from." No chance of that now. He was too deep in Arlene's life to back out now, and she his.

He pulled her to him. Curled up together in front of the monitor, a curtain drawn behind the seats, he told her about Rena. Arlene had to know exactly what the stakes were.

"So what I'm saying is that it could dangerous," he finished. Rena hadn't been the kind of woman who would use someone else to get to him. But then, Rena had gone to the other side, hadn't she?

In the glow of the monitor he saw the look on Arlene's face when he described Rena. "I want you to know what she looks like in case you ever see her, so you can give her a wide berth—and me, as well, should she turn up."

"She sounds like she is a beautiful young woman."

He laughed at that. "In her case, beauty is definitely only skin deep."

Then he told her about himself. He was sick of secrets and he didn't want any between them. But also he wanted her to know who he'd been, *what* he'd been, because he knew they couldn't escape their pasts. He wanted her to know him. Know him in a way Bitsy never had.

"You killed people." Arlene said it so simply, without judgment, without reproach, when he'd finished.

"For my country," he said, his tone laced with sarcasm.

"It haunts you."

"Oh, yeah."

She snuggled against him, her head on his chest. "You and I have that in common, don't we? We both wish we could rewrite the past."

He stroked a hand down her slim back. "I guess we're just going to have to make the best of every minute. Have you ever made love in the back of a van?"

She shook her head as his hand slid inside her shirt to cup her breast.

"Then you definitely haven't lived."

Just before daylight, Arlene dozed.

It wasn't until a little after seven in the morning that the garage door on the Foster house finally purred open once more.

Chapter 10

Violet Evans had done everything they had asked. She'd been working at one of the nurses' stations as required by the doctors, hating every minute of the horrible graveyard schedule they'd given her and the mind-numbing monotony of the work.

Every day it was harder to pretend to be one of the sane ones. It had been easier to pretend to be crazy. How crazy was that?

She had too much time to think about her life. To remember things she'd forgotten, things that began to haunt her. She'd been a disappointment to her mother, but sometimes when she thought about it, she didn't hear her mother's voice—which surprised her.

It was her grandmother she heard belittling her. *You'll never get that girl married off, Arlene. You'd better teach her to cook. It's the only hope she has of ever getting a man.*

Her grandmother's irritating voice seemed to follow her through her daily duties. At night, Violet would take one of the pills the doctor had prescribed for her after she'd complained of headaches, and that quieted her grandmother for a while.

But lately the voice had been getting more insistent.

Violet had been forced to steal extra pills just so she could get some peace.

That girl is a malingerer, Arlene. You going to let her get away with that?

"*Shut up!*" Violet screamed.

"Violet?"

She looked up and realized she was still at the nurses' station, and now the nursing supervisor was watching her closely, looking worried.

"Sorry," she said meekly. "I was talking to myself. It's a song that I got in my head this morning and can't get out," she added, smiling sheepishly. "It's driving me crazy." She realized what she'd said. "You know what I mean."

The nurse nodded, but Violet knew the woman would be keeping a closer eye on her. That's all they did around here—watch you. It was as if they *expected* abnormal behavior, waited for it. Who wouldn't go crazy here?

And she still didn't have a release date. She felt as if it had all been a trick, as though they were pushing her to the edge, seeing if she would break so they could keep her here.

The irony was that she'd put herself in here. She'd used her intelligence to fool the law and the doctors into believing she'd had a breakdown. It had kept her out of prison. She'd pretended to be crazy. And now she was pretending to be sane. No wonder she felt…confused.

That girl is crazy, Arlene. Certifiable. Remember that wagon with the dead cats?

Violet shook her head frantically. *I didn't do anything to the cats. It wasn't me. I didn't do it. Noooooooo.* She looked up, hoping she'd only thought the word—not spoken again.

"I think you've worked enough for one day," the nurse said.

"No, I'm fine. I need to finish filing these." Violet stared down at the papers in her hand. Is that what she'd been doing? Filing? She couldn't remember.

The nurse gently took the papers from her. "You're overwrought. Why don't you lie down for a while?"

Violet nodded and stepped out from the behind the desk. She stopped in the middle of the hall, and for a moment she couldn't remember where her room was. Stress. It shortfused her brain. That and all the drugs they'd given her.

Well, at least now we know what happened to those cats that kept disappearing, don't we?

"Violet?" the nurse asked behind her. "Are you sure you're all right?"

"Tired," she said, realizing that she'd put her hands over her ears to shut out the sound of her grandmother's voice. How crazy was that, since her grandmother was dead? "I didn't realize I was so tired."

She heard a bell ding behind her and an instant later a young orderly was at her elbow.

"Show Violet to her room," said the nurse. "Make sure she takes her medication."

Violet felt a hand on her elbow and then she was moving down the hall in a direction she would have sworn she'd never been before.

Do you need any more proof that something is wrong with that girl, Arlene? A wagon full of dead cats. It's enough to scare the wits out of you. You can't let this get out. Imagine what people would say about this family if they knew. And we all know who they'd blame, don't we, Arlene?

"I didn't do anything to the cats," Violet whimpered as the orderly led her down the hall. "I found them like that. I thought I could…" But she couldn't remember what she'd planned to do with them.

As she crawled up onto her bed into a fetal position, she

saw herself at her bedroom window watching her mother in the yard below with an eerie kind of fascination. Her mother had been crying. Violet could tell by the way Arlene's body seemed to jerk with sobs. She'd never seen her mother cry before, especially like that.

It had been strange watching her usually stoic mother digging a hole and dropping the dead cats into it, her body convulsing with sobs, face stained with tears, her strangled words barely audible through the open window, "Violet, oh, my baby girl, what have you done?"

Arlene woke to daylight and Hank still watching the monitor. The street was quiet, as was the Foster house, but the sun was up. She could feel the glow of it coming through the curtains and wondered, as she did every morning, where Charlotte was and if she was all right.

A part of her still believed that Charlotte had taken off with some man. Just as Hank had told Meredith, the girl lied so much that it was hard to believe she hadn't told yet another man that he was the father of her baby—and probably had, if the mood struck her.

"Good morning," Hank said more cheerfully than she would have had she stayed up all night.

"Good morning." She sat up, knowing he'd seen the worry on her face and was doing his best to relieve her mind. She thought of his confession last night and knew how hard that had been for him. As hard as her telling him about her children and the terrible job she felt she'd done with them.

"Cold pizza," he offered.

She shook her head. "I'm fine."

He reached out and stroked her cheek. "You look beautiful in the morning."

"I can well imagine," she said with a laugh.

Suddenly his gaze darted to the monitor, and she instantly sobered as she watched the garage door yawn open.

"Let's get dressed," he said as John Foster drove out in his black sports car and the garage door slid shut.

"What about Meredith?" she asked as she quickly shed what little clothing she was wearing to put on the utility workman uniform, complete with cap.

"If we have to, we'll trick her out of the house, but I'm willing to bet she doesn't spend a lot of time cleaning the place," Hank said. "Even pregnant, I'd bet she has a very active social life. Also, if she has Charlotte, then she will know she's being watched. After last night, she knows that even her husband is watching her, so she'll stick rigidly to her normal schedule."

John Foster fought panic as he drove to work. Those FBI agents, even working in an unofficial capacity, asking questions about the girl, had him more than rattled. Add to that the strange way Meredith had been acting. He'd tried to write it off as her just being pregnant, hormones, as she'd said.

But he was worried. If Meredith had known about the girl, what would she have done?

He felt sick and scared, and it was all he could do not to get on the interstate and make a run for it.

We couldn't be happier, could we, John? Meredith's voice echoed in his head from the night she'd announced she was pregnant.

He couldn't leave his child. Wasn't that exactly the reason Meredith had gotten pregnant?

She'd never wanted children. She'd made that perfectly clear. At one point she'd even demanded he have a vasectomy. It was one of the few times he'd stood his ground. Had he known then that he would try to leave her one day? That he might want a chance for happiness with another woman?

He and Meredith hadn't been intimate for months after that. Hell, they hardly were now. He was surprised she'd managed to get pregnant.

Except she'd been more loving after he'd returned from Whitehorse, he thought now. Oh, God, had she known even then?

If not, she'd suspected. He'd been such a fool. Her getting pregnant, and the girl, Charlotte Evans, getting pregnant with his child, as well. He wasn't stupid enough to think it was a coincidence, not knowing Meredith the way he did. She knew about Charlotte. And now she had him trapped.

Not that he hadn't felt trapped all his life. His family and Meredith's had been friends from before the time the two were born. Just a year apart, the families had always joked that John and Meredith would marry.

Unfortunately his father and Meredith's were also in business together, and it became quite clear to John that he was expected to marry Meredith. He'd made the mistake of dating her a few times to appease his parents. Meredith had given herself to him and he'd taken her up on it. Hell, sex was sex. But then two months later she'd called him to tell him she was pregnant.

John had felt he had no choice, had never had a choice, not about going to work for his father or about marrying Meredith. It wasn't until after the huge, expensive wedding when they were on their way to St. Thomas for their honeymoon, that Meredith told him she'd lost the baby.

He'd suspected she'd never been pregnant. He had tried to make the best of it. Meredith had made it clear early on that they were married for life. John knew what he would lose if he left Meredith: his job, his family, everything he'd worked for. He'd be lucky to get out with his life.

After ten years of marriage, he'd gotten to the point that he couldn't take it anymore. Willing to give up everything to be free, he'd asked Meredith for a divorce. He'd left the house not caring what happened.

He'd gotten into his car and headed north, not having any idea where he would go or what he would do. The freedom was intoxicating. He found himself in the small western town of Whitehorse, Montana. He'd rented a motel room and gone out to dinner. A young blond woman had waited on him. She didn't even look of legal age.

John had gone back a second time. He felt sorry for the girl. She'd dropped some dishes. He'd given her a large tip. She'd been grateful and had asked him to wait for her, since she was getting off for the night, something about needing a ride home.

That was the last thing he remembered except for nightmarish bits of memory until he woke up in a strange motel room with the reek of the young blonde's perfume all over him and the girl in bed beside him.

He'd never been unfaithful to Meredith. That morning with the girl in his bed, he could just see the headlines when he was arrested for sleeping with an underage girl. He'd hightailed it out of Whitehorse, running back to Meredith. A mistake, of course, in hindsight.

He'd never dreamed he might have gotten the girl pregnant. Or that Meredith would find out and trick him into getting her pregnant, as well.

And now the girl was missing and the FBI was involved. They knew what he'd done, believed him to be the father of the baby, probably thought he'd done something with the girl.

John Foster couldn't imagine things getting any worse.

Unless, of course, Meredith had done something to that poor pregnant girl.

Hank watched the monitor and waited. He'd been a little jumpy ever since he'd heard that Rena was on the loose again, but he'd tried to hide it from Arlene.

What had worried him as he'd stayed awake last night on the surveillance was why *hadn't* Rena settled the old score with him?

It had been almost a year. How many kills had she done in that amount of time? Or was the one in Prague the first? Where had she been all this time?

In a hospital recuperating? Strange how that thought pricked him to his soul. Doing away with enemies of the state was one thing. Wounding one of them was another.

What a screwed-up job he'd had. No wonder Bitsy hadn't been able to take it. He'd never told her exactly what he did. Had she suspected? All Bitsy had known was that he'd worked with a female operative for a while. Until Rena had defected to the other side. Until she'd become enemy number one.

"Are you all right?" Arlene asked.

He glanced over at her and nodded. It hadn't just been Rena who'd kept him up last night. He was worried about Arlene because he feared that they might already be too late to save Charlotte and the baby.

Worse, he feared that if Meredith Foster had abducted Charlotte, it was because of the lie Charlotte had told about John Foster. A lie that could have already cost Charlotte her life. And all because Charlotte apparently didn't want anyone knowing that Lucas Bronson was the father of her baby.

Oh, the tangled web we weave, he thought.

He'd considered taking what circumstantial evidence they had to the sheriff. Better yet, the FBI. But he knew that with Charlotte's phone call and the note, coupled with her past behavior with the law, they wouldn't get more than lip service.

Also, Hank knew how the FBI worked. The agents wouldn't have been doing any more than he was doing right now. Actually, a lot less, he thought, since the phone tap would have been illegal without a warrant and they couldn't have gotten a warrant with such flimsy evidence.

The garage door opened again and he breathed a sigh of relief. He could feel the clock ticking and hoped to hell he was doing the right thing by not turning this over to someone who wasn't involved with the mother of the alleged missing girl. Would Arlene forgive him if he made the wrong move and Charlotte and the baby suffered for it?

As the back of the SUV swung up, Meredith Foster appeared with a dry-cleaning bag and several department store shopping sacks, as if returning items. She was dressed up for her luncheon engagement with her friend Cara.

She slammed the trunk door, looking very pregnant, and disappeared back into the garage. A moment later, the silver SUV backed out and sped off down the street toward downtown Billings, making him wonder if he wasn't chasing the wrong suspect.

Hank called the home phone just to make sure that Delores was gone as Meredith had said. The live-in's car wasn't on the street where it had been last time. He'd seen it and run the plates.

The phone rang and rang and finally the answering machine picked up.

He hung up without leaving a message and looked over at Arlene. "Ready?"

* * *

The Foster house had a security system, state-of-the-art, the kind Hank had been trained in years ago.

Within minutes he and Arlene, dressed in their utility company uniforms, with him carrying a toolbox, headed for the back door.

Within seconds they were in the house, the system disarmed. He handed Arlene a pair of latex gloves. "Put these on. Leave everything just as it was. You start upstairs." He handed her a small two-way radio. "I'll signal you if we need to get out quickly."

She nodded, clipped the radio to her belt as he had done and snapped on the gloves, her face set in determination.

"Ten minutes. See what you can find," he said, knowing he didn't have to explain to her what they were looking for.

He took the office. The entire place was too neat and clean. It felt like one of those model homes where no one lives. Even Arlene's, with the plastic covers on the couch and chairs, was more inviting.

The office, which he found at once, contained little. One three-drawer cherry file cabinet that matched the desk and chair. The top desk drawer had the usual: pens, extra box of staples, thumbtacks, paper clips, white-out and stamps. The two other drawers contained envelopes, paper and bills to be paid.

Hank sorted through the mail twice seeing nothing except the usual household bills. No rental records for some hideaway to keep a young pregnant girl. He hadn't expected Meredith Foster to be that foolish. She hadn't been.

The file cabinet was locked. He found the key under the box of staples in the top desk drawer.

Like the rest of the office, the file cabinet offered nothing of interest except insight into the Fosters. Both seemed to be meticulous to the extreme.

If either of them had something to do with Charlotte being missing, then the abduction would have been well planned.

Something was bothering him. He couldn't put his finger on it until he had searched the rest of the downstairs.

He backtracked to the office. Medical bills. John Foster had said his wife was having a difficult pregnancy. Meredith had indicated the same thing. But he couldn't remember seeing any in the mail.

He opened the file cabinet again and pulled out the file marked *Medical* and riffled through the papers.

Dr. Florence Springer. Hank memorized the name and address. He knew why he hadn't picked up on it earlier. There were only a couple of paid bills from Dr. Springer in the file.

Maybe Meredith had been seeing a specialist. But then, where were the invoices?

In the back of the file cabinet was a box marked *Canceled Checks*.

One quick peek was all he needed. All of the checks were signed in Meredith Foster's no-nonsense neat hand.

Of course Meredith would do the bills. No checks to another doctor.

As he closed the file cabinet, locked it, replacing the key in the drawer, he heard Arlene come into the room and looked up. One look, and he knew she'd found something.

Arlene clutched the book in her hands to keep from shaking.

"What did you find?" Hank asked.

"This was next to her bed, on the bookshelf with some other books about babies and pregnancy."

"Nothing unusual about that, since she's pregnant," Hank said.

"Except this one was wedged behind the others." She handed him the book, her hand trembling from the shock of what she'd found. "Check out the pages she has marked."

He glanced at the title of the book, then let the pages fall open to the receipt Meredith Foster had been using as a bookmark.

Hank closed the book after a moment to study the title. She watched him school his expression.

"C-sections aren't that unusual, especially in high-risk pregnancies," he said. "She'd read up on them."

"It's a *medical* book." Her voice broke. "Why would she need to know how to perform the surgery?"

"Put the book back exactly as you found it," he said, glancing at his watch. "We have to get out now."

"Hank—"

"We can talk in the van. I'll meet you in the kitchen."

She'd hoped he would relieve her growing fear about Charlotte and the baby. He'd tried, but she knew that the medical book and the marked page had upset him as much as it had her. Only he was better at hiding his reaction.

She hurried up the stairs to the spare bedroom where it was clear that Meredith had been staying and did as he'd instructed, trying not to let her fear get the best of her. Now more than ever she couldn't fall apart.

She was waiting in the kitchen, standing on the expensive Italian tile, not touching anything, making herself as small as possible, when he suddenly appeared.

She'd never known anyone who could move so quietly. He motioned toward the back door they'd come in. She followed. Once outside, she took a gasping breath. The air was hot and close and she felt as if she were suffocating.

He reset the alarm, stripped off his gloves. She did the same, stuffing them into her pocket just as he had done. Then he took her arm as he led her along the side of the house until they were almost to the spot where the elaborate landscaping that blocked any view of the neighbors ended.

He stopped to pick up the toolbox from where he'd ditched it. Arlene made sure her hair was tucked under her cap. He gave her a thumbs-up and, with toolbox in hand, walked casually to the service van parked at the curb.

It wasn't until they were inside the van and several blocks away that she finally felt she could breathe. She fought the fear that threatened to overwhelm her. She could feel the clock ticking. Charlotte could have the baby at any moment. Maybe already had.

Was she alone? Scared?

Arlene fought back the tears that closed her throat. What if something horrible had happened to Charlotte and the baby, and that it was too late? *They* were too late?

Hank parked the van. She felt his hand on her arm. She turned to him.

"I know you're scared. But, believe me, I'm trying to find her as fast as possible."

She nodded. "I know. Thank you. Meredith did something with Charlotte and the baby, didn't she?"

"I think it's possible given what we know now. Let me see what I can find out, all right? Will you be okay out here for a few minutes?"

"Don't worry about me. Just do whatever it is you do," she said, just then realizing that he'd parked in front of a cell phone company.

"I'll be right back."

She watched him go, wondering what she would have done without him. Certainly not have broken into anyone's home. Or even tracked down John Foster. And she knew how far she would have gotten with law enforcement.

As she waited, she did something she'd never done. She prayed.

Hank bought a cell phone and some minutes, then dialed numbers he'd told himself he'd forgotten.

"Need some medical information on one Meredith Foster. Doctor's name is Florence Springer." He gave the name of Meredith's insurance company, complete with address. "Looking for pregnancy information. Need it ASAP. Will hold."

He stood in the shade of the building, watching his SUV. He could just make out Arlene inside. When he'd seen the medical book, the chapter on C-sections falling open too easily where it had been marked, he'd tried not to let her see his concern.

But Arlene was sharp. She knew. She'd known when she found the book.

"Information ready to transmit," the voice on the other end of the line acknowledged. "Protected e-mail address?"

He rattled off a secure e-mail address. What would they do without computers? "How soon should I have that?"

"Sending it now."

He hung up and walked back to his vehicle and Arlene. Reaching behind his seat, he picked up the laptop computer and turned it on. The van came stocked with wireless Internet. Once on the Internet, he checked the special account he'd set up.

There it was. Quickly he scanned through Meredith Foster's confidential medical records, once, twice—and let out an expletive as he looked up at Arlene.

"Tell me," she said and seemed to brace herself.

"Meredith Foster *isn't* pregnant."

Chapter 11

They watched the Foster house from a distance via the monitor in the back of the van. Hank had gotten them more food before returning to the house. He'd checked to make sure no one had been there since they'd left earlier.

No one had.

It was almost six in the evening by the time John Foster's little black car pulled into the drive.

Meredith hadn't returned, and Hank had felt his worry escalate with each passing hour.

"Doesn't look as if John will be getting a hot meal tonight," Arlene said. "You don't think she—"

"We're about to find out," Hank said as he started the engine and drove down to the Foster house.

John Foster was just getting out of his car and hadn't even had time to close the garage door. He looked up as the van roared up.

The man stood like a deer caught in the headlights as Hank and Arlene got out and walked toward him. They still wore their utility service uniforms, but Arlene saw that John recognized them.

"I thought I answered all your questions," he said, already sounding panicked. If he wondered why they were dressed as they were, he didn't ask.

"Where is your wife?" Hank demanded.

"My wife? She's gone to visit a friend. You upset her. She's pregnant and could lose the baby." He sounded distraught.

"Let's step inside," Hank said calmly.

John Foster fumbled his cell phone out. "I think I'm going to call the police. This is harassment."

"Your wife isn't pregnant," Hank snapped. "She never was. She faked the whole thing. And, unless I miss my guess, she abducted Charlotte Evans and intends to take her baby—one way or the other." He stopped. "I thought you were going to call the police?"

John Foster had frozen in motion, the cell phone in his hand. Suddenly he dropped the phone. It hit the concrete garage floor and bounced.

Hank caught it before it could bounce again and handed it back. "We need to find your wife before she does something we're all going to regret. Now, shall we step inside?"

John nodded and turned to lead them into the house. Hank closed the garage door behind them and followed.

"Where did she say she was going?" Hank asked as soon as they were standing in the kitchen.

"She didn't say. She was angry with me and said she needed time alone to think. She knows about me and Charlotte."

Hank swore. "I called Meredith last night and told her it wasn't your baby. You never slept with Charlotte. She drugged you and only planned to tell you that you'd impregnated her. Apparently she'd planned to have you help with expenses. She never got around to doing that, right?"

His eyes widened. "No. Meredith knew last *night?*"

"I guess she didn't tell you," Hank said.

John Foster pulled out a chair at the breakfast nook and dropped into it.

"I'll make coffee," Arlene said and Hank nodded his approval.

John looked stunned as he dropped his head in his hands.

"Where would she go?"

"I don't know."

"She has a cell phone with her, right?"

He nodded.

"What's the number?" As John gave it to him, Hank scribbled down the number into a small notebook.

Arlene watched for a moment, then asked, "Where do you keep the coffee?"

John shook his head. He looked dazed. "I don't know."

Hank heard Arlene going through the cupboards. She found the coffee and got a pot going, the smell filling the kitchen as he continued to question John Foster.

"Does her cell phone have GPS on it?" Hank asked.

John shrugged. "I suppose so. She always likes the best that money can buy." He looked alarmed that he'd said that. "Not that she doesn't deserve it."

"Your wife *lied* to you."

"I just can't believe Meredith would do anything like this."

"Can't you?" Hank asked.

John Foster took the cup of hot coffee Arlene offered him, clutching it in both hands like a life raft. He took a sip, then another, and seemed to grow a little stronger.

"Look," Hank said. "Meredith has to be checking on Charlotte, so wherever the girl is being held must be close. Do you have a summer cabin, a condo, a favorite place you go? A friend who she might have watching Charlotte?"

His head came up slowly. He blinked. "She has a friend

who owns a place in Red Lodge. It's about thirty miles south of here in the mountains."

Hank shot Arlene a look. "Is there a phone up there?"

John shook his head. "No cell phone service either."

"Can you draw us a map how to get there?"

John nodded as Hank handed him the notebook and pen.

Hank swore. He'd watched Meredith load a lot of things into the SUV—from the rear. She'd wanted them to see her. She'd known they would be watching. Just as she had to have known her phone was tapped. That's why she'd made the luncheon appointment on her land line. She'd probably canceled it via her cell phone later.

He'd been had. He should have followed her. But if he hadn't gotten into the house, he wouldn't have known she wasn't pregnant. Not that that information didn't seem pretty worthless right now.

It wouldn't help find Charlotte. But at least he had a pretty good idea of why Meredith had taken Charlotte. She wanted the baby. Apparently planned to try to pass it off as her own.

What had she planned to do with Charlotte, though? That worried him. That and the fact that Meredith knew they were onto her. How did that change things?

Would she make a run for it? Or did she think she could still get away with this? There was no evidence against Meredith at this point. If Charlotte was never found…

He didn't want to go down that road. He had to find her—and fast.

As meticulous as Meredith was, she'd planned ahead, probably taking a suitcase to wherever she had Charlotte stashed—maybe even before she'd abducted the girl. She probably had the rest figured out, as well, a story about her

baby being born earlier, away from a hospital, then showing up with Charlotte's baby. No one would have been the
wiser, since apparently she'd had John fooled from day one.

Meredith could have gotten away with it.

"We're going to need a photograph of your wife," he told
John as he tore the map from the notebook and handed it
to Arlene. While John went to get a photo, Hank asked Arlene, "How you holding up?"

"Okay," she said.

He smiled at her, dropping a hand to her shoulder to rub
her neck for a moment. He could tell she was on edge but
trying hard to remain strong. He'd never met a more cou-
rageous woman. If this had been his daughter, his grandchild...

John returned with the photo and Hank asked Arlene to
wait for him in the van. Then he turned to Foster.

"If you hear from your wife, you call me immediately.
Do not tell her that we were here or that you know she isn't
pregnant. If you do that, she will have no reason to keep
Charlotte Evans or her baby alive. Do you understand?"

John shuddered. "Meredith wouldn't—"

"Your wife is in a very delicate mental state right now.
One little push..."

"I understand."

"Good. Give me your cell phone number. I want to be
able to reach you."

Foster seemed more together as he gave him the number, but still Hank worried.

"If you hear anything from her, you'll call me, right?
You still have my number?"

John Foster nodded. "What will happen to Meredith if
all this is true?"

"It will depend on if we can stop her in time."

* * *

Arlene tried not to think. But it was impossible. She could imagine Charlotte, pregnant and afraid, being held prisoner by some stranger. Her baby girl. Charlotte had never been strong. She was the sensitive one, the one who seemed the most affected by any problems in the family.

With an awful feeling in the pit of her stomach, Arlene thought about how Charlotte had taken up for her sister Violet, taking that pain out on drunks at the bar. She shivered. What would Charlotte do under these circumstances? Unable to defend even herself, let alone her baby.

If Hank hadn't persisted… Arlene hated to think how badly she'd wanted to believe the phone call from Charlotte, the note. She hadn't wanted to face that anything could have happened to her daughter. That some crazy woman had abducted her and—

She brushed at the tears that burned her eyes as she watched Hank hurry toward the van. She couldn't panic. She'd been holding it together. That's what she'd always done. She was the strong one. She was the one who had always protected her family as best she could.

And now she had Hank on her side.

Meredith didn't know that they knew she wasn't pregnant. She wouldn't hurt the baby. If Charlotte hadn't had the baby yet, if she was being held in this cabin…

They would find her. Get there in time. Charlotte and the baby would be safe. And Meredith Foster would be locked up for a very long time.

She had to believe that.

"What is it?" she asked as Hank climbed behind the wheel of the van and she saw the frown on his face.

"Nothing." He sighed, looked over at her and added, "It's Foster. The guy worries me, that's all."

"Worries you how?" she asked as Hank started the van and they took off south toward Red Lodge.

"His reactions seem all wrong. Maybe it just takes him longer to assimilate what's going on." He gave her a reassuring smile and reached for her hand. "It's probably just me."

Arlene doubted that. Hank had great instincts. From the beginning he'd thought Charlotte's disappearance was suspect.

The elevation changed more than two thousand feet as they drove from Billings to Red Lodge at the base of Red Lodge Mountain. They drove through the turn-of-the-century downtown, with its sandstone and brick edifices of the late 1800s. Red Lodge was best known as the start of the sixty-eight-mile-long Beartooth Highway, a gateway to the high country.

"According to the map, you go out of town toward the Red Lodge Mountain ski resort for four-point-four miles," Arlene said, reading what John Foster had written.

The day cooled as they reached the dense pines at the foot of the mountain.

"Take the next right."

Hank did, then pulled off the road and into the trees. "I'm going on foot from here." She watched him strap on a holster and check the gun to make sure it was loaded.

"I'm going with you." It must have been her tone.

He glanced over at her, seemed to hesitate, then nodded. "Just stay behind me. And if all hell breaks loose, you dive for the dirt."

Arlene followed him as they kept to the trees. The evening was hot. Only the shade of the pines cooled the still air. According to the map, the cabin was just over the next rise.

Hank stopped, motioned her to silence as he pulled out a pair of small binoculars and crawled up the hill. She followed, doing as he did. When she reached him, he handed her the binoculars. She peered down at a small log cabin. There were no vehicles in sight. But there was a barn not far from the cabin.

She lowered the binoculars and handed them back to Hank.

"We'll check the barn first," he whispered, and she nodded, seeing no other place Meredith could have stashed her silver SUV.

The sky darkened behind the mountains as the sun made its descent and the first breath of cool air moved over them. The fragrant scent of pine grew stronger as they worked their way through the trees to the barn.

The barn was old, probably part of a ranch that had since subdivided. Hank tried the door, keeping his eye on the cabin. Arlene fought the urge to storm up to the cabin. If Charlotte was in there…

The barn door yawned open with a groan. Dust motes danced in the dim light, the smell of hay as strong as that of old manure. No silver SUV.

Hank turned to her and motioned toward the cabin. Arlene was sure that, like her, he suspected they would find the cabin empty, as well.

This wasn't where Meredith had taken Charlotte. Arlene felt the weight of her worry drag at her as they worked their way to the back of the cabin. Hank peered in one of the windows and shook his head.

The cabin was small and open. And empty.

"Where's Delores?"

Hank looked over at Arlene behind the wheel of his

SUV. She'd offered to drive, since he hadn't gotten any sleep last night. He hadn't been able to sleep, though, too keyed up and upset.

He hadn't been paying any attention and now saw that they were almost back to Whitehorse. They hadn't passed another car in miles. The land lay dark beneath the starlit big sky, the headlights carving a narrow swath of gold through the darkness as they sped along the two-lane road. For the last hundred and fifty miles there had been no towns, nothing but open country.

"Delores?" he repeated, tired and discouraged and starting to feel the effects of no sleep.

"I don't think she's been at the house since the first time we were there," Arlene said. She'd obviously given this some thought. "Didn't you notice the dust?"

"Dust?"

"And when I was looking for coffee, I saw that the refrigerator was almost empty except for some frozen dinners."

It took him a moment to catch up. He was still back on the dust. The Fosters were meticulous. The house spotless. At least the first time he and Arlene had been there.

He sat up, coming fully awake, his brain finally catching up. "Delores."

He snatched up his cell phone. "I need everything you can get me on a woman named Delores. No last name. She is in the employ of John and Meredith Foster of Billings, Montana, and I suspect has been for some time."

"It was just a nightmare," Violet repeated for the third time. She'd come out of the dream to find two orderlies holding her down on the bed and the doctor standing by, looking concerned.

"Perhaps we should try a different medication," the doctor said as he studied Violet now.

She noticed that the orderlies hadn't left the room. What were they expecting her to do?

"I'm fine. Of course I was combative. You would have been, too, if you woke up and two men were holding you down." She just wanted them to leave. "I just need to go back to sleep."

He frowned. "Have you been having trouble sleeping?"

She knew better than to lie. "It's excitement. Isn't it normal that I'm excited about the idea of life outside these walls?" *Escaping this hell hole.*

"I can understand that," he said slowly. "Are you worried you might not be able to cope on the outside?"

She warned herself not to answer too quickly. "Not *worried.* Of course I'm anxious. But I feel, after all the help I've gotten here with you and the other doctors, that I can do it. I want to do it. I want to make you proud."

He beamed and rose from the chair he'd pulled up beside her bed. "Good."

"How much longer do you think it will be?" she couldn't stop herself from asking.

"Well…" He didn't look at her and she knew. That bitch of a nurse had reported her odd behavior, and now this. "I'm thinking a few more weeks couldn't hurt. Let's see how you are then."

It was all she could do not to start screaming again, only this nightmare was real. She was never getting out of here.

She looked down and blinked away tears of fury. He put his hand on her shoulder. He had no idea how much she wanted to grab that hand and break every bone in it.

"Patience. You're doing well at your in-patient job here. That will look good to the board. You've made such miraculous improvements while here that we want to make sure there is no backsliding. You're our prized case."

One irony after another, Violet thought. She'd done such a good acting job that now she was their prized case and they were afraid that she would embarrass them. Just great.

"What's a few more weeks?"

Was the man insane?

She said nothing, couldn't have spoken a word. No, if she had tried, she would have howled, and he would have seen a side of her that would have struck fear to his very core and put those stupid thug orderlies on her again.

Part of her wished she could have let her fury fly, just let it loose on him, just to see the expression on his face.

A few more weeks.

As she lay back down and closed her eyes, Violet knew she couldn't stay here any longer. She'd been paying attention to deliveries, even flirted with one of the older drivers a few times.

She wouldn't be staying a few more weeks. She wouldn't even be staying a few more days.

That girl is a cunning little thing, Arlene, the way she always manages to get her way.

"Yes, Grandmother," Violet whispered and smiled as the doctor and orderlies closed the door behind them. "Aren't I, though?"

Her name is Delores Gonzales formerly of Mexicali, Mexico.

"An illegal?" Hank asked as he paced the floor. He'd been pacing ever since he'd dropped Arlene off at her house and returned home. Time was running out. Once Charlotte had her baby…

"*Was* illegal, but her employer, Meredith Foster, helped her get American citizenship."

Hank let out a low whistle. Delores would be indebted to Meredith in a big way. She would probably do anything her employer asked of her—even keep a pregnant girl prisoner.

He thought about what Meredith had said about Delores having a family emergency.

"Any family in the States?"

"An older sister. She is applying for citizenship through the Fosters, as well, and is also employed by the Fosters. Juanita Gonzales Mendez. Husband Juan deceased."

Hank swore under his breath. "Do you have an address?"

"Both are listed at the Foster residence."

He remembered the red minivan he'd seen parked in front of the Foster house. "What do they drive?"

"Delores Gonzales drives a minivan." He read off the make, model and plate number. It was new and expensive. Meredith either paid her well or provided the ride. "The other doesn't have a license. Nor a car listed in her name."

"Thanks. I owe you."

"Yeah, you do." The man dropped his voice to a whisper. "It hasn't escaped anyone that you've been getting inside assistance. Thought I should warn you."

"Thanks." Hank hung up as he heard the sound of a motorcycle coming up the drive. He walked out to the porch as the rider dismounted and came toward him. "Lucas Bronson, right?"

The young man was tall and lean, clad all in black leather except for the red bandanna tied around his head. No helmet. Kids his age didn't believe they were mortal. Hank remembered that age well. Hell, he still thought he was immortal at times.

Lucas stopped at the bottom of the porch steps to narrow his eyes at Hank. "Arlene said you're trying to find Charlotte."

"What do you want to know?" Hank asked.

"I want to know where Charlotte is," Lucas snapped. "I want to help find her." There was a strained passion in the young man's voice that Hank felt.

"Come on in, then," he said and turned and walked back into the house.

Lucas came in like a dog that's been beaten for coming in the house.

"Have a seat," Hank told him. Bitsy used to say he felt more at home with homeless people than with polite society. He smiled at the memory because it was true.

Lucas eyed the leather furniture for a moment.

"Sit. Tea or a soft drink?"

"You got a cola?"

Hank came back with a cold cola from the fridge. Lucas was perched on the edge of one of the leather chairs. Hank handed him the pop and dropped into a chair across from him to keep from pacing.

"So what did you find out about the old guy?" Lucas asked.

Hank smiled, knowing the "old guy" Lucas was referring to was John Foster, who was a good ten years younger than himself. A part of him wanted to challenge the punk kid to an arm-wrestling match just to show him what a really "old guy" could do. But that was such an "old guy" thing to do.

"John Foster?" he asked instead.

Lucas nodded.

Hank filled him in on what they knew. "You have any ideas?"

Lucas shook his head, worry in his expression. "She

could be having the baby right now." He met Hank's gaze. "I'm the father. She didn't run around with other guys. She never has. I know she's done some things she shouldn't have, but she's a good kid. I love her and I'm going to marry her."

"That's just it, Lucas—she's a kid. And now that kid is about to have a baby. You're still a kid yourself. How do you plan to support her and yourself, let alone a baby?"

"I've got some ideas."

"Any of them include an education? Maybe an occupation?"

"Yeah, as a matter of fact, Charlotte wants to go to college. She just didn't think Arlene could afford it with her old man splitting like he did."

"Arlene can afford it," Hank said confidently. "But she said Charlotte's never had any interest in going. Charlotte barely finished high school."

"Yeah, well, maybe she's changed. She wants the best for her baby," Lucas said. "That's why she was thinking about giving it up like her mother wanted her to."

"But you plan to talk her out of that," Hank reminded him.

Lucas shrugged and swigged down some of the cola. "I want the best for my kid, too. I don't want him having a family like mine."

"Him?"

"Yeah, didn't Charlotte tell Arlene? The baby's a *boy.*"

After Hank left, Arlene started up the porch steps, but then she heard Bo's stereo and wasn't in the mood to fight with him, so she walked back into the trees behind the house. She could hear the phone if it rang. Floyd had had a bell put in so he could hear the phone when he was working in the barn.

She didn't have to ask Bo to know that he'd made no effort to get a job. Or move out. She'd have to pack his things, leave them on the porch, have the locks on the house changed. How did other parents handle it when their grown children returned home and refused to leave?

She had no idea. All she knew was that she had to put him out. It was the only way he would ever become a responsible adult. Things couldn't keep going the way they were.

It was easier to worry about Bo than Charlotte. Just the thought of her youngest daughter was like a toothache that just kept getting worse until she didn't think she could stand the pain any longer.

Earlier, she'd called Bo on her way home. He'd said there hadn't been any more calls from Charlotte. No more mail either.

She sat down on the old picnic table under the big cottonwoods. She needed to be alone. To think.

It was hard not to panic. If Lucas was right, then Charlotte was nine months pregnant. Her first baby could come late. Maybe there was time.

Or maybe Meredith Foster would get antsy, especially now that she knew they were onto her.

Arlene wouldn't let herself think about what Meredith might do now. Her only hope was that a woman like Meredith was so used to things going her way she wouldn't panic and do anything stupid.

But where did she have Charlotte hidden?

She had abducted a very pregnant woman. She wouldn't have been able to drug her for fear of hurting the baby. So what had she done? Tied her up? Held her at gunpoint?

It was a three-hour drive from Whitehorse to Billings. How could Meredith try to make Charlotte as comfortable as possible—and yet at the same time keep her from getting away?

She pulled out her cell phone and dialed Hank's number. She needed to hear his voice. But she also had a feeling so strong she couldn't ignore it any longer.

"I have a theory," she said the moment he answered. She spelled it out for him.

"I was just getting ready to call you. Delores Gonzales was an illegal. Meredith helped her get her U.S. citizenship. She also helped Delores's older sister, Juanita. I think Meredith has them taking care of Charlotte."

Arlene grasped onto the news, telling herself at least someone was with Charlotte, taking care of her. "Charlotte isn't down by Billings. She's up here somewhere. Maybe close by. I feel it, Hank. Isn't there some way to find out where? You asked about GPS on Meredith's phone...."

"That only works if there is service in that area," he said. "But we tried another way. You know how parents can tell if their kid is where he said he was going to be via computer and the kid's phone? It didn't tell us where Meredith is. But by expanding the area outside of Billings, it did tell us where she isn't."

Arlene felt her throat choke off, her eyes filling with tears. "She's up here, isn't she?"

"It appears that way," Hank said. "Are you sure you wouldn't feel better here with me?"

She wanted nothing more than to be in his arms right now. "No, I need to stay here." In case Charlotte showed up. She knew it was crazy. But if Charlotte managed to get away...

* * *

John Foster couldn't sit still. He'd tried to reach his wife, but she had her cell phone turned off. He'd left messages. She hadn't returned his calls.

He wanted to kill her, feared he would if she came in the door right now. How could she do something like this? Was she crazy?

The periodic unexplained disappearances. Delores leaving so abruptly. Juanita already gone somewhere. Meredith's supposed risky pregnancy. The way she'd moved into the spare bedroom almost at once and kept him at arm's length.

He'd been relieved. He hadn't wanted to have sex with her anyway. But she wasn't even pregnant. Just like the first time.

His wife was a liar and worse.

What if they couldn't catch her before she did something to that poor pregnant girl? Meredith didn't really still believe she could get away with this, did she?

Knowing Meredith, she did. She would come home with a baby. His baby. Except now he knew it wasn't his baby. And she knew it. DNA tests would prove it.

No, even Meredith didn't think she could get away with this now. She would have to cover her tracks. He shuddered at the thought.

The phone rang, making him jump. He stared it as it rang again. Meredith? He recalled what the FBI agent had told him as he started to answer it.

If he told Meredith that he knew she wasn't pregnant, what would she do?

Turn herself in. Return the girl and the baby unharmed. The court would probably be lenient with her. She could be out of prison in a matter of years. Because of who their families were, she might not even have to serve a day in prison.

But what if she tried to get rid of the evidence—and got caught? Murder one. She'd never get out of prison.

John Foster picked up the phone as it rang again. He knew his wife better than she thought. She wouldn't be able to admit guilt, to throw herself on the mercy of the court. The public shame would be too great for her.

No, if Meredith were told that the FBI were not only onto her but also now knew she wasn't pregnant, she would cover her crime. It would just be their word against hers—without the bodies. Delores and Juanita would never talk.

He smiled as he said, "Hello? Is that you, Meredith?" He could see himself on some tropical island. If he sold the house, he could afford a nice boat. He and Meredith had saved enough money that he could live the rest of his life in relative luxury. Without working for his father and father-in-law. Without giving up a dime of his hard-earned money. Without Meredith.

"Meredith, I'm so glad you called."

Chapter 12

Hank stayed by the phone. Outside the ranch house, the sky darkened to a soft black velvet. No stars, no moon, no northern lights tonight. Clouds blocked out any light, giving the night an eerie ambiance.

Hank had talked Lucas into staying for a while. They'd made a snack and given up on conversation after a while as they'd waited for the phone to ring.

Lucas hid his nerves well, but Hank could see that the kid really was concerned about Charlotte and the baby—and no doubt beating himself up for leaving her the way he had.

Regret. It wasn't a good way to start a relationship. Hank just hoped to hell the two would get a chance. For the baby's sake if nothing else.

When the call finally came in, he snatched up the phone.

"We've got a GPS reading," the voice on the other end of the line announced.

Meredith had turned on her phone, gotten service and made a call.

As Hank wrote down the longitude and latitude of where Meredith's call had originated, he glanced over at the map he had spread out on the table.

"Who'd she call?" he asked.

"The John Foster residence."

He found the location on the map. Arlene was right. Meredith hadn't taken Charlotte to Billings or anywhere near it. He hung up and found the spot where Meredith had made a call to her husband just moments before.

Was it where she was holding Charlotte? Or had she been forced to drive somewhere to get cell phone service?

According to the topographical map, there was nothing but open country where the call had come from.

Hank looked up at Lucas. "Do you know that area?"

"Hell, yeah," the biker said studying the map. "I can take you right to it."

That was what Hank had been hoping the kid would say.

The problem was how to get there. "According to this map, there aren't any roads into that country."

"There are roads. Well, trails. You just have to know how to find them."

"How far?" Hank asked.

"Twenty-five, thirty miles. Rough road. We could go there on my bike."

Not a chance. "Draw me a map."

Lucas straightened, met Hank's gaze and shook his head. "You won't be able to find it without me. Trust me. Especially in the dark."

He didn't know whether to believe Lucas or not. But clearly he wasn't going anywhere without the kid.

"Okay," Hank said. "Let me call Arlene." He stepped into his office and dialed her number. She answered on the fourth ring. "Arlene, I think I've found Charlotte. I'm on my way there. Lucas is going to take me." He heard the rumble of the bike outside the ranch house and swore. "Gotta go." He hung up and raced toward the living room.

Damn kid was planning to take things into his own

hands. Hank grabbed the keys and the map off the table and raced outside to his SUV. He could make out the tail-lights on the motorbike. He started the engine and went after him, promising himself he'd kick the kid's butt when he caught him.

Lucas was cooking down the highway, but Hank wasn't about to let him out of his sight. The SUV had a big gas-hog of an engine, and right now Hank was damned glad of it.

The night was bottom-of-a-well black, clouds low, stars nonexistent. The only thing he could see was the white line of the highway in his headlights. No one else was on the road tonight but him and Lucas. Nothing unusual about that in this part of Montana, even in early summer.

This was austere country, wild, open and rolling. The only thing breaking the distant horizon was the purple out-line of the Little Rockies. The sky was immense. Only a few trees appeared out of the darkness, huddled around a creek bed or a small pond.

Hank had the feeling that he could keep driving forever and never reach the other horizon.

Ahead, Lucas braked, the light on the back of the bike brightening as he slowed to turn off the highway. They were headed into the country to the south of Whitehorse known as the Breaks. Hank had driven some of the bad-lands. Miles and miles of isolated country and only a few roads, most impassible when wet. Fortunately there hadn't been a rain for days.

He swung onto the dirt road and took off after Lucas. He could barely make out the bike's taillights for the dust the kid was kicking up.

Hank was swearing when his cell phone rang. "Yeah?"

"Thought you'd want to know. She made another call,

then a third call, this one from a different location. We have a second reading on her."

He felt around until he found a pen, then in the light of the dashboard he wrote down the new reading on the edge of the map. No way could he check the map and keep up with Lucas. "How far is that from where she made the first call?"

"About fifteen miles."

Meredith must have taken off right after making the call. What the hell?

"She called an Arlene Evans from the first location after calling John Foster. Then she called John Foster from the second location a few minutes ago."

Hank disconnected and speed-dialed Arlene's number. "Arlene!"

"Meredith called," Arlene cried.

"Tell me—" The T in the road came up too fast. He dropped the phone as he had to brake hard, gripping the steering wheel with both hands, and still he barely made the turn. The dust wasn't quite as bad on this more narrow road. He could make out the bike's taillights from a farther distance.

Groping on the floor, he found the cell phone. "Arlene? Sorry, I had to drop the phone. Tell me exactly what Meredith said."

He heard Arlene pull herself together. "She said that if I wanted to see Charlotte or the baby, I was to tell you to back off. She still thinks you're FBI."

"Okay. That's good."

"Hank…" Arlene's voice broke. "I could hear Charlotte in the background. She's in labor!"

That meant that Charlotte had been at the first location that Meredith called from. The one that Lucas was rushing toward right now. But why would Meredith leave with Charlotte in labor? Had she gone to get help? Or was she making a run for it?

"Arlene, I need you to do something for me. Do you have a map of the area?"

"Yes."

"Get it." He waited, driving at a little slower clip, but keeping the bike's lights in sight.

"I have it." Her voice was growing more distant. He was about to lose service.

"I need you to check this longitude and latitude and tell me where it puts you, okay?" He held what he'd written up in the dash light and read it off to her. "Can you find it on your map? Try to hurry. I'm afraid I'm going to lose you." Silence.

Then Arlene's voice, tight, scared. "Hank, if I'm reading this map right, she's headed right for—"

"Arlene? *Arlene?*" He swore and tried to redial, but the no-service signal came up. Disgusted, he tossed the phone on the seat next to him and concentrated on his driving. From what he could tell, they were now about twenty miles south of Whitehorse. He could make out the jagged dark edge of the pines that marked the Missouri Breaks.

After the most recent ice age, the Missouri River changed course, flowing along the southernmost edge of the glaciers, cutting a gorge a thousand feet deep on its way to the Mississippi.

Ahead, Lucas made another turn, slowing down, obviously realizing he wasn't going to lose him. Then suddenly, almost before Hank could react, the bike stopped in a flare of brake lights.

Hank braked, coming to a dust-boiling halt. He jumped out of the SUV and had Lucas by the throat before the punk could get off his bike. Out of the corner of his eye he saw what had stopped Lucas. Someone had felled a huge old cottonwood across the road—and recently.

"What the hell did you think you were doing?" Hank demanded.

"I lost my head," Lucas croaked. "I wanted to be the one to save her. I *needed* to be the one."

Hank gave the kid a shove. He stumbled backward. "That was stupid. Had you found her and gone busting in, you could have gotten her killed." He shook his head, wishing he didn't understand Lucas's reasoning so well. Lucas wanted to make up for the past. Didn't they all? "I'm actually trained in this sort of thing. So trust me, okay?"

Lucas nodded.

"Is there another way?"

He shrugged. "All these ridges lead to the reservoir. We just take the next one over. We'll have to backtrack—"

"Leave your bike," Hank snapped as Lucas started for it. "You're coming with me. One way or the other."

Lucas eyed him in the glow of the SUV's headlights, clearly not liking taking orders. But maybe he also saw that Hank was in no mood to argue. "Okay."

Hank could have told the kid that he'd be waiting in the SUV once they reached their destination. He had a pair of handcuffs in the glove box and would make sure of it. But right now he just needed Lucas to show him where to go.

They backtracked a mile or so up the road, then took what looked more like a trail.

Hank sensed rather than saw the movement out of the corner of his eye. His gaze shot to the rearview mirror.

He almost ran off the road as he found himself looking into Rena's green eyes—and the dark barrel of the weapon she held trained on him. She hadn't been in the back this whole time. That meant she'd followed them and had gotten into the SUV while he'd been arguing with Lucas.

Hank swore under his breath. He hadn't even thought to look for a tail. Especially someone driving without headlights on.

"Where are we going?" Rena asked, sounding amused as Lucas let out a surprised curse. "Tell your biker friend to be cool."

"Do as she says," Hank said as Rena pressed the barrel of the gun into the back of Lucas's neck.

Rena knew him too well. He would have tried to disarm her if the gun had been on him any longer. But he wouldn't chance it with Lucas.

"There's a young woman," Hank said. "Eighteen, she's having a baby and being held by a desperate woman who wants her baby and her dead. I'm on my way to try to save them both."

Rena cocked a brow and smiled at him in the rearview mirror. "You always were such a champion of the underdog. By all means, let's go save the girl."

Arlene had lost Hank. Frantically she tried to reach him again on the cell phone, needing to tell him that according to her map—

She felt the hot breeze skitter across the kitchen floor and realized someone had just opened the front door and was now standing in the doorway.

Bo? She'd gotten into an argument with him when she'd come in to answer the phone, and he'd left, walking down the road, calling someone on his cell phone to no doubt come get him.

So when she turned toward the open front door, she was

curious why he would have come back. She'd figured he would be gone for the night.

But it wasn't Bo standing in the open doorway, and she felt her heart leap to her throat as she saw Meredith Foster—and the gun she was holding. She looked very different—no longer pregnant, dressed in jeans, a T-shirt, a jean jacket and sneakers, her hair messed and no makeup.

All Arlene could think was that the coordinates had been right. Meredith had called her just a few miles from here.

"Is anyone else in the house?" Meredith asked.

Arlene shook her head. "Where is my daughter?"

"She needs you."

"I know she's in labor. Is there someone—"

"Yes, now stop wasting time. Let's go." Meredith waved the gun in the direction of the door.

"You're taking me to her?"

"Why else would I be here?"

That was the question Arlene was asking herself. "Is something wrong with Charlotte? The baby? You're here because I need to call the doctor—"

"No." Meredith shook her head impatiently. "Delores and her sister are with her. They have delivered hundreds of babies in Mexico. They assure me she and the baby are doing fine."

Arlene looked from the gun to the woman, trying to make sense of what the woman was here for. Not to take her to Charlotte, Arlene feared. "I don't understand."

"Your daughter needs you. There is nothing more to understand. She's in labor. She's screaming for her mother."

Just the thought of Charlotte screaming for her made Arlene move quickly to the door. A part of her still didn't believe Meredith was taking her to her daughter. But if there was even a chance... She hurried out to the silver SUV parked outside, still running.

"You drive," Meredith ordered.

"You don't have to hold that gun on me," Arlene said as she climbed behind the wheel and Meredith slid into the passenger seat.

Meredith gave her a tight smile as Arlene shifted the SUV into gear and backed out of the yard. "Turn right," Meredith ordered, still holding the gun on her. "It's about fifteen miles from here."

Fifteen miles on this road would put them in the middle of nowhere in the Breaks.

Meredith couldn't believe how good it felt not to be wearing that stupid maternity form. She pitied pregnant women everywhere, waddling around, eating lunch off their protruding tummies like snack trays.

Arlene Evans hadn't even blinked an eye when she'd seen her without the form. So what John had told her was true. That bastard. Apparently everyone knew what Meredith Foster had done. Or if they didn't, they would soon.

She let out a silent oath under her breath as she rehashed her upsetting phone conversations with her husband. This was all his fault, and he was acting as if there was something wrong with *her?*

Well, it wasn't over yet.

She'd been underestimated her entire life. Had she been born a man, she would have been running her father's and father-in-law's company. Instead she'd had to marry John. As if he would ever be able to take over the business.

Just the thought of John made her cringe. He'd told her that the FBI knew everything, knew that she wasn't pregnant, knew that she'd taken Charlotte Evans, and they were closing in on her. Unless she got rid of all the evidence…

It was the excitement she'd heard in his voice. She'd never been able to elicit any excitement from the son of a bitch. Until now.

"Imagine the newspapers," John said. "They'll have a field day. You'll never be able to show your face in this town again."

Oh, she really did wish she didn't know him so well. "They'll never catch me. I covered my tracks too well," she'd told him.

"So you killed that girl and her baby. You're going to fry," John had said, sounding both horrified and delighted.

"Montana state doesn't 'fry' people, John," she'd said sarcastically. "They hang them. And they have never hanged a woman." At least that she knew of.

"Then you're going to spend the rest of your natural life in prison." He'd sounded just as thrilled by *that* thought. "I'm putting the house up for sale. I'm buying a boat and sailing around the world."

"John? Are you drunk?"

"Not yet, but I'm thinking about it," he'd said with a laugh. "You've made my life miserable for years, Meredith, but that's over now. I'm free of you. The FBI will catch you. I'll tell them what you told me. Even if they can't find that poor girl's body—"

She'd hung up on him, too angry to even speak. Why she'd called him back, she had no idea.

"Meredith, is that you calling for bail money?" he'd said with a laugh when he'd answered the second time. "I'm sorry, but I can't in good conscience allow someone like you back out on the streets."

He'd definitely been drinking. Celebrating.

She'd hung up without a word. Which wasn't like her.

Neither was changing her plans. John wouldn't expect that. Once she had a plan, she stuck to it come hell or high water. He would expect her to panic. To do something stupid that would if not get her killed at least get her caught. Wouldn't he be surprised that she'd changed her plans at the last minute?

Clearly she wasn't herself.

Chapter 13

The narrow road ran along the sharp backbone of a rocky ridge, erosion eating away at its edges, which dropped precariously down vertical coulees thick with giant scrub juniper and tangled copses of cedar.

Hank had never been on a road more remote or desolate. He half expected a chunk of the earth to break off and drop away, taking them with it. He was beginning to think that Lucas didn't have a clue where they were—let alone that this was a back road to the location they'd been given. Charlotte couldn't be out here.

He did his best to ignore the fact that a hired killer was in the backseat holding a gun on Lucas. He had to concentrate on driving. But his mind reeled. What did Rena have planned? Clearly she could have killed him back down the road. But she wanted something more. Him to suffer? The people around him to suffer? Thank God Arlene wasn't with him—and she would have been if he'd had his way. He'd wanted her near, thinking he could comfort her, protect her.

As the road started to fall way toward the river bottom, he caught the dim light of a house in the distance.

Lucas must have seen it, too. Hank could almost hear the young man's mind at work. The kid was going to do something stupid. Lucas was young, already had regrets when it came to Charlotte. And he was a fearless kid who Hank figured didn't always consider the consequences.

Hank wanted to warn Lucas not to do whatever it was he was thinking of doing, but he didn't dare call attention to the kid. It would only give Rena the edge when Lucas ignored whatever he said and did whatever crazy thing he had in mind.

As they topped a small rise, Hank heard a soft click. Before either he or Rena could react, the passenger-side door swung open and Lucas threw himself out, disappearing over the edge of the road to drop into darkness and nothingness down a steep ravine.

The SUV couldn't have been going more than ten miles an hour at the time because of the road. The kid fell off the backbone of the ridge. If the fall didn't kill him, Rena sure as hell would.

Hank had hit the gas the moment he heard the click of the door opening, throwing Rena off balance. She got off one shot, the boom inside the SUV drowning out most of her expletive.

In his business, Hank had learned to never pass up an opportunity, especially one when it looked as if things were going to hell in a handbasket. Gas pedal to the floor, he jerked the wheel toward the drop-off to the right, grabbed his door handle and bailed.

He knew Rena would anticipate the move. She did. She got off another shot. As he hit the hard ground, tumbling head over heels down the steep slope, he felt a searing pain in his side. But that pain was quickly forgotten as he careened downward through a thick stand of junipers, the limbs scraping, scratching and jabbing as he continued to plummet down the coulee.

In the distance he heard something large crashing through timber. His SUV.

Hank finally managed to grab a limb and stop falling through the blackness of the coulee. He lay for a moment, assessing the damage. The fall had tweaked his left shoulder and left him feeling beaten to hell.

But it was his side that had him most concerned. Although the bullet apparently hadn't hit any vital organs, he'd lost quite a bit of blood. Bracing his feet against the base of one of the larger juniper trees, he took off his long-sleeved shirt, folded it and pressed it to his wound under this T-shirt.

That was the best he could do for the moment. Glancing back up the coulee, he could make out the line of the road above him, the sky a smidgen lighter above it.

He hadn't fallen as far as he'd thought. Which was good, since it was going to be difficult climbing back up. Using the branches of the junipers and small cedars, he began to climb. He wondered where Lucas was. He hoped to hell the kid hadn't broken his fool neck.

At least Lucas had been dressed in all leather. He probably hadn't gotten as scraped up as Hank, blamed kid.

But it was Rena who Hank worried about as he topped the ridge. The road was empty. He listened, heard nothing human. He could see the light of the house just down the road.

He hesitated only a moment. He knew by following the open road down to the house he would be a sitting duck. But he had little choice given the terrain—and the ticking clock.

Meredith had Arlene turn off the road onto a trail atop a ridge. Arlene had hunted some of this country with her father when she was younger, before her mother insisted she was too old for such foolishness. Hunters had made most of the roads trying to get to the Breaks, where there were elk, deer and antelope.

If she wasn't wrong, this one was called the Middle Eighth Ridge on a topographical, but it was hard to tell. They all looked the same on a dark night. And it wasn't as if there were signs out here. If you couldn't read a map, you were lost.

Obviously Meredith could read a map.

The road switchbacked down a steep hill, and Arlene caught sight of water—a huge surface of dull silver. Fort Peck Reservoir, with a shoreline that was longer than the entire California coast.

Arlene felt her heart drop. Meredith wasn't taking her to Charlotte. She was driving her out here to kill her. It would be months before some bow hunter found what was left of her remains. Animals would carry off most of the bones. After the vultures picked them clean.

Arlene glanced over at Meredith, thinking she would see this woman in hell first.

"Watch where you're going!" Meredith snapped as Arlene hit a rut in the road, jarring them both as the SUV came down hard, the gun in her hand never wavering.

"You'd better hope my daughter and the baby are all right," Arlene said, gripping the wheel tighter. "And that you're really taking me to her."

"Don't make threats you can't back up," Meredith said with disinterest. "I've taken good care of your daughter and her unborn baby."

"You can't possibly think you can still get away with passing this baby off as your own," Arlene said.

Just then she saw a light ahead in the distance. Was it possible Meredith had been telling the truth? She could make out a small log building. One of those hunting camps used during the season. Closed the rest of the year. Completely isolated.

The only thing Arlene could think was that no one would hear Charlotte's cries. Or her own.

"Watch out!" Meredith bellowed.

Out of the corner of her eye Arlene saw a large dark figure lurch up onto the road. She hit the brakes as a body careened off the right front of Meredith's fancy SUV and disappeared over the side of the road, into the darkness.

"Keep going," Meredith ordered, shoving the barrel of the gun into her side hard enough to make Arlene gasp.

"But we just hit someone," Arlene snapped.

"Drive. Think of your daughter."

Sick to her stomach, Arlene put the SUV into first gear. The vehicle lurched forward.

Who had she just hit? She couldn't believe someone else was out here. Her heart began to pound. Oh, God, what if it was Hank?

"Stop here," Meredith ordered as they reached a wide spot.

Arlene could see the log structure in the distance. If Charlotte was in there and they were this close…

"Stop!" Meredith ordered, jabbing her again with the gun barrel. "Now get out. You can walk from here."

She couldn't see any vehicles. Just an outside light. Arlene feared Meredith would shoot her once she stepped from the vehicle, but what choice did she have? If there was even a chance that Charlotte was down there…

She put the SUV into Park, pulled up the emergency brake and, unsnapping her seat belt, climbed out.

Meredith quickly slid over behind the wheel and, without another look, turned the SUV around and took off back the way they'd come.

Confused, Arlene looked up the road they'd come down, thinking of the person she'd hit.

A blood-curdling scream rose from the darkness below her. Charlotte. Arlene took off running toward the sound.

Hank heard the scream. He was almost to the lit building, all his senses on alert. He'd seen where his SUV had left the road, the tracks in the soft earth, the bright-skinned bark of the closest juniper. But it was too dark to tell where the SUV had finally landed. Or if Rena had gotten out before it crashed over the side.

He stopped. The whine of a vehicle engine carried on the breeze, and he thought he saw lights through the trees on another ridge in the distance. But the lights were headed in the opposite direction. Someone leaving?

He quickened his pace. The loss of blood made him feel light-headed. He pressed his now-soaked shirt to his side and kept moving.

A small log cabin came into view, rising up out of the darkness and trees. It sat precariously on the edge of the Breaks, overlooking Fort Peck Reservoir, the dull dark sky reflected in the water far below. A dense copse of ponderosa pines flanked the building on three sides.

Hank headed for the trees, weapon in hand. A breeze stirred the pine boughs, making them emit a low, mournful moan. A few stars broke free of the clouds. Silence settled around him.

He didn't know where Lucas had gone, and that worried him. Nor could he see Rena.

He hadn't gone far when he saw the red minivan parked in the pines. No sign of Meredith Foster's silver SUV, though, he noted with concern. Was that who he'd seen driving away?

Hank was to the cabin when he felt the presence in the darkness. An instant later the cold steel of the barrel was pressed to his back. He froze.

"You know how this has to end," Rena said quietly behind him. Her voice held no emotion, but she seemed to be breathing hard, and he suspected she'd been injured. That would only make her more dangerous—if that was possible.

"So what are you waiting for? Shoot me. End it." A breeze stirred the pines nearby, a whisper in the dark. He could smell dust from the vehicle that had left and the unmistakable scent of water close by.

In the distance a flock of geese made an inky ebony vee across the night sky, their soft honks barely audible over the thud of his heart in his ears.

Hadn't he always known this was how it would end for him? Just a few more feet, though, and he would have been inside the cabin. He could hear Charlotte's screams of pain. He felt his gut clench with fear for Charlotte and her baby. His pain was about to end. But hers…

Arlene was almost to the cabin when she caught movement by the door. While she couldn't make out any more than the shapes of two people, she could almost feel the tension in the night air. She slipped into the shadow of the building and held her breath.

One of the figures spoke. A woman, her voice low, sounding almost pained. But it was the second figure's voice that sent a chill skittering up her spine. Hank. So that hadn't been him on the road.

Her relief was short-lived as his words registered. He'd just told the woman to kill him.

Rena? The woman Hank had told her about?

Arlene's eyes had adjusted to the darkness enough that she could make out a woodpile behind her against the side of the building. She eased back to it, quietly lifting one of the more manageable logs into her hands, then she worked her way along the side of the building to the corner again.

The sound of her movements was hidden by her daughter's cries of pain inside the cabin. With each, Arlene felt her heart break. Charlotte was still in labor, having a rough time of it. Arlene desperately needed to reach her daughter's side.

The only thing blocking her way was a hired killer.

"This is between you and me," Hank was saying. "I don't want anyone else hurt."

"You and me?" The woman let out a humorless laugh. "There is no you and me. Not anymore."

"You went to the other side," Hank said. "You knew the price. You knew who would be coming after you."

"Indeed, I did. That is why I'm still alive."

"Rena…"

Arlene didn't dare wait a moment longer. She rounded the corner quickly, the log clutched tightly in both hands as she swung at the smaller figure.

The woman sensed her at the last moment—but not quickly enough.

Hank had seen Arlene come down the hill. He'd desperately wanted to cry out a warning for her to go back, but he knew her better than that. She had to get to her daughter. And Arlene wasn't one to back down just because the going had gotten rough.

He reacted the moment she made her move. He spun around, going for the gun, knowing that Rena would have heard the movement behind her. That she would be half turned.

There was a flare of light, an ear-splitting boom and a shower of splinters as the bullet tore through the log in Arlene's hands. But the shot didn't slow down Arlene's swing. The log struck Rena, knocking her into the side of the cabin.

Inside the house came an instant of silence, followed by Charlotte's screams.

The second boom followed swiftly behind the first. This time the shot went wild because Hank was on Rena, fighting for the gun. The third shot was muffled, followed by a groan, then silence.

Hank didn't realize he was all that was holding Rena up until she let go of the gun. Those amazing green eyes of hers met his gaze. She smiled, nodding slightly, as she dropped to her knees, blood blossoming from her chest and streaming down her face from a head wound she must have gotten when she'd jumped from the SUV before it went over the ridge.

She fell to her side, and he saw that the head wound wasn't her only injury. There was a jagged tear in her leg that showed bone. He knew that revenge had been the only thing keeping her standing those last few minutes of her life.

Hank moved quickly to shield Arlene from the corpse, looping an arm around her as he opened the cabin door and, stepping through, drew her in after him. He could feel his side, knew it was bleeding again. He fought the light-headedness. Just a little longer...

Arlene could hear Charlotte as Hank ushered her inside the cabin, making sure there was no one waiting to ambush them. The first room was empty. Charlotte's cries were coming from down a short hallway. A light bled out onto the floor from an open doorway.

Arlene practically launched herself at the light. Hank tried to keep in front of her, but her need to reach her daughter was suddenly so urgent, so primal....

She could hear the soft, encouraging murmur of voices in between Charlotte's moans and cries of pain.

As she and Hank reached the doorway, he motioned for her to wait. It was the hardest thing she'd ever done, but rationally she knew what they did in the next few minutes could be a matter of life and death.

One look at his face as he peered into the room and all reason left her. She rounded the edge of the doorway to find two Hispanic women, one at the foot of the bed and the other at the head, near Charlotte.

Arlene had been prepared to see her daughter tied to a bed. Held at gunpoint. Or worse.

Instead the room had been prepared much like a hospital room. Charlotte was propped up, her feet splayed. Delores, the younger of the Hispanic women, was holding the girl's hand, offering words of support in her broken English. She looked up as Arlene entered the room but didn't seem surprised to see her.

"She's my daughter," Arlene said as she rushed to Charlotte's bedside.

The other Hispanic woman at the end of the bed gave her and Hank only a glance and went back to what she'd been doing.

"I'm here," Arlene said as Charlotte burst into tears.

"Mama!" she cried. "Mama."

Arlene hugged her daughter. "It's okay, baby," she said, smoothing back Charlotte's long blond hair from her damp face.

The older woman snapped something in Spanish. Delores translated, "She needs to push with the next contraction."

Arlene nodded and turned to her daughter. "You can do this."

Charlotte was crying and shaking her head. "You have to get me to a hospital. Something is wrong."

"Listen to me," Arlene said, taking her daughter's face in her hands. "Women have given birth for centuries. In the middle of fields. In the backs of cars. This woman knows what she's doing. It will be over soon. You have to do as she says."

Charlotte's sobs lessened as another contraction began, making her suck in her breath.

"Push," Arlene ordered. She glanced toward the woman at the foot of the bed, hoping Meredith had been right. That there wasn't anything wrong. That these women knew what they were doing. Because it was too late, the hospital too far away. Getting a doctor here was out of the question.

"You're doing great," Arlene said to her daughter as Charlotte let out a pained breath and sagged back on the bed.

Delores translated again from the older woman. "She must push very hard at the next contraction."

Arlene nodded. "You did great, Charlotte. It won't be long now."

Her daughter actually smiled at that. Charlotte looked older but none the worse for wear. Apparently Meredith had taken good care of her.

Another contraction seized her and she bent forward, gripping Arlene's hand as she pushed.

The woman at the end of the bed said something in Spanish.

"What?" Arlene demanded.

"She can see the baby's head."

Everything happened quickly after that. Arlene was only vaguely aware of Hank in the room. Or that at some point Lucas had come in looking scraped up and limping. Arlene didn't put it together that he'd been the person she'd clipped with Meredith's SUV. She didn't question what he was doing here or how he'd gotten here or where he'd been. Her only thoughts were with her daughter.

Arlene concentrated on her daughter, feeling each pain as intensely as Charlotte did.

And suddenly, at the end of a long contraction, the baby was expelled. Hank, she saw, had stepped forward to offer his assistance, grabbing some clean towels piled on a table next to the bed.

The older woman gently laid the infant into the thick white towels that Hank held out to her, while the younger woman worked to bind off the cord.

As the baby began to cry, an angry full-lunged howl, Arlene finally let herself feel. Like the baby, she began to cry. Charlotte, exhausted, had tears in her eyes, as well, as she lay back in the bed.

The women took the baby from Hank to clean it up as the infant squalled. Then they handed the baby, wrapped in a clean blanket, to Hank.

He looked down at the baby, smiling as he stepped around the end of the bed to where Arlene stood.

"Would you like to hold your grandson?" he asked.

She nodded and he put the wriggling, crying baby into her arms.

Charlotte sat up to look at her son for a moment, a look of wonder in her gaze.

It was only then that anyone noticed Lucas. At some point in the delivery he'd keeled over.

As he came to on the floor, he said, "It really is a boy?"

That's when Arlene noticed the blood. "Oh, God, Hank, you're hurt."

Chapter 14

At daylight, the emergency room at the Whitehorse hospital was bursting at the seams, between the injured patients, the newborn baby and her mother and the local sheriff's department.

"I'm going to need a statement from both of you," Sheriff Carter Jackson told Hank and Arlene.

The two Hispanic women had been taken into custody, and an APB had been put out on Meredith Foster. Both Hank and Arlene asked for clemency for the Hispanic women.

"If it wasn't for them…" Arlene said, her emotions to close to the edge.

"I understand," the sheriff said. "Arlene, I want to apologize. I'm sorry I didn't take your concerns more seriously."

"It's all right," she said, no doubt surprising him. The old Arlene Evans would be threatening to sue the department and everyone in sight. "Charlotte and the baby are fine. That's all that matters."

The sheriff still looked upset with himself.

"Aren't you getting married in a few hours?" Arlene asked. "Isn't today the Fourth of July?"

He frowned. "Yes, but I—"

"I'm sure your deputy can handle this," she said. "You should go get ready for your wedding. We're all fine."

Lucas had a few cuts and bruises. Even being clipped by Meredith's SUV hadn't been any worse than some of his motorcycle accidents, he said.

Arlene liked watching him with the baby and Charlotte. Maybe there was hope for Lucas yet. Maybe there was hope for all of them.

The gunshot Hank had taken hadn't hit any vital organs, and while he'd lost a lot of blood, the doctor said he was in great shape for his age—didn't she know it—and that he should be up and around in no time. He'd have to recuperate for a while, though.

"Don't worry, I'll take care of him," Arlene told the doctor, then looked over at Hank. "That is, if you'll let me."

He shook his head. "I want to take care of *you*. You saved my life, Arlene."

She brushed that off. "We're even then. You saved mine in more ways than you can imagine. Not to mention that if it hadn't been for you…" Her voice broke. "I don't know what would have happened to Charlotte and my grandson. But all that aside, I'm going to take care of you as long as you need me."

Hank smiled and pulled her to him for a kiss. He'd seen a lot of things in his life, but he'd never seen a baby born before.

It had done something to him that he could hardly comprehend. All he knew was that he'd glimpsed his future in the birth of that baby. A future of grandchildren, long horseback rides across the prairie. And maybe someday he and Arlene would travel the world as he'd originally planned. Or maybe they would just sit on the porch and watch the sunset and count their blessings that they'd been given a second chance for happiness.

All of that would have to wait, though. Until he was on his feet again. And then he'd have to take it slow. Arlene would have a lot to adjust to with helping Charlotte plan a wedding and spending time with her new grandson.

But he felt they had all the time in the world now.

Hank had put in a call to one of the numbers he'd told himself he'd forgotten. He'd given the person who answered the information about Rena and the coordinates, and by the time the sheriff's department had reached the cabin, all evidence of Rena was gone. To all accounts, she'd never existed.

He'd told the sheriff that he must have shot himself when he'd taken a fall. Lucas was smarter than he looked. He'd backed up Hank's story of losing control of the SUV on the road.

Rena was dead. That part of his life was truly over.

Arlene finally talked the sheriff into leaving to get ready for his wedding, which was taking place at the Whitehorse Community Center this afternoon, followed by a fireworks show.

"You should go to the wedding," Hank told Arlene.

"I'm not leaving you. The doctor's going to admit you to the hospital. Charlotte has a room down the hall. The doctor said she's sleeping peacefully. She's going to be all right. This has changed her, Hank. She knows now how her lies led to what happened. I'm just so thankful that Meredith took good care of her, probably made her eat better than I was ever able to."

"And the baby?"

"At the nursery. That's where Lucas is. He's so young to

be a father, but he's determined to make a life for the three of them. He's already lined up a job on a ranch near here."

"You don't have to stay with me," Hank said. "Don't you have cookies to bake for the fair? A wedding to go to? A fireworks show? A grandson to gaze at?"

Arlene laughed, took his hand and smiled down at him. "I'm right where I want to be."

It wasn't until later that day that they heard Meredith Foster had been arrested. She'd given herself up and had made a full confession—including the murder of her husband John.

In her statement, according to what the deputy told them, Meredith said that unlike pretending to be pregnant, shooting her husband had actually been pleasurable.

"She could have gotten off easy on the other charges," the deputy said. "After all, she took Arlene to her daughter and she made sure there was someone there to deliver the baby. But cold-blooded premeditated murder?" He shook his head. "You got to wonder what she was thinking, huh?"

The Whitehorse Community Center was overflowing. Everyone in several counties had shown up for what they were all calling "the wedding of the century"—the marriage of Eve Bailey and Sheriff Carter Jackson.

If it happened.

Bets were being taken at the local bars.

Even Eve Bailey's sisters weren't too sure.

"Would you stop eyeing me like that," Eve snapped. "I'm *fine.*"

"Of course you are," her sister McKenna said, giving their youngest sister, Faith, a wink. "If you were any more fine, we'd have to peel you off the wall."

"I *love* Carter," Eve said. "I'm *marrying* him. *Today.* And nothing is going to stop that from happening. I heard what happened down by the Breaks. But Carter will be here."

McKenna and Faith exchanged looks behind her back.

"I saw that," Eve said and pointed to the large mirror against her bedroom wall. The two laughed and plopped down on their sister's bed.

"It's all going to come off without a hitch," McKenna assured her. "Carter wouldn't miss this. Wild horses couldn't keep him away."

Eve clearly wasn't convinced. "Even if he's late…"

Just then they heard the sirens and all raced to the second-floor window. They could see all the cars parked for a good half mile around the community center—and a cloud of dust coming up the road toward Old Town.

The siren died off as the patrol car skidded to a stop in front of the center. A cheer went up. Eve began to cry. "It's Carter. He made it."

"Of course he did," McKenna said as she and Faith hugged their sister.

"The Whitehorse Sewing Circle decorated the center with fresh flowers," Faith said. "It really is gorgeous."

"What about the food for the reception?" Eve asked, excited and nervous and anxious.

"Laci and Bridger have it covered," McKenna told her.

"I hate to have my brother have to work on the day of my wedding," Eve said, frowning.

"You know Bridger wasn't about to let anyone else cater this wedding," Faith said. "It's his present to you. Don't you think we should get down to the center?"

"Yes," their mother said from the doorway. Lila Bailey Jackson wore an emerald jewel-tone dress that was stunning on her. "May I speak to Eve alone for a moment?"

she asked her other two daughters. "We'll meet you at the community center in the bride's room in a few minutes."

"If this is going to be that mother-daughter talk you've been putting off," Eve joked. "It's a few years too late."

Lila smiled and shook her head. "There is nothing I can tell you about life that you haven't already figured out for yourself. There's someone downstairs who needs to talk to you."

Eve felt her heart leap to her throat as she let her mother lead her downstairs to where Pearl Cavanaugh sat in her wheelchair in the kitchen. Eve's twin brother, Bridger, stood at the window. He turned as she walked in.

"I wanted to give you your wedding present early," Pearl said, her speech slow from her stroke but clear enough that Eve had no trouble understanding her.

Eve saw what the woman held on her lap and frowned. Pearl held Eve's quilted baby blanket, the tiny quilt the Whitehorse Sewing Circle had made for her when she was born—just as the women had done for all newborns in the area.

Only her birth hadn't been here. She and her twin brother had never known where they were born. They had each followed the thread of their lives to this spot, Old Town Whitehorse. The rest of the answers had been lost. All they knew is that they were two of the babies who were found homes through an illegal adoption ring run by the women of the Whitehorse Sewing Circle.

"I don't understand," Eve said as she glanced at Bridger. She saw that his quilt was neatly folded in a plastic bag on the table, as it no doubt had been done by his mother for safekeeping.

She met his gaze and saw that he had brought it but didn't seem to understand any more than she did. For months the two of them had been trying to find out who their birth mother was and the circumstances of their birth.

"I told myself that it was best to leave the past where it was," Pearl said. "But the two of you made me see how badly you needed to know about your birth parents." She nodded toward the quilt in Eve's hands. "The answer is in the stitching." Pearl stopped, out of breath.

Eve stared down at the quilt in her hands. The answer is in the stitching? She saw it then, the tiny flowers, each carefully stitched along the border. "The files we found. Flowers. That's the—"

"Key to the code," her twin brother answered for her as he picked up his own quilt, drawing it from the plastic bag to cradle it in his hands. Each quilt apparently had a different flower that matched up with the records the doctor had kept.

Eve met her brother's gaze across the table, tears springing to both their eyes. They both moved to Pearl as one.

"Thank you," Eve said, leaning down to press a kiss to the older woman's smooth cheek.

Bridger took Pearl's hand, and she was smiling her lopsided smile up at him. The two had become close over the last few months, closer than Eve had imagined.

"The truth comes with its own burden, though," Pearl said. "I have kept the secret all these years. But I'm old and I realize I can't let it die with me. So I am passing it to the two of you. Others will come to you over time, seeking the same answers you have. You will have to decide when to share the secret—or if keeping it would be kinder. It is a heavy burden, one I am glad to be free of."

Eve thought of her sisters. Like her, they were adopted. Would they one day change their minds and want to know about their birth mother?

"I trust the two of you to make those decisions in the future," Pearl said. "I guess I knew this day would come when I had the women stitch in a different flower border on each quilt."

The church bell at the community center began to ring.

"Don't you have a wedding to get to?" Pearl asked Eve, smiling up at her.

Eve nodded. "Thank you. You don't know how much this means to me."

"I think I do," she said as Bridger put his quilt back into the plastic bag for safekeeping and placing it in Pearl's lap, pushed her wheelchair toward the door. "I just hope it brings you the peace you so desperately seek."

Epilogue

Arlene hadn't been to the Whitehorse Sewing Circle in months. She'd told herself that she could never hold her head up in that room with those women again. Not after everything that had happened with her family.

That's why she'd sat in her pickup for so long, parked outside the center. Just that morning she'd gotten a call from the state mental hospital. Violet had tried to escape. Her condition seemed to be worsening. The doctor felt she would need more treatment. Violet wouldn't be getting out. At least not for the foreseeable future.

"I think your daughter might be a harm to herself or others at this point," the doctor had said.

"Yes. I wish I had gotten her treatment earlier." As the mother, she should have done something more.

As she got out of the pickup, she prayed it wasn't too late to help Violet and that someday her oldest daughter would be well.

At the Whitehorse Community Center door she hesitated, took a deep breath and pushed, bracing herself as she readied to face down her own demons.

The women around the quilt frame glanced up in surprise as Arlene stepped inside. Just her luck, most of them were here today. Alice Miller, Corky Mathews, Muriel

Brown, Ella Cavanaugh, Helene Merchant. Even Pearl Cavanaugh in her wheelchair.

"Hello, Arlene," Pearl said in her slow post-stroke voice. The others murmured their greetings and continued working, sneaking looks at her. "I like your hair that way. It flatters you."

"Thank you, Pearl." Arlene walked across the room and quietly pulled up a chair, several of the women moving aside to give her room to join them around the quilting frame.

Her fingers trembled as she picked up a needle and threaded it. She knew everyone was watching her, but when she looked up, she found them all intent on their sewing.

"Whose quilt are we working on?" she asked after a few moments.

"Your grandson's," Pearl said and smiled a lopsided smile.

Tears stung her eyes. She swallowed the lump in her throat and took a stitch. A comfortable silence seemed to settle over the room.

Arlene remembered when she would have tried to fill the silence with anything she could think to say, usually a bit of gossip she'd heard. Silence had made her nervous.

But today she settled into the work as she made a neat, small stitch on her grandson's quilt, then another one.

Each stitch—even hers—would eventually make up the whole. And for the first time in her life Arlene felt part of something bigger than herself.

* * * * *

We hope you enjoyed reading

Best-Kept Secrets

by *New York Times* bestselling author

LISA JACKSON

and

Second Chance Cowboy

by *New York Times* bestselling author

B.J. DANIELS.

Both were originally Harlequin® series stories!

From passionate, suspenseful and dramatic
love stories to inspirational or historical,
Harlequin offers different lines to
satisfy every romance reader.

New books in each line are available every month.

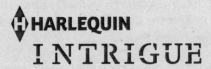

HARLEQUIN

INTRIGUE

SEEK THRILLS. SOLVE CRIMES.
JUSTICE SERVED.

Harlequin.com

⬧ HARLEQUIN

INTRIGUE

SEEK THRILLS. SOLVE CRIMES.
JUSTICE SERVED.

Save **$1.00**

on the purchase of ANY

Harlequin Intrigue book.

Available wherever books are sold,
including most bookstores, supermarkets,
drugstores and discount stores.

- ✂

Save $1.00

on the purchase of ANY Harlequin Intrigue book.

Coupon valid until November 22, 2021. Redeemable at participating outlets in the
U.S. and Canada only. Not redeemable at Barnes & Noble stores. Limit one coupon per customer.

52617166

Canadian Retailers: Harlequin Enterprises ULC will pay the face value of this coupon plus 10.25¢ if submitted by customer for this product only. Any other use constitutes fraud. Coupon is nonassignable. Void if taxed, prohibited or restricted by law. Consumer must pay any government taxes. Void if copied. Inmar Promotional Services ("IPS") customers submit coupons and proof of sales to Harlequin Enterprises ULC, P.O. Box 31000, Scarborough, ON M1R 0E7, Canada. Non-IPS retailer— for reimbursement submit coupons and proof of sales directly to Harlequin Enterprises ULC, Retail Marketing Department, Bay Adelaide Centre, East Tower, 22 Adelaide Street West, 40th Floor, Toronto, Ontario M5H 4E3, Canada.

5 65373 00076 2   (8100)0 12506

U.S. Retailers: Harlequin Enterprises ULC will pay the face value of this coupon plus 8¢ if submitted by customer for this product only. Any other use constitutes fraud. Coupon is nonassignable. Void if taxed, prohibited or restricted by law. Consumer must pay any government taxes. Void if copied. For reimbursement submit coupons and proof of sales directly to Harlequin Enterprises ULC 482, NCH Marketing Services, P.O. Box 880001, El Paso, TX 88588-0001, U.S.A. Cash value 1/100 cents.

Love Harlequin romance?

DISCOVER.

Be the first to find out about promotions, news and exclusive content!

[f] Facebook.com/HarlequinBooks

[t] Twitter.com/HarlequinBooks

[o] Instagram.com/HarlequinBooks

[p] Pinterest.com/HarlequinBooks

[You Tube] YouTube.com/HarlequinBooks

ReaderService.com

EXPLORE.

Sign up for the Harlequin e-newsletter and download a free book from any series at **TryHarlequin.com**

CONNECT.

Join our Harlequin community to share your thoughts and connect with other romance readers!
Facebook.com/groups/HarlequinConnection